M000306221

COUNTERATTACK

S.A. VAN

INFINITY
PUBLISHING

All rights reserved. No part of this book shall be reproduced or transmitted in any form or by any means, electronic, mechanical, magnetic, photographic including photocopying, recording or by any information storage and retrieval system, without prior written permission of the publisher. No patent liability is assumed with respect to the use of the information contained herein. Although every precaution has been taken in the preparation of this book, the publisher and author assume no responsibility for errors or omissions. Neither is any liability assumed for damages resulting from the use of the information contained herein.

Copyright © 2013 by S.A. Van

ISBN 978-0-7414-9753-6 Paperback
ISBN 978-0-7414-9754-3 eBook
Library of Congress Control Number: 2013912542

Printed in the United States of America

This is a work of fiction. Names, characters, places, and incidents either are the product of the author's imagination or are used fictitiously. Any resemblance to actual events or locales or persons, living or dead, is entirely coincidental.

Published August 2013

INFINITY PUBLISHING
1094 New DeHaven Street, Suite 100
West Conshohocken, PA 19428-2713
Toll-free (877) BUY BOOK
Local Phone (610) 941-9999
Fax (610) 941-9959
Info@buybooksontheweb.com
www.buybooksontheweb.com

The Counter Series

COUNTERPLAY
COUNTERACT
COUNTERATTACK

coming soon...

COUNTERPOINT
COUNTERBALANCE

Acknowledgments

For always keeping me grounded when the *Counter Series* characters want to take on a life of their own, I express my deep appreciation to Kim Wilson, my manager and good friend.

To my editing team of Joan Murphy, Kathy Nerlinger, Shannon Peters, and Karen Roth, my sincere gratitude for making sure the words in print jump off the page in the right direction.

To my friend and co-author Lynn Kellan, many thanks for your optimistic and upbeat cheers.

And to my husband Steve and daughter Caitlin, who are always there to make sure I can tackle it all, including the ominous, soon-to-be-tipping-over ironing pile, you two are simply the best.

For ANM,
step forward with determination
and you'll go far

"…I intend to stage a counterattack at any cost."

Prologue

December 1978
Brussels, Belgium

Scream! I beg of you...scream!
The reflection from the shiny blade danced in her eyes...almost to the point of blinding her. Blinking several times, she willed it to go away, but the knife still hovered. Purposely.

He was a monster...wanting to kill her in front of her parents. Slowly...deliberately.

All the while he smiled his vicious smile...and teased her, twirling the blade between his fingers.

Seeing the look of horror on her mother's face, he pressed the knife closer to the young girl's neck, nicking her first, and then drawing a very thin trickle of blood across her neck.

A cascade of droplets wet the top of her white collar, staining it a bright red.

God, I hate the color of red...scream, child! This is your chance...scream now!

The madman was laughing...getting high on the thrill of tormenting such an innocent child...while his partner stood frozen in the shadows.

Fear gripped him. A paralysis he couldn't explain...except the debilitating numbness turning his blood cold. Mason Hamilton had never personally witnessed Renault's reign of terror before...and he certainly wasn't prepared to be an active participant.

Forced to watch such atrocities was making him nauseated. Disgust riddled inside him. Any moment now, Mason knew he would have to run into the next room to retch. Shutting his eyes, he turned his face away to hide his shame and cowardice. He should have stood up to Renault when he had the chance. It was too late now.

Be a man, Mason. For once, be a man. Mason could hear his late father's words echoing in his head, and he almost yelled back in response.

I don't want to be that type of man...ever.

Mason thrust his hands inside his coat pockets. He couldn't let Renault see how much they were shaking.

A true man never reveals his weaknesses, Mason Sr. had quoted on several occasions, almost to the point his son could recite it backwards and forwards.

Mason *Sr.* The most arrogant, self-serving bastard he knew, aside from Renault. They were quite the pair, and as far as Mason *Jr.* was concerned, they could both go to hell. No doubt where his father was residing at this very moment.

Thinking of his father's constant criticisms belittling him at every turn, and the showering of endless praise for Laurence Renault made Mason even more depressed.

How could my father actually believe Renault is the better man?

Mason wiped his lips with his monogrammed handkerchief and saw the blood stains. He had been too preoccupied to notice he was chewing on his bottom lip. No wonder.

Forcing himself to pay attention, Mason watched Renault's horrific performance play out in front of him. It didn't take long to lock eyes with the young girl, and immediately he regretted doing so. Mason was mesmerized, too terrified to break free.

Her knees were knocking together as she stood inches from Renault's chest. He was keeping her steady, not allowing her body to sway naturally.

It was too much to bear...too hard to watch.

The child uttered no sound even as ripples of shock convulsed her body.

Why isn't she screaming? Is it fear or defiance in her eyes?

The absence of even a whimper was more frightening than taking the brunt of the knife himself. Mason tensed for the exact moment when the knife would slice her throat. He turned his head away, unable to watch.

Scream! Just scream!

Scream for me.

For the guttural sounds I wish to God I could make right now.

2

Impossible. Reacting in such a way would be unmanly. Renault wouldn't think twice about turning his hideous weapon in my direction. I have to stand still. There is nothing...absolutely nothing I can do. Mason steadied himself. Sweaty fingers pressed into his palms. Nails grazed the middle of each hand, and Mason was sure he was drawing blood.

From his lips and his hands. Blood drawn as easily as the knife tearing into her throat. A blood sacrifice. A blood bonding. They were forever linked now.

Despite his fervent desire to separate himself from such inhumane actions, Mason realized from that moment on he would never forget her haunting eyes and the hatred she was communicating on a non-verbal level.

All because of a *business* transaction. *How pathetic.*

Of all the potential business partners with whom he could have built legal, professional relationships, he now had the misfortune of being tied criminally to Laurence Renault.

Mason practically choked on the bile rising in his throat. *"You need Renault, Mason," his father had lectured after his initial meeting with the young, charismatic entrepreneur Laurence Renault. "You need him and he needs you. A perfect partnership. Mark my words, Mason, this alliance will take you to heights you never knew existed."*

Mason breathed through his nose, forcing oxygen to rejuvenate his dwindling resolve. It was no use; Renault's sadistic game had reduced him to a spineless coward, incapable of taking control of the situation. All he could do was stand in the darkness several feet away, and pray the night would end...

The girl was fisting her hands now, Mason noticed. Intrigued by her show of bravado, he fixated his eyes on her face. She caught him staring at her again.

Scream!

Oh, God, why won't she scream?

She's trying to be brave...for her parents.

Bound with thick, coarse rope and gagged with dirty rags, the girl's mother and father were being forced to watch in horror as Renault wielded his instrument of sheer terror upon their only child. Taken from the safety and warmth of their home in the middle of the night, they had been brought to this desolate, cold and dank warehouse on the outskirts of Brussels. Surprisingly, they had not resisted much…seeking only to assure the safety of their child.

Renault smiled insidiously. He knew he was in control and he relished the splendor of it. He had taken the most precious person in their lives, and suddenly turned their world upside down, threatening to slice her tender neck wide open in front of them.

No, they would not try to escape. There was no chance of that happening. But Renault had insisted on another precaution just in case.

Mason gulped as his eyes darted to the small gun resting on the overturned barrel beside him.

The weapon he had no idea how to use.

He had tried to tell Renault he had never even cradled a gun in his hand before, but all Renault did was laugh, telling him he was overdue for a lesson.

A man has to take charge of every situation, good and bad. And turn the bad situations into opportunities.

Renault's words rang too loudly in his ears now, and Mason wrestled with the moral consequences. There had to be other ways of persuasion…other than this, Mason convinced himself.

This was a detestable way to do business…

Mason's stomach lurched. Torn between being loyal to a knife-wielding madman and having the decency to do what was right. To fight for the innocence of the child who was pleading with him with her steadfast, blue eyes.

Mason was too mortified to return her painful glance. He couldn't take it anymore. He just wished she would vocalize her anguish. Even with the wind howling through the broken windows and the rain pounding outside, Mason strained his ears, eager to hear even the slightest cry.

There was none.

Mason wanted to run to her, pick her up into his arms and carry her far away from this God-forsaken place. To return her to the safety of her home, and help her forget the horrific acts she was being forced to endure.

He dared not move.

Renault wouldn't hesitate to kill everyone in the room, including Mason. Renault had no conscience, no morals. *How could he?*

He was disfiguring a child in front of her parents for the sole purpose of blackmailing the museum curator into accepting their business proposal. To extract priceless artifacts and replace them with replicas. Renault would then arrange for their sale on the black market through private dealers. The reproductions would be kept on display through the promotional period and then they would be returned to their owners who would simply assume their original masterpieces were intact. All the while Renault and Mason would make a hefty profit. By the time the forgeries were discovered, the museum's statutes of liability would be long over, exonerating them from any culpability.

A perfect arrangement.

Mason Sr. would be proud. His son had done well.

Mason turned his head to spit out a clot of blood. He had unconsciously bitten the side of his mouth, clenching his jaw so tightly.

"Stop, please!"

The girl's father had worked his gag down below his mouth and was now struggling to stand.

"Stop! I beg for your mercy! She is just a child." Tears drenched his face and his words became inaudible.

Mason's eyes darted towards Renault, waiting and watching for an answer. He wanted nothing more at that moment than to tackle Renault, toss the knife to the ground, and carry the collapsing child to her parents. To weep along with them, apologizing profusely until his mouth was dry, and willingly taking the punishment allotted to conspirators.

Renault's look made Mason's body stand rigid. There would be no rescue, and there would be no peace of mind. He would do exactly as Renault commanded.

Whatever Renault commanded.

Renault's eyes showed no emotion as the blade deepened its bloody pathway across the girl's neck. Not a fatal wound, but certainly sufficient to draw as much blood as necessary to intensify the moment.

You bastard, Mason thought, forcing his lips closed. *Enough is enough.*

Mason shook his head, unable to watch the remaining few seconds. The tragedy would forever be etched in his brain. When

S.A. Van

he didn't hear the girl's body crumple to the floor, Mason looked up again and was totally surprised at Renault's hesitation.

He was sparing her life. But why? Surely Renault had every intention of finishing what he started.

Renault straightened, letting the knife drop to his side. He still held the girl's tensing shoulder, ready to take an alternative action should the opportunity present itself. One sudden jerk in movement and his hands would mingle with her blood, strangling the last breaths out of her body. She was no challenge for him; her death would be quick.

"Your answer?" Renault insisted as his fingers dug into the girl's bony shoulder making her cringe.

Her father nodded repeatedly as tears mixed with grime and sweat covering his face.

"Say it. *Now.*"

"Yes, yes! I will do as you say. Please...stop!"

Renault smiled vengefully. Another victory to his credit. As usual, he had gotten the answer he expected. Another compliant curator willing to do his bidding. If only Mason could see it that way.

Renault snorted, disgusted at Mason's obvious lack of back-bone. Such a stark change from when Mason stood in the limelight as the spokesman for the Hamilton-Knox Foundation. There was no mistake. Mason could charm the media, but underneath the expensive suits and perfectly-styled hair was a gutless coward who preferred to let others dirty their own hands.

Renault had his work cut out for him, trying his best to honor the wishes of Mason's father.

I'll make your son into a true man. Renault remembered his promise made the day before the elder Hamilton took his last breath.

Renault paused. Challenges had always been his specialty. He certainly had risen to the occasion once again.

The wind gusted, this time taking with it a chunk of loose glass from one of the cracked windows. The noise startled Mason as he cast his eyes once again in Renault's direction. He took a deep breath, realizing the child had only been wounded, not killed.

Let her go...please, Renault. Mason's words were on the tip of his tongue, but voicing them held too many risks.

He wouldn't and couldn't stand up to Renault. Mason faced that fact now. At least not here. There would come a time, though, Mason was sure of it.

As the child's eyes lifted and she stared in Mason's direction, both of them experienced the same revelation. One day Renault would pay dearly.

"I will expect your full cooperation. When my team arrives tomorrow afternoon, you will have the Gauguin canvases boxed and ready for transit. Do I make myself clear?"

With a sudden jerk of his hand, Renault pushed the girl forward until she fell at her parents' feet. Her mother had fainted several minutes ago from the sheer shock of seeing her only child victimized. Her father inched closer until he could lay his head against her small, trembling body.

Mason stood immobile once again as Renault wiped his hands on a rag and tossed it aside. With no regard for what he had done except to acknowledge his victory with a quick wink in Mason's direction, Renault shrugged on his overcoat. "We're done here."

Mason looked back at the struggling family, hoping to see that they had begun to untie themselves. All he saw was the three of them lying together, crying and shaking. "What about them?"

"They can find their own way home." Renault sloshed through deep puddles on his way to the driver's side of their rented Audi.

"But, I think…"

"That's entirely your problem, Mason. You think too much. I made my point. They got the message. We are done here. Let it go. Now, get in the car."

Mason threw himself into the passenger seat with a huff. He fought hard to quell the incessant voice inside him wanting badly to lash out at Renault for his barbaric behavior and his holier-than-thou attitude. He dared not broach the subject. He feared Renault's wrath more than anything.

"You do not believe in my…methods of *persuasion*, Mason?" Renault laughed callously. "Unlike you, I am not opposed to using force when the situation warrants it."

Mason couldn't hold back his temper any longer. "For God's sake, Laurence, she was just a child!"

"No, Mason. She was just a *means to an end*, nothing more. Fear is the best motivator. I simply brought fear to a personal level her father would indelibly understand. Which I might add, was rather ingenious on my part."

Mason shook his head in disgust.

"One day, you'll understand this, Mason. Any man can be brought to his knees with the right motivation...*enticement*, whatever you wish to call it."

"Torture? Is that your preferred method? You could have warned me what you were planning to do tonight, Laurence. Instead, you made me witness such a...display of..." Mason suddenly found himself at a loss for words as the young girl's eyes once again rallied to the forefront of his mind. "She was an innocent child and you...forced such cruelty upon her. She will never recover; I assure you."

"And your point, Mason? I don't give a damn about her recovery and neither should you. If we want to succeed, sacrifices will have to be made. Surely, as a businessman, you can fully appreciate profit and loss. I have no problem sacrificing anyone or anything to get what I want. What we *both* want."

"I'm not sure, Laurence, if we want the same thing."

Renault slapped the steering wheel with such forcefulness the car swerved, jerking them both.

"Of course you do, Mason. We both know you have high aspirations set in motion by your father. He laid the groundwork for your success, and you would be foolish to step aside now. The Hamilton-Knox Foundation is poised to become an international powerhouse, showcasing museum collections for years to come. Don't be an ass and discount the sacrifices your father made to ensure your place at the helm."

"My father was entirely self-serving. He never understood me or wanted to. It was always about him."

"Nonsense, Mason. He understood plenty. That's why he purposefully sought me out, asking me to befriend you. Your father was a visionary. A great man *you* never appreciated. Admit it."

Mason sat dumbfounded, finding it hard to look Renault in the face. His own father had recognized his weaknesses and purposefully found someone to take up the slack.

"My father allied himself with you for the wrong reasons, Laurence. I won't make the same mistake. You and I will be strictly business partners; nothing more. I don't need your..."

"Oh, you need me, Mason, more than you think. Without me, you'll fail. I'll be the one in the shadows who handles the messy situations while you continue to stand in the spotlight as the head of H-K. In return, we'll both profit immensely. You will come to realize, Mason, our partnership will be the best decision your father ever made for you."

"I'm not so sure about that."

"Well, let me know if you need to be reminded."

Within seconds, Renault brought the car to a sudden stop and withdrew a knife from underneath his seat. He flicked the knife back and forth in full view of Mason's widening eyes. "I do have *special* talents, Mason." Renault slowly drew his fingers down the edge of the razor sharp blade, nicking his thumb in the process. "You will learn to appreciate every last one of them."

"Don't count on it, Renault."

Mason turned his eyes away. He could no longer look at Renault with any degree of respect.

Only the sheer desire to destroy him...

Chapter 1

Falling backwards, her body absorbed the stark reality of the pain shooting through her like the steel-edged blade of a knife.

It was happening *again*.

Another threatening note, another picture which sought to suffocate her, to strip her lungs of every breath.

This time, Mason Hamilton had gone too far.

Jenna Reed knew without a doubt Mason Hamilton was to blame...directly or indirectly; it didn't matter. The picture didn't lie. It caught the full magnitude of Hamilton's wrath...at the hands of someone he had hired.

Fear gripped her insides, as Jenna's trembling fingers struggled to hold the small picture of her younger brother, Austin and his fiancée, her best friend Kelly. Restrained with cable ties around their wrists, and gagged with handkerchiefs as they lay in the back of Austin's car.

The most distressing part of the picture was a mysterious hand holding a gun to Kelly's stomach, threatening the life of her unborn child.

Jenna clenched her teeth. "How could he do this...to his own daughter and future grandchild? What kind of a man...?"

Chase Garrett shook his head. Jenna's anchor in her otherwise tumultuous life, Chase was speechless at the moment.

Austin and Kelly were missing, and the picture presented its own horrifying theories he dared not mention. Jenna was right...this latest turn of events had *Mason Hamilton* written all over it.

Just a few months earlier, Jenna had received unsettling news inside another tan envelope. At that time, a picture of Austin indicated he had been abducted and Hamilton was the prime suspect.

Déjà vu.

Mason Hamilton was up to his old tricks again, all for the sake of the precious treasure pieces.

Mason Hamilton's obsession.

Five small gold animal figurines believed to be the Lost Treasure of Blackbeard. Reportedly worth millions, Hamilton had proven he was willing to stake the lives of *anyone* in order to collect all five pieces.

Regrettably, Jenna had been the one to find the treasure pieces hidden for over thirty years in the basement of her family's beach house. Purposely buried in the bottom of an old metal cabinet by her mother...at the request of her best friend, FBI Agent Maria Turette.

The pirate treasure still casting its fateful curse for centuries.

Death comes to those who dare to hold all five pieces of tainted gold.

"The pirate curse...," Chase began. "It's holding true. I told you, Jenna, and you didn't want to believe me."

"Well, I'm a believer now," she said firmly. Slipping out of Chase's grasp, she fell flat on her ass on the hard wooden floor. Staggering to her feet, she steadied herself by placing both hands on the kitchen table.

"He's not giving up...and neither am I," she asserted, resisting the temptation to tear the picture into tiny shreds. "He's pushed me too far this time. For God's sake, Chase! Kelly is pregnant!"

Jenna wanted so badly to scream. Maria Turette had been right; this was all just a game to Hamilton. He knew exactly which pawns to use and what moves to make keeping everyone on the verge of exploding. "I'm not giving up, Chase! Not now, not ever! He's not going to win."

Chase covered her hands with his own. "But at what price, Jenna? You know what Hamilton is capable of...and he has people on his payroll who are ruthless. Every step you make is met with a lethal maneuver. Are you sure you want to keep baiting him?"

Jenna turned and swallowed hard. Chase was right, of course. She knew it deep down, but at the same time there was no way she could stop now. She had vowed to finish what her mother had started.

To keep the treasure pieces far away from Hamilton for as long as possible.

"I'm in this to the end. Just like Maria."

"Then I'll stand with you." Chase closed the distance between them. Drawing her back against his chest, Chase planted a light kiss on the back of her head.

Jenna attempted a small smile. She spun around and lifted her hands to Chase's neck. "Might not be the best decision you ever made."

"Oh, I don't know about that," Chase said with a twinkle in his eye. "Meeting you was one of the best moments in my life. And spending time with you certainly has added a dimension of thrill to my lifestyle. I wouldn't trade a minute of it." Chase paused for a moment, then squeezed Jenna's waist. "Actually, I could have done without the gun threats, finding you unconscious inside the museum and watching you bleed from a gunshot wound. But other than that…"

Jenna didn't wait for the rest of the sentence. She grabbed Chase's face then kissed him long and hard. "That's for being my anchor and keeping me sane." Jenna picked up the picture from the kitchen table and took a deep breath. "We need to find my brother and my best friend as soon as possible."

"Hamilton is playing you, Jenna."

"Maybe…but he has no idea what I'm capable of…*this time*." Jenna ran her fingers over the picture as rage emanated from her pores. Turning it over, she re-read the taunting message as she grimly imagined the fate of Austin and Kelly.

Welcome Home, Jenna Reed. I'll be in touch.

The insidious cat-and-mouse game which had begun in early summer was now escalating to a new distorted level. Jenna had no doubt Mason Hamilton was at the controls once again, primed and pumped to inflict his wrath upon those who dared to defy him.

The first figurine, the gold elephant, had been forcibly taken from her in New York when she had gone to Hamilton's office to plead for her brother's release. Suffering mercilessly at the hands of Hamilton's side-kick, the hideous ogre Hans Kliric, she finally passed out, almost dying from the multiple wounds he inflicted across the top of her chest with his honed knife.

The scars had only just begun to heal when Jenna offered her help to Damian Pierce to find his wife Maria. Heading to Texas, Jenna risked her life in an attempt to rescue Maria, narrowly missing an explosion at a storage facility. Assuming the coast was clear after the dust settled, she made the critical mistake of jumping from her hiding place too soon. A bullet from an unknown assailant burned into her shoulder, and yet again, Jenna found herself in the hospital.

Most sane people would have given up by now, her conscience bellowed.

"Not going to happen," Jenna asserted, under her breath. Letting Hamilton win was not an option. She couldn't let Maria down...and she couldn't give up on her mother's quest to keep the treasure pieces away from Mason Hamilton.

Bringing Hamilton to justice was the only viable solution. He had caused too much pain and death already.

People alive...and dead...were counting on her. Especially Austin and Kelly.

Catching her breath, she found the nearest chair and slid into it. "Son-of-a..."

"This is exactly what he wants." Chase began to pace. "For you to get so riled up, you'll think about doing something crazy. I'm calling Damian and Maria. They need to get on board with this...*right now.*"

"Pierce."

"Damian, it's Chase. My God, we just got the worst possible news! We're in Cape May. Hamilton left another calling card. This time it's a picture of Austin and Kelly...tied up and gagged, lying in the back of a car. Might be Austin's car since it's not in the driveway."

"I'm putting you on speaker, Chase," FBI Special Agent Damian Pierce said as he hit the Bluetooth speaker button on his steering wheel. "Maria is with me. We're headed in your direction."

"Chase, is Jenna right there?" Maria asked.

"I'm here, Maria."

"We'll find them, Jenna. I promise you. Stay put and wait for us. Text me Austin's license plate number as soon as you can. I'll get Jacoby to send out an alert."

"Austin's car is probably abandoned by now, Maria," Damian added. "Hamilton only hires the best...with the exception of Kliric."

Maria didn't wait for Jenna to respond. "Even the best criminals have flaws, Jenna. We just have to find out what they are. We'll go through standard protocols anyway. It's a place to start."

"I won't let anything happen to her, Maria." Chase tugged on Jenna's hand.

"Good to know," Maria added before she ended the call.

Chase sulked. "She still doesn't trust me."

"Well, you did take a swing at her, Chase. Maria knows you were dealing with the drug interaction, but all the same, you attacked a senior FBI agent."

"She needs to get over it. I'm one of the good guys."

Jenna fell into Chase's arms. "And for that, I will always be grateful." She kissed him lightly, then laid her head against his chest. She sighed, feeling his arms loop around her.

"We'll get through this together." Chase stroked her back. "I won't let you deal with this alone. If I ever get the opportunity, Hamilton is as good as dead."

Jenna reached up to cradle Chase's face. "Don't say that, please. Don't ever stoop to his level. If you kill him, I'll lose you. We can't let this diminish who we really are. If we do, we have nothing left. Maria and I will..."

"You'll do what...exactly? My God, Jenna, do you hear yourself? You can't be thinking straight! You and Maria cannot go up against Hamilton by yourselves. Maria might be hell bound to finish this, but I can't let you....I'm afraid I'll be the one to lose you!" Chase buried his face in Jenna's hair. "I can't...lose you."

"No chance of that," Jenna added, feeling Chase's heart beating rapidly against her palm. Her anchor, her safe haven...was struggling to stay grounded.

Being drugged in Texas and succumbing to erratic changes in behavior, Chase had lost control. Losing sight of the situation, he lashed out...attacking Jenna physically and emotionally. Had it not been for Maria's insistence that Chase be checked for drug poisoning, Jenna dared not think what would have happened.

Instead of tearing them apart, the experience deepened the bond between them. She couldn't even begin to imagine life without Chase, even though the past week had worn her down.

Jenna looked into Chase's eyes and found her much-needed point of balance. She drew an imaginary line along his jaw. "I love you," she whispered.

"And I love you, Jenna. I hope you never forget that," Chase added. "I know I've hurt you...but it was never intentional."

"I've forgiven you. It's over. Let's get past this...right now." Forcing her trembling lips to recover enough to kiss him, Jenna moved closer.

Chase stopped her before their lips met. "I won't forget what I did...and I know you won't either. You can't just erase the slate. I hurt you, and I can't...forgive myself for that." Breaking free of Jenna's embrace, Chase moved across the room and folded his arms. His head hung low in shame.

Jenna rubbed her neck in anguish. Chase was the one hurting now, and if they were to move forward, she had to bridge the gap between them. Starting with truthful forgiveness. In three strides she was standing before him, lifting his chin to stare in his eyes.

"Don't ever pull away from me again," she said firmly as she began to untangle his arms. As a half-smile emerged on her face, she locked her arms around his back. "I need you, and you need me.

"Looks like you're *my anchor* now."

"Then you're in trouble." Jenna tried to smile.

The joke hit too close to home. Chase knew he was going to have to push Jenna away for her own safety, but every time she touched him, his resolve decreased another notch. Love was keeping him anchored, but it was also dangerously getting in the way.

Balancing his heart and his sense of duty was driving Chase crazy. He was getting too close now to give up...no matter what the cost.

A daunting thought which spiked his adrenaline...and scared him at the same time.

*****

"I'm going to kill him this time!"

Maria was hyperventilating. Shouting obscenities as her husband floored the accelerator on Interstate 95 wasn't making her

S.A. Van

feel any better. Her nerves were fraying as fast as Damian's Nissan GT-R sped along the freeway.

Pounding her fist against the door panel in frustration, Maria immediately regretted her action. Smartness from the blow reverberated up her arm.

"And that is precisely why I'm driving." Damian rubbed Maria's shoulder. "Take it easy, sweetheart."

Maria crossed her arms in defiance. "One chance, Damian, I swear to you, that's all I want. One chance to take him out. I will not hesitate; believe me!"

Damian reached out to take Maria's hand. "I'll be right beside you."

Maria's breathing steadied as the warm touch of her husband's fingers and his sexy, scratchy voice soothed her temperament. Damian always knew exactly what to do to bring her back to Earth.

"You are the best, Damian."

"Care to elaborate?" Damian winked.

"Not right now. Maybe later...when we're not in crisis mode. I need to call Jacoby." Maria dug her cell out of her pocketbook she had tossed on the floor of the car. "Hey, Genius," she said after two rings.

"Miss me already, Turette? You're getting soft. What will the guys think of their fearless leader?" FBI Special Agent Brett Jacoby teased.

"All along I thought that was you," Maria retorted followed by short wisps of laughter. "I have no doubt you're running a tight ship in my absence."

"Always do. Can't let my guard down, or they'll take advantage. Longer lunch hours, punching out early...you know how it goes."

"Do what you need to do, Genius. Listen, we have a problem. I need you to alert the state police in the mid-Atlantic region. Austin and Kelly are missing. Jenna got another threatening note and picture. We think...."

Jacoby whistled, cutting Maria off. "Hamilton, right? One damn thing after another. Ok, I'm on it. Austin used to live in Philly, right? I can get his license number from the Pennsylvania DMV. No need to bother Jenna. We'll put a BOLO out on it. In fact," Jacoby paused for just a second. "I'm sending a request over now. I'll ring you back when we get a hit."

"You amaze me," Maria said, shaking her head. "Another thing. Get the Atlantic City field office to send a couple of agents down to the Reeds' beach house. Just to keep an eye out until Damian and I get there. We're still hours away."

"On it, boss."

Maria snickered. "You haven't called me *boss* in quite a while. Letting down your guard, Jacoby? You're the one getting soft."

"Don't let that rumor fly. Keep in touch, Turette. Don't make me come and get you this time."

"Good-bye, Genius, and tell Thompson to get a posse ready. As soon as you find Austin's car, I want him on it."

"Roger that."

Maria laid her head against the headrest. Tiredness and trepidation were too often competing for her attention these days. "Kidnapping his own pregnant daughter! I really don't put anything past Mason this time. He's descended to a new all-time low.

"Maybe he doesn't know Kelly is pregnant."

"Do you really think it matters, Damian? Mason is heartless. He doesn't care about anyone but himself. Kelly has been down in Cape May since she left New York. Unless someone was spying on her, Mason would have no idea. She just started showing a few weeks ago according to Jenna."

"Then whoever abducted them may have given Mason the news. I'm sure that's thrown a wrench into his plans. Mason doesn't care about anyone. He's too self-absorbed...except when he's trying to yank your chain."

"This isn't about me," Maria emphasized. "Mason is switching gears. He's focusing on Jenna again. This is a direct attack on her. He knows she'll do anything to get her family back. He's playing her. I just hope she doesn't try to take him on by herself. He's obviously got some other players involved besides Kliric and The Closer. I dare to think who else has signed on to do his bidding."

Damian nodded. "The list keeps growing. Must be costing Hamilton a small fortune to keep all his players happy. Good thing for us, we're teaming up to bring them all down."

"Yeah, how exactly did you make that happen?"

"I have my connections, sweetheart," Damian said, staring straight ahead. The less Maria knew, the better. "Relax; I have nothing but good intentions. I just...made some arrangements to allow me to take care of a few matters and stay by your side for a little while. Who knows? You might need my special skills."

"I'm assuming you're referring to your sniper expertise and not those *special skills* I'm more familiar with on a private level?"

Damian laughed heartily. *"Whatever* you need, sweetheart, I'm your man."

Chapter 2

Mason Hamilton licked his lips to savor the tingling moment. He never got tired of the brief burning sensation from repeated shots of his most favorite whiskey, Macallan. At seven hundred dollars a bottle, he appreciated the fine taste enveloping his mouth. The closest thing to heaven in a bottle he could ever imagine.

His staff had a standing order to keep the Waterford decanter full and at least four glasses polished on his marble mantle. Heirloom quality and collectible significance were concepts for which he had little appreciation, but Ellen had insisted all the glassware in the house would be Waterford. Nothing else would do.

He had given in only to silence her protests, a feat he rarely undertook. He was certainly the master of the household and held all the cards. Except for the glassware, apparently.

Even in death, Ellen's memory was still spiting him.

Why do I care? Mason made up his mind not to dwell on such trivial matters.

Tonight he raised his glass high, congratulating himself on a wise decision. Convincing the newest member of his team, Logan McHenry, to have no qualms about kidnapping Kelly and bringing her to New York was pure genius. As soon as he laid eyes on Kelly once again, another long-suffering chapter of his life would be brought to a close. How long had it been now? Twenty-eight years...of living a lie? Convincing the world he had fathered a child and was a happily-married man.

Rubbish, to say the least.

But necessary to maintain his public image, as his father had drummed into his head.

Mason tossed back another shot. Even after all these years, his father was still irritating the hell out of him from the grave.

Ghosts from his past...still taunting him, never letting go. Ridiculing him, eating away at his sanity...until there would be nothing left.

Mason gulped too fast, choking. Calloused thoughts continued to plague him. He had taken his father's advice all those years ago, marrying a woman he didn't love and assuming the responsibilities for her illegitimate child he didn't sire. *Why wasn't that enough?*

Cursing out loud, Mason resisted the urge to toss his glass across the room. Had the media ever found out about his inability to father a child, they would have had a field day. A rare infection contracted when he was a child and the experimental treatments which followed had made him sterile. A secret no one needed to know.

Not then and certainly not now.

Besides, once Kelly was out of the picture the need for his perfect family image would be a moot point. The media could focus its attention on yet another tragedy in the life of Mason Hamilton. He would take the public's pity and milk it for all it was worth.

"Gullible fools." Mason almost tipped the decanter on its side. Carefully replacing it on its matching crystal base, he sucked in a deep breath.

"No more…loose…ends." He was slurring his words…his father's words. Mason felt an eerie sensation creep along his neck.

"Ties are too binding, Mason, remember that," the old man used to say. *"Stay in control, and never allow anyone…through any means…have dominion over you. Personal relationships are damaging…and will cause you immeasurable pain. You must stay focused on the task at hand, foregoing any ridiculous notion of becoming enamored with anyone. This wisdom, my son, will serve you well."*

Mason sputtered, drooling whiskey down his chin. He wiped his face with his silk monogrammed handkerchief, and suddenly felt ill.

He had become his father.

The sad truth hammered at Mason until his head hurt.

It was too late to turn his life around. Too late to make amends. He had to finish what he started: the methodical, sadistic foray with Agent Maria Turette, the quest to retrieve the rest of Blackbeard's lost treasure from his newest adversary Jenna Reed, and the murder of Kelly McBride, his *pretend* daughter.

The three components of his *end-game*.

Mason snorted, remembering Renault using such a word to describe how their repeated threats to the international museum community would result in major profits and heightened satisfaction for their partnership. A sullied thought, Mason recounted. Putting himself in an alliance with Renault had been the biggest mistake of his life, and he was still paying for it.

He rarely slept for more than a few hours at a time, and here of late, those times were prefaced by the consumption of several glasses of whiskey or wine.

I'm afraid to close my eyes. She's always there...

The nightmares had never really stopped, only retreating to dormant stages periodically. The memory of that fateful night in Brussels still tormented him. Mason could still see the intensity of the young girl's eyes, impaling him into a frozen stance. She was still menacing him...making him recoil for his past atrocities. She was the one...in control.

And always would be.

He recalled the chill in the air from the dampness in the abandoned warehouse, the blood dripping in slow motion down her white shirt, and the cold, revengeful look of her piercing, blue eyes.

Damn those eyes!

She had chosen to communicate with him in silence, sending the most disturbing thoughts and premonitions his way in lieu of her screams. Her fortitude gripped him and hung on. Paralyzing him and changing him forever.

Though Renault had done his best to condition Mason into becoming heartless and unsympathetic, he still harbored a cowardly fear he had shared with no one...that she would one day enact her revenge.

Mason couldn't get the glass to his lips fast enough. He needed to wash away troublesome memories before they consumed him to the point of madness. He needed to regain control, to force apparitions of his former life back to the unreachable trenches of his mind. Mason's nervous laughter bellowed through the hollow corridors of his prestigious mansion.

"I am...in control," he said, slurring his words. Mason's thoughts drifted until he could vaguely see the outline of Laurence Renault's face, making him seethe with resentment.

The absolute audacity of that man!

Coming to Ellen's memorial service and showing his face after all these years! Scaring the living daylights out of him in front of such a massive crowd.

Renault would pay dearly for his little show of egotistical retaliation, Mason vowed.

Renault and his daughter would pay the same price; Mason would make sure of it. Whatever and *whoever* it took.

Deciding to hire Logan McHenry and The Closer had been sheer brilliance. Mason sneered, allowing himself yet another round of congratulatory thoughts. Two hit men at his beck and call. A perfect arrangement.

A strange calmness engulfed him. Knowing he could make demands and have them fulfilled made Mason relax for the first time that evening. It was time for bed.

Dragging his exhausted body to his first floor bedroom, Mason paused briefly to ponder why Suzanne, his administrative assistant and current lover, had not returned his repeated phone calls. He could have used her explicit calming skills right about now. After three attempts to reach her, he gave up.

"Sick and tired...of the women...in my life." Mason pitched forward onto his bed, never taking the time to undress.

Or realizing uninvited guests had infiltrated his home, and were watching him from a distance.

*****

"How pathetic, don't you think?"

Laurence Renault kept his voice low. He nodded to Jonathan Knox as both men peered into Mason Hamilton's bedroom. "The big man can't hold his liquor. Never could, although he's always tried to convince himself otherwise. Oh, how I find this so entertaining. Makes me reminisce of days gone by."

"I'd rather not know."

Jonathan regretted the fact he had allowed Renault to talk him into such a fool's errand. Breaking into Mason's home had been the easy part. Mason had long since provided Jonathan with the access codes to his estate as a precautionary measure. Keeping out of sight while Mason drank himself into a stupor was another matter altogether.

Jonathan would have been perfectly content to stay in the adjacent garage until nightfall, but Renault saw no reason to waste time. Mason's routine hadn't changed in the past three decades. As soon as he was home, he kicked off his shoes, loosened his tie, and headed straight for liquid comfort.

Tonight was no different.

Renault had called this one, much to Jonathan's surprise. Yet Renault still hadn't told him exactly why it was necessary to catch Mason off-guard.

"Follow me," Renault announced after several minutes had passed and Mason hadn't stirred from lying on the bed. "He's out. We can walk around freely."

"Where's Kliric?"

"Who?" Renault asked, preoccupied with setting the timer on his watch.

"Kliric, Mason's right-hand...whatever. He could be here."

"I sincerely doubt it. My associates made a scan of the household with their infrared camera. The staff was dismissed hours ago. Mason is the only one here...besides us."

"You're positive Kliric isn't lurking about?"

Renault finally looked up. "Yes. Stop worrying, Jonathan. I know what I'm doing."

"Well, I have no idea what I'm doing, or why in the hell I should even be here in the first place. I think it's time you level with me."

"We're here to save my daughter. To beat Mason at his own game. If he's successful in bringing her back here, he'll kill her. I can't let that happen."

Jonathan was at a loss for words. He would certainly do whatever Renault required if it meant he could save Kelly's life.

Even though she wasn't biologically his sister.

Just another shocking reality thrown at him the past couple of months. First, finding out his real mother was FBI Agent Maria Turette, then realizing her affair with Mason Hamilton had brought about his own birth had nearly knocked him flat on his ass. But there had been a silver lining. He and Kelly were siblings.

Of course that theory lasted only weeks. When Renault appeared at Ellen Chandler Hamilton's memorial service and introduced himself to Jonathan, he also mentioned that Kelly was his real daughter. So much for brother-sister bonding. The best he could now hope for was to be a surrogate brother to Kelly, and to get her out of harm's way as soon as possible. If that meant linking arms with Laurence Renault, then so be it.

Renault retreated into a small hallway, motioning for Jonathan to follow. "We have work to do. We need to disengage the double-room. Mason won't hesitate to put Kelly in there. She won't survive."

Jonathan grabbed Renault's arm and swung him around. "Talk, Renault, and not in riddles. What is this *double-room*? Some kind of personal torture chamber? I've been here several times. I have never seen anything out of the ordinary."

"Because Mason never wanted you or anyone else to see it."

"Maybe it's not here anymore. This could just be a wild goose chase."

Renault broke out of Jonathan's grasp. "Listen to me and stop jumping to your own conclusions. I'm telling you the double-room exists. I helped Mason design it. We needed a private place in which to...*entice* others to cooperate. As much as it appalls me to recant my former lifestyle, I ask you to keep an open mind."

Jonathan felt bile rising in the back of this throat. "An open mind? You disgust me, Renault. I've only agreed to help you because it involves Kelly."

"Fair enough." Renault noted Jonathan's resistance. "I don't expect us to become friends, only allies." Casting a nod over his shoulder in Jonathan's direction, Renault retreated back into the hallway. Retracing their steps through the dining room and into the back of the house, they soon found themselves at a side door just off the kitchen. Renault stopped shortly before placing his hand on the doorknob. Jonathan slammed into Renault's back.

"What's the matter? Did we trip some type of alarm?"

Renault shook his head. "I...just wanted to make sure you were..."

"Open the damn door, Renault, and let's get this over with." Jonathan shoved Renault forward.

Renault switched on the light in the stairwell. He and Jonathan descended the steps. Turning left at the landing, Renault led Jonathan into a small passageway. The first doorway they came to was locked.

Withdrawing a small key from his pocket, Renault easily unlocked the door and pushed it open. "I've kept a key all these years. Never expected I'd have another opportunity to use it, but here we are." He opened the door slowly at first, then swung the door wide open, revealing a wide viewing panel and a couple of metal chairs covered in a thin layer of dust. Straight ahead was a large, empty room separated precisely in half by a wall of glass.

Shock rendered Jonathan motionless. Although the room was immaculate, indicating nothing bad or otherwise had ever taken place here, the mere thought of a modern-day torture chamber sent icy chills up his arms.

Sensing Jonathan's apprehension, Renault took a step backwards. "You're curious. You want to know exactly what we did down here, don't you? You want to know...but you're afraid to ask." He opened a door to the right which led to a small booth overlooking the double-room.

Jonathan could barely catch his breath, let alone utter a response.

"Verbal threats were useless maneuvers, I told Mason over and over. Actions spoke so much louder back then." Renault stared into space. "We placed the curator on one side of the room and a member of his family in the other. Usually a child, if possible. The younger the better." Renault's hands hovered above the silver knobs on the control panel. "Slowly, we would reduce the air flow in the child's room, making it difficult for..."

Jonathan held up his hand. To be in the presence of a man capable of such atrocities was one thing, but to hear Renault describe such vile acts was incomprehensible. "I don't want to hear any more, Renault. What you and Mason did...makes me sick. I find it hard to believe you're ready to repent of your past sins."

"I cannot turn back the clock, nor can I erase what happened. It's a part of my past. I must move forward with what little time I have left. To atone for my past mistakes by making sure my daughter is safe."

"Really? You expect me to buy that? You're doing all this...all for the daughter you never knew." Jonathan folded his arms, not believing a single word. "That's the biggest bunch of bull..."

"I love my daughter. I always have. Even though I have kept my distance." Renault's voice cracked.

"Love? You wouldn't understand the concept. You just admitted to using this room for...torture, and yet you can stand there and tell me you're capable of loving someone." Jonathan pinned Renault against the wall. "You're the reason Kelly is in danger. You came to Ellen's memorial service. You just couldn't stay away, could you? Now you've got Mason all riled up and he's fighting back. The only way he knows how. Revenge. He knows you'll spill his little secret...about Kelly's true parentage. Isn't that right?"

Renault relaxed his arms as Jonathan backed away. "How little you understand, Jonathan. Mason has been planning this for quite some time. He waited for Ellen's parents to die, leaving her with a vast fortune. By now, I'm sure he has figured out Ellen changed her will when Kelly was born. She and Mason are co-beneficiaries. With Kelly out of the way, he inherits everything."

"You're sure about this?" Jonathan leaned against the control panel, knocking a small leather-bound notebook to the floor. Picking it up, he began to skim through it.

Renault waited for Jonathan to react.

"What the hell is this?"

"A log book; nothing more."

Jonathan couldn't believe his eyes. Dates, names of curators and family members, varying methods of control, explicit descriptions of... "You son-of-a-bitch. You kept a record of what you did. A brag book, Renault? This is beyond...disgusting. I've had enough. You and Mason deserve each other." Jonathan dropped the book on the control panel and had almost reached the hallway when Renault stepped in his path.

"Don't be too hasty to leave. Your fingerprints are now on the log book. You've read the contents, or some of them. How can you possibly deny any knowledge of the double-room and what it was used for when you have immersed yourself into our little horror story just by following me here?"

Rage emanated from Jonathan's face, making his eyes burst. "You planned this! Right from the start, didn't you, Renault? I was stupid to trust you."

Renault tried not to sneer. He had Jonathan right where he wanted him. "Don't be a fool, Jonathan. If you leave now, you'll be on your own. My driver will refuse to take you anywhere. Let us finish what we came here to accomplish. You can blame me later for my underhanded ways of corruption."

Jonathan huffed. "What do we need to do?"

"Open the cabinet door underneath the panel. Crawl underneath. That's it," Renault said as Jonathan knelt down and got inside the small area directly below the control board. "Do you see the black and yellow wires running from the middle of the board to the left edge?"

"Yes."

"Good. Here's a pair of scissors. Cut the wires from the back of each connector. We can't take a chance even the slightest spark will ignite some type of reaction. We have to make sure..."

"I get it, Renault. Now what?"

"Next, I want you to disconnect the wires running along the right side of the board. They are black and green. Do you see them?"

"Yes. Cutting them now. Got them. Anything else?"

"No. We've taken care of the immediate access." Helping Jonathan to his feet, Renault placed the log book back on the top of the control board. He gestured for Jonathan to follow him out of the booth. "If and when Mason does decide to use the double-room, he'll get the surprise of his life! How I wish I could see his face when that happens!"

"Well, let's just hope he doesn't get that far." Jonathan followed Renault up the stairs. "Because if I know Mason, he'll have a back-up plan. He'll just find another way to hurt Kelly."

"Then we must not let that happen," Renault affirmed. "We must do *whatever*...is necessary to save my daughter."

Chapter 3

Sweat matted her hair, plastering several blond strands to her face. Or was it the multitude of tears flowing from her eyes? Kelly couldn't be sure.

Not that it really mattered.

Her body hadn't stopped trembling from the moment the blanket had been carefully thrown on top of them as she and Austin lay in the backseat of his car, and the unmistaken barrel of the gun had been pressed against her stomach. A threat worse than any words could portray.

She and Austin had been cuddling together in the old burgundy arm chair, talking about their upcoming wedding. Kelly remembered the look of excitement in Austin's eyes as he cradled her and ran his fingers over her growing baby bump. They were both so happy. She couldn't imagine anything more wonderful than to be married to her incredible man, and awaiting the birth of their child.

Yet in the back of her mind, Kelly couldn't help but wonder if true happiness was just a wasted thought. Her father was still attempting to keep her on a short string in order to make her new life with Austin a living hell.

When their unknown attacker had surprised them in the living room just a short time ago, Kelly had seen the shock registered on Austin's face. Although she had been caught off-guard, she had half-way expected some form of retaliation.

After all, she did disobey.

A sin her father, Mason Hamilton, would never forgive.

As her body shook with deep-rooted fear for the safety of her future husband and their unborn child, reality struck her like a blinding flash of light.

She was responsible for bringing this terror upon all of them.

If she had just gone back to New York to take her punishment...none of this would be happening right now. Austin would be safe, and better off if he had never met her. He wouldn't have had to suffer two beatings this summer, the latter one almost claiming his life. He could have spent another carefree summer, enjoying a laid-back lifestyle, never being afraid to look over his shoulder.

Instead, Kelly found out she was pregnant. Austin immediately proposed, promising her he was in love with her and the baby was just an added blessing. She had wanted so much to believe him, and before she knew it, he was putting an engagement ring on her finger.

Making a commitment to her.

Something he probably shouldn't have done. For his own well-being.

Kelly squeezed her eyes shut, ashamed to gaze in Austin's direction. He was lying close to her, touching her with as many fingers as possible despite the strange angle of his shackled wrists. Because he knew how much she needed to feel him.

Austin's touch…a source of comfort, love and a promise for a better future together…was hurting her now. It was a constant reminder of the pain she had caused him. *Again and again.*

By betraying him to trust her and fall in love with her…by looking the other way when her father's men kidnapped him and took him to New York…by making a foolish run back to her father which backfired after just a few miles away from Cape May, and now *this*…

Why couldn't Austin see how much trouble she was?

Stinging tears brought her back into focus.

He's in love with me. No matter what happens…Austin is in love with me.

Kelly stretched her arms until the tips of her fingers reached Austin's hand. Then she had to withdraw for fear of falling off the backseat as the car kept up with the flow of traffic. She assumed they were on the expressway due to the increased speed. Most likely north towards New York. To her father.

Holding them at gunpoint, their assailant had specifically laid out his own ground rules. She and Austin would do exactly as they were told, or suffer the consequences which he promised would be extremely unpleasant.

It was nothing personal, the man wearing the aviator glasses and baseball cap had said as he withdrew cable ties and two bandanas from his pocket. *Just a business deal*, the details of which he refused to discuss.

Austin had glanced at Kelly, wanting to dart away, to create a diversion for just a moment so he could overpower the assailant. The fear in her eyes told him to stop at the precise moment the man aimed his pistol at Kelly's stomach. One slight move and their baby would die before it was born, the man threatened.

Forced to lie down in the backseat away from each other, the man secured Austin and Kelly's wrists, then tied gags around their mouths. Next he told them to shut their eyes and lay still. Snapping a picture with his camera phone, he then tossed a blanket over them, warning them to keep down. Slowly pulling out of their driveway, he casually drove down Congress Street, confident he was not drawing attention to himself.

He could blend into any lifestyle and town. Adapting to various cultures had become one of his specialties.

Logan laughed silently. How gullible people were…unsuspecting of the guy next door. In fact, when he had flirted recently with the cute brunette who had taken up residence in the house next door to his Cape May rental, he had almost let his guard down. Flirting was a dangerous pastime he rarely allowed himself to enjoy. But it had felt good.

Logan continued to dwell on his chance meeting with the sexy, athletic-built woman who had charged up the steps and locked eyes with him. Almost to the point of distraction, Logan couldn't help but remember the look on her face when she admired his sculpted abs. Her eyes had widened along with her smile. She was impressed, no doubt. He certainly didn't mind.

Logan swore out loud. He narrowly missed hitting a squirrel who had the misfortune to try and navigate Broadway's two-lane road just a few feet before it intersected with Route 47. Logan's quick reflexes had prevented the car from swerving into oncoming traffic.

He didn't need this…not today. Besides diverting his focus from reminiscing about the brunette, the sudden jerking of the car had made his captives fall to the floor. He hastily pulled onto a side street and idled the engine. "Get back on the seat," he ordered.

Kelly and Austin did as they were commanded, fighting against gravity and awkwardness. They fell against each other breathing heavily, waiting for the kidnapper to speak again.

"Here's how this is going to play out. We'll be at a rest stop soon where we'll be changing cars. If...you behave yourselves, I will allow you to use the bathrooms one at a time. Any contact with another person, and I'll know about it. Which won't end well for either of you...or your baby."

Austin reached protectively for Kelly's hand. As the sinister threat sent shivers up his spine, he felt her trembling beside him.

"Do we understand each other?"

Nodding as their eyes locked, Austin and Kelly sought momentary comfort through touching each other. Words were impossible at the moment, with or without the gags.

"Good." Logan tossed the blanket on top of them, then turned back around. Hesitant to carry on too much of a conversation with his back turned, he pulled back on the road. Quickly blending into traffic, he exhaled. No more stopping until the rest stop, he promised himself. Not even for suicide squirrels.

He couldn't take the risk. Right now it was more important to go with the flow, like the polished chameleon he was.

A habit perfected in such a short time, but a necessary one he had relied upon for survival.

Driving in silence once again allowed him to concentrate on his achievements, and the next phase of his plan. In the middle of a sunny day, he had accomplished the impossible. Kidnapping two people at gunpoint and driving off in their own car. He had timed the abduction perfectly.

Logan prided himself on a job well done. Or at least, the first phase of his mission. Everything was going according to his plans, and his captives weren't giving him any reason to change course at this point. He had them right where he wanted them.

Obedient and quiet. *For now.*

The rest stop wasn't much to look at. A few vending machines set inside a three-sided concrete alcove, two covered pavilions and a small building which housed the restrooms. No on-site custodial staff to get in the way. At this time of the day, only one other car was in the small parking lot. A black Chevy Tahoe with Virginia plates.

His getaway car.

Logan got out of the driver's seat, stretching his arms. Opening the driver's side back door, he crouched down, blocking the view of the backseat, just to make sure no one came upon his car unexpectedly. Cutting the ties on Austin's wrists, Logan motioned him to get out of the car.

"Two minutes. I'll keep your lady-friend company while you're away. "Don't do anything stupid, Reed."

"I heard you the first time." Austin walked at a fast pace, wanting nothing more than to reach the closest phone and dial 911. But the fear in Kelly's eyes made him nix that fleeting notion. He wasn't going to do anything to put her or their baby's life in jeopardy. No heroic action was worth the chance of losing his family.

"Time for us to get acquainted." Logan slid into the backseat next to Kelly. Immediately sensing her tension, he wasn't surprised when she made every possible effort to widen the distance between them.

He couldn't blame her, naturally, for wanting nothing to do with him. Forced out of her home, threatened repeatedly, bound and gagged. Scared out of her mind.

He had to relieve her fears, if only for a brief second. He had no intention of hurting her. *How could he?*

Spying on her through concealed cameras, he had seen practically every inch of Kelly McBride naked and vulnerable. But up close and personal, she was surreal. Logan was captivated, stunned beyond words. Blond, wavy hair and strikingly blue eyes. *The perfect woman.* He couldn't stop staring. He had to touch her.

"You're beautiful, you know that?"

Kelly recoiled, pressing herself against the car door. With Austin gone and her hands restrained, she couldn't possibly defend herself. She was at this man's mercy...if he had any to begin with.

Logan was surprised at how much her spurned reaction caused him pain. He had trained himself not to react to anyone...to *any* type of feelings. To be cold-hearted...and lethal. He couldn't afford to let his emotions get the better of him.

But it was happening now...and he was having a lot of trouble staying in control.

Austin's approaching footsteps made Logan snap to attention. He jumped from the back seat, shoving Austin inside. After fastening new ties onto Austin's wrists, he replaced the bandana across his mouth.

"Lie down and keep quiet. I'm going to take your girl to the ladies room. If I see the top of your head rise above the seat, I'll shoot her first, and then come back for you."

Walking to the other side of the car, Logan opened the back door and slit the ties off of Kelly's wrists. He removed the bandana from her mouth and stuffed it inside the front pocket of his jeans. Before he pulled her from the car, Logan tossed the blanket on top of Austin. "Let's go. Move nice and easy."

Wrapping his arm around Kelly's waist, he guided her along the brick pathway to the entrance of the ladies room. Her body was warm, and it felt so good to be close to her. Logan was disappointed the short walk had not given him enough time to touch her. Frustrated, he pushed her gently towards the door. "Don't be long, or I won't hesitate to come in and get you." Keeping a watchful eye on the car, he leaned against the concrete wall and folded his arms.

Sweat poured down his arms and across his forehead. Not from nerves, but definitely in reaction to the way Kelly felt against his arm. A feeling he desperately fought to avoid at all costs.

Lusting after her would only cause him trouble.

What have I gotten myself into?

He was a contract killer, not some highly-paid errand boy hired by Mason Hamilton. Kidnapping had never been part of his repertoire. He certainly wouldn't have entertained such a ridiculous notion if Mason Hamilton hadn't forced his hand.

Blackmail wasn't boding well with Logan McHenry even if it did make him step up his game. Logan spat on the ground. *How had he been so stupid to trust Hamilton in the first place?* Taking Hamilton at his word when he had been invited into his grand mansion, Logan had regrettably learned later their conversation was being recorded for Mason's own sense of self-preservation.

Logan would never forget the shock, knowing full well Hamilton had played him from the beginning. What began as an invitation to join Mason at his estate to go over the details of a new mission had ended with a threat of exposure.

His father had been right about one thing.

Trust was an over-rated concept.

One that snuck up and bit him right in the ass.

Now he was forced to do Mason's grunt work, no matter how condescending and degrading it was. Logan couldn't take a chance Mason was bluffing about the surveillance equipment installed inconspicuously in every room of his mansion. Or the fact Mason had every intention of sending a modified version of the recording to the FBI.

Usually Logan was quite adept at reading people, but not this time. Mason Hamilton had thrown a curve ball right at Logan's head.

Logan paced outside the ladies room, careful to avoid the security camera mounted on the outside corner of the building. He had done his recon several days ago, memorizing the placement of the three security cameras and the approximate sweeping range of their motorized scans. "Let's go," he called to get Kelly's attention. When she emerged Logan grabbed her elbow a little too roughly, causing her to jerk against him. "We need to get back on the road."

"Why are you doing this? For money? I'm sure my father is paying you plenty to…"

"I'm not discussing the terms of our business deal. Your father is…quite generous…and he has high expectations. You already know that, don't you, Kelly?"

Kelly cringed hearing her name cross his lips. "I don't want to talk about my father. Now…or ever."

"That's what I thought," Logan said drolly as they neared the car. He withdrew a cable tie from his pants' pocket. Quickly, he fastened the cable around her wrists and secured the bandana again around her mouth. As his fingers grazed her cheeks, he felt his own body shiver in response.

He was mesmerized with her. *How could he possibly hurt her…or allow her father to kill her?*

Mason hadn't made any qualms about what he intended to do when Kelly arrived in New York. He practically gloated, making Logan sick to his stomach. She was his daughter, and he would do whatever he wanted despite Logan's warnings. Mason Hamilton had made that perfectly clear.

Kelly would never see the light of day once she stepped inside Mason's house. Nor would her body ever be found.

Logan's previous conversation with Mason was weighing heavily on his mind. He was leading Kelly straight to her death.

The mere concept practically suffocated him every time his eyes fell across her beautiful scared face. He had absolutely no idea how he could pull it off.

Unless he double-crossed Mason Hamilton.

He could make Mason think Kelly was on her way to New York when in fact Logan would make sure she was travelling in the opposite direction. It just might work, Logan considered as he yanked the blanket off of Austin.

"Get out. Time to switch cars."

Chapter 4

"Got a little field assignment for you, Cowboy."

FBI Special Agent Brett Jacoby stopped in front of Trent Carroll's desk at the D.C. home office and sat on the corner.

The junior agent looked up from his pc and did a double-take. Shocked that a senior agent even remembered his name, Carroll sputtered, spewing coffee across his keyboard. "Yes, sir!" His thick, Texan accent coupled with his rugged swagger had earned him the dubious nickname. He took the ribbing in stride, never feeling the need to retaliate towards ill-bred Easterners who didn't know better. The less people who knowingly delved into his past, the better.

Searching his desk drawers for a paper towel, Carroll was surprised again as Jacoby handed him one from his jacket pocket. Carroll wondered what he had done to deserve field duty. His days were usually spent analyzing surveillance data or designing ingenious ways to infiltrate audio and video feeds. Mundane work, but intellectually challenging for the majority of the FBI agents. Carroll was the go-to guy for anything techno when Brett Jacoby wasn't around.

"Need you to get to Cape May, New Jersey ASAP. Agent Turette will already be there. She's en route now. You and Bromley are her back-up. I'm needed here. Got any questions?"

Carroll shook his head, jumped from his chair, and smoothed his tie. "No, sir. I'll grab my travel bag from my trunk and meet Bromley in the garage. Do we have a car reserved?"

Jacoby nodded. "Just called it in. Keep an eye on Bromley. He's still hell-bent on..."

Hearing his name, Agent Bromley smirked as he sidled up alongside of Jacoby. "No more heroics. I get it, Jacoby. We'll pack the vests, just in case." Lack of common sense on an earlier assignment in South Carolina had earned him a trip to the local hospital and a scar from a bullet hole. "Let's saddle up, Cowboy."

"Good," Jacoby retorted, raising an eyebrow. "Turette will apprise you of the situation when you arrive. Suffice it to say, you'll be assisting the locals with a kidnapping. Austin Reed and his fiancée Kelly McBride."

"Jenna's brother, right? God, she never gets a break. If it isn't one thing, it's something else."

"Who are you talking about?" Carroll tried his best to make his desk look presentable. Jacoby was still hovering and he needed to make a good impression. "Jenna Reed. I'll fill you in on the way. Don't worry, boss. We've got this. We'll check in when we get there."

"Do that," Jacoby called over his shoulder. A slight smile curled on his lips. Watching the two younger agents pick up the pace as they headed towards the elevator, Jacoby walked back to Turette's office. He had taken the liberty of using her desk when she wasn't in town, giving him more of an authoritative edge with the junior agents. His rightful place as her second-in-command.

A fine line he continued to walk while he also reported directly to her husband, Senior Agent Damian Pierce. Although, his connection to Pierce was purposely undocumented, Jacoby understood the covert reporting structure better than most people.

He had been Damian's right-hand man almost as long as he had been partnered with Maria Turette...without her knowledge. Jacoby's first assignment after being chosen to join the elite Joint Task Force was to infiltrate Maria's unit and keep a watchful eye.

Damian Pierce never had doubts about his wife's ability to be one of the only female agents in charge of an all-male FBI team, but he wasn't taking any chances. If one of her unit decided to back-stab her, Pierce wanted to make sure someone was watching her back...literally. There was no better watchdog than Agent Brett Jacoby.

Pierce knew his wife wouldn't have the heart to accuse any of her men of wrongdoing, but Jacoby had no reservations. He was the man for the job, and Pierce never regretted his decision. Jacoby soon became indispensable to Turette while at the same time he reported back to Pierce, keeping him apprised of every assignment.

One day though, Jacoby mused, he'd have to come clean and tell Turette the whole truth, but that day wasn't today. He was still being tasked with figuring out which one of Turette's team could possibly be a traitor, and it was driving him crazy.

He had carefully reviewed background checks on every agent in the unit and no one seemed outright suspicious. On Pierce's recommendation, Jacoby had consulted Simon Delarian, Pierce's old buddy at the CIA, but even Simon was baffled. Maria's unit was solid, yet Pierce was still harboring his betrayal theory, and wouldn't let go of it. It was almost an obsession.

Jacoby had his own theories which he fully intended to pursue. Starting now with Trent Carroll.

Carroll was fully capable of field duty, Jacoby thought, yet he seemed perfectly content to spend his days staring at computer screens, constantly analyzing data. Carroll was young, muscular, and tough. Transferred from the Austin Field Office a few years ago, he seemed like a fish out of water trying to navigate his bearings around D.C., but Jacoby hadn't quite paid too much attention to the Texan. Just rumors flying within the unit which Jacoby immediately dismissed. He didn't have time to speculate on Trent Carroll...until now.

Carroll was an enigma, a puzzle with the corners missing. He was an exemplary employee, never late, and always prompt with reports when Turette needed some intense research. Either he was trying to impress the boss, or he was a candidate for the next cloning project. Carroll almost seemed too good to be true.

Jacoby shook off his suspicions about Carroll. He'd deal with them later. Right now, there were more pressing issues. He speed-dialed Turette. "Wanted to give you a heads-up. The posse is on its way. Bromley and Carroll."

"Thanks," Maria said, barely acknowledging Jacoby's call. "I'm sorry...just tuning out for a few moments. How are things on your end?"

"I got in touch with the AC Field Office. They've just dispatched a couple of agents to Cape May." Jacoby glanced down at his watch. "Actually, they should be arriving soon."

"You never cease to amaze me. Are you keeping everyone in line while I'm away?"

"Running a tight ship, as always. You keep making excuses to avoid the office, Turette, and I might even take over your coffee cup. I've already made myself comfortable at your desk so disregard the heel marks on your desk blotter."

"They better be gone when I get back," Maria threatened jokingly. "And don't mess with my chair. You know I can't stand it when you move the height lever and my feet dangle. I'm on to you, Jacoby."

Jacoby snickered. "You got nothing, Turette. I always wear gloves."

"I doubt that, but I'll take it under advisement. Keep in touch."

*****

Damian hit the button on his steering wheel activating his Bluetooth speaker phone. "Simon, please tell me you have good news for me, and make sure you behave yourself. I have a lady in the car."

Simon Delarian laughed before responding. "Oh, I do hope you have the lovely Maria by your side."

"Always a pleasure, Simon," Maria said with a smile. "Are you behaving yourself these days?"

"Maria, Maria...I always behave...it's that rogue husband of yours we need to worry about. So glad to finally hear your tantalizing voice again. Now, what laws can I break for you today?"

Maria laughed. Simon Delarian never changed. He had the same personality he always did, and the same catch phrase. Simon was always the talker but never confident enough in person to follow through with any of his suggestive remarks. He was harmless enough except when it came to his clever sleuth skills in the field of surveillance. If anyone harbored a secret lifestyle, Simon had ways of finding out all the intricate details, good and bad through legal...and sometimes illegal channels.

"I think I'll keep my husband for a little while longer, Simon. But if he acts up, it's good to know I have other...*options*." Maria sneaked a wink in Damian's direction as his hand slid off the wheel, grabbing hers in mid-air.

"I plan on keeping my wife very happy, Simon, so you may be waiting a while." Damian kissed Maria's hand quickly, then returned his hand to the steering wheel. "What did you find out?"

"Permission to speak freely?" Simon asked warily.

"Go ahead, Simon," Maria interrupted. "Damian finally confessed he dragged you into his little seek-and-find game. I'm holding him accountable, not you."

Simon chuckled. "Nice to know who wears the pants in the family."

"Absolutely," Damian lied. "Maria has on her tight, black leather pants as we speak. Try not to salivate, Simon. Now, what do you have?"

Simon cleared his throat, trying to shake the mental picture of Maria Turette donning black leather above or *below* the waist. Known for her rigorous routine of jogging, kick-boxing and weight-lifting, Maria's sculpted body never gave her age away. "Anyway...here's the skinny...Jacoby and Thompson, check. Bromley and Michaelson, check. Good so far, right?"

"No-brainers, Simon. What else?" Damian asked, shooting a glance in Maria's direction.

"A few cobwebs here and there."

"What is that supposed to mean?" Maria spoke up, annoyed with the whole run-down of her team. As much as she wanted the matter cleared up so they could move forward, she knew it was going to be a painful process as Simon persisted with his thorough, yet somewhat condescending reviews.

"Easy...easy. Don't shoot the messenger. Anyway...here's where it gets a bit dicey. Carroll, or *Cowboy*, as you like to call him, has a few blips on the radar. Could be nothing but there are two years where I can't find anything about him in the system. Maybe a data glitch. Who knows? Even the CIA's most sophisticated systems have problems. Bad data in, bad data out. Simple math. But it does raise a few miniscule flares. You want me to pursue it, Pierce?"

Damian debated what to do. Carroll had never given Maria one bit of trouble in the five years he had been on her team. Still...unexplained data didn't sit well with him. Damian's reluctance to answer promptly caused Maria to punch him in the arm, forcing his hasty decision. "Move on, Simon. I don't think it's a big deal."

"Finally...the voice of reason." Maria folded her arms in protest. "I hope my husband's little side project isn't taking you away from your actual job, Simon."

"On the contrary. I'm a bit bored anyway. This little project, as you like to call it, is quite...intriguing to say the least. I'll call you when I have more updates. Oh, and Pierce, don't forget. Fifty-yard line. I won't take anything less...unless the seats are in a dark corner of the stadium...with *your wife*."

Maria tried not to laugh as she batted her eyes at Damian.

"In your dreams, Simon. Just keep checking, and I'll see what I can do," Damian said, unappreciative of Simon's risqué remarks.

"Anything for you, Agent Pierce...and the lovely Maria. Over and out."

Damian was still frowning when Maria tapped the back of his hand. "He pushes your buttons, doesn't he?"

"He tries to, especially when he's making suggestive remarks about my sexy wife. I'm not planning on sharing you with anyone else, sweetheart."

"Keep that thought and we'll get along just fine. How much further?" Maria asked, yawning and stretching her arms above her head.

"About another hour or so. Do you want to check in with Jenna and Chase again?"

"No. I'm sure they're fine. Anyway, the AC team should be in place watching the beach house by now."

"Maybe it's a good time to call Jonathan. He was supposed to fly into Atlantic City sometime today. He needs to know what's going on."

"I've sent him two texts. He's either too busy to check his phone, or he's ignoring me for some reason," Maria said in a worried tone.

"He can handle himself, Maria. He won't take any unnecessary risks."

"Really? Do you hear yourself, Damian? Jonathan has been doing *nothing* but taking risks ever since he met Jenna Reed. When it comes to her, he doesn't think clearly; that's for sure. He's doing all this to impress her; I just know it. Jonathan is going to get hurt...physically, emotionally or both."

Maria sighed. She wanted Jonathan to be happy, but she wondered if Jenna was the one who could truly make him happy. Torn between making a commitment to Chase and dealing with her obvious attraction to Jonathan, Jenna always appeared to be overly distracted in Maria's mind.

"Jonathan needs to face the facts. Jenna belongs with Chase."

"Maybe, maybe not. She's wavering between the two of them. Jenna keeps trying to convince herself she's committed to Chase, but she can't completely push aside her feelings for Jonathan. Just a big, confusing love triangle. Thank God I never had that problem. I knew I loved you from day one."

Maria tugged on Damian's hand until their fingers were linked. She laid their clasped hands on the console between them.

"Good to know," Damian said in his low, raspy voice. "You know I feel the same way. I always have."

"Oh, I know." Maria smiled. "I know all about you, Damian Pierce...the good *and* the bad."

Damian was glad Maria had chosen that exact moment to look out the side window at the passing landscape. She narrowly missed the brief closure of his eyes and the regrettable shake of his head. Keeping secrets from his wife...had *never* been easy.

Chapter 5

"Oh, this is just what I need!"

Ann Bailey couldn't help but notice the shiny, black Suburban pulling alongside the curb next to the Reeds' beach house. Standard issue, rugged SUV. Dark-tinted, impenetrable windows. A small triangular-shaped beacon positioned in front of the luggage rack. Even before the passengers got out, she had no doubts who they were.

Feds.

But what were they doing here? Did Turette request backup? Was she expecting some type of trouble and didn't quite have a comfort level that Ann could handle it?

"Thanks for the heads-up," Ann said with a huff. Pulling the linen curtains aside, she peered out of the front window of the house she was using to spy on Jenna Reed. The house Turette secured with her multiple connections was directly across from the Reeds' beach house. Disappointment mixed with curiosity kept Ann at a distance. She fought the urge to race down the steps, confront the agents who had stepped out of their car, and demand to know what was going on.

Of course making such a bold move would blow her cover and draw unnecessary attention. Neither of which were compelling enough reasons to make her do something stupid she would later regret. Still, Turette should have at least warned her the cavalry was coming. Out of courtesy.

Ann continued to watch the actions of the two men dressed in dark suits and sunglasses. They looked so out of place at the beach, she couldn't help but laugh.

"Discreet, fellas. Very discreet."

As the two agents made a cursory sweep around the perimeter of the Reeds' house, Ann speculated as to the reason they had been summoned. Nothing seemed out of the ordinary when Jenna and Chase had arrived about an hour ago, except that Chase had raced down the side steps and searched the pebble driveway like he had lost something. Jenna had stayed inside, and as far as Ann could tell, there was no cause for alarm. No other local police had arrived. No ambulance or fire rescue.

Something had definitely happened to require the services of two federal agents. Something Turette undoubtedly knew about...yet was unwilling to share.

Ann fumed. She hated being kept in the dark, and was ready to call Turette when her cell buzzed.

"Hey, how are you doing?" Special Agent Maria Turette asked.

Ann ignored the perfunctory greeting. "We have company."

"Jacoby requested some back-up from the AC field office. Wanted to make sure you knew about it. Guess I'm a little late calling."

"A little. They just got here."

"Sorry. Too much going on. Austin and Kelly are missing. A picture was left on the kitchen table for Jenna. Looks like they were taken against their will earlier today."

"I...didn't see anything. Must have happened when I was out running. I take a morning jog almost every day. Trying to fit in."

"Not your fault. I asked you to keep an eye on Jenna, not Austin and Kelly."

"Still...I'm right across the street. I feel responsible."

"Ann, stop beating yourself up. This could have happened when they were out shopping. There was no way to predict Austin and Kelly were going to be kidnapped. Whoever did this is a professional or extremely brazen. In the middle of the day of all times. This was well-planned. I guess I don't have to tell you, Mason Hamilton is at the top of my list. Actually his hired hands, who at this point, could be practically anyone willing to do his bidding."

"What do you need me to do, boss?"

"Sit tight. Don't interact with the other agents; you'll blow your cover. Jenna doesn't need to know she has a bodyguard right now. That will just upset her more knowing someone is watching her every move. I'm on my way. Probably should arrive in another forty minutes or so. I'll call you when we get there, then we can figure out our next move."

Ann tossed her Blackberry on a nearby chair. Frustrated at her own incompetency, she shook her head and rolled her eyes. A kidnapping had occurred right under her nose, and she hadn't seen or heard anything. Maria was right; whoever had kidnapped Austin and Kelly knew precisely what he was doing with perfect timing.

Too perfect. Had she been set up?

Ann wondered if the kidnapper had figured out she was staking out the Reeds' house, and somehow had worked his plan around her schedule. Anxiety and paranoia body-slammed her at the same time.

Maybe the house was bugged? At this very moment, he could be listening...or watching...

Ann wasted no more time. She began sweeping the house for micro cameras and audio feeds. She checked windowsills, lamps, each piece of furniture, and all the drapes on the lower level until she was covered in sweat. She found nothing but she still didn't have a comfort level.

Electronic recording devices could be planted inconspicuously almost anywhere. Refined over the years, she knew for a fact the tiny bugs could take various shapes and could be well-placed and hidden from even highly-trained agents. She needed specialized equipment to track the tiny frequencies inaudible to human ears.

She needed "*S*", her mysterious partner who had made sure she was well-connected with firearms and video surveillance upon her arrival. Ann ran down to the basement and withdrew the small folded note she had found in the duffel bag containing her small arsenal.

Welcome to Cape May!
This is idiot-proof. Follow the instructions attached to the back of this note and you'll do fine. Call me if you need help. S.
202-555-5357

Ann returned to the living room to find her cell which was wedged between the side of the armchair and the seat cushion. Hurrying outside using the back door off the kitchen, she typed in the number from the note. Within seconds, an unfamiliar male voice answered.

"I'm assuming you need my help."

"Yes, and I suppose you're not going to tell me your name."

Seconds ticked away with no response.

"Well?" Ann persisted.

"I'm thinking."

"Think faster. I've got security issues. I need a sweep."

More pauses. This was starting to claw at her nerves.

"Interesting…"

"I can't function if…" Ann protested.

"Patience, Agent Bailey." His voice took on a confident, authoritative tone. "I've just dispatched an agent to your location. He will arrive within the hour, dressed as a plumber. I'm assuming he can park his van in your driveway or along the curb?"

"Yes. What about your name? You obviously know who I am. I should expect the same courtesy."

Silence bounced back at her for the third time. *Enough already.* "Look, I don't know who the hell you think you are but…"

It didn't take her too long to realize the call had ended. "Son-of-a…doesn't surprise me."

Ann hurried back up the steps. As long as the elusive "*S*" came through for her, she didn't care what his initial stood for. She had plenty of suggestions that didn't bear repeating.

It didn't matter, really. As long as she got the help she needed. Denial. Lies. Obscurity. Came with the badge.

Unfortunately, sometimes it was a disadvantage. But not now, Ann thought as she tried to hide a smile. The elusive "*S*" had come through for her once again, and she wasn't about to discredit his assistance.

Quite the opposite.

She needed "*S*" more now than ever. As Ann made her way back into the house, she couldn't help but wonder what type of twisted and lethal perpetrator they were dealing with. A man…or woman so devious and manipulative to take Austin and Kelly from the safety of their home in pure daylight…who threatened them to such a degree they didn't hesitate to go along. Their abductor had no fear and no regard for Kelly's pregnancy.

Merciless and deadly. The worst possible kind of criminal element.

Shivers trickled down Ann's spine. As she began to mentally profile the person responsible for such a brash offense, Ann stood rigid at the front window watching the two agents pace up and down the sidewalk. The severity of the situation hit her hard as she recalled the two kidnapping cases she had worked on earlier in her career.

Neither had ended well.

Ransoms were paid, and the kidnappers were never apprehended. But the bodies had been found.

Revealing each victim had been tortured, then brutally murdered.

*****

"Enough scurrying around in the dark, Renault. I have to leave," Jonathan Knox protested as he and Laurence Renault got inside the car waiting to take them back to New York City. Their act of espionage in Mason Hamilton's mansion had concluded for the evening. Much to Jonathan's relief.

"Patience, Jonathan. You must learn…"

"I've wasted enough time," Jonathan complained. "I'm needed in Cape May. You made me miss my plane. The least you can do is drop me off at the airport." Jonathan folded his arms in disgust. He couldn't wait to get as far away from Laurence Renault as was humanly possible. What he had seen and heard this evening was too revolting.

"Of course. Raul, head straight for JFK," Renault called to his driver who nodded in response. "Mr. Knox needs to catch a plane."

"I think you need to keep your distance, Renault," Jonathan said, forcing himself to stare directly at Renault. "In fact, I don't want you anywhere near Kelly. She means a lot to me and you'll only upset her."

"How gallant of you, Jonathan. Chivalry isn't dead by a far stretch," Renault joked sarcastically.

Jonathan shifted his gaze to the side window hoping Renault would disappear into thin air. "You and I both know you don't give a damn about my relationship with Kelly. Your intentions are entirely self-serving."

"On the contrary, Jonathan. My sole mission is to save my daughter's life."

Jonathan rolled his eyes. He didn't believe one word out of Renault's mouth. "You came back to the States for revenge. Why don't you just admit it?"

"Merely a side adventure, I assure you. Mason needs to atone for his past sins, as we all do. I was forced to re-evaluate my lifestyle, when news of my untimely death was broadcast over Europe. I had to live...through precarious means for many years. Have you any idea what that is like? Never coming out in the light of day unless I was wearing a disguise and changing my voice? I was a prisoner, Jonathan, of my own life...and Mason was fully responsible. I have never forgiven him. Mason Hamilton is an evil man. So, yes, you are correct. I have every intention of enacting my revenge...but first I must make sure I do everything possible to keep my daughter safe."

Jonathan snorted. "Feeling pious, Renault? Don't waste my time. I really don't care about your resurrection. As far as Mason's concerned, go ahead. Duke it out. I don't trust either one of you."

Renault sighed. "Then I must find a way to earn your trust. What can I do to assure you...?"

Jonathan whipped his head around. "Nothing. I don't want you to do anything...especially now. For God's sake, Renault, Kelly is getting married in a few days. She's looking forward to the best day of her life...and she deserves to be happy. Please don't take that away from her. Do you have any idea what your news will do to her?"

Before Renault could answer, Jonathan continued. "You want to do the right thing? To really prove how much you love your daughter? Then give her the gift of a peaceful wedding day. No surprises, *no rising-from-the-dead-I'm-your-father* speeches. Just a day filled with beautiful memories. Give that to her...please."

Renault looked Jonathan straight in the eyes...and lied. "Of course. I will do as you wish."

The remainder of the ride to the airport was met in daunting silence. Jonathan refused to prolong the conversation. As soon as the car pulled up alongside of the curb, Jonathan jumped out, not waiting for Renault's assistant to help him with retrieving his suitcase from the trunk.

Renault watched Jonathan jog into the airport as a smile creased his lips. "Find a parking space, Raul. We're taking a private charter...to New Jersey. Jonathan is a fool if he believes I won't see my daughter on her wedding day."

*****

Logan McHenry was perspiring more than usual. A sure sign regret was about to give him a swift kick in the ass.

He had let Mason Hamilton talk him into a bad situation. He wasn't a kidnapper, let alone a man who was risking the life of a pregnant woman. He was a gun for hire, nothing more. Until today.

What choice did he have? Not much, Logan lamented. Not much at all. If Mason made good on his threat to expose him to the FBI, Logan wouldn't have a chance in hell of getting across any border or flying back to Europe. Not without going to extremes and a lot of trouble.

Logan paused for a brief second to consider the impact of his actions. Hearing Kelly groan in the backseat was eating at him. He wished he could trust her so he could release the binding on her wrists, to make her more comfortable. So she would be less afraid, if that was even possible.

But he dared not take the chance. Not with her boyfriend by her side.

Austin Reed, whom Mason held in such low regard.

"Austin Reed is nothing but a slacker. His relationship with Kelly was an unfortunate by-product of a miscalculated mission. Do whatever you feel is necessary to rid yourself of this complication." Mason's words rang loudly in Logan's ears, making him shift uncomfortably in the front seat.

Austin Reed didn't deserve to die, and for the first time, Logan wished he hadn't chosen his present profession. Logan shook his head to clear it of any uncertainties. He needed to focus on his mission, pushing away any crazy regrets. He was a professional, racking up enough kills to make a name for himself. He had no time or energy for self-doubts, especially those threatening to cloud his vision and increase the chances he would make a mistake.

No mistakes, Logan recited silently to himself. No mistakes...and no regrets. Just a couple more miles and he would pull into his destination...his safe house in the Poconos. A far cry from Mason Hamilton's mansion, but at least it would give him some time to figure out his next move.

It was difficult enough to navigate the terrain due to the fog which frequently engulfed the Pocono Mountains. Logan had made the journey many times before; he knew it like the back of his hand. Still, the dense weather conditions caused him to reduce his speed several times on the back roads leading to his private property. Just as well, Logan thought. At least he wasn't drawing any attention to himself.

Pulling onto the dirt road at the front of his multi-acre property, he couldn't help but breathe a sigh of relief. He had made it this far without any problems and his captives hadn't given him a bit of trouble. *So far, so good.*

He stopped short of the ten-foot barbed-wire fence which barricaded his house, leaving the rest of the wooded grounds in their natural state. More or less.

Two years had passed, and no one had come calling. Of course baiting the property with a sophisticated alarm system and multiple traps had been well worth his efforts. Even if some nosy tourist had found the trail off the main highway and followed it straight to his electronic fence, he doubted they would have stayed long. Posting *Government Testing Facility* signs to several trees and on the fence itself would most likely have made most people run for their lives.

Logan chuckled to himself. People were so gullible and easily fooled by the simplest interventions. As he typed in his security code, he waited patiently as the dual-gates opened widely. He paused briefly, surveying the small yard in front of his house. It was just as he had left it the last time he passed through on his way to Canada. Nothing seemed out of place. Extra barbed-wire and steel poles were piled in a heap next to his side door, almost blocking the entrance. Several spare tires were tossed randomly across the front stone walkway, and his wood-pile on the far right corner was surprisingly still upright.

Confident the security of his private domain hadn't been breached by human or creature intervention, Logan pulled the

Tahoe inside, swung his door open, and jumped straight into a large mud puddle on his way to secure the gates.

"Shit," he swore in a low tone. His Keen hiking shoes were soaked through as well as his socks and the bottom of his jeans. "Welcome home," he grumbled as he walked back to punch in the reset code on the lock, securing the gate.

The frequent rainstorms the past couple of weeks had made a mess of his driveway, making Logan wish he had taken the time to lay down another layer of gravel. The initial foundation had practically washed away due to the slight incline leading up to the house. He didn't have time to worry about his lack of landscaping detail.

Logan yanked open the back door of the Tahoe, and pulled out his duffel bags. Slamming the rear tailgate, he circled around to the side door. "Get out. Watch your step. It's muddy."

Austin shook off the blanket and sat upright. He first glanced at Kelly to make sure she was alright, then nodded his head. His first thought was to kick his way out of the truck, and then attack his assailant with enough strength to knock him out. However, fearing the retaliation that would surely come if he wasn't successful, Austin did as he was told. He couldn't take a chance the bastard would take his frustration out on Kelly, hurting her and the baby.

"Stand over there," Logan said gruffly, pushing Austin aside. Then he climbed inside the truck and tugged gently on Kelly's wrists. "You're next," he ordered, trying hard to soften his tone.

Kelly wiped a tear with the back of her hand before she slowly edged her way along the back seat. Stepping down into the soft mud, she winced, as the thick wetness seeped into her sneakers. She took a step closer to Austin but was quickly pulled away.

"She stays with me," Logan announced as his arm slid around Kelly's waist. "Walk towards the side door of the house, Reed. Any sudden moves and she'll take the brunt of your dumbass decision."

Austin trudged forward up the small incline, slipping once and almost falling to his knees.

"Inside," Logan barked. "Door's open. Kick off your shoes and socks. Roll up your pants. I don't want mud in my house."

"Then untie us." Austin responded.

"Shut up, Reed. Make do for now." Logan nudged Kelly inside until she bumped into Austin's back.

"Sorry," she whispered as her fingers eagerly sought to grasp a clump of his shirt.

Austin took off Kelly's shoes first then her socks. Rolling her jeans up her calves, he lingered briefly to caress the back of her legs. A small touch of comfort was all he could give to her now.

Logan was paying attention. "You know I was quite entertained when I was watching the video feed from your house. Better than HBO. The two of you are...*very extreme*. Even by my personal standards. Especially the time..."

"We get it. You bugged our house and probably enjoyed reporting every last detail back to Hamilton. Am I right? He gets off on that kind of thing, doesn't he?"

"Just for the record, I didn't give Mason any descriptive details about your sex life. He didn't ask and I didn't tell." Logan grabbed a knife from the block on the counter and twirled it with his fingers. "Don't underestimate me, Reed...ever." Logan paused for effect. He cut the plastic ties binding their wrists, then motioned them towards the living room. "Sit on the sofa, and enjoy my...*hospitality*."

Before Austin stepped forward, Logan lunged sideways and nicked Austin's neck, drawing several droplets of blood.

Kelly gasped as her hands flew to Austin's neck. Blood trickled down two of her fingers as she tried to keep them steady. Her eyes darted around the kitchen until she saw a stack of napkins on the counter behind her. Grabbing several, she applied pressure until the bleeding eventually stopped. Her lips were trembling so much she couldn't even say his name.

"I'm ok, Kel." Austin draped his arm around her shoulders and moved them both towards the sofa.

"He's going to kill us, Austin. I'm so sorry..." Kelly turned her face away so Austin wouldn't see her shame.

"For what, Kel?"

"For all of this. If I had just done what my father wanted...gone to New York...you wouldn't be here right now. You wouldn't be hurt."

"Enough talking," Logan ordered. "We move out at dawn."

Chapter 6

Jenna woke the next morning with a migraine headache threatening to keep her brain in a vise grip.

Once again, too much tension was consuming her life with very little breaks in between. Worried about the fate of her brother and her best friend, Jenna did little but toss and turn most of the night. Bumping into Chase and apologizing at least twice, Jenna finally fell asleep out of sheer exhaustion.

For only a few hours. She was wide awake now.

Jenna bolted upright in bed, cradling her throbbing head. "I've put them in danger! This is all my fault! If something happens to Austin and Kelly...Chase!"

Chase's strong arms did little to comfort her. Resting his chin on her shoulder, he gave her waist a small squeeze. "Go down and talk to Maria and Damian. They might have some updates by now. I'm going to hit the shower. Save me some coffee." He kissed her cheek before jumping from the bed.

Another wave of pain crossed Jenna's eyes when she got to her feet. Navigating the stairs took a great deal of effort. "Hi," was all she could say before making a beeline for the Advil bottle on the kitchen hutch.

"Coffee?"

Maria didn't wait for Jenna to respond. She filled a mug of steaming black coffee and set it on the table. "Damian and I made ourselves at home, raiding your coffee supplies. We're caffeine addicts. I personally have no problem justifying at least six cups a day." Maria uttered a small laugh then stopped as she took in Jenna's drawn face. "You look like hell."

"Couldn't sleep."

"Understandable." Maria refilled her own mug and sat down across from Jenna. Bags under her eyes were a tell-tale sign she hadn't slept either. "Damian just got a call. Jersey State Police found Austin's car about an hour ago. They're processing it now for prints."

Jenna's mouth dropped.

"Don't go jumping to any conclusions. We're waiting on details."

"Maria...what if...?" Jenna's bloodshot eyes started to mist.

"No blood. No sign of struggle. A partial print. That's all we've got so far. We're running it through IAFIS. If he's on the radar anywhere...we'll get him."

"Sorry...*IAFIS*?" Jenna questioned, wincing from another sharp jab of pain.

Damian strode into the kitchen, stopping behind Maria's chair. "Integrated Automated Fingerprint Identification System. We got a match. Ever hear of Logan McHenry? Went rogue a few years back. Walked off an Army base in Germany without a trace. Word on the street is...he's back on the East Coast. Been tracking him in Europe the past couple of years. Not sure why he's stateside, but it wouldn't surprise me in the least if he's hooked up with Hamilton."

Maria took Damian's hand. "I don't like this. What else do you know about McHenry?"

"Army Special Forces, sniper-trained. A contract killer but different than The Closer. Young, probably mid-to-late twenties. A risk taker...but very creative. Doesn't have a signature style. Likes to mix things up, confuse everyone. He blends into his surroundings very easily; that's probably why we can't nail him. Methodical, very dangerous. A charmer and a con artist rolled into one. Good with disguises. If he's added kidnapping to his repertoire, then he's diversifying."

Maria reached over to touch Jenna's arm. "We'll get him. It's only a matter of time. He's used to travelling alone, not with two hostages. This will throw off his game. Some-one...somewhere will see him or he'll slip up. Jenna, trust me. We're going to find Austin and Kelly very soon. I promise."

"Hamilton is pulling the strings, isn't he?" Jenna's voice cracked. "I just know it."

"Unfortunately, we can't tie McHenry to Hamilton at this point," Damian confirmed. "Hamilton is too clever. If we can find one shred of evidence linking the two of them together, we can bring Hamilton in; hit him with an accessory charge. We have to be sure this time."

"Wishful thinking," Maria added. Without concrete evidence, she knew the DA's office would never bring charges against Mason Hamilton. They had been shot down too many times before, made to look incompetent with too much bad press.

Jenna seethed. "There's only one way to end this...and we all know what that is."

"Stop thinking like that," Maria said.

"Let us do our jobs, Jenna." Damian reaffirmed Maria's appeal. "Austin and Kelly are depending on us. Ok?"

Jenna nodded reluctantly. "I know you're right, Damian, but I can't help but feel responsible. If I had just given Hamilton the rest of the treasure pieces, he would have left Austin and Kelly alone."

"You don't know that." Maria rose from the table. "What's our next move?"

"I'd like to hear this, too." Chase leaned in the doorway, keeping his eyes on Jenna.

Damian drained his coffee mug and set it in the sink. "State Police all along the East Coast have been notified. They've got McHenry's army picture for reference, although I'm sure he's changed his appearance enough that it really doesn't matter. Anyway, we've pulled some agents from D.C. to monitor traffic cams, bridge cameras, airport, train and tunnel recordings. The FBI has jurisdiction and I'm heading up the investigation. I'm getting picked up within the hour. Setting up base in northern New Jersey for now until we need to shift gears. Jacoby is flying up from D.C. to assist. I want all of you to stay put for now."

Jenna started to stand but Chase pushed her back down in her seat. "Don't get any ideas." He firmly squeezed her shoulders then popped a kiss on the top of her head.

"The minute you find anything...I'm joining you, Damian." As much as she appreciated Chase's attempt to keep her grounded, she wished for once he would just let go.

"Jenna, let us handle this...please. As much as I can appreciate your concern for your brother and your future sister-in-law, our team doesn't need one more person to worry about," Damian insisted.

Jenna glared first at Damian, then Maria. "You're ok with this? Come on, Maria. You're just going to stand by and watch this unfold?"

"I have to be, Jenna. Damian is point on this one. He's coordinating the efforts of several agencies, and I'm needed here.

Just in case Hamilton pulls another trump card. Two of my men are en route from D.C. We want to make sure everyone here stays safe."

"What you really mean…is that you're keeping an eye on me. I'm not the one in danger. Can't you all see that? Hamilton is striking out by going after people I care about. He's getting to me that way instead of a direct attack."

"You were shot in Texas, and for all we know, The Closer was behind it. You're still in danger whether you want to believe it or not. So, yes, we are keeping an eye on you."

"Great, Maria," Jenna lamented. The Advil was just taking the edge off, although her head was still hammering.

"You think McHenry is heading north, Damian? Why not stake out Hamilton's house and office? Isn't that the obvious trail?"

"McHenry isn't known for doing the obvious, Chase. My gut tells me he's switching gears. We need to be ready. I'm covering as many bases as possible. I've got a team en route to New York who will follow Hamilton everywhere he goes. If McHenry does surface, we'll move in. But I think Hamilton is smart enough to keep a safe distance."

"I don't get this. What could McHenry possibly gain by kidnapping Austin and Kelly if he doesn't plan to take them to Hamilton?"

"I haven't finalized that theory yet. There are too many players in this game."

"And not enough winners," Maria added as an uneasy hush fell over everyone in the room.

*****

"Where the hell are you?"

Mason Hamilton's patience was wearing thin. He had tried to impress upon Logan McHenry the importance of providing regular, on-time reports. A concept The Closer blatantly disregarded.

"A very secure location. My captives can't escape."

"*Captives*…as in the plural sense?" So that was it, Mason mused. McHenry was still saddled with Austin Reed. "I would have thought by now you would have…"

"Not yet."

"You're wasting time. *My time* and I'm not happy about it."

"I have everything under control."

"Is that so? I have no problem sending Hans your way if you need assistance. He's perfectly capable of..."

"I work alone, Mr. Hamilton. I thought I made that clear to you." Logan didn't back down.

"As you did, my boy. However, I merely wanted to present the offer. Hans is available, and his services would not complicate your mission; only enhance it."

"I can handle it. Keep Kliric out of my way."

"Two days, Logan. I want this wrapped up very soon."

"Not a problem."

"Good. Don't disappoint me. I expect great things from you."

Logan stared at his cell, surprised Mason had hung up without another word. "Arrogant bastard," Logan cursed. He pulled his gun from the holster left on the bedside table. It felt heavier than normal, and he knew the reason why.

Austin Reed didn't deserve to die. Not like this.

Logan paced the floor of his bedroom as conflicting arguments swirled in his mind. He had to make a stand and it had to be right now. If he was determined to cross Mason Hamilton, and he was pretty sure that was the only way to go, then he needed to make a move before Mason got wind of his defection.

To save Kelly McBride's life, he would cross into Canada. His friends lived in Ogdensburg, a border town on the New York side, and they wouldn't hesitate to help. It was a good plan. It would work.

Only if he was travelling with one hostage.

This presented Logan with two options.

Kill Reed or leave him behind.

Logan tossed the gun on his bed. He was sticking by his own set of rules. To kill only when warranted. Mason Hamilton could fume all he wanted.

Unzipping his duffel bag, Logan withdrew a small syringe. As he opened his bedroom door, he inhaled sharply and told himself he was doing the right thing. Although he was sure Kelly wouldn't understand, he hoped at a later date she would actually thank him.

Logan took small steps making sure neither Austin nor Kelly could hear him approaching. Both of their heads were tilted downward giving him the impression they were both asleep. *Good,* Logan thought. *This will be quick and painless.*

Austin woke suddenly, feeling a pinch on his arm. In less than a minute, he felt overly drowsy. He reached for Kelly, trying to wake her. She wasn't responding. Austin tried again until his arms went slack and his eyes closed. His head rolled to one side. He was out.

"Get up," Logan whispered as he bent down close to her ear. "He can't hear you."

Kelly's immediate reaction was to shake Austin and call his name, but from the look in Logan's eyes, she knew it would be of no use. "What did you do to him?"

"Gave him a sedative. He'll be out for a few hours. Get up," Logan repeated, pulling Kelly to her feet. "Now, do as you're told and we'll get along just fine. I won't hurt you…or your baby, but you need to listen to me."

There was nothing she could do. She had no way to defend herself or Austin…or their baby. Nodding, she allowed herself to be led into the back bedroom. Kelly froze when they were both facing the bed. "Please…don't make me…!"

Logan relaxed his hold on her arm. "This isn't what you think. I couldn't hurt you…or any other woman, for that matter…in that way."

"Then why did you bring me back here?"

"To escape." Logan opened the sliding door to his sparsely-filled closet. Kneeling, he pushed aside two shoeboxes. In the far right corner, he felt along the carpet until his fingers connected with a small half-moon handle, inconspicuously hidden by the rug fibers. Pulling upward, the hatch revealed a passageway and a ladder. Logan tossed down a flashlight along with two duffel bags. "Climb down. Hang on tightly and take one step at a time. You'll be fine, and I'll be right behind you."

Kelly gingerly lowered herself down the small ladder which only consisted of six metal rungs. She picked up the flashlight and shone it around her feet, praying no rats or other small creatures were in the immediate vicinity. The underground tunnel had been carefully dug and supported by wooden beams. He had planned this escape route for quite some time, she gathered. Just like he had carefully planned to kidnap her and Austin.

Logan wasted no time. He tossed the duffels over his shoulder and grabbed Kelly's hand. It wasn't long until they reached another ladder. Pausing briefly, Logan considered what he was about to do. Move forward and be on the run from Mason Hamilton, the police, and the FBI...or turn back, reunite Kelly with her boyfriend, set them both free...and hope Mason Hamilton didn't send someone else to kill her.

One look at Kelly's tear-soaked face was all the motivation he needed. "Up you go." Logan gave Kelly a slight push towards the ladder. "There's a car parked a few feet away. Get in the back seat and lay down." He withdrew a small remote from his pocket and showed it to her.

"What's that?" Kelly asked, afraid of his answer.

"My insurance policy. Hopefully I won't have to use it. The house is wired. As long as you don't try to escape, everything is going to be just fine."

Kelly drew in a sharp breath. She sensed he meant every word he said, and each one cut her deeply. "Where are you taking me?"

"Somewhere...safe."

Chapter 7

"Finally!"

Jonathan grabbed his suitcase from the luggage carousel and sprinted towards the Enterprise rental counter. He had just landed in Atlantic City, a delay of several hours from his original arrival plans.

All because Renault wanted to do a little recon at Mason's estate.

I've really fallen in the hole this time. Reached a whole new level of stupidity.

Breaking and entering. Destruction of personal property. Associating with an international criminal.

Maria is going to kill me…if she ever finds out.

Jonathan took a deep breath before speed-dialing his mother. "I'm ok…before you start jumping to conclusions."

"Why on earth would I do that?" Maria asked curiously. "Just because Damian and I carry concealed weapons most of the time, there's no need to…"

"How are you?" Jonathan changed the subject. "Your shoulder ok?"

"Fine…and not so fine. Still hurts. Not bouncing back as fast as I'd like to. When are you getting here?"

"Hopefully within the hour. I'm at AC Airport. Just got in. Delayed flight," Jonathan lied. "Should see you in a little bit unless I hit traffic…*Mom.*" It still sounded strange calling Maria that, but he was slowly getting used to it. Finding out who his real mother was just months earlier had been shocking, but not totally out of the ballpark. Jonathan had always suspected he was adopted, and when Maria admitted she was his real mother, he couldn't be happier. Raised by one of Maria's college friends, Jonathan had enjoyed a very cohesive family arrangement with unlimited love. But after both parents died of medical issues, he felt abandoned. His adoptive grandmother Mabel had done her best to fill the gap along with her constant barrage of rescue dogs.

"I'll be happy to see you. Drive safe."

"Kelly and Austin a bundle of nerves by now? I can't wait..."

Maria wished she had ended the call sooner. "I...was waiting until you got here. We've had some bad news. Kelly and Austin...are missing. We have reason to believe they've been kidnapped."

The severity of Maria's words hit Jonathan like a brick wall. He could barely respond without sputtering. "I...can't believe this." Remembering Renault's fear that Mason was enacting revenge, Jonathan swallowed hard.

"Go ahead and say it."

Jonathan didn't hesitate. "Mason's behind this, isn't he?"

"We're thinking alike. Not sure if that's good or bad, but that's exactly my theory as well. We can't prove anything at this point. We don't even know who's taken them. Got a partial print to go on, but it's not enough. Oh, and another thing. When Jenna and Chase arrived, there was a picture waiting. One of Mason's calling cards, so to speak. Kelly and Austin were tied and gagged in the back of a car."

"This can't be happening..." Jonathan felt his legs going weak. He found the nearest chair and sat down.

"I know; it's devastating. With Kelly being pregnant, it presents another level of complications. I'm staying here with Jenna and Chase. Damian left a few hours ago to team up with Jacoby. They're leading the search and rescue mission."

"How is Jenna holding up?" Jonathan gripped the metal arm of the chair so hard his knuckles were turning white.

"Not too good, as you can imagine. This is the second time someone has taken Austin against his will...and now her best friend. She's overwhelmed."

Jonathan coughed, choking on his own anxious reflux. "You said Garrett is with her? I'm assuming they've made up?"

Maria paused. "Yes, Jonathan. Jenna and Chase are together. You're going to have to accept..."

"She needs both of us," Jonathan blurted. "The sooner Jenna realizes that, the better..."

"She can't have both of you. She'll have to choose. If you force her right now, Jenna will probably..."

Jonathan took his turn at interrupting. "I don't want to force her to do anything. But Jenna needs to see the broader picture. Garrett is just...*wrong* for her."

"That's her decision to make; not yours. I'm warning you. Now is not the time to pressure Jenna into making a decision. You need to back off and give her some breathing room. If you care enough about her, you'll do that." Maria wondered if her motherly advice was getting through at all.

Jonathan didn't immediately answer. "I don't trust Garrett; you know that."

Maria sighed. "Well, Jenna does. So, until you have concrete proof Chase is up to no good, you better tread lightly or risk losing your friendship with Jenna."

Jonathan laughed. "You're good at this mom stuff, you know."

"I'm trying."

"Good to know. I'll see you soon. Bye, Mom." Jonathan headed back towards the Enterprise counter. Thoughts of Chase Garrett refused to leave him alone. There were too many unexplained scenarios involving Garrett, and not enough answers.

Such as the mysterious gun appearing in Garrett's duffel bag in Texas. Not to mention all the phone calls to unlisted numbers Jonathan had tracked on Chase's cell when Jenna was distracted.

Maybe it was time to tell her...

The more he dwelt on Garrett's questionable behavior, the more Jonathan felt himself starting to internally combust. He didn't have any concrete evidence, as Maria had put it. Just a gut feeling that irritated the hell out of him.

Many little nuances about Garrett weren't adding up. Jonathan wished he would have jotted down a couple of the unlisted numbers on Chase's cell so Damian or Maria could have checked them out.

"There has to be a way," Jonathan muttered to himself as he dodged traffic leaving the airport. Swerving to stay in his lane, Jonathan gripped the wheel. Pent-up anger throbbed inside him. The mere thought of Garrett doing something underhanded to threaten Jenna's life was consuming him to the point of recklessness. He had to learn to control himself.

As much as he wanted desperately to be his own man with his own set of values, Jonathan knew deep down he had inherited a malicious streak from his biological father. Every time Jonathan dared to acknowledge Mason Hamilton's tainted blood was coursing through his veins, he struggled with the urge to get violently ill. Even now his hatred towards Garrett was taking him down a path he never wanted to take. He would willingly go there if it meant keeping Jenna away from someone who had ulterior motives.

Garrett's recent behavior certainly had ulterior written all over it. The drugs found in Garrett's bloodstream were listed as the only contributing factor causing him to lash out at Jenna, but Jonathan wasn't buying it.

How could Garrett have possibly hit the woman he supposedly loved?

Jonathan wracked his brain for a coherent answer but found none. He couldn't see clear when it came to Garrett. Maria was right. He was just itching for a fight.

Now that Garrett was himself again, Jonathan wondered who would throw the first punch. Garrett's jealousy had ignited when the drugs were flowing through his system, but it had always been there lying dormant. It wouldn't take much this time to push Garrett over the edge. Besides, Jonathan contemplated, if Garrett lunged at him first, no one would blame him for defending himself.

Jonathan's lips turned into a twisted smile. All he had to do was find a way to push Garrett's buttons a little at a time. Discreetly, of course. Jenna could draw her own conclusions. It was a good plan but one he'd have to work on a little bit more once he arrived.

A distraction to keep his mind off of Laurence Renault.

Sweat beaded on Jonathan's forehead. Maria and Damian couldn't find out he had snuck into Mason's house with Renault. Even if their intentions were honorable...disconnecting the wiring to a torture room, they had committed breaking and entering. A felony charge Mason would surely press without hesitation. Jonathan saw the end of his managerial career flash before his eyes in addition to the lashing he'd receive from his mother.

Renault knew exactly what he was doing. Purposely involving Jonathan in a plot to outsmart Mason when in reality Renault was blackmailing Jonathan into keeping his mouth shut about their

S.A. Van

new alliance. One word to the FBI and Jonathan would incriminate himself.

That whole bullshit about Renault wanting to protect Kelly was just a cover story...and unfortunately, Jonathan had fallen for it. Jonathan tensed as he realized how stupid he had been to believe a single word out of Renault's mouth.

Renault had returned to the States with one goal in mind...revenge against Mason Hamilton who had taken his livelihood away. Kelly was nothing more than a pawn in the vicious game Renault intended to play with Mason. She was being used...once again.

Jonathan's heart ached. He couldn't imagine growing up with Mason as his father as Kelly had done. It was bad enough receiving the news as a grown man. What she must have lived through...succumbing to Mason's threats, being forced to spy on Jenna who had become Kelly's best friend, and now...being kidnapped just days before her wedding. *How much could one person endure?* Jonathan wondered as he saw the first sign for Exit Zero, the Cape May ramp off the Garden State Expressway.

Yet Kelly had survived, becoming one of most remarkable people he had ever met. Strikingly beautiful, kind, compassionate...his *sister*.

Jonathan didn't dwell on her biological parentage. In the past couple of months, he had bonded with Kelly as a sibling, and as far as he was concerned, that wasn't going to change. She needed a brother; she had told him so.

They were family now...and that's all that mattered.

*****

Austin woke up groggy, disoriented. Rays of light beamed through the slits of the musty, dark gray curtains. It had to be morning. A quick glance at his watch indicated it was just past seven o'clock.

He wasn't home; that much he knew. The sofa he was sitting on was torn and lumpy. Not that he had noticed the night before. His attention had been drawn to Kelly...who was no longer beside him.

Austin jumped to his feet as his eyes darted around the dimly lit room. "Kelly?"

64

"Kelly!" Austin screamed. Frantic visions were flying through his brain at record speed. He stumbled, trying to get his bearings.

It didn't take long. He remembered where he was…and why.

Austin raced through every room in the small house, searching for any clue as to where Kelly may have been taken. A cursory glance out the front window indicated the car they had travelled in was still parked in the same spot and the gate was closed.

"How in the…?"

The house was surrounded by wired fencing. They had to be on foot. That was the only reasonable explanation. Somehow they had left without his knowledge…

Austin smacked his forehead. The needle. He had been drugged. Too out of it to save Kelly. Austin fell to his knees in desperation.

Time was ticking away and Kelly was getting farther away from him and closer to a new level of danger. Facing her father. Mason Hamilton would surely kill her and not think twice about it, whether or not word had gotten back to him about the baby.

The baby. Our baby.

"I can't let anything happen to our baby." Austin choked on the last few words. "I have to find them…somehow."

Austin darted to the car. Fortunately, the driver's side door was unlocked. He fell into the driver's seat and reached his hands underneath the steering column.

"Thank you, Lenny Lex," Austin said, yanking the ignition wires free from the plastic casing. So grateful his friend from Philly had taught him the art of hot-wiring a car a couple of years back, Austin told himself he would have to remember to thank Lenny the next time he saw him.

As the ignition turned over, Austin slammed the car into reverse, positioning it as far back as possible. He hesitated momentarily. This was a stupid move for sure. Driving through the fence could instantly kill him. Then who would save Kelly?

He had to test his theory first. Austin glanced over at the pile of debris piled up alongside of the house to the right of the side door. Wood planks, extra fencing, broken pipes, odds and ends of car parts. Junk.

Maybe not.

He raced from the car and selected a couple of metal pipes. Standing a few feet from the locking mechanism, he tossed the pipes towards the fence. Expecting to see sparks flying, Austin covered his face and turned sideways.

The pipes clanked against the metal lock and fell to the ground. No sparks, just an annoying noise when metal hit metal.

Surprised but elated, Austin picked up the pipes and threw them again at another section of the fence. This time he watched carefully for the slightest indication the fence was wired with electricity.

Nothing.

That was all the proof he needed.

Revving the car engine, Austin slammed the accelerator to the floor. Right before he hit the fence head-on, Austin covered his face with his hands, praying he hadn't made the wrong decision.

He had to find Kelly and their baby...even if he died in the process.

Chapter 8

Jonathan was calling. *How downright decent of him…*

Mason ignored his cell phone until the very last ring before it went to voicemail. Making Jonathan wonder if his call was going to be answered would most certainly infuriate him. Perhaps even cause him to hang up and try again.

Serves him right…

Mason finally gave in. "Why, Jonathan, so good of you to call. Will you be gracing the office with your formidable presence today?"

"You know why I'm calling Mason, so cut the crap. Where is she? What have you done with Kelly?"

Mason bellowed with laughter. "And how would I have the slightest idea where my errant daughter is at the moment? She disregards my phone calls, shows me no respect, and can't be bothered to attend her own mother's funeral. Furthermore, I'm curious as to why you're taking such an interest."

"She's missing, Mason."

"Missing?" Mason repeated mockingly. "Don't waste my time, Jonathan. Kelly knows exactly what she's doing. Purposely ignoring me. Now, if you have anything else you'd like to talk about…such as your responsibilities here at Hamilton-Knox, then I would…"

"Mason, for God's sake, listen to me! She's missing and may have been kidnapped. If you had *anything* to do with this, I swear…"

Mason's twisted smile deepened. "Why, this is disturbing news. Have you contacted the police?"

Jonathan cursed under his breath. "Of course they've been contacted, Mason. They might be knocking on your door soon. I'm sure you're on their list of interested persons."

"You're spending too much time with the FBI, Jonathan. If I was you, I…"

"You're not me, Mason, and I have no aspirations to be you. So we're even. As to your smartass remark regarding my interest in Kelly, let's just say someone needs to have her best interests in mind. But I can understand now why you don't. She's not your daughter." Jonathan let his words sink in before he continued. "You pretended she was your daughter just like you pretended you loved your wife. All for the camera. How am I doing? Getting the facts straight?"

Mason struggled to provide a response.

"Thought so. Called you on the carpet, didn't I?"

"Your accusations are unfounded. And I would caution you to keep your ludicrous assumptions to yourself. No one will believe you. I have provided for Kelly all her life. Given her apartments, substantial bank accounts, cars, jewelry…"

Jonathan had heard enough. "All material objects which you felt the need to take away the moment she rebuffed your attempts to control her this summer. The best thing Kelly ever did was finding Austin Reed…and getting away from you."

Mason paused for effect. "Again, I'm curious, Jonathan, as to why you're taking the time to question me about my family?"

"Because someone needs to. Your charade has gone on long enough. I won't be dragged down along with you, Mason."

"Jonathan, I resent the implication. Stop trying to read between the lines. You're needed here at H-K. If Kelly is no longer in Cape May, then there is really no need for you to stay down there. Perhaps she and her lackluster excuse for a boyfriend have run away together. Has anyone undertaken that line of thought?"

Staying on the phone while driving was making Jonathan too distracted even with the speakerphone. "They were planning their wedding. They didn't run away. A picture was left for Jenna…of Austin and Kelly tied and gagged in the back of a car. I don't suppose you know anything about that, Mason?"

"Sounds like a depraved individual seeking attention."

Jonathan resisted the urge to make a guttural sound. "The FBI is conducting a search and rescue."

"As they should. And I will expect regular reports. Who is in charge?" Mason's change of tone was intentional.

"Screw your expectations, Mason. If you're so determined to get in touch with the FBI, you can call Special Agent Damian Pierce. I'm sure he'd love to hear from you. Especially if you're willing to turn yourself in. Save them a lot of time and effort."

Mason fumed. Jonathan wasn't backing down as expected. In fact, he was getting more hostile with every passing minute. "Well, then. I'll expect *you* to call me with any details as they arise."

"Not going to happen, Mason. My whole purpose in calling you was to let you know how happy I was to learn you're not Kelly's biological father. I plan on sharing that news with her the first chance I get. Might be the perfect wedding gift." Jonathan landed his final punch.

"Be careful of the side you choose, Jonathan. Not everything is black and white."

Jonathan laughed. "That's exactly what Renault said."

"You really do need to be wary of the company you keep. Laurence Renault is…"

"Kelly's biological father. Ellen's lover. I know the story."

Mason was quick with a comeback. "You only know *half* the story, and I would venture to guess the details were extremely distorted. Come home, Jonathan. I would be happy to relay the truth to you."

"The truth? Oh, please. How naïve do you think I am? Your version of the truth would take years to decipher. I don't have the patience for it."

"Pity." Mason cleared his throat. "One last thing, Jonathan. Due to your blatant disregard for your business responsibilities, I've decided to postpone my retirement until you can prove yourself worthy to succeed me."

The line went dead before Jonathan had a chance to utter another sound.

Mason had just leveled the playing ground.

*****

His teeth were chattering so badly, Chase could hear an echo.

A game of shivers was playing tag throughout his entire body, making him hug his chest until his arms hurt.

The same type of drug interaction he had experienced in Texas, but worse this time. He knew what would follow, and he braced himself for it.

Pain would start in his chest, then spread to his limbs, paralyzing him and making him almost crazy. Then he would collapse and everything would go dark. A brief interlude would follow when he woke only to be followed by an intense desire to hurt someone.

He couldn't let that happen. Not again.

Chase tried hard not to topple off the bench. He had stumbled to the nearest bench along the Promenade after leaving the house for a walk. Telling Jenna he wanted some time alone and offering her no further explanations, Chase had sought some private time to figure out his next moves.

Time he didn't have.

As soon as the first round of painful jabs tore through him, Chase knew it was starting all over again.

But how? Who was doing this to him? And for what purpose?

There had to be an underlying reason someone wanted him to be out of control. The answers weren't coming fast enough. With each passing minute, he was losing the ability to think straight.

Chase rubbed his eyes. They were tired and heavy. He hadn't slept well and neither had Jenna. She kept waking up and bunching the covers in her fists. She had been fighting, too…in her dreams.

He could do little to help her. God knows, he was hardly able to help himself. Chase grabbed his cell phone and hit the first number on his speed-dial, cursing himself for not being man enough to handle this on his own.

"You're up early," the deep, scratchy voice said after two rings. "Where are you?"

"Promenade. Across from Molly's." Chase glanced over his shoulder at Molly's Pancake House, already busy with its first round of breakfast customers. The restaurant, extremely popular year-round with the locals, was a gold mine in summer when the tourists arrived.

"What's going on?"

Chase groaned. "I'm getting the same symptoms again but worse this time. I don't know how long I'll be able to…stay in control."

"Well, that theory didn't work in Texas. Did it? I'm worried. You're playing with fire."

"Then I'll just have to stay away from Jenna."

"Get away from her now. Don't take any chances."

"It's not that easy. She wants to be with me...and I want to be with her. I love her, damn it. Don't ask me to give up on that." Chase's hands dug into the wooden bench too hard. He wondered if he had just driven splinters under his skin. He shut his eyes, debating his options.

"Last time you hurt her. Do you want to do that again? I'm pulling you from this assignment...before you end up killing yourself or putting anyone else at risk."

Chase rode another crest of pain, slamming against the bench. "I can handle it for now. Don't pull my cover. Not yet. All I want to do is nail him. I'm very close; I can feel it. For all I know, he's behind the drugs."

"On that we agree. He's our number one suspect. He's using you, Chase. Be careful. If you get in too deep, we won't be able to save you. You're putting your partner's life on the line, too. Think about that before you make any rash decisions."

"I got it, boss."

"I sincerely hope so," Damian said before the line went dead.

*****

"You'll be interested to know your nemesis is heading up the search and rescue party for my daughter."

Mason cradled his cell in his perfectly manicured hand. "How apropos, don't you think?" Mason took a step closer to his mantle, eyeing the crystal box which housed two small gold animal figurines. The elephant and the tiger. Plenty of room for three more.

His coveted treasure pieces...once belonging to the infamous pirate Blackbeard, or so the legend said. Five small gold animal figurines, cursed for all eternity. Mason scoffed at such nonsense, although he had committed the ridiculous rhyme to memory.

Death comes to those who dare to hold all five pieces of tainted gold.

Mason puffed out his chest in contempt. He had better things to do with his time than dwelling on childish matters.

"Damian Pierce?" The Closer tried not to act surprised. "Where is Pierce setting up the command post?"

"How should I know that?"

The Closer was glad Mason had chosen to call rather than deliver this piece of information in person. Had he been foolish enough to unleash this bit of news without prior warning, The Closer wouldn't have been able to control himself. "You should have asked."

"Jonathan wasn't forthcoming with that information."

The Closer drummed his fingers on the side of the phone. "I'll find out myself. Did you call me for any other relevant reason?"

Pompous ass. Mason suddenly grew silent realizing history was repeating itself. An alliance with Renault had proven to be an extremely bad decision several decades ago, and now The Closer was challenging him at every turn. "Take the information and do with it as you will. Personally, I think you should…"

"I don't care what you think, and I don't need to be reminded how to do my job. Unless you've forgotten, and I'd be happy to remind you, my allegiance to you is only dependent upon my willingness to do a job, and your ability to pay."

"Of that I am well aware." Mason clenched his hands.

"Good. We understand each other. Now that you've managed to insult my intelligence, I'm raising your fee."

Mason was furious but held his tongue. The Closer could demand whatever he wanted and Mason would pay it. There was no one else he completely relied upon. "As you wish. However, there is one small matter I want you to resolve before I pay another dime."

The Closer covered his cell with his hand, nodding to his associate and lover, Mallory Kincaid. "We have him," he mouthed as he watched her lips turn upward into a contemptuous smile.

"Fair enough," The Closer said quickly before hearing Mason's request. "What is it?"

"I want you to kill Logan McHenry."

*****

72

Kelly twisted against the coarse ropes binding her hands and feet. Her skin was bloody and raw where the prickly rope fibers had rubbed off several layers of skin. Pain shot up her arms and legs each time she moved, but there was no use screaming.

No one could hear her.

The bandana was tied too tightly around her mouth. She couldn't take the chance he would retaliate and hurt her...and the baby.

Our baby.

Dried tears caked her face. Kelly couldn't remember when she had stopped crying. All she could think about was leaving Austin, and what he must be thinking right now. Devastated, frantic. Austin would do something crazy trying to get away. She just knew it.

He would put himself in danger to find her.

Oh, God! Don't let him find the trap door!

Kelly envisioned the small house exploding, taking her breath away. She fought hard to stop shaking. The blanket fell downward below her face. She tried to shield her eyes from the bright sunlight by turning her head sideways but doing so only aggravated the sores on her ankles and wrists. It was uncomfortable enough lying in the same position in the backseat of the car for hours, but she dared not protest.

She had so much to worry about, and little she could do to prevent any of it. Forcing herself to think of her baby's well-being, Kelly took several deep breaths until she felt her body going lax.

It wasn't long before the car pulled to a stop. Kelly tried to sit up but her shoulders ached from lying in the same position for so long.

"Get out."

The back passenger door opened swiftly. When Kelly didn't move, Logan reached inside to pull her towards him. Terror filled her eyes.

"I'm not going to hurt you. I...just thought you needed to stretch your legs. We're at a construction site and there's a Port-A-Potty just off the side of the road." Logan pulled the bandana down around Kelly's neck. He untied the ropes on her wrists and ankles, finally noticing the sores. "I...have something in the trunk for that," he stammered. "Stay in the backseat for just a minute."

Kelly squinted at the bright sun. She guessed it was early afternoon. Her watch was missing. Most likely it was still at the beach house on the ledge above the sink where she had forgotten to put it back on after her last shower. She felt dirty and grimy being in the same clothes for all this time, but she had more important things on her mind.

Survival.

And getting a message to someone...somehow.

"Hold out your wrists."

Logan squeezed antibiotic cream over Kelly's wrists, then wrapped them gently in gauze. He did the same with her ankles while he watched her face. She was wincing from the pain, and would probably whimper if she wasn't so scared.

"Thank you," she said with notable tension in her voice.

Logan stuck the tube and gauze in his back pocket. He took her hands and pulled Kelly to her feet. "Do you need me to walk with you?"

Kelly shook her head firmly. There was no way she wanted his hands on any part of her body. She'd crawl before she'd let him touch her again unless it was absolutely necessary. "I'll be...fine."

Logan admired her defiance, wishing he had met her under different circumstances. "Five minutes. We need to get back on the road." As he watched her limp away, deep remorse struck him hard.

What am I doing? Why am I hurting her like this?

Will she ever understand I'm just trying to help her?

Kelly returned while Logan continued to stare into space.

"I'm back...please don't tie me up again. I'll be quiet...I promise."

Logan nodded without saying a word. He helped her back into the car, handing Kelly a bottle of water and two packets of crackers. It was the best he could do for right now until darkness came again.

His favorite time of the day...when everything went still and he could blend into the night.

Chapter 9

Jenna rammed her cell into the front pocket of her well-worn denim jacket and headed for the front door. Before her hand had barely even reached the doorknob, she caught Maria's wary glance. "I won't be gone long. Don't worry about me. Just getting some fresh air."

"No need to explain." Maria folded her reading glasses and looked up from her laptop. "You've got a lot on your mind."

"Yeah, I do. I want to find Chase. He got up very early, and I think he said something about heading to the Promenade. I was half-asleep. Call me if…"

"Will do. If you happen to bypass that coffee shop on the mall…"

Jenna shook her head. "Can't do it. Damian made me promise to cut you off at six cups."

"Damn that man!" Maria pretended to be annoyed. "Mr. Pierce will have to be punished for such underhanded tactics."

Jenna smiled. "He's a lot bigger than me, Maria. I had no choice. He intimidates me…sort of."

"Don't give him that satisfaction, Jenna. He's just a big teddy bear. He might flex his muscles, but let me tell you, he's just messing with you."

Maria peered between the wooden slat blinds. She watched Jenna run down the front steps of the beach house, and cross North Street. Within seconds she was hitting her speed-dial. "Jenna just left. She's on Congress walking towards the beach. Get on her tail…*now*."

"Copy that," Ann Bailey responded before grabbing her keys and her Nike windbreaker. She hustled down the steps of the house across from the Reeds', and picked up her pace, making sure she kept a safe distance.

When Ann was finally out of sight, Maria returned to her laptop, put it in *sleep mode* then laid it on the side table. She was too keyed up from her caffeine indulgence to study Jacoby's probability reports any more. Unless he was right beside her to explain the various calculations, she was at a loss.

Tired eyes and a stiff neck were causing her enough irritation. Both symptoms she blamed entirely on her husband. In Damian's absence, Maria had occupied her time staring for hours at her laptop. Reading emails from her junior agents, catching up on division memos, and trying to fine-tune her multi-page dissertation required at the end of every month justifying her unit's activities. A task she usually delegated to Jacoby, but he had his hands full.

Another annoying fact she blamed on Damian. Taking her right-hand man. Maria was seeing stars. "Damian, how could you pull rank on me!"

Frustration was eating at her nerves, not to mention the fact she and Damian had parted on less than friendly terms. Hurtful words had been exchanged without either realizing how little time they had to apologize. Damian had been whisked away by the AC Field Office team while Maria had stubbornly refused to look in his direction.

Her eyes stung now from the tears she had pushed back. She was as much to blame as Damian; neither willing to take one step closer on principle.

Maria wondered if Damian was feeling the aftershocks as much as she was…or if he had shrugged off the whole ordeal. After all, he had a job to do and orders to follow.

Which had included telling Maria she was side-lined until further notice.

She was helpless and powerless. It was a miracle Damian had allowed her to keep her gun and the extra clips. Only after she had practically begged him. For protection, she had insisted. Finally after several choice words mixed with tears, he had relented, telling her he was going against protocol. To which she had refused to make another comment for fear he would renege on his promise.

She had accused Damian of using her forced administrative leave to perpetuate his goal of making her retire. A concept she wasn't ready to consider despite his best efforts. He had been harping on the subject for months now, telling her it was time to give up such a risky job, although he had no intention of doing the same.

Maria could almost recite their last conversation which had drained her and infuriated her at the same time.

"I love you, sweetheart. You don't need to put yourself on the line anymore. You've put in your time. I worry too much about you."

"So this is about you...not me?" Maria had countered. *"Oh, please, Damian. Don't make this into something it's not. Don't try and turn me into someone you think I should be. That's not fair to me. I can't just stay home to clean the house and make you dinner every night. I would go crazy! Damn it, Damian. Don't do this to me."*

"You're doing this to yourself, sweetheart. You're crumbling and you just can't see it. It's killing me to watch you fall apart. I don't want to lose you, Maria. You'll be off on one of your hot and heavy pursuits, and then I'll get the call none of us wants to hear."

"I knew the risks when I took this job, Damian. So did you. You married me anyway. Regretting that now? You could have had anyone...you settled for me."

Spitefulness was surfacing. It was too late. The damage had been done.

"You know it wasn't like that. I wanted you, Maria. I didn't have to settle for you...I had to have you."

"Why? So you could control me? That's it, isn't it? This is all about control."

"Stop it!" *Damian had grabbed Maria by her upper arms, practically lifting her off the floor.* *"You're not hearing a word I've said. You're wasting your time...our time...trying to catch Hamilton. We're drowning in this. For what, sweetheart? To get revenge? Guess what? It's not happening. Give it up, Maria. You've tried your best, and I admire you for that, but it's over. You can't win this."*

Maria had folded her arms in defiance, turning her head away. "It's not over."

Damian grabbed his gear bag and slung it over his shoulder. "No, I suppose it's not. I was a fool to actually think you'd listen to reason." He hated talking to Maria when she had turned her back. "It won't be over until one of you is dead."

Storming out, Damian didn't look back. There was nothing else to say. Stubbornness was a character flaw they both embraced.

To the detriment of each other's tender emotions.

It didn't hit Maria full force until she watched the FBI's SUV pull away from the curb.

They hadn't kissed good-bye.

Through all the years of juggling careers, facing insurmountable dangers and forced separations, not once had they left each other without a kiss.

Until now.

A wall had just gone up in their marriage, one they had fought so hard to prevent.

"What have I done?" Maria felt an aching hollowness swelling inside her. Her tenacity had always been one of her best assets, an unyielding driving force propelling her forward to succeed, but now…it was pushing her farther away from the man she loved.

She was alone and miserable.

Not the best way to start the day.

Maria's head drooped. Tension crept into her shoulders like a million tiny ants descending on their prey. Deliberately and furtively. Threatening her to succumb.

It was her fault the argument had escalated to the point of an impasse. Her strong, passionate, logical-thinking husband had done his best to make her see the inevitable truth…she was fighting an uphill battle with little or no chance of winning.

Over three decades, Maria had tried unsuccessfully to find some small shred of evidence linking Mason Hamilton to a crime…*any* crime which would put him on trial. But each and every time, he slithered his way around the criminal justice system. She couldn't give up now. Too many people, alive and dead, were counting on her. Why Damian couldn't see that, she didn't know. Or maybe he did, and he just didn't want to admit it. Either way, her job wasn't done by a far stretch. He'd have to *deal with that.*

Forcing herself to concentrate on something other than her marital strife, Maria attempted to log into her agency email. It was suddenly blocked. "Oh, here we go," she muttered to herself as her eyes rolled. Briggs was starting to play games.

Senior-Agent-In-Charge Elias Briggs was overseeing the task force Damian was coordinating. Which meant he would take the credit and do none of the work. Briggs was nothing more than a big mouth with a cocky swagger. A twenty-year veteran who had made it his business to know everyone else's business, earning him quite a few degrading nicknames. He did the job no one else wanted to do...Internal Affairs, and he was always looking for his next conquest. Once an agent found himself caught in Briggs' web, it was only a matter of time before he or she bit the dust.

Briggs had elevated himself through improper channels, as practically every agent outside of Internal Affairs would attest. Stepping on the backs of unsuspecting agents, he took great satisfaction in personally persecuting the younger, more inexperienced agents. Making sure his superiors were well aware he was ridding the FBI of trouble before the agency felt the wrath of public humiliation, or word got to budget-conscious legislators. Briggs had won favor with the Director many times for saving the reputation of the Agency.

It just didn't make sense why Briggs would be put in charge of a search-and-rescue mission. Seemed to be out of his element. Even a demotion. *I wonder*, Maria thought to herself. *I wonder if this was done on purpose.*

Damian's mission was going to be scrutinized from the start, criticized at every opportunity, and then pistol-whipped for good measure. Briggs only operated one way. His own. He had no concern for anyone's way of thinking unless it directly benefitted him.

Damian was on shaky ground.

Maria wished to God she could be right by her husband's side, taking the brunt of Briggs' wrath. Damian shouldn't have to suffer because of her, and that's exactly what would happen. Briggs' would take this assignment and turn it into an opportunity to crucify Damian for his wife's errors.

That's exactly what was happening.

It was Briggs who had insisted she be put on administrative leave following the unforeseen attack at the Livingston Museum of Art. Briggs was out for blood; making a case which implied Maria was entirely to blame. Art exhibits had been destroyed, two agents had died, and other law enforcement officers had sustained significant injuries. The press had intensified the problem, making the FBI look like a bunch of incompetents. *"Someone's head has to roll,"* Briggs had been quoted in one of the New York papers, and Maria knew who he was referring to...even without directly mentioning her name.

Now Briggs was pumped up and ready to take his frustration out on her husband just for spite.

Maria reached for her phone to warn Damian with a quick text then decided to alert Jacoby instead. Damian was probably still mad at her, and she didn't need to incite him any further.

They both needed to cool down before other poorly-chosen words got them deeper into trouble.

*****

Jenna quickened her pace. Nearing Beach Avenue, the first street running parallel to the ocean, she glanced over her shoulder. At first it had just been paranoia, but here of late, the casual gesture was becoming part of her lifestyle.

Reaching the corner of Beach and Congress, she spun around and looked both ways. No one immediately caught her eye as being overly suspicious. Locals mainly, she assumed, going about their daily routines. Getting on with their life. Without a care.

When am I ever going to get on with my life?

Jenna was half-afraid to utter the answer. Instead, she turned left, walking towards Molly's Pancake House. Seeing the all-too-familiar landmark, her heart warmed. Austin had agreed to manage Molly's as a special favor to Teresa Maylor. When Teresa had visited him in the hospital, she had offered Austin the job, knowing he was a financial consultant. Teresa had more confidence in Austin's abilities than his own family. Jenna regretted the ways she had criticized her brother's laziness, wanting to spend every summer at the beach when he should have been gainfully employed. Little did she know, he was a very successful money manager with several high-end clients who paid him quite generously to issue a few monthly reports.

I never gave him any credit, Jenna bemoaned. Cutting behind Molly's, she waited a few seconds. A woman with shoulder-length dark hair, wearing a faded *Life is Good* baseball cap and Oakley sports-style sunglasses was walking fast, looking in both directions. Not exactly power-walking. More like...*keeping-an-eye-out* curiosity-walking.

Jenna tensed, debating her options.

I'll lose her on the Mall.

Making a mad dash down Perry Street, Jenna crossed at the side entrance of the Blue Pig Tavern, Congress Hall's premier restaurant. Bypassing the urge to sneak inside the Cape May Popcorn Factory diagonally across the street to grab a sample of warm caramel corn, Jenna swiftly headed for the Whale's Tale gift shop, just a couple of doors down.

Keep your head down...

Jenna was careful not to make any sudden moves inside the gift shop. She blended easily with other customers, browsing at the wide variety of beautiful seashells, one-of-a-kind jewelry made by local artisans, and a wide variety of fragrant, organic candles. Making her way through the children's section in the middle of the store, she was stopped by a little girl holding two puzzles.

"Tigger or Pooh Bear?"

Jenna hesitated, looking around for the girl's mother.

"Mommy is trying on a bracelet. Which puzzle should I get? Tigger or Pooh Bear?" She repeated, frowning because she couldn't decide.

"Definitely Tigger. He's my favorite," Jenna said with a wink.

"Mine, too," the girl replied. Looking up, she started to smile and then realized she was alone again. "Mommy!"

Jenna hoped the child could navigate the store and find her mother. But it was just the distraction she needed. When she came to the back part of the store where several racks of greeting cards and Victorian glass ornaments were displayed, she paused long enough to catch her breath and look casually over her shoulder.

The same woman in the cap and sunglasses had entered the store and was scanning the people inside. It was so obvious she wasn't here to shop. Bells clanged in Jenna's head.

Get out of here...now!

Jenna rushed out the side door. Running as fast as she could down the side street behind the mall, Jenna hung a left on Ocean, finally stopping at the information kiosk. Right behind her was her favorite store in Cape May, Winterwood. She let out a sigh of relief, then jogged up the steps.

She knew it was a crazy concept defying any type of logic, but Jenna had always felt safe and secure inside the multi-level shop which celebrated Christmas in grand splendor every day of the year. Displays on the lower level in the front part of the store were changed for various holidays, but everywhere else, top and bottom, it was Christmas-time. A child's dream where no bad men dared to enter.

Or bad women?

Jenna choked back her stifled laugh, nervously sticking her hands in the back pockets of her jeans. She made her way to the back of the store, and pressed her head against a bare space on the wall. Taking in ragged breaths made her keenly aware she needed to take action...some type of action before it was too late.

"I'm being followed." Jenna turned her back to camouflage her phone conversation. There were only a few patrons shopping at this hour, and she practically had the lower level to herself.

"Take it easy." Maria rushed to the back bedroom to grab her sneakers and her gun. "Tell me where you are."

"I'm at Winterwood, the Christmas shop on the corner of..."

"I know right where it is. I'll be there in a few minutes. Stay on the phone with me, Jenna." Maria sprinted down the front steps and broke into a run, her gun jostling inside her jacket pocket. "I'm on my way. Give me five minutes...tops. What's he look like?"

"She...has dark brown hair...a little past her shoulders. Not much taller than me. Athletic-built, wearing Oakley's and a baseball cap. God, I don't know, Maria! I didn't have too much time to..."

"Calm down. I'm almost there."

Maria slowed her pace. There was no need to rush now or panic. A whiff of pine mist greeted her when she opened the door to Winterwood. Snow-crested artificial Christmas trees were everywhere with different motifs ranging from traditional decorations to beach themes. Maria had to navigate her way through several themed areas until she came to the back of the store.

Wandering around the Boyds Bears display, Maria finally found Jenna leaning against the back wall. "Shop here much?"

Jenna fell into Maria's arms. "I'm sorry I called you. You're going to think I'm crazy! I didn't mean to..."

Maria stepped back to give Jenna some breathing room. "Sure you don't want a job in law enforcement? You're getting good at picking up a tail."

"What?" Jenna looked nervously around the store.

"Ann?" Maria waved her hand and looked behind her. She turned her attention back to Jenna. "Jenna, meet Ann Bailey...your *stalker*. Actually, she's your bodyguard."

Ann stuck out her hand towards Jenna. "Been away from Langley too long. My covert skills are a little rusty. Ann Bailey, CIA. Nice to finally meet you *officially*, Jenna Reed."

"You know each other?" Jenna tried to comprehend what was going on. "You look so familiar to me. Have we met?"

Ann exchanged a smile with Maria. "Twice as a matter of fact. I was undercover as a nurse. You were pretty much out of it when I first came to see you in New York. Then in Texas, I...gave you your mother's ring."

Jenna felt herself swaying. She was grateful when Maria grabbed her elbow. "You...told me my mother was alive. No one would believe me." She paused. "I don't know what to believe any more."

"The truth, Jenna. Always believe the truth." Maria firmly gripped Jenna's hands to steady her. "Lois is alive."

Chapter 10

"That is quite unfortunate."

Tumi Carile returned his cell to his jacket pocket, and stared for a few moments out the passenger side window. More disturbing news had just been shared, and he was trying to find the right words to articulate his discontent.

Thoughts, unpleasant and unnerving, were sounding as loud as blaring trumpets in his head. Glancing over at Phillip, his personal assistant, Tumi shook his head.

"You have not received good news, I take it," Phillip commented, still focusing his eyes on the road. "You are silent, Tumi. And you are filled with melancholy. Please, talk to me."

"You know me well, my friend."

"Enough to know you are hesitant…to voice your concerns. Damian is well-equipped to handle this matter. I am quite certain he will find Kelly and Austin before matters get out of hand."

Tumi tilted his head. "I fear they already are. The stakes are higher this time. Kelly's pregnancy could be placed in jeopardy. Any effort the FBI makes must take that into consideration. However, I cannot assume Elias Briggs will make that a top priority when he countermands every move Damian attempts to make. I assure you, Phillip, this will be quite a complicated assignment for my brother. Briggs is…"

"Ruthless in his own right," Phillip interrupted. "Yes, I am well aware of Elias Briggs and his sordid reputation. Damian would bode well to stay as far away from him as possible."

Tumi furrowed his brow. "Indeed. My brother's hand will be constantly compromised as long as Briggs has a presence. I foresee trouble. It is very disconcerting."

"Then we must eliminate the obstacles." Phillip smiled, knowing Tumi would agree. "You've already sent Markus to Cape May to keep an eye on matters. Now, we must enlist…"

Tumi interceded. "Thomas Movell. Yes, Phillip, I've already made the call. Movell has agreed. He is en route as we speak. I trust he will be successful. Movell has ways even more…cunning than my own. I have the utmost confidence he will find a resolution."

Phillip laughed. "Movell is almost as legendary as you, my friend."

"Thomas Movell has never ceased to amaze me, Phillip. I trust him with my life…and the lives of the people for whom I am responsible. I do not question his…methods, and he does not apologize for them. We have that understanding."

"Then it is done. Movell will make his move soon?"

"Yes, Phillip. You can be assured of it. Movell will penetrate the grottos of the FBI and find the traitor lurking within. Then, he will simply eradicate the problem."

"Perhaps it is better if we do not learn the details."

"Yes, I do not think we would want to know them at all."

*****

"Mason."

Mason struggled to stay upright in his seat. He absolutely detested The Closer's impromptu meetings, especially those which invaded the privacy of his home. "I am…surprised to see you."

"I suppose you are. I hadn't planned on making an appearance so soon…however, when our last phone call ended, I thought a meeting in person was warranted."

Mason coughed, as air stuck in the back of his throat. "I thought I made myself quite clear. I would contact you if the need arose …"

"We have business to discuss. I know you usually prefer a private setting rather than the office; however, if you want me to make an appointment, I can call your secretary. What is her name again?"

The Closer smirked, hoping Mason would read between the lines. He knew full well Suzanne Carter wasn't at the Hamilton-Knox receptionist's desk anymore. He had seen to that. Scaring the living daylights out of her to be exact. Drugging her, stripping her naked and tying her to her bedposts. Threatening her with the cold, steel edge of his favorite hunting knife resting against her bare thigh.

Such a tried and true technique. A salacious smile creased his lips. Suzanne was attractive, even when she was begging for her life.

"Suzanne," Mason stuttered. "She...has taken a leave of absence, I'm afraid. A...sudden illness...in the family."

Bullshit, The Closer thought. Mason had no idea where Suzanne was. Unless she was a total idiot, Suzanne had left town, never to return again. Mason could lie all he wanted.

"What...business did you want to discuss?" Mason asked nervously, changing the subject.

"Our long range plans. A partnership, so to speak. Interested?"

Mason leaned across his desk to hear The Closer's words. As usual he spoke in a low droning tone, adding to Mason's irritability. "My last partnership ended rather...abruptly, so you can imagine my reluctance to step into another one."

"You chose the wrong partner...obviously. That won't be a problem this time."

Mason loosened his tie, feeling the pressure mount. "Why would you assume that?"

"Because what I'm going to propose is based on needs, not trust. Renault was a fool to trust you. I won't make that mistake. Trust is a concept I rarely entertain. It's kept me alive and well."

"Then why bother to debate the issue of a partnership?"

"Needs, Mason. Pay attention." The Closer sat on the edge of Mason's desk. "You want Renault out of your life once and for all? I can make that happen, but first we need to agree to terms. I'll take care of your *needs*...and you will take care of mine."

"I can't imagine a man of your...*standing* would have any needs that would possibly concern me. You seem to be well-equipped to handle anything or anyone that comes your way."

"That is true; however, there is one little matter you can take care of for me."

Mason choked on his glass of water, sputtering droplets across his desk. He quickly grabbed his silk monogrammed handkerchief from his breast pocket and dabbed at the water marks on his blotter. "I'm listening."

"Call off the hit on McHenry."

Mason pushed his chair back as far as it would go until it hit the wall. He wanted as much distance as possible between him and The Closer. "I...don't know what you're talking about."

The Closer slammed his fist down on Mason's desk, making the ice cubes in his glass crackle. "I told you before...my community is a small one. We pay close attention when one of our own has a price on his head. Call it off immediately."

"I...wanted you to kill Logan McHenry. I have..."

"And this is precisely the reason why I don't trust you. You tell me one thing, then do something else. I know for a fact you put a hit on McHenry even though you asked me to take care of the job. You're working this from both angles, and it's insulting, not to mention a complete waste of time. Make the call...*now*."

Mason reached for his desk phone with shaking hands. "Hans, call Chavez and tell him the McHenry issue has been...*resolved*. No further action is to be taken. Yes, Hans. Do it now."

The Closer grabbed the receiver out of Mason's hand, slamming it down. "You trust that idiot to make the call to Chavez? He'll screw it up for sure. Might even end up putting a hit on himself. Why you bother keeping him around is a mystery all its own."

"Hans has...a certain usefulness."

"Only in your eyes, Mason. Now, let's discuss the Jenna Reed matter. She still has three treasure pieces. Even though you've managed to get your hands on the first two, I'd be a little worried. She's not backing down. Kliric tortured her, I shot her, but she's still giving you a run for the money. You have to admit, Jenna Reed isn't going down without a fight."

"I don't spend my days worrying about her...of all people."

"Well maybe you should. She's getting quite chummy with the FBI. Your nemesis...as a matter of fact."

Mason huffed. "I'm well aware Ms. Reed and Agent Turette have bonded. However, I would think the FBI has better things to do with their time than offer up their senior agents as bodyguards. Surely..."

"Then you haven't heard?"

Mason swiveled in his chair. "Heard what exactly?"

"Turette's on administrative leave. Apparently, her superiors aren't too forgiving for what happened at the museum. She's the scapegoat, and from what I hear, they're out for blood. Won't be long until Turette is out the door. Guess your worries are almost over. You won't have Turette on a string to play with. Better start setting your sights on someone else, Mason. Turette's as good as gone. My contact tells me the powers-that-be are gunning for her resignation…unless she's fired before she has a chance to submit it."

Mason ran his fingers through his silver wavy hair, staring in disbelief. Turette's predicament was definitely a boon to his plans, but he had wanted her to go down fighting, not relegated to the sidelines. "That is quite unfortunate."

The Closer shot Mason a confused look. "I would think you'd be happy."

Mason looked up with determination. "The game's not over…yet. Agent Turette and I have…unfinished business."

*****

Jonathan pulled alongside the curb at the Reeds' beach house later than he anticipated. No matter how many times he had driven down from the Atlantic City airport, he still managed to get into a traffic jam. *Was fate intervening?* He certainly hoped not, but his track record said otherwise.

Maybe it was the alluring scent of the gentle sea breezes he immediately sensed as he stepped from his rental car, a very nice Lincoln MKS sedan in silver with dark grey leather seats. Or maybe it was just the fact he was within a few steps of coming face to face with Jenna Reed again.

Jenna.

Jonathan's mind wandered to a time not too long ago when he and Jenna had almost succumbed to their temptation, taking each other to new levels of excitement as they struggled passionately in the front seat of his car. She was only there because he tricked her. Convincing her she was in danger and had to escape Cape May, when in reality the only danger at that precise moment was his wandering hands and deceitful mind.

Jonathan smiled, remembering Jenna's hands in his hair, caressing him and pulling him closer. Oh, there would definitely be a next time. All he had to do was find a way to eliminate the competition and turn her attention completely around.

Right. Good luck with that, his conscience hammered.

Jenna Reed had become his ultimate challenge.

The one woman who had the unmistaken ability to captivate him beyond compare. He just hoped this time he wouldn't have to jump through rings of fire to make her notice. Rescuing her brother after he had been kidnapped should have earned him a few points. Or what about figuring out Chase had been poisoned in Texas?

Damn it, Jenna, Jonathan swore under his breath. *What else do I have to do?*

Jonathan reached the landing at the top of the staircase and took a deep breath before knocking. "Anyone home?" Jonathan called after a few minutes of silence. He tried the door; it was locked. Racing down the steps, he stopped short, almost bumping into Markus' massive frame.

"No one is home at the moment. How are you Jonathan?" Markus grinned as he vigorously shook Jonathan's hand. "Fortunate for you, I have a spare key."

Jonathan dropped his hand, trying not to wince from Markus' strong grasp. "Where's Tumi? Is he here as well?"

"No. Tumi and Phillip have gone to help Damian. Tumi sent me here…to help and to protect."

"He's expecting trouble?"

"I do not know…specifically. Tumi asked me to come, and here I am." He withdrew a key from his pocket and stomped up the steps to unlock the door. "See? I am already a help, yes?"

Jonathan laughed. "Yes, Markus, you are quite helpful…as usual. Where did everyone go?"

"They all left at different times. I am not certain. Perhaps it would be best to call Maria to let her know you have arrived?"

Jonathan waved to Markus who descended the steps and headed to the Maylors' house next door. At first Jonathan was puzzled, but then remembered Maria saying there was plenty of room at the Maylors since the house was now vacant and soon to be on the market.

Teresa Maylor, Maria's friend and colleague at the CIA from years past, had been murdered several weeks ago. Stabbed from behind, the autopsy had indicated Teresa died within minutes. One thrust with a forceful twist. Very little blood splatter. The work of The Closer, Maria had surmised when Damian had given her the news. There could be no mistake.

Which had led Maria to believe George Maylor had met the same fate, although his body was never recovered. So in the absence of Teresa and George Maylor, Maria had taken it upon herself to be the temporary landlord of the Maylors' beach house. She knew Teresa would have no problem offering her home to Maria's friends and colleagues; she had made that perfectly clear on several occasions.

But despite the sexual tension with Jenna, staying next door with Markus was out of the question. He couldn't help himself.

Jenna Reed was a temptation he couldn't say no to…not now anyway. Jonathan firmly believed Jenna needed both him and Chase Garrett even though she was too scared to admit it.

Wandering through the lower level just to make sure he was alone, Jonathan finally headed upstairs. He peered inside the only bedroom on the left previously belonging to Jenna's parents. Linens were laid out on the bed but the room seemed otherwise empty.

This will do, Jonathan thought to himself as he quickly undressed. He needed a shower and a shave to be presentable.

Presentable…and *seductive*.

Chapter 11

Stay in control. Force yourself...

Labored staccato breaths. Accelerated heartbeat. Sweat pouring down his sideburns.

It was happening all over again.

First in Texas, now in Cape May.

Someone had slipped him another dose of...Chase wracked his brain. He couldn't remember the name of the drug, but what did it matter now?

Whoever was responsible was close...and if he could hang on, he could trap the bastard. Bringing him one step closer.

If...

Another wave of nausea gripped him and he doubled-over, struggling to walk upright. He had made it this far returning from the Promenade...escaping early this morning so Jenna wouldn't have to see his transformation.

Or be scared *again*.

Chase feared Jenna's reaction more than anything. He had gone crazy in Texas, lashing out at her. Bruising her inside and out. Splitting her lip.

Spilling her blood.

He hated himself for what he had become.

And only through the grace of God had he been able to keep her. She had forgiven him the moment she learned his erratic behavior was the result of some type of organic drug compound slipped to him without his knowledge. She had actually felt sorry for him.

When he didn't deserve her pity...or her love.

"Jenna," Chase moaned as he grabbed onto a fencing post and held on as tightly as he could. "Can't see me...like this."

He prayed Jenna wasn't watching him from the front windows of the beach house. She wouldn't understand...and he couldn't explain it. As much as he wanted to tell her everything, now was certainly not the time.

He couldn't risk it. Whoever had poisoned him in Texas was making sure they got his attention again...here in Cape May. He was being followed...and targeted. If his assumptions were correct, Chase was determined not to lose control.

Not this time.

Everything was on the line. He just had to take it slow, put the puzzle pieces together, find a way to outsmart The Closer and take him down. Without putting anyone else at risk.

Including Jenna.

A person could only take so much pain, and Jenna was reaching her breaking point. Her eyes didn't lie, and neither did her body. Jenna wasn't the same woman he had fallen in love with several months ago. Her beautiful brown eyes had lost some of their sparkle and she was finding it harder every day to smile.

She was stressed enough waiting for some type of answer about Kelly and Austin. She didn't need to deal with one more crisis. She didn't need to worry about him, too.

Maybe Damian was right, Chase pondered as he drew in a sharp breath. *I need medical help. I can't fight something or someone I can't see.*

As Chase weighed his options, he knew the risks were coming at him faster than the answers. Too many questions would raise discrepancies. His DNA was on file, like any other federal officer, and his cover would be blown.

Lies upon lies.

He was tired of living that way. Wanting nothing more than to be totally honest with Jenna, Chase agonized over his decision. He was driving a wedge between them with no end in sight. It would be well worth it to keep her safe.

Jenna's safety meant everything to him. He couldn't let her down. She loved him, and that was all the motivation he needed.

Chase staggered to the street sign at North and Congress, breathing deeply. Blinking several times to clear his blurry vision, he pushed onward and crossed at the intersection.

He had made it to the Reeds' beach house. Finally. Without falling down.

When he reached the landing at the top of the front steps, he dug out the spare key he had taken from the small pewter bowl on the dining room table. His hands were shaking but somehow he managed to insert the key into the lock.

Chase stumbled inside, barely shutting the door. Instead of collapsing into the nearest armchair or sofa, he moved slowly towards the staircase just off the kitchen. The house was quiet, and he assumed no one was home. That was a good thing. At least if he managed to get to Jenna's bed, he could pretend to be asleep...or he could just pass out.

Firmly grasping the wooden railing, he heaved himself upward. Both feet on the first step, then the next. At this rate, it was going to take a lot of time and stamina.

Chase gasped, unsure if he could make it up the flight of steps without breaking his neck.

He had to try.

Halfway up, his body swayed. One hand flew off the railing, and his right foot slipped. He just couldn't hold on anymore. His fingers slowly uncoiled. *It's alright*, he kept telling himself. *Don't be afraid to fall...*

"Garrett, what is wrong with you?" Jonathan shouted as he raced down the stairs. Dripping wet with only a towel draped around his waist, Jonathan caught Chase under the arm before he lost his balance. With a lot of effort, he was finally able to pull Chase to his feet, swinging his arm around his waist. They hobbled together until Jonathan dropped Chase onto Jenna's bed.

"Thanks," Chase mumbled, sighing with profound relief.

"You look like crap, Garrett. Worse than usual." Jonathan maintained his irritated stance. "Tell me what's going on."

Chase had no energy to respond.

"Garrett? You still with me?" Jonathan repeated, nudging Chase's foot.

Chase didn't move.

"Figures." Jonathan wheeled around, then his eyes widened. "What did you do to him?"

Jenna was standing in her doorway, glaring. Forcing herself to look past Jonathan's glistening chest, she saw Chase lying across her bed. Pushing Jonathan aside, Jenna rushed forward. She laid her hand against Chase's forehead. "He's burning up. You just couldn't wait to kick him while he was down, could you?"

Jonathan folded his arms in annoyance. Jenna had only caught the tail end of what was really happening. She was driven to make the wrong assumption given the circumstances, and the undisputable fact Garrett was not on his favorite-person list. Still, he had a right to defend himself. "Did it ever occur to you for one minute that I might be one of the good guys? Garrett wouldn't have made it to the bed without me! He almost fell down the steps. For once, give me the benefit of the doubt."

"Oh, let's not go there."

"I think we should." Jonathan moved closer and the towel around his waist draped lower. "You need to see..."

Jenna held up her hand. "I've seen plenty, believe me. As far as I'm concerned you don't qualify as a good guy. Every chance you get you find a reason to make Chase look bad. Well, guess what? I don't give a damn. I know what a good man he is, and I've known from the start. So, don't start lecturing me on my choice of men. If there is some shred of truth to what you're saying, then thank you for breaking Chase's fall. Otherwise, get the hell out of my room."

Jenna bounced off the bed, rushed to the bathroom to wet a washcloth, then returned to lay it across Chase's forehead. She purposely avoided glancing in Jonathan's direction. With only a towel draped around his waist and water dripping from his bangs onto his chest, she dared not spend another minute ogling him. It could lead to nothing good.

"I can think of several ways you could show me your gratitude."

"Out!" Jenna pointed towards the door. "Now!"

Jonathan stifled his laugh. "I'll be right across the hall. Call me...if you need *anything*."

Jenna flung her pillow across the room, knocking the door shut. She had no patience for Jonathan's blatant display of flirtation. From the corner of her eye, she had caught him purposely untying his towel. Just another ploy to distract her. *Jackass.*

Turning her attention to Chase, she stroked his cheek.

"Talk to me, Chase," Jenna pleaded. "Tell me what's going on with you. I want to help you."

"No help," Chase murmured. He rolled over without another word.

"Don't push me away." Jenna picked up his hand and brought it to her lips. "Please, don't."

Chase didn't respond. His hand fell limp when Jenna let it go.

Sliding off the bed, Jenna sat on the floor wondering what to do. Her hands began to shake. Wrapping her arms around her knees, she dropped her head and began to cry.

Her life and everyone in it were spiraling out of control.

Her brother and best friend were missing...almost certainly in danger God knows where. She was scared out of her wits thinking she was being followed only to find out Maria had arranged for a personal bodyguard to track her every move. Coming to terms with the fact her mother was alive was one thing, but to be told she couldn't see her or be taken to her was something Jenna couldn't understand.

Feelings of helplessness and worry weighed down upon her shoulders like tons of massive bricks. Jenna rolled to her side, curling into a ball. Unaware her cries could be heard outside her bedroom, she let the tears flow until they dried on her face. Finally, she succumbed to exhaustion, and fell asleep.

Jonathan poked his head inside Jenna's doorway. Her cries had stopped minutes ago, but he hesitated grabbing the doorknob. In retrospect, he had acted like an ass. Jenna had every right to put him in his place. Even though he couldn't possibly understand her devotion to a man whose actions were conflicted and unpredictable, Jonathan admitted to himself he had acted rather poorly. Instead of airing Garrett's dirty laundry, he should have focused on turning Jenna's head in his own direction. On a more positive level.

He deserved what he got. Front and center.

It was time to make amends.

Surprised to see Jenna asleep on the floor, Jonathan walked slowly towards her. He wrestled with the temptation to pick her up, and place her on the bed next to Garrett, or even carry her across the hall. Not wanting to take a chance Jenna would awaken and slap him for making such an overt gesture, Jonathan took the safe way out. Grabbing the crocheted blanket lying across her wicker chair, Jonathan draped it lightly over Jenna. He kissed her forehead, understanding for the first time how deeply she could be devoted to someone.

Jonathan wanted to believe he was in love with her, too.

*****

Maria leaned against the back of the weathered wooden bench facing the gazebo and squeezed the bridge of her nose. The time for regretting past actions was well over. Now the healing could begin.

If Jenna could ever forgive her.

Maria sighed, as Ann sauntered up to her and held out a large coffee cup.

"Drink up," she said. "You need it."

"Not according to my husband."

"Damian isn't here. I think you're entitled after the morning we both had."

Maria nodded before taking a sip. So much for cutting back. She was already on her seventh cup of the day, and it wasn't even noon yet. "Speaking of my husband, I started off the morning having a major fight with him. Something...we rarely do. Fight. I mean...we have disagreements, and occasionally, I let him win." Maria forced a smile. "But today...I think we were both on the losing side. Now this whole mess with Jenna. Today is turning from bad to worse."

"She's not upset, Maria; Jenna is just in shock. Finding out her mother is alive is unbelievable news. Give her some time; she'll come around." Ann stared off into the distance.

"I wish it was that easy." Maria gulped down her coffee. "I betrayed her trust, Ann. Jenna will only see this as another lie forced down her throat."

Ann tossed her cup in a nearby trash can. "You did what you had to do. You've kept Lois safe all these months. Let's face it, Hamilton was getting too close. Lois would be dead if it wasn't for your quick thinking. Jenna will have to realize that."

"Not right now, she won't. Jenna has been through too much in such a short period of time. It's a wonder she hasn't gone over the deep end. I feel like I'm partially to blame. I should have told her from the start about Lois. At least we would have started out on the right foot...with honesty." Maria's voice waned. "I'll be lucky if she ever trusts me again. I screwed up."

Ann grabbed Maria by her shoulders. "Do you hear your-self, Maria? This is crazy. You saved Lois Reed's life, not to mention countless other people over the course of your career. If anyone's to blame, it's me. My tracking skills sucked. I scared her. I'm the one who should be having regrets; not you."

"Thanks for the pep talk. Sometimes I need one."

"Not a problem."

"Really? Seems like this assignment has been nothing but problems. I'm sorry I involved you, Ann. Maybe it's time for you to go back to D.C. Right now you could be..."

"Forget it. I'm here to stay."

Maria continued to notice the gray clouds which seemed to be following her as soon as she left the beach house. "Alright, but try not to be too obvious. Keep an eye on Jenna. I'd feel better if I knew someone had her back."

"And who has your back, Maria? I thought you said two of your guys were driving up from D.C.?"

In all the confusion of the morning fight with Damian, and then rushing to find Jenna, Maria had completely forgotten about Bromley and Carroll. An unsettling feeling suddenly crept up her arms. She hit the speed-dial for Jacoby but it went straight to voicemail. "Call me ASAP. Bromley and Carroll haven't arrived. I'm worried. They should have checked in by now or at least called me. Thanks."

"Did you try their cells?"

Maria started walking in the direction of the beach house, quickening her pace with each step. "I will when I get back to the beach house. I don't have them saved in my contact list; Jacoby usually handles these things. Something's happened. I don't have a good feeling about this."

"Neither do I," Ann murmured. "Not one bit."

*****

Mallory Kincaid kicked off her Jimmy Choo peep-toe sandals as soon as she entered David's apartment in Upper Manhattan. Choo was her favorite designer, but she had to admit, wearing the platform five-inch heels all day made her feet tired. She wasn't cut out for this eight-to-five routine, and despite David's repeated requests to stay on the job to keep an eye on Mason Hamilton, Mallory was extremely tempted to throw in the towel.

Mason was an ass and a fool. His frequent stops at the receptionist desk had no business relevance. He was overtly flirting with her. Apparently, having no clue she was the same woman who had impersonated his dead wife just weeks earlier. Hair dye, fashionable glasses, and sexy, professional attire had done the trick. Mason hadn't put two-and-two together. Mallory doubted he ever would. All Mason seemed to care about was a new conquest.

Mallory sighed, wishing David would finally pull the plug on her assignment. She didn't know how many more days she could tolerate Mason's suggestive remarks and prolonged stares. It would only be a matter of time before he followed her into the storage closet or insisted she join him in his office for a private meeting.

"Never going to happen," Mallory affirmed to the empty apartment. She checked the antique pendulum clock on the wall. Six-thirty. David had promised they would eat together tonight.

Simple promises from a man who shouldn't be making them at all. David's life was so unpredictable. His jobs took priority over Mallory's needs and wants, and if she was being totally honest with herself, she hated what their lifestyle had become.

David was away more times than he was home. Even if it was just for a day or two, Mallory felt the loneliness never quite leave her. Depression would set in, then anger. Before long, she was ready to kill him herself.

A constant cycle she wished they could break.

They needed some down time. Time to focus solely on each other for more than a few hours or minutes each day. It wasn't like it used to be when David had taken less elaborate assignments in Europe. They had more time to be together...more time to thoroughly enjoy each other...before he had to rush home and play house with Francesca Tulane, of all people.

Thank God the manipulating bitch is dead, Mallory thought as she began to unbutton her blouse. Mallory had barely tolerated hearing about Francesca when she was alive. Now that she was the only woman in David's life, Mallory had no intention of competing with a memory.

Besides, Mallory mused, *memories won't keep David warm at night*. She smiled, thinking of the many creative ways she planned on entertaining David this evening.

Stepping out of her short pin-stripe skirt, she tossed it on the ivory chaise next to their bed. Sitting down, she slowly slipped off her thigh-high stockings, wishing David was the one taking them off of her.

Mallory had thought about keeping them on, and donning one of her provocative Victoria's Secret teddies, but working such long, boring hours was taking its toll. All she wanted right now was a long hot shower to rejuvenate her body and pump up her libido, if it could get any higher. David was in for a wild night of hot sex. They both needed to work off their frustrations.

Mallory fanned herself as she felt her body getting warm. Instead of heading for the bathroom, she wandered back into the kitchen to fill a wine glass with ice cubes. Several varieties of Chardonnay and Riesling were tempting her in the fridge. Adding a couple of fresh strawberries, Mallory chose a bottle of Chardonnay at random. Chilled wine didn't give her quite the instant buzz of red wine, but it didn't matter. She needed something to distract her until David came home.

Two sips later, the door opened. Mallory set her glass down on the dining room table, then propped one hand on her hip. She didn't have to wait long. David was in her arms, and they were falling to the floor. Mallory's eyes widened with delight.

"Missed me? Thought so." David found her neck extremely inviting. The faint smell of fruit-infused Chardonnay on her lips was driving him crazy. "How was your day?"

"I don't want to talk about my day…or about Mason Hamilton…or about anything in particular." Mallory distracted him with her roving hands. "I don't want your lips doing anything but…"

David laughed at her brazenness. "We have all night, baby. I'm all yours…remember?"

"Of course I remember," Mallory said as she fell into his arms again. "I just want to make sure…*you remember.* I love you, David."

Chapter 12

Bursting glass shot at him from all angles making Austin realize what a dumbass decision he had made. Too late for regrets. It had been a hasty decision, and not one he'd probably ever undertake with a rational mind. What he did was based entirely on instinct, realizing it was his only chance to get out of there and find Kelly as soon as possible.

Never considering the risks. He was bleeding...badly.

"Damn it!" Austin quickly brushed away the slivers of glass that had accumulated in his lap. Blood was on his hands, his arms, and the worst of it was saturating his jeans. Piercing pain radiated from his right leg just above the knee. A glass shard, approximately four inches in length, was sticking out of his leg. Blood was pooling around the entrance wound. Austin cried out several times before he had the courage to grasp the shard and pull upward.

Pressing his hand over the gaping wound did little to stop the steady blood flow. It would only be a matter of time until he lost consciousness. Staggering from the car, he shook off more glass chips from his head and neck, thankful he was still able to move. But after a few steps, the pain was insurmountable. His leg was growing weaker.

Falling to one knee, Austin struggled to regain his balance. He pitched forward hitting the gravel road. His eyes searched the area around him until they glazed over.

Drifting between consciousness and darkness for several minutes, Austin fought to stay awake.

"Kelly!"

Austin was sure no one was close enough to hear his cries, but it didn't matter. He needed to say her name, to keep her close. To keep him from going crazy imagining something worse was happening to her.

Catching his breath, Austin managed to pull himself up on his left knee. His other pant leg was soaked dark red but at least the wound had stopped gushing. A good sign the blood had clotted. He still had a chance of some movement. Maybe it would be enough.

Austin heaved his right leg up. He took one small step, and instantly saw stars. The pain was intense, but not as blinding as it had first been. He could make it, even if he had to drag his bad leg behind him.

He wasn't giving up.

Kelly needed him, and he needed her.

More than anything.

*****

"I don't want excuses, damn it! Just find that car!"

Damian Pierce fought the urge to slam his cell phone down on the hood of the police cruiser. His temper was escalating with each minute that passed. It had started the moment he raced down the side steps of the beach house and into the AC Field Office's waiting SUV.

His bull-headed ways had gotten him into trouble once again. Pushing Maria too far this time, it was no wonder her defenses had flared.

You just couldn't leave it alone, could you?

Wanting her to change is only half the battle...and you're on the losing side.

Damian swore under his breath. This time he had managed to drive a wedge in their relationship...a point of no return. He hurt Maria today in a way no words of forgiveness would ever cure. Just shy of a betrayal. The one thing he had promised he would never do.

Maria won't forget this. Damian's mind played out several scenarios. Maria was probably pacing right now, so furious she could barely speak. Or worse, she was crying...or holding back tears until they flowed uncontrollably. Maria would take the silence approach...the worst punishment of all...and Damian would feel the sting of her broken heart, condemning him to suffer over and over.

I'm the one who won't forget this. Damian glanced around to make sure he hadn't said the words out loud. Frustration was hitting him like a double-barreled shotgun.

Table it. Damian knew he had no time to dwell on his own personal tragedy. He was in charge of a multi-state search and rescue mission, coordinating the efforts of state, local and federal authorities. He had to stay in control, maintain objectivity, and make productive, rational decisions. As he turned to greet Agent Brett Jacoby, on loan from Maria's unit, Damian forced himself to calm down.

Jacoby was toting his iPad as usual, glancing down at the screen every few seconds. Data scrolled down four separate quadrants, each calculating a different statistic, yet all were connected to a common goal...determining the probability that Kelly and Austin would be found alive...or not at all.

"Nothing yet?" Jacoby saw the answer on Damian's face before he heard it.

"McHenry knows we'd try to track him with the Facial Recognition Database. He's three steps ahead of us. He knows all the tricks. We're getting played."

"Then we just have to play harder." Jacoby handed his iPad to Damian.

"You expect me to understand any of this?"

Jacoby frowned. "Does the word *luddite* mean anything to you?"

"Don't push me, Jacoby. My day has gotten progressively worse. And I don't appreciate being called names I'm sure are offensive."

"If you and Turette would just embrace technology a little more," Jacoby started to say but stopped when he realized his attempt at dry humor was going nowhere. "Keep the faith, Pierce. We're making good strides. At least we have plenty of help this time. Checking traffic cams, toll booth surveillance. Somewhere...someone is going to track them. Just takes time."

"Time is a luxury we don't have. McHenry is unpredictable. He has no standard calling card just a whole deck he likes to mix up. He'll use that to our disadvantage."

Jacoby scanned the multiple windows streaming data on his iPad. Maps of two different regions were taking up the left side of his screen while probability stats calculated in a small box at the top right. Text messages from different points of contact scrolled at the bottom.

Damian felt dizzy looking at the tablet for more than a few seconds. "I don't know how you stand that thing."

"It's great for multi-tasking. Does practically everything."

"Except make coffee."

"Doesn't need to." Jacoby pointed to a portable coffee and bagel station set up a few yards away.

"Feeding the troops. Good call. Maria is going to be upset when I finally take you back into the fold."

"Not a good idea to get her riled up right now."

Damian tried again to focus on the iPad. "Too late. Lost quite a few points this morning. Pushed too many buttons."

"Bad habit, Pierce. Wouldn't worry about it though. Turette doesn't hold grudges."

"No, she doesn't, thank God."

Jacoby reached for his iPad realizing Damian had stopped looking at it. "Let me give you a rundown."

Damian nodded, zipping up his windbreaker. The air was damp and getting cooler. Matching his demeanor. "Enlighten me, *Genius*."

"Don't start. You know I only tolerate it when Turette calls me that. I haven't granted you privileges yet." Jacoby switched screens to display a map of the region spanning Pennsylvania to the Canadian border.

"Fair enough. What do we have?"

"Delaware, New Jersey and Pennsylvania State Troopers all pumped up and ready to go. BOLOs out. Media's been notified to broadcast pictures on all the major networks. Just in case McHenry's inclined to switch modes of transportation, we've notified Amtrak and all airports from here to New York. I don't think he's brazen enough to take public transportation with two tagalongs, but you never know. Personally, I think he'll stick to back roads, ferret around in the dark, start fresh in the morning...maybe even change cars again. But he'll screw up or chicken out; it's inevitable."

"Your confidence amazes me."

"We have the upper hand whether he realizes it or not. We're narrowing his trail. There are only so many places McHenry can hide and keep moving." Jacoby tapped his earpiece and took a step backwards. "Are you sure? Good work, fellas." He turned back to Damian. "Pennsylvania Transit Authority just called in an ID. Ran it through Facial Rec and we've got a high probability match."

"Meaning?"

"Meaning...we have a better than average chance McHenry's been spotted. Heading north and west. Clocked them on I-476. My guess is they're bound for the Poconos. A detour, maybe? Definitely bypassing the New York corridor and...Mason Hamilton. Interesting," Jacoby paused. "Looks like he's running away from Hamilton...but why?"

"I'm not putting anything past McHenry. If, and I say this lightly, if he's taken it upon himself to circumvent Mason Hamilton, then he's a ticking time bomb. Hamilton will retaliate if he realizes McHenry is playing by his own rules. Mark my words, McHenry just put a price on his own head," Damian surmised.

"Could be a detour to throw us off."

"Maybe...or not. This situation just got more complicated. If McHenry has gone against the grain, and he's not bringing Kelly to her old man, then it wouldn't surprise me if Hamilton brings in the big gun."

"The Closer?" Jacoby swallowed hard. Bringing in The Closer severely reduced Kelly and Austin's chances of survival.

"I'm just theorizing."

"Your favorite pastime. You know, Pierce, you and Turette need to get a life. You have too many theories, and not enough answers. It's wearing the both of you down."

Damian shrugged, accepting Jacoby's observation. "That was the basis of our fight this morning. I want Maria to back off. Retire. She's running in circles because of Hamilton, and we're both getting too old to deal with it."

"You actually *told her* to retire?" Jacoby whistled. "I'm surprised she didn't deck you."

"Didn't have to. When Maria starts swinging, it's mostly with words. They cut deeper and she knows it. Let's just say, I came away with a few new scars. When she gets her back up against the wall..."

"She pushes back. Yeah, I know. But you're handling this the wrong way. Turette is..." He stopped short, drawing Damian's attention to the man walking towards both of them.

"Pierce...and Jacoby. Always a...*pleasure.*" Senior-Agent-In-Charge Elias Briggs stopped a few feet away from invading their personal space. With a smug smile on his face, he took an ostentatious stance, folding his arms. "I'm the first to admit, I don't appreciate being awakened at four this morning and told to get my ass in gear, but here I am."

"What are you doing here, Briggs?" Damian didn't mince words. He couldn't stand the brutish, overweight and overbearing Briggs for more than a few minutes at a time.

"I'm not here to play nice, Pierce. The brass wants someone with accountability in mind on the job. You, on the other hand, seemed to be lacking in that department. Could be...because of the company you keep, or should I say sleep with?"

Damian's face bulged with anger.

"I'm here for damage control. Should have been in New York a few months ago when that whole mess at the museum went down. Could have spared the agency quite an embarrassment. Turette needs to learn a little more finesse...and crisis management skills. She..."

"Did you come up here to bad-mouth my wife or assist with the mission, Briggs? Which is it? I've got work to do." Damian turned to leave.

"Not so fast, Pierce. The Director wants periodic updates...from my office. He's expecting your cooperation." Briggs ran his fingers over his sparsely covered head. He did it more out of habit than need. With each passing month, Briggs bemoaned the fact the gray hairs on his head were decreasing at the same rate his waistline seemed to be expanding. Middle-age was a bitch.

Not that he cared much for his personal appearance. Actions, decisive ones, counted at the FBI a lot more than a perfect body, or at least Briggs tried to convince himself of that. All he needed was one more win, one more chance to prove to the Director he was worth a seat at the head table. Or at least a door down the hall from the Deputy Director.

All he had to do was find a way to bring Damian Pierce and Maria Turette to their knees. To prove their unworthiness, to strip them of their badges and showcase their weaknesses. A crowning achievement with the potential to elevate him to star status.

Finding blemishes in junior agents' records was chump change. Briggs was sick and tired of making cases out of bad decisions. Inexperience and ineptitude were solid enough reasons to rid the Agency of less-than-stellar agents who shouldn't have made the cut to begin with. *Nothing more than housekeeping,* Briggs told himself regularly.

A few years shy of retirement, now was the time to make his move. To go out with a glowing review, make the Director proud. Maybe even name a wing after him.

As Briggs glared at Damian Pierce through mirror-reflective sunglasses too old to be called stylish or even retro-chic, his lips creased. *One wrong move, Pierce. That's all you need to do. Hand me my promotion on a silver platter.*

"I said, do you want an update...or not?" Damian repeated with annoyance. "I don't have time to stand here while you make up your mind. We have lives at stake, Briggs."

Briggs felt the first few rain pellets take him by surprise. Gray clouds had overtaken the sky rather quickly, forcing the sun to retreat. He had no desire to stand outside much longer and get drenched. "Give me the rundown, Pierce, and make it quick."

"We're tracking McHenry north and west...*sir*," Pierce said with disdain. He hated the man...and what he stood for, pure and simple. But it was out of his control. Briggs was here on the orders from a higher level, and as much as Damian wished the circumstances were different, he couldn't do anything about it.

"I see. Let me get this straight. You've got police and federal agents in four states ready to make a move because, and I quote, *'you are relatively sure'* McHenry is our man. You're basing your entire operational rationale on a single piece of evidence...a partial, not a full fingerprint. You are convinced Logan McHenry single-handedly abducted Mr. Austin Reed and Ms. Kelly McBride from their residence in Cape May to take them...where? Somewhere...north and west? Did it ever occur to you, the evidence...the fingerprint...could have been planted as a decoy?"

Damian's face reddened. Briggs was making a mockery out of his trained observation, and mission directives. "Of course I considered that," Damian growled. "For the record, I was right. A bridge cam just picked up the car. Ran it through Facial Rec. It's a match. We anticipate he's headed for the Pocono Mountain Region. We need to get moving. Cover as much ground in that area as possible before nightfall, or he'll burrow down somewhere."

"Another *guess*, am I right? Seems to be a family trait…guesswork." Briggs turned up his collar as the rain became more insistent. "Pierce, let me make myself clear. When you screw up, I'll be right here to slap your hand and push you aside. The Director is expecting results, not some lame-ass excuse for a rescue mission."

Jacoby shoved his iPad at Damian, driving a distance between him and Briggs. "Your updates, Pierce."

"Leave Maria out of this, Briggs." Damian's posture stiffened. "She has nothing to do with this."

Briggs smirked. "How right you are, Pierce. Turette has absolutely nothing to do with this mission, and we're going to keep it that way. This is all you, your show. Go ahead and prove me wrong. Find McHenry and bring him down. Save Reed and McBride. Get all the accolades you want, but rest assured, I'll be one step behind you making sure we do this right. By the book. *My book.* You got that?"

Damian seethed. "Yeah, I got it."

Briggs retreated just as the storm clouds opened. He ran for cover, pushing aside an agent who was about to climb into one of the agency vans.

Jacoby stuck his iPad inside his jacket, motioning for Damian to follow. They jumped inside a waiting SUV just seconds before the downpour erupted. "He's a jackass." Jacoby tilted his head towards the direction in which Briggs ran. "Don't let him get to you."

"Already has. I was this close to decking him. Thanks for running interference."

"No problem. Anytime." Jacoby started to laugh. "No contest anyway. You'd nail him in two seconds flat. Brigss would have to limp back to D.C."

"Then he'd write me up for sure."

"Probably so. I'd love to write *him* up. Just once."

"Good luck with that." The smile left Damian's face fast. "He knows how to yank chains, doesn't he? Bringing up New York."

"It's his *thing*. It's what he does. Briggs and his little perverted fetish. He loves to annoy people, get under their skin."

Damian grabbed the door handle, so tempted to rip it off. "He's acting like Maria was the only one in New York. She couldn't possibly have planned for an ambush coming from inside the museum. Intel indicated the building was empty. The team she sent in never had a chance. She did her best recon, and she's being punished for it."

"I know. I was there. Remember?"

"I'm surprised Briggs isn't trying to run you out of town along with the rest of us."

"Let him try. Briggs and I have...history. I don't think he's stupid enough to tangle with me." Jacoby watched the rain run down the front windshield in wide, continuous torrents. "Before I joined your ranks...I did a little time in Internal Affairs. Briggs was just starting to get noticed back then. He was gearing up to make a name for himself."

"Nothing's changed."

"Not much, except he's on better behavior these days, if you can believe it. Briggs narrowly escaped a very nasty sexual harassment charge several years back. Almost brought his career to a standstill. Then some idiot stepped in and made all the charges go away. Mysteriously, the female agent resigned, and get this, the case file...*disappeared*. How friggin' convenient."

"So there's no record of the charges? Nothing in the computer? You've got to be kidding me!" Damian could hardly sit still.

"You have to understand, the pc system back then was ancient. It barely functioned, was always going down. Anyway, there was more to that story which always bothered me. The female agent came straight from Quantico. I mean, she was only in the office a day or two before Briggs made his move. Got too personal. Offensive touching...behind closed doors. Just shy of rape, if my memory serves me right. Her word against Briggs', who had already caught the Unit Chief's eye. Do the math. Guess who was asked to leave? Swear to God." Jacoby threw his hands in the air. "So, just to keep it on the up and up, I was asked to do a *cursory* investigation. What a crock that was. Every time I tried to contact the victim, I got nowhere."

"What finally happened?"

"Nothing. Briggs came in the next day cocky as always. Took his seat, did his job and life went on. The whole incident got shoved under the carpet, and it never set well with me."

"That's the reason Briggs avoids you like the plague."

Jacoby leaned back in his seat. "Could be. One day when I have some free time and I'm not running referee, I'll figure it out."

"I'm sure you will. Enough about Briggs. What else do you have on McHenry?"

Jacoby tapped a screen on his cell phone. "Frequents the town of Ogdensburg, New York at the Canadian border. No known associates, but I'm assuming he's made friends who live there. I think that's where he's going. Ok to send a team up that way?"

"Do it. That way we can prove to Mr. High-and-Mighty we're not overlooking any possibility."

Jacoby laughed. "You sound just like Turette. Except she wouldn't be so diplomatic even after listening to my sound advice."

"That's one of Maria's downfalls. She doesn't hold back. She'd tell Briggs where to get off and land herself four weeks of anger management sessions." Damian's cell buzzed. "Speaking of my beautiful...and hopefully forgiving wife."

"Five minutes, Pierce, and then I'm getting back in the car." Jacoby slammed the door shut before Damian had a chance to respond.

"Hi, sweetheart. Listen, I..."

"I'm sorry," Maria blurted out. "Don't be angry with me."

"Maria." Damian's voice deepened. "I've been a wreck ever since I left you. I didn't kiss you good-bye. I'm sorry, sweetheart."

"I know the feeling. I love you, Damian," she added softly.

"If you were here right now, I'd..."

Maria laughed. "I know what you'd do, and that's enough for me right now. I won't keep you. I know you're busy. I...just needed to hear your voice." Thinking of Damian's sexy, scratchy voice brought a smile to Maria's face.

"Well it's not nearly enough for me," Damian insinuated.

"I refuse to have phone sex with you, Agent Pierce. Might get yourself written up."

"That's a distinct possibility. Briggs is here and I can tell he's on the warpath."

Maria sighed. "Watch your back, Damian. Briggs can't be trusted. You and I both know that."

"I'll try to behave."

"Do more than try. For me, please."

"Yes, dear. Anything for you." Damian began to laugh.

Chapter 13

Another betrayal.
By a friend.

Jenna slammed the side door of the beach house, never looking back. Her temper was rising faster than she was speed-walking. It didn't dawn on her until she was almost a block away that she never checked to see if the glass door panel had survived. Coming home to broken glass all over the landing would just be the icing on the cake.

The unbelievable, good news she had received about her mother was being overshadowed by one distinct fact.

Maria had lied to her.

Jenna power-walked down Congress Street a couple of blocks. Breaking into a full-paced run, she fought hard to put Maria's deception behind her. Playing devil's advocate, Jenna almost spoke out loud, not caring if anyone was listening.

Maria had her reasons. She was keeping Mom safe. She was keeping me safe.

"Oh, the hell with this!"

Jenna sucked in too much air, dropping her hands to her knees. Her hard-core jogging had lasted about four blocks.

The only thing she was running away from was herself.

Jenna steadied herself against an oak tree. Her eyes fell to the roots protruding from the cracked cobblestone walkway, and she felt just as broken and torn in too many directions. Overwhelmed with a barrage of emotions, she was barely functioning anymore.

At the intersection of Broadway and Beach, Jenna stopped short at the wooden plank just off the concrete Promenade. It was too inviting not to walk across the sand. Ditching her sneakers and socks by the Broadway Beach sign, she sighed the moment her toes sunk into the sand.

For a few precious seconds, she closed her eyes and breathed in the sounds and smells of the surf. The best way she knew to calm her nerves, Jenna wished she had more time to savor the peaceful sensation. The sand felt cool and refreshing, so different from the scorching heat of summer when flip flops were mandatory.

Fall was different at the beach, and Jenna had forgotten just how much she loved this time of year. Mid-to-late October was the absolute best time. Warm enough to still wear sandals and capris, but chilly at night to warrant a sweatshirt.

Too many weekends to count, Jenna had made the trek down to Cape May to help her parents winterize the beach house. She never minded. It gave her an excuse to hit the beach a few more times before the winter storms, even if it was just a brief stroll along the shoreline with her mom.

Her mother's face seemed so distant. She could hardly distinguish the features.

"This is crazy."

Jenna fingered a clump of sand, letting the particles sift away as her mind wandered. She was drawn back to the days preceding the double funeral for her parents. Pieces were staring to make sense now. Why she and Austin had never been asked to identify any remains. Why the funeral home had apologized profusely when they told Jenna her parents were cremated by accident. A miscommunication not explained by the funeral director until the funeral service was over.

"How convenient."

Jenna shook her head, realizing just how gullible she and Austin had been. In their state of shock, neither had questioned the competency of the funeral home, or demanded a more detailed explanation. The funeral went on as planned with closed caskets, never giving any family or friends the slightest notion something had gone wrong.

Everything had gone wrong. Dad hadn't survived the staged accident, and Mom had to go into hiding.

Jenna stared into the ocean, praying it would provide some much-needed relief. Digging her toes deeper into the sand crests, she let her mind go completely blank. She didn't want to think of lies, betrayals, kidnappings, or murder.

She wanted her normal life back again.

She wanted happy, innocent times with family and friends.

She wanted to fall completely in love with the right man.

So many things out of her reach.

Jenna didn't realize she was crying until tears dropped to her knees. Visions of her father swiped across her mind. She couldn't let them go. She didn't want to.

It was more painful now to think of her father, knowing her mother was alive and well. His loss seemed so much stronger now. Jenna couldn't explain it. She was re-grieving, giving into the raw agony she had pushed to the far reaches of her mind. She had promised herself she would always remember her parents in a positive light and not dwell on the terrible circumstances which took them from her.

Just another example of how bad she was at keeping promises to herself. She hadn't been able to swear off men for the summer, and now she couldn't get past hurtful memories.

Her dad never had a chance. He was doomed from the start, panicking at the last minute. Setting the whole operation in jeopardy, risking her mother's life, and making the ultimate sacrifice.

Jenna couldn't wrap her head around it. What Maria explained to her didn't make any sense. Why had her mother waited until the last possible moment to tell him who and what she was? Why couldn't Lois just be honest with her husband who had shared her life and loved her unconditionally?

"Why, Mom?"

The crescendo of the waves gave no solace or answers. Jenna continued to watch its natural movements, hoping a divine response would somehow reach her.

Why did Dad have to die?

Once a spy, always a spy.

Isn't that what Maria had said a few times? Jenna hadn't appreciated the significance of such a casual comment until this very moment. When the picture came into focus. When she finally could grasp what her mother had done.

Why she was holding her accountable.

This is on you, Mom. Dad died because of you.

Jenna fisted her hands, never feeling the tiny granules cutting her between her fingers because she was squeezing them together. She wasn't feeling anything physical right now. Just a hollowness of sadness.

Despite Maria's best efforts to explain how she and Lois had staged the accident last December, Jenna still could not forgive her mother for her last minute expulsion of the truth. Lois had waited too late to reveal her true identity and purpose. Naturally, Jim Reed had reacted the way he did. Having only a few minutes to comprehend what his wife was telling him. He had no second chance.

His fate had been sealed. One error in their calculations had caused his seat belt to malfunction. The agent assigned to help him from the car had finally given up knowing full well the bomb was ready to explode.

Lois hadn't looked back before hearing the blast. She had assumed everything had gone according to their plan, and Jim was fine on the opposite side of the embankment. It wasn't until she reached the rendezvous point that she was told her husband was dead, his body consumed in fire when the bomb went off.

Jim Reed had burned alive.

Jenna's hands flew to her cheeks, drenched with tears. Envisioning her father's body engulfed in flames was too much to take. She couldn't get the horrible picture out of her mind.

Or the fact her mother could have prevented it.

Jenna drew her knees up to her chest. She rocked back and forth, weeping once again for the loss of her father...another innocent life taken because of turmoil surrounding the cursed treasure pieces.

He had trusted, loved...and suffered because of it.

Was she destined for the same fate?

Attempts had been made on her life...and somehow through unfathomable miracles, she had survived. Jenna wondered when her luck would run out. Just sitting here on the sand, she was a prime target. Her body sagged, mirroring her resolve. She had been too trusting, too naïve. Too stupid to see through all the lies and deceit. The people she cared about, and who supposedly cared about her...were no longer trustworthy. Keeping her in the dark, concealing secrets...supposedly for her own good.

The hell with all of them.

They had used her...in more ways than one. Putting her and her family in danger unnecessarily...convincing her to search for the cursed treasure pieces...which had made her life spiral out of control. *For what, really? Revenge?*

She was sick and tired of being on the losing end. This had to end...right now. Reaching into her jacket pocket, Jenna pulled out her cell. Dialing a number she had committed to memory several years ago, she closed her eyes wondering if she was making just another stupid mistake. Daring to trust someone else.

"Baby Girl, what a surprise."

"I need your help," Jenna confessed, sniffling back tears. "Austin and Kelly have been kidnapped. And I'm having major trust issues. The FBI flat out lied to me. I just don't know who…"

"No need to explain. I'm here for you, Baby Girl. What do you need right now?"

Jenna hesitated only briefly. "A gun. I need a gun, Lenny Lex."

*****

Thomas Movell moved fluidly through the sixth floor of the FBI's main office in Washington, stopping abruptly at the door of Internal Affairs Division Chief Raymond Konecki. Tall, lean and dark-skinned, Movell embraced his Jamaican heritage with quiet dignity and style. Sharing an uncanny resemblance to his confidante and best friend, Tumi Carile, Movell also shared Tumi's fine taste in tailored white linen suits.

Straightening his royal blue silk tie and matching handker-chief in his left breast pocket, Movell made slight movements, always aware he was being watched. Tiny cameras placed inconspicuously in every elevator and hallway recorded the time and location of every visitor. Imbedded in the visitor tag Movell now wore clipped to his jacket pocket, was yet another tracking device. It made no difference to Movell. The FBI's internal surveillance team could track him for as long as they wanted. He was on their turf, and he would be respectful of their internal controls.

Besides, he wasn't a stranger to this corridor. He had been here before…always to see the same person.

Konecki was indebted to Thomas Movell for saving his life. A debt Konecki had not yet repaid. A matter of obligated reciprocity Tumi Carile was counting on. As he had so eloquently phrased it, Movell was to "appeal to Konecki's sense of duty and honor."

Movell was here because Tumi had asked him to be, not because he expected Raymond Konecki to return any favors. He had followed Konecki's career from a distance, and felt certain their sense of values and morals would never meet in between; however, Konecki was a prominent player and a seasoned agent, a fact Movell did not discount. As much as he abhorred the idea of using Konecki to ensure his ultimate goal, Movell was motivated purely by allegiance to Tumi Carile.

Knocking twice then three times in rapid succession, Movell wondered if Konecki would take the hint, knowing exactly who was on the other side of his door.

"Come in, Thomas," Konecki called without getting up from behind his massive steel-cased desk. As soon as Movell closed the door behind him, Konecki looked over his reading glasses. At fifty-eight, Raymond Konecki was on the shorter side of retirement, and he was quite comfortable delegating outside assignments to younger agents eager to spread their wings. He had put on weight the past couple of years, resulting in a larger stomach and sagging jaws, but he was well past caring about his overall appearance. He was biding his time, relying on fewer alliances, and keeping his head low. He neither cared about elevating his position any higher on the FBI's hallowed ladder nor amassing a larger Internal Affairs Unit. *Scraping by*, Konecki always kidded himself, until it was time to hang up his badge and put the past behind him.

Besides, he had trained deputy directors and senior agents to handle the bulk of the job tasks he couldn't be bothered with. Now, he was perfectly content to sit back, review reports, and make the critical decisions. He was held accountable for every termination and suspension his senior staff recommended, and he could live with that. He was doing the FBI a service, although a thankless one at times. His position was considered to be one of the less glamorous and less respected, but one which was necessary for optimal efficiency.

It wasn't his present position which made him go home every night and befriend his vodka. It was the sins of his past, and the likelihood they would catch up to him.

Maybe they already had.

Ten years ago, almost to the day in fact, Konecki had made probably the worst decision of his life. There was no turning back.

Brash and bullish, Konecki had developed quite a no-holds-barred rep as a field agent, but this time he had done himself no favor by taking on one of Miami's most-feared drug cartels. His confidential informant had promised him the Intel was good, and Konecki had no reason not to trust him. Not bothering to call for back-up, his first mistake, Konecki had gone alone to the plumbing warehouse at night with only one fully-loaded pistol.

He had gotten the call on his way home from a late night football game, tickets he had won the week before at a poker game. Prime seats he just couldn't pass up. He was mildly-drunk, having consumed more than his share of beer and hot dogs, but coherent enough to get home, just a couple of miles from the stadium. At first, he could barely understand Luis whose broken English was at times so heavily-accented; words seemed like an entirely new language. After three renditions, Luis had gotten his point across, and Konecki didn't hesitate to react.

Arriving at the plumbing warehouse just five miles away, Konecki never bothered to grab his spare gun from the glove compartment. There was no time. He had a short window of opportunity to catch the drug runners in action. If he wasted even one minute, they'd be gone and more importantly, the drugs would be gone.

Nearing the side door of the warehouse, Konecki could hear voices, all speaking in Spanish. Although he considered himself fairly fluent, he was having a hard time detecting what exactly they were saying.

Hearing footsteps, he knew he had screwed-up bringing only one gun and not requesting back-up. There was no way he could outrun four men with guns. The best he could hope for was to take a couple of them down before he took his last breath. Konecki took cover behind several large metal storage units stacked three high behind the warehouse. He breathed heavily, wishing to God he hadn't been stupid enough to forget his other handgun. Survival training 101 – don't be caught with your pants down, or in this case, without back-up...gun power and manpower.

A mistake he knew could be fatal.

Except for today.

Konecki had never expected what happened next.

Thomas Movell materialized out of nowhere, stepping out from his hiding place inside the warehouse. Konecki could see through the partially-opened side door and was caught speechless. Movell, who he didn't know at the time, was standing in front of the men, all of whom were heavily armed with some type of assault rifle. Although Konecki couldn't hear what was being said, he could sum it up rather quickly.

The tall, dark-skinned man held a small gun at his side and was commanding the drug runners' full attention. He snapped his fingers with his right hand and within a few seconds two cars exploded across the parking lot from Konecki. The armed men retreated, running in the opposite direction, directly past the storage units while Konecki held his breath.

It wasn't his day to die. He had someone to thank for it. As he stepped cautiously away from his concealed location, he shouldered his weapon and outstretched his hand. "Thanks," he managed to say. "Raymond Konecki, FBI."

Thomas Movell merely bowed and shook hands. "Thomas Movell. Stay safe, Raymond Konecki." Then he took off running before Konecki could say another word.

The beginning of the strangest, most complicated alliance Konecki would ever know. Also the one which haunted him the most due to Movell's international reputation as one of Tumi Carile's most-trusted and obscure partners.

Konecki felt tension creep into every muscle of his body. He told himself it was just his arthritis acting up, but deep down he knew better. As Movell gracefully entered his office, looking like the years had never touched him, Konecki suddenly felt old like a racehorse who had outlived his livelihood.

He had agreed to meet with Movell on several occasions since the night they met. Even though Konecki's main objective was to keep tabs on Tumi Carile, he had done his best to camouflage conversations, never giving up his underhanded intentions. He suspected Thomas Movell had figured out his little scheme but nonetheless, he was willing to share a few tidbits of information. For all Konecki knew, Movell was playing the same game with his own hidden agenda.

Such as now.

Without expression, Konecki extended his hand, making Movell reach over the desk to shake it. "Long time, Thomas."

"Indeed. Eighteen months, if I am correct."

Konecki tilted his bald head, disregarding the sweat building on top of it. "What brings you to D.C.? I presume you're not sight-seeing."

Movell uttered a small laugh. "No, I am afraid not."

"What then?" Konecki persisted. For Thomas Movell to travel from Jamaica and show up on his doorstep unannounced, there had to be an intriguing reason. Konecki folded his hands on top of his desk, his curiosity piqued. "Now tell me, what does the great Tumi Carile need of my services?"

Movell bowed his head. "Tumi sends his regards, Raymond, and thanks you for considering what I am about to ask. I do not mean to inconvenience you or any member of your team, to be sure. However, I must ask that you keep my request confidential."

"Everything I do is *confidential*, Thomas. You know that."

"Of course." Movell took a seat in one of Konecki's guest chairs and crossed his legs. "My request is simple. I merely wish to observe one of your operational units."

Konecki leaned back in his chair, spinning it from side to side. "Observe? Really, Thomas, you can do better than that. We're old friends. Level with me. Tell me exactly what you're hoping to gain by *observing*, and I'll do my best to save you the trouble." Konecki's impatience was showing through his forced smile.

Refusing Movell's request would be foolish; it would cost him. Movell and Tumi Carile had connections which were far-reaching. Legal and not-so-legal channels. *No*, Konecki thought to himself as he watched Movell sit stoically in his guest chair, this was not the time to negate relations with one of Carile's right-hand men.

"Suffice it to say, Tumi believes there are traitors in your midst. I am here to…identify them and…"

Konecki slammed his fist on his desk. "Damn it, Thomas! I can't permit you to conduct your own witch hunt! We have laws, good ones, and I can't just look the other way when you're about to break them."

Movell never changed his expression. "I meant no disrespect, Raymond. I would never ask you to compromise yourself. I merely wish to conduct a private investigation, the results of which I am most happy to share. All I ask is that you establish my presence as a visiting law enforcement officer, a member of the Jamaican consulate, who wishes to observe unit operations as an *educational* experience. Nothing more."

Konecki stared at Movell for several seconds before looking away. "Of all people, don't you think I would know it if one of our own was dirty? Under my own roof? It's what I do...every day I walk through these doors. You're insulting me and my team."

"I'm doing no such thing. Quite the contrary, Raymond." Movell tried his best to sound reassuring. "Objectively, I believe this exercise will rid you of the *undesirable* element in your ranks. I would think that would be very beneficial to you."

"Who do you suspect?"

"Elias Briggs, for one."

Konecki's mouth dropped. "Briggs? One of our senior agents? This is ridiculous, Thomas, and you're completely out of line. Briggs has an exemplary record. I'm not going to tolerate your unsubstantiated accusations. Whatever Tumi thinks he has on Briggs is entirely wrong. I would personally vouch for him."

"His record...is not entirely *unblemished*."

Konecki twisted nervously in his swivel chair. "What do you know of that?"

"Would you like me to recant the details?" Movell started to remove a slip of paper from his jacket pocket. He stopped when Konecki waved his hand.

"That won't be necessary."

Movell hid his smile. "Perhaps you would consider an alternate request?"

"I'm listening." Konecki cracked his knuckles.

"I wish to infiltrate Maria Turette's unit. We have reason to believe an infidel is sabotaging her missions from within. I would like to conduct my own research. When I..."

"If this backfires, you're on your own. I will deny this conversation ever took place."

"As you wish."

"You may be treading in dangerous waters, my friend."

Movell bowed one final time, playing with the silver falcon dangling from his shiny Rolex watch. "Perhaps, Raymond. Perhaps."

Chapter 14

"That's the first time I've seen you smile all morning."

Ann Bailey handed Maria a glass of iced tea. "Damian's not mad at you anymore, I take it."

Maria shook her head after taking a sip. "We're back on track, I suppose. Long distance apologies don't really work for us, but we'll make it up to each other."

Ann leaned against the kitchen counter in her rental. She and Maria had followed Jenna home then decided to give her some space. Watching Jenna from a distance as she sat on the beach and cried was hard enough to take. Jenna deserved some private time.

"Let's take these to the living room."

When they were both seated, Ann finally broke the uncomfortable silence. "You didn't have a choice, Maria. Jenna was bound to find out about Lois. It was just a matter of time. I think you handled it rather well, actually."

Maria took a long drink then set her glass down. "I should have been honest with her from the beginning. Jenna had a right to know her mother was alive. I had no business keeping that from her. I know...we were both concerned for Lois' safety, but, Ann, let's face it, we caused Jenna unnecessary anguish. God knows she's had plenty of that already. She probably hates me right now."

"Jenna will see the logic in keeping Lois in protective custody once she calms down. I'm sure she doesn't hate you. You're her friend. You did what you had to do to protect her mother."

Maria laid her head back against the chair cushion as she slid a little lower. "I hope I haven't pushed Jenna over the edge."

"She's been heading in that direction on her own," Ann added. "What do you want me to do?"

"Keep an eye on her. I'm sorry...I know I sound like a broken record but I can't help it. She'll be in danger until I can wrap this up with Hamilton. I can't take any more chances. I've already made enough mistakes." Maria drained the rest of her glass.

"Then make up for them. Take Jenna to see Lois. Maybe being reunited with her mother will calm her down a bit so she doesn't think she needs to take care of matters on her own. Lois could talk some sense into her."

Maria shook her head, disagreeing. "Not yet. It's too risky. We need to tread lightly. The minute we bring Lois out of hiding, she's in danger, too. Then we've got another problem on our hands."

"Something we don't need right now."

Maria got up and took Ann's glass. "We're officially off-duty. I'm making us Long Island iced teas."

*****

Bromley never knew what hit him.

He had grown impatient waiting for Carroll to return from the men's room. They were finally making good time after spending hours sitting in traffic on I-95 North just above the Harbor Tunnel. As soon as they hit the Delaware Memorial Bridge, Carroll announced he needed to make a pit stop. Grumbling, Bromley had finally relented not wanting to cause a riff. He and Carroll had never been partnered together before, and this was no way to start out.

The tie-up on the interstate was nerve-wracking. A wiseass tractor trailer driver had switched lanes, swerving to pass a slow moving van, only to end up jack-knifing the cab and spilling his cargo across the four-lane highway. Safety restraints had burst upon impact, sending two-by-fours, drywall panels, and stainless steel beams sprawling across the East Coast's most travelled highway. Highway patrols were doing their best to re-route traffic in a single lane around the wreckage, but it was slow going. Then if that hadn't been enough, the bridge traffic had been reduced to two lanes due to construction. By the time they reached Penns-ville, the first exit over the bridge, both Bromley and Carroll had reached their breaking points.

"Pull in the Exxon," Carroll gestured. "This coffee is going straight through me."

"Hurry up. We're not stopping again until we see the Cape May lighthouse."

Carroll bolted from the car making Bromley grin. Cowboy could hold his beer but not his coffee. *Figures*, Bromley thought. *The Texan can out-drink all of us on a Friday night, but when it comes to riding around with a coffee cup, his kidneys can't take it.* Bromley promised himself he would rib Cowboy about this for quite some time.

Twenty minutes later, Bromley had lost his sense of humor. He was hot, tired and his patience had just run out. "Carroll!" Bromley knocked on the door of the men's room. "Let's go. We've got two more hours to drive, and I'm getting damn sick of being in the car. Hurry up."

No response.

Bromley pushed the door wide open, finding the rest room empty. *Strange.* Even stranger was the fact the gas station had cleared out. Not a car in sight except for the one he and Carroll had arrived in and the tow truck parked in front of the office. Bromley swatted a fly away from his neck then released the safety latch on his holster.

A radio was blasting from the open bay of the garage. Cautiously approaching the mechanic's area, Bromley found it to be abandoned also.

"What the hell?"

Tools were scattered across countertops and on the floor along with soda cans. Whoever was here had left unexpectedly. Bromley drew his gun. He circled around to the side of the building where his search had begun just minutes earlier. "Carroll!" Bromley called again. If Carroll had wandered off to the McDonalds across the street without telling him, he was in for a shitload of trouble. Bromley reached for his cell right before he heard a loud noise coming from the back parking lot.

Bromley stuck his head around the corner. He saw no movement of any kind. Just a pile of discarded tires about eight feet high, three barrels marked *used motor oil*, and an air pump with a long, tangled hose. No sign of Carroll. No sign of anyone else.

"I don't get this..."

Breaking glass shattered his focus. Before he could turn around, blinding pain hit the back of his head.

The bullet exited his forehead before his body hit the ground.

Malcolm removed his sunglasses then nodded to his two assistants who were also wearing mechanic's overalls. Bromley's body was dragged into the office and covered with a huge, black tarp. "Shut the garage doors," Malcolm ordered as he turned the cardboard sign on the front door to *Closed*. "I'm setting the timer for ten minutes. That should give us plenty of time to get out of here...and light up the sky."

*****

"I don't know where they are, Turette."

Jacoby had activated the Bluetooth speaker in the SUV just minutes after hanging up from Michaelson in the D.C. office. "Tried pinging off their vehicle's GPS, but no luck. Both of their cells go straight to voicemail. Something's happened."

"I find it hard to believe two federal agents and their vehicle have disappeared into thin air. Did you check with the State Police who monitor the bridge traffic?"

"Already put in a request. Waiting on a call back but it's doubtful I'll get a report for a few more hours. Have to wait till the system refreshes so they can pull the video stream. Even if they crossed the bridge, that's only going to give us a wide timeframe of twelve hours plus."

Maria paused. "What about OnStar?"

"They can't locate the vehicle. No signal."

"Get Thompson on board. I know he's being pulled in ten different directions, but tell him this is a priority. Get in touch with the AC Field Office. See if they can run point with the bridge techs. You and Damian have enough going on."

"I'll call you later, sweetheart." Damian cut in.

"Be careful...the both of you."

Jacoby pushed the Bluetooth button on the steering wheel. "Might be a late call. Command's been set up at the Stroudsburg Field Office. By the time we get there, run a briefing, and review the probability reports, might be after midnight."

"Maria won't go to sleep until she talks to me." Damian shifted his focus on the map of the Poconos that was spread across his lap. "Did you get anywhere with the Canadian Border Patrol?"

"They're cooperating but they're not happy about it. Don't like it when they have to bail us out, so to speak. If McHenry crosses over and they can nab him, they'll hold him until we get there, but only as a courtesy. They'd rather not get involved."

"How neighborly." Damian frowned.

"Can't blame them. Not their responsibility. If we can't catch McHenry, it's on us, not them. Not that they want a criminal crossing their border, but at this point, they have no beef with him. If he doesn't force Kelly to cross the border, he hasn't broken any of their laws."

"McHenry won't make it look like he's forcing her. We have to find them before they get to Canada." Damian traced the distance on the map between the Poconos and Ogdensburg.

"So far we only have one possible traffic cam that's picked them up and this is a long shot. Can't make a positive ID of the vehicle or the license plate. McHenry knows how to beat the system."

"So much for modern technology. I'm old school. We're going to find McHenry by beating him at his own game. Mark my words."

*****

Chase lifted one eyelid and quickly shut it. He had survived another round of whatever drugs had been coursing through his body.

Thank God.

His determination to withstand the symptoms until he could find out who was poisoning him was admirable, Damian had told him, but stupid. Chase grimaced as he rolled to his side, his body still sore from thrashing back and forth, trying to ward off the alternating waves of pain and nausea. Falling asleep earlier, he hadn't expected to wake up to Jenna's soothing voice and the cool touch of her fingers caressing his forehead.

He wanted to reach out and draw her into his arms. Tell her everything was going to be ok, make her believe he could withstand the pain. Let her know he was still her rock...her anchor.

Chase hadn't been able to do any of those things. He was barely able to move or speak. Jenna had seen the anguish on his face before he turned away, too ashamed to acknowledge his own weaknesses.

Jenna had slid to the floor beside the bed, sobbing...and all he could do was listen, too far gone to be any help to her.

Why is she still with me?

Jenna Reed had amazed him from the first time he had met her. Finding her way to the small conference room at Convention Hall where she had come to interview him for the Gazette, Cape May's newspaper. Her sparkling brown eyes and natural smile had mesmerized him, capturing his heart and never letting go. Chase had known then what he firmly believed now...Jenna was the one woman he would want forever.

But loving her meant pushing her away....for her own safety.

Chase moaned. He couldn't let Jenna become a part of what he was about to do. She had suffered too much already.

Chase feared the worst. The drug interactions would continue incrementally until he could no longer fight them off, and he would lash out again. It had to stop. He couldn't take any more chances with Jenna's life. She was in danger just being with him.

Chase gripped the sheet beneath him. Vivid memories of his horrible metamorphosis rattled his brain, forcing him to relive what he had done to her. He'd never forget the look of sheer panic in her eyes, and the blood dripping from the lip torn open by his fist. She had since forgiven him, being so understanding after the doctors in Texas had explained Chase couldn't possibly be held accountable for his actions.

Chase knew in his heart, Jenna might forgive but she would never be able to forget. *How could she?*

He had to find a way not to let that happen again.

But how?

He knew what he had to do, and it was killing him.

Leaving her now would take Jenna out of harm's way...at least the harm he was capable of inflicting. There was no other choice, no other options to consider.

He had to leave...*now.*

Chase took several deep breaths before sitting up. Grabbing a pillow, he wiped his face with shaking hands. As long as he could get down the steps and out the door, all would be well. He could call his partner for back-up and arrange an extraction.

Then he would be out of Jenna's life...never looking back, but knowing she was safer without him.

Convincing himself he was doing the right thing, Chase staggered to the door of Jenna's bedroom. He leaned against the doorframe and glanced down the stairwell. If he took the steps one by one at an extremely slow pace holding on tightly to the wooden railing, he'd make it.

Chase reached around the doorway and gripped the top of the railing. Easing his legs down the first step with success, he sighed in relief. One down. He could do this.

Half-way down the stairwell, Chase was practically knocked sideways as Jonathan bounded up the steps.

"Garrett, we meet again...in the stairwell. Imagine that? Maybe this time I should let you fall and break your neck."

"Get away from me, Knox."

"Fine. I didn't expect your gratitude anyway. Go ahead, Garrett, make a total ass out of yourself. Break two or three bones. I don't really give a..."

Chase let go of the railing to bypass Jonathan. He began to stumble, losing his balance.

Jonathan grabbed Chase's belt to steady him. "Shit, Garrett. What are you trying to do? Kill yourself?" Jonathan hoisted Chase back up the steps into Jenna's room. "That makes two, Garrett. Two times I saved your sorry ass. The least you can do is thank me."

"Thanks," Chase said as his eyes drifted close.

"You're welcome. Get some sleep. Better get Jenna to call a doctor. Something is definitely wrong with you...physically," Jonathan added with a twinge of sarcasm before shutting the door. Turning around he came face to face with Jenna.

"What are you doing in my bedroom, Jonathan?"

"Saving Garrett from taking a flying leap off the stairs. This is twice now he's tried to navigate the staircase with dire results. If I hadn't been here, he would have..."

Jenna didn't wait for the rest of Jonathan's explanation. She burst into her room and climbed up on the bed. "Chase, what is he talking about?" Jenna took Chase's hand into her own.

"If you'd just let me explain..." Jonathan followed Jenna into her room.

"Get out!" Jenna shouted. "Now, Jonathan. You're not helping. Shut the door on your way out."

"One day you'll appreciate me," Jonathan added, crossing his arms and leaning against the doorjamb.

"Now!" Jenna turned her attention back to Chase when she heard the door shut. "Chase, look at me. Tell me what's going on."

"I'm sorry," he said, feeling their fingers interlocking. "I'm sorry...for everything."

"Oh, Chase." Jenna stroked his forehead then kissed him where her fingers had been. "Don't say anymore. Just hold me." Jenna lay down next to Chase, draping his arm around her. She buried her face against his chest.

"I'm afraid for you," Chase began as he stroked her arm. "So afraid...I'll hurt you again. Jenna, please...you have to leave...right now...or I have to."

Jenna lifted her head enough to kiss the side of his face. "Not going to happen. I'm staying right here...right beside you. I love you. I'm not going to leave you."

"Jenna...please...you don't know what you're saying."

"I know exactly what I'm saying." Jenna nuzzled Chase's neck. "And I know where I need to be."

Chase winced, frightened by the sacrifice Jenna had no idea she was making. "I love you," he said, turning his head to face her. Memorizing every inch of her face, he wanted so badly to remember her the way she was at this very moment.

Loving, caring, and so vulnerable.

And never suspecting how much hurt he was about to cause her.

Chapter 15

"You're calling to update me?" The Closer activated the speaker button on his cell while continuing to sharpen his favorite hunting knife, creating an annoying high-pitched echo in the background. "Need I question your outcome or are you merely calling to gloat?"

"I've taken enough insults from you over the years so I'm barely hearing the sarcasm anymore. It's done. Nice and clean as always. The bodies are on their way to the Pine Barrens for an improper burial." Malcolm snickered. "You know, if the Jersey boys ever get wind of my local dumping ground, we could all be in a lot of trouble."

"Doubt that will ever happen. You're too creative, Malcolm. I'm curious, though. What did you do with the car? The Feds will have to itemize their loss." The Closer laughed at his own joke.

"At first, I thought about lighting it up with the rest of the gas station but then I decided it would draw too much attention. You know, some little techie would find a partial serial number and then the trace evidence boys and girls would have a field day. Anyway, it's en route to one of my favorite chop shops in South Jersey. No fuss, no worries. As usual. How are things in New York? Mallory behaving herself?"

"Do you really need me to answer that question?" The Closer asked as a smile crept onto his lips. Mallory never behaved, and that was one of her endearing charms. "Tell me about Garrett. I want to know if our little plan is proceeding on schedule."

"As far as I know, your man in town is doing just fine. We've had a tail on Garrett since he arrived, and he's fading fast. Shouldn't be too long now."

"Good. You know how I hate dragging things out. Step in if you feel the need."

Malcolm hesitated in responding. He was in the clean-up business, not a sidearm mercenary like The Closer. He had no desire to involve himself any further in the Garrett matter.

"Still there?" The Closer asked as he tested the edge of the blade by making a small slit in his thumb. A trickle of blood ran down the back of his hand and he wiped it on his jeans. His weapon was prepped once again, and would not disappoint him.

"Yeah, I'm here. But I have to tell you, I'm not too comfortable stepping in to move Garrett to the next level. Get someone else to do your dirty work, Caldwell. I've got enough going on with your on-demand clean-up jobs."

The Closer laughed heartily. "Malcolm, how do you ever intend on rising above your current station if you're not willing to do extracurricular activities? Relax. Everything is going according to plan. I just need you to stay on alert in case my man needs some assistance. He won't call you unless it's absolutely necessary."

"Fine by me."

The Closer ended the call rather abruptly. He was marginally annoyed Malcolm seemed reluctant to take more of an active role when it came to the downfall of Chase Garrett. It was more surprising than aggravating. He expected more from Malcolm.

Malcolm was reliable, though, and the best at what he did. So for that reason alone, The Closer was willing to cut him some slack. He needed Malcolm and his special blend of *clean-up* services which mainly consisted of body retrieval, transportation and elimination. Not to mention the meticulous eradication of trace evidence linking him to the crime scene. Never had Malcolm's team disappointed him. The Closer had come to rely on the quirky man with the kinky hair and small wire-rimmed glasses who made his home on the outskirts of Cape May, more than adequately blending in with the locals.

Enough about Malcolm, The Closer thought. Malcolm was quite capable of taking care of himself. It was time to check in on his other associate in Cape May, the one who had the most tedious job...of slipping drugs to Chase Garrett without his knowledge.

"I wasn't expecting you to call...now," the heavily-accented voice answered after three rings.

"Just checking in." The Closer sheathed his knife and laid it aside. "Malcolm indicated you're still on schedule."

"Yes. Chase Garrett is exhibiting symptoms as you predicted. I'm watching him very carefully. I've already given him two doses. He's nearing his breaking point. He won't be able to control himself much longer. As soon as I have confirmation, I will contact you."

"Excellent. I knew I could count on you. Keep me informed. Especially with the *aftermath*."

"As you wish," the husky voice added before hanging up.

*****

Even Jake's pizza couldn't cheer her up, and that was saying something.

Jenna swallowed the last bite of veggie pizza, her all-time favorite from the best pizza shop in Cape May. Jake's was her go-to place for beach comfort food. She had been a repeat customer for years, and all the owner had to do was look up, see her face, and a fresh veggie pie was popped in the oven. He never asked any questions, just offered a familiar smile, and Jenna's mood usually changed within seconds.

Not today.

Despite the enticing aromas tantalizing her senses, Jenna was too far gone. She found herself wandering aimlessly for several blocks, miraculously arriving at Jake's on Sunset. Fate had brought her here, or her growling stomach. Tossing her plate in the trash can next to the outside picnic table, she stopped briefly at the pick-up window to wave good-bye.

Jenna glanced at her watch. Chase had been sleeping for several hours. He needed to get up, eat, and maybe even go for a walk. Spend time with her.

The house was quiet when she returned a few minutes later. Grabbing a bottle of water from the fridge, Jenna trudged up the stairs. Opening her door just a crack, she poked her head inside. Her heart sunk. Chase wasn't lying in her bed anymore.

Pushing the door wide open, Jenna suddenly realized the mistake she had made.

She wasn't the only one in the room, and the door had now locked behind her.

*****

Two beers down, and Jonathan finally noticed he had a beautiful woman sitting next to him.

I'm out of practice, he thought as the faint scent of her floral perfume wafted through his nostrils. Turning ever so slightly on his barstool, he gave her the once-over. He was glad he did. She was smiling back.

Athletically-toned with high cheekbones and shoulder-length brown hair, she was definitely a looker. Jonathan didn't mean to stare; he was reacting the way most men probably would to the dark intensity of her eyes, the subtle curves of her body, and the tiny bit of skin showing when her shirt rose above the top of her jeans. Exuding the perfect blend of femininity and boldness, this woman was making him anxious and curious at the same time. He doubted it was pure coincidence she had chosen the barstool next to him when several others were available.

Jonathan didn't have to wait too long to find out.

Ann nodded to the bartender who winked at her then placed a cold Molson in her hand. "Thanks, Bill," Ann replied after taking a swig. Spinning sideways, she tapped her bottle against Jonathan's. "Hi. Ann Bailey. I'm a friend of your mother's. So, go ahead and stare all you want. I won't tell…if you won't." Ann twisted her lips into a smile.

Jonathan sputtered, spewing beer on top of the bar. Wiping his mouth hastily with a cocktail napkin, he shook his head. "Was I really staring?"

Ann took another drink. "Yeah, you were."

"Sorry…but most of my mother's friends are Feds…and you certainly don't…"

"Look the part? I'm flattered. Sorry I have to burst your bubble. I'm CIA. Want to see my badge?" Ann winked, moving her left hand off the bar.

Jonathan caught her hand before both of them realized what he was doing. He held it for several moments until both of their palms became sweaty. "Don't know why I did that actually. Two drinks and I'm getting brazen. Sorry about that."

Ann slapped the bar and held up two fingers, getting Bill's attention. It wasn't long before two cold Molsons were pushed in front of her and Jonathan. "Here's to getting a little more brazen." She handed Jonathan the beer and touched the long neck.

Jonathan coughed then set his drink down. "Are you packing?"

Ann threw her head back and howled. "Really? You just met me, and that's the first question you want to ask? You certainly have a way with women, Jonathan Knox."

"Tell me about it." Jonathan guzzled the rest of his beer.

"Girl trouble?"

"Yes, as a matter of fact."

"Maybe you're just spending your time worrying about the wrong girl."

Jonathan smacked his lips, wishing he hadn't reached the bottom of the bottle so soon. He was starting to get a buzz, although he wasn't too far gone to realize Ann Bailey was flirting with him. "Maybe," he replied, and for once found himself at a loss for words.

Ann caught Bill's eye again, and in short order, two more beers found their way to her corner of the bar. "Drink up, Jonathan. You obviously need a distraction."

"How right you are. The next round's on me." Jonathan laid two twenties on the bar and pushed them forward. "Did my mother tell you to come and get me?"

Ann didn't flinch even though she somewhat resented Jonathan's implication. "No. Maria gave me the night off. I'm here because I want to be. I like Carney's. Reminds me of this little pub outside..."

Jonathan leaned on the bar and stared directly into Ann's eyes. He liked what he saw. Ann was beautiful, confident and intriguing. Jonathan was having a hard time convincing himself he didn't want to spend more time with her.

"....couldn't understand one word they were saying," Ann continued. She laughed without caring if she was getting a bit too loud. "I kept telling them I spoke English, and they just..." Ann finally caught Jonathan staring at her. "Sorry...I go off on tangents occasionally." She licked her lips after draining the bottle.

Jonathan swallowed hard. He wanted to lick the taste of Molson off her mouth at this precise moment more than anything.

Ann felt the intensity of Jonathan's gaze pouring over her. It was time to go. She knew that look, and based on prior bad experiences, Ann had to be the one to make a move before matters got out of hand. She was beginning to become overstimulated, a condition which would make her lose control. Grabbing her jacket from the barstool on her other side, she tossed two more twenties on top of the ones Jonathan had previously laid down. "Nice drinking with you."

"Is this where you tell me you're supposed to walk me home?" Jonathan asked, waiting anxiously for Ann's response.

Ann's face reddened. "I told you before I'm not here to babysit you. In fact, I could care less if you stay here all night."

Jonathan stuck out his arm, stopping her. "I deserved that."

"Yeah, you did. Now let me go." Ann's anger diffused when Jonathan's grin appeared. "If this is how you try to pick up women, I can see why you're still single."

"Ouch! Guess I deserved that as well. I'm not making many points with you, am I?"

"Not really. Want to start over?" Ann stuck out her hand, putting her other one on her hip. "Ann Bailey. And you are?"

"Jonathan Knox. Now if you wouldn't mind...I would like some company walking home." Jonathan got up from his barstool too quickly, losing his balance. He started to pitch forward just as Ann grabbed him around the waist. "Good reflexes."

Ann laughed. "Oh, I'm just getting started. Bottled beer doesn't have much of an effect on me. Try drinking pints with the locals in Chesterfield. They pack a wallop; believe me. Let's go."

As soon as they exited through the side door of Carney's, the night air hit them both sharply. Almost immediately, Jonathan regained his posture. Breathing deeply, his head began to clear.

Ann slowly dropped her arm from his back, wishing she had some excuse to leave it there. Jonathan Knox was incredibly handsome and there was no mistake they were exchanging sexual vibes. As much as she struggled to keep her mind focused, her body was betraying her. If she touched him again, Ann was afraid she wouldn't be able to let go. She had to stay on track, leaving her fantasies locked up where they needed to be. "Hey, I do need to talk to you about something. I need your help."

"I'm listening." Jonathan zipped up his jacket and stuck his hands in his jeans. It was cooler than he had anticipated but he wasn't ready to go back to the beach house just yet. Ann was piquing his interest in more ways than one.

"It's about Jenna. She's...not too receptive to the fact I'm her bodyguard. Maybe you can convince her...to cooperate. We...ah...had a parting of the ways earlier this afternoon."

Jonathan shot Ann a curious look, prompting her to continue.

"Maria and I finally told her...Lois is alive."

"What!" Jonathan stopped in his tracks. "Jenna's mother, Lois Reed, didn't die in the car accident?" Jonathan did a double-take. "How did Jenna take the news?"

"She's confused. Happy that her mother is alive, but shocked she wasn't told until now. Hopefully when Jenna calms down, she'll understand we had to protect Lois. If word gets out she's alive, Hamilton will do his best to find her. He's figured out Lois was one of the five women in The Circle. That had to be why he sent someone to threaten her last December. Maria had to act quickly. She had to make everyone including Jenna and Austin believe Lois and Jim Reed were dead."

"What about Jim Reed?"

"There were complications with the rescue; he didn't make it."

Jonathan ran his fingers through his already wind-blown hair. "I can't believe my mother kept this news a secret...after everything Jenna has gone through. Ann, watch the company you keep. You're swimming with sharks."

"I can take care of myself. I made a promise to Maria and to Lois. I'm not backing down. So, if that makes you think less of me, so be it. Oh, why am I bothering?" Ann pushed ahead then stopped, spinning around. "You're a jackass. You take advantage of Jenna when she's vulnerable, and you don't think twice about it. Yet you have the nerve to question your mother's good intentions. It's a wonder you haven't pushed Jenna over the edge by now."

"What's that supposed to mean?"

"You know *exactly* what it means. You make your move when Jenna is frustrated, tired and almost out of her mind. Then you confuse her with your sexual advances. How am I doing?"

"No comment."

"Find your own way home, Jonathan Knox." As Ann started to walk away, Jonathan reached for her arm. Within three seconds, she had twisted Jonathan's arms behind his back, and pressed him against the side wall of Carney's. With their bodies touching, both could feel the sexual vibes flowing all too easily between them. Breathing was getting harder. It was only after

Jonathan began to squirm against Ann's hold that she regained her focus.

Dropping her arms, she stood frozen with embarrassment. "I'm...sorry. I...shouldn't have done that. I reacted..."

"The way you should have. Although, I have to admit, I usually don't get rejected in that way. Maybe a slap to the face, but certainly not a Rambo move."

"Actually, it's a Krav Maga move. My instructor at Quantico said I was at the top of my class. Guess I need to tone down my...*reflexes*."

Jonathan held out his palm. When Ann finally placed her hand in his, he surprised her by lifting her hand to his lips. "I have a few moves of my own, Ann Bailey." When he saw her lips part in wonder, he released her hand. "You're my new best friend."

"That's the Molsons talking."

"Let them talk." Jonathan chuckled. Ann was feisty and a lot of fun. He wanted to spend more time with her.

Stopping in front of the Reeds' beach house, Ann leaned in to kiss him on the corner of his mouth. "Good-night, Jonathan Knox." Crossing the street without looking back, Ann felt Jonathan's eyes on her from the moment they parted.

And it wasn't just his eyes she wanted on her.

Chapter 16

I stand on a different shore now...touching the same indomitable ocean. I am weaker; not the stalwart warrior of my youth. Fear threatens to cripple me in ways I have never known. My child is beyond my reach...I cannot protect her.

She needs me...yet, my presence will undoubtedly cause her to question why she was conceived, and the telling of that tale alone will cause her much discomfort...or happiness? I cannot imagine...how she will take the news.

I want to be her father...even for the briefest moment.

The joy of a lifetime...in a single smile.

Is it possible?

Or will the truth cause her more harm than good...?

Laurence Renault never flinched as the chilly waves lapped between his toes. The frigidness did little to divert his attention. He was too lost in his thoughts. Memories of walking hand-in-hand with Ellen along the water's edge at Plage Royale in southern France were painful reminders of the love he had left behind. So oblivious to the underhanded ways of Mason Hamilton, Renault had rushed into his affair with Mason's wife with no regard for what lay ahead. Ellen had found and captured the darkest part of his soul, turned it inside out and changed him forever. She had loved him.

The first and only time Renault had let himself be completely taken by anyone. Ellen Chandler Hamilton had been lost herself, devastated to be turned away on her wedding night, and fell hopelessly and helplessly into Renault's willing arms. What began as a one night stand for both of them, had miraculously been a turning point neither could deny.

Their affair was reckless, initially based on physical attraction and the rush of knowing they were defying conventional boundaries. Ellen was a married woman now despite Mason's reluctance to consummate the wedding vows. She had duties to fulfill to support her husband in or out of his bed, but she had no desire to do any such thing. Her heart quickly made another commitment...to her lover and only to him. Wishing she had never promised to love and obey Mason Hamilton, Ellen devoted herself to finding every possible reason to go her separate way...into the arms of Laurence Renault.

Another wave crashed higher, wetting his rolled pant legs. Renault merely looked down, having no desire to change his present stance. As the tide receded, his memory of Ellen's last tears faded away.

She had cried so many times back then. Happy tears when she told him how much she loved him and how wonderful it would be to have his child. Sad tears when they both realized how a child would complicate their many secret rendezvous...and frightful tears when Ellen relayed Mason's threat and plans.

Renault tensed. He had committed to memory what had become their last conversation. The final time he had looked deeply into Ellen's red and swollen eyes, promising her he would find a way to bring them together. The very next day Mason tried to kill him.

Renault looked across the skyline at this early hour and prayed.

Ellen had found peace. He regretted never being able to honor his promise, and hoped she had forgiven him. Their love had been profound, unequivocal and fateful. The true essence of that love still remained.

Kelly.

Renault wasn't ashamed to admit he had spied on his only child from the day she was born until now. He had paid dearly for each and every photograph, and short videos his private investigators could capture and relay back to him. Kelly had never been privy to such an invasion of her privacy even though Renault felt it was highly necessary. He couldn't come to her, but he was able to bring Kelly to France, in a manner of speaking.

Renault lamented those lost years with Ellen and his daughter, wishing he had taken the risk of arriving in the states and facing Mason once and for all. He could have ended speculation he had died in the botched attempt on his life in a fishing accident; thereby putting Mason in his place and telling the world he hadn't fathered a child. He could have claimed Ellen as his lover, taken her away from society's hurtful ridicule of being an unfaithful wife, and insisted she and Kelly return with him to his private villa in southern France.

He did none of those things.

Mason had too many connections stateside and in international circles. Men he handsomely paid to do his bidding and keep an eye out for anyone attempting to blackmail him. It was too risky to resurface back then.

Now…it didn't matter.

With Ellen gone, Kelly's layer of protection had significantly diminished. She was in danger, and it was time her father came to her rescue.

I waited much too long…

I should have been here for you…

Had it not been for Kelly's close-knit friendship with Jenna Reed, Renault feared Kelly would have been pushed over the edge or close to it by now. Jenna had saved his daughter, giving Kelly a chance at happiness and as it turned out, part of a real family for the first time.

Kelly had made her own stance with Mason this summer; staying with Austin Reed instead of giving in to Mason's repeated attempts to bring her to New York. Renault admired her tenacity but also feared she was placing herself in harm's way. He knew first-hand what it was like to defy Mason Hamilton.

Mason had learned from the master.

Any man can be brought to his knees with the right motivation…enticement, whatever you wish to call it. You just need to find the right method of motivation.

Renault's own words put into action against him and his daughter. Mason couldn't have dug the knife deeper.

"We should go," Raul cautioned, sensing uneasiness in the air. Renault paid the six-foot-three muscle man a hefty salary to watch his back, and pay close attention to anyone else who might be looking as well. Raul cracked his knuckles, a mindless, nervous gesture he had developed ever since agreeing to become Renault's bodyguard. He didn't like to be in situations, such as this one, where he couldn't protect Renault in the open-air. Raul much preferred to be sequestered inside the hotel room where he could at least have the benefit of a door and walls protecting his boss. "You are not dressed for the beach. Your attire will draw unnecessary attention. I suggest that…"

Renault held up his hand to interrupt. "Of course, Raul. There is no need for that." Gathering his shoes and socks, Renault followed Raul towards the wooden plank leading to the Promenade. He was followed by Jason, his other attendant of Latino descent who spoke very little English, but understood his requests perfectly.

Renault wiped the sand off his feet, and then replaced his socks and shoes. He wished he had simply brought his sandals, allowing the crevices between his toes to dry completely, even though it was just a short drive back to their hotel.

Raul's eyes darted left and right, vigilantly searching the surrounding area for any dubious persons casting a glance in their direction. When he was satisfied no one was paying them the least bit of attention, he turned back to confront Renault. "You must limit your public visibility. It would only take one person to recognize you."

Raul nodded to Jason then pointed to their car parked across the street. "Bring the car."

"You're worried, Raul." Renault said, buttoning his jacket.

"You pay me to worry."

Renault chuckled at Raul's attempt at humor, but he valued his aide's sense of duty. "Yes, I suppose I do. You've become very good at it, I might add."

As Jason pulled the sedan parallel to the exit ramp of the Promenade, Raul yanked open the back door before Renault could even reach for the handle.

Renault stared back at the ocean, longing to return to watch the crescent waves. As the car merged into traffic, he wondered if he had made the right choice coming to Cape May in the first place.

*****

Rain beat into the ground, shooting tiny stone fragments against Austin's eyelids. He woke trying to blink them away, feeling disoriented as his surroundings startled him. Then he remembered where he was…and how he had gotten there. All too well.

He hadn't been dreaming; he was living the nightmare.

Through some miracle, he had survived the crash when the car slammed into the fence barricade. The windshield had shattered on impact. His hands had covered his face, but the rest of his body had been fair game.

Glass slivers cut into his neck, chest and arms. A larger shard had pierced his leg. Blood was everywhere. Pain was everywhere.

Then numbness...and darkness.

Floating between consciousness and light-headedness, Austin had finally passed out.

In the moment right before he closed his eyes, Austin had prayed hard...that Kelly would somehow know he had died loving her.

Austin pushed himself to a sitting position. Pain still resonated with every move, but at least the bleeding had subsided. He was wet and cold. No telling how long he had been lying next to the car or how he had managed to get there in the first place.

Austin knelt, then steadied himself against the driver's side door. He brushed away as many glass pieces as he could from the seat, then heaved upward falling back behind the wheel. The rain was still saturating the dashboard, but at least his head was covered. Breathing hard, Austin wiped his hands on his jeans. Hot-wiring the car once again wasn't going to be easy.

I have to keep trying.

The wires had untangled most likely when the crash occurred, jarring everything inside the car including the ignition connection. Austin wondered if there was a slim chance he could get the car to turn over.

The wires were dry; a good sign. Austin held his breath as he twisted them together. The car jumped a little as the ignition fired. Austin laughed, realizing it was still in drive. He had forgotten to downshift to park after the crash.

"Alright!" His adrenaline was pumping to a new level as he slammed his foot on the accelerator.

Amazingly, the old Tahoe wasn't going down without a fight. Neither was he. Austin followed the dirt road as it curved to the left. When he reached a paved roadway, he nearly jumped for joy.

"Thank God!"

Which way to go?

Austin tried to recall the turns but his memory was foggy. *A concussion?* Not a good state to be in behind the wheel.

No choice. No time.

Austin turned right. The direction didn't matter; he had to get to a telephone as soon as possible then to a doctor. His head was pounding. The aftermath of the crash and the tension building inside him was making his body shake.

Have to keep moving...

His palms were sweaty, slick against the steering wheel. Austin tightened his grip, wishing he could turn back the clock. If he and Kelly had just gone out to the grocery store an hour before, they wouldn't have been home...when the intruder turned their lives upside down.

Austin shouldered the blame. He had taken his sweet time getting up that morning while Kelly had risen early to prepare for Jenna and Chase's arrival. She outdid herself, getting up at five a.m., putting a roast in the crock pot, cleaning the bathroom and straightening the house. She had let him sleep, kissing his forehead and running her fingers through his hair. Then he had rolled over, hugging her pillow and fell back to sleep. Waking two hours later, Austin had moved in slow motion from that point on.

Until the man with the gun threatened both of them unless they did exactly as he said.

Austin could barely focus on driving as his mind regretted every stupid move he had ever made, putting Kelly's life in jeopardy. He should have figured out a way to outsmart their captor before the tables were turned. He should have protected Kelly with his life.

He forcibly blinked tears away, cursing when they rolled down his cheeks.

Snap out of it, and pay attention!

Before he knew what was happening, the car swerved to the shoulder, hitting the guard rail. Austin jerked the wheel to get the car back on the road, breathing deeply to keep himself calm. He kept one foot on the brake, preventing the car from accelerating as it descended the steep road.

He was driving down a mountain.

The Poconos.

He remembered now.

When the blanket had slipped off his face about a half hour before they had stopped for the night, Austin recalled seeing a road sign for Bushkill Falls. He knew right where they were. He had spent a long weekend there with some college buddies about five years ago.

If he could get to a phone, he could call the police. They could get in touch with Damian.

Taking a quick glance at the gas meter, Austin's heart sank. He had less than a quarter tank left.

Would it be enough to take him somewhere...anywhere to get help?

Chapter 17

It was getting colder the farther north he drove.

Brisk air snapped at his face causing Logan to shut his window. He always preferred to drive with his window cracked even a couple of inches in winter allowing fresh air to keep him sharp and alert. When he didn't have to think of anyone but himself.

The way he preferred to live his life...or the way it had been forced upon him. Until now.

His eyes shot to the rearview mirror, and Logan felt his defenses softening. Kelly was having that effect on him. She was tearing down a wall built upon years of hardening his persona to avoid emotional entanglements. She was breaking through without even trying.

And he was letting her.

Never having to think of anyone else's welfare, Logan was confused and disoriented. Worrying about Kelly McBride was threatening to reduce his competencies, to make him do something foolish. To get caught.

Logan shook his head in defiance, promising he would never let that happen. He had to stay strong, stay focused. He couldn't allow the tears in Kelly's eyes to weaken him, even for a minute.

Glancing up to the mirror again, he locked eyes with her. She was crouched down in the backseat with the blanket pulled up to her chin. She was staring straight ahead. *At him.*

Logan broke away, forcing his eyes back on the road. Back to neutral ground and away from the temptation to scrap this insane mission and just let her go.

No, he couldn't do that. Not yet anyway. Mason Hamilton would just send someone else to kill her.

I have to protect her.

His unorthodox concern for Kelly had thrown him off-guard, unprepared for the long drive to the Canadian border. They had left his safe house in a hurry. A last minute change in plans when his brain was in overdrive, his adrenaline pumping so hard he could barely rationalize what he was doing.

Grabbing a few extra clothes, snacks and water bottles, Logan had forced Kelly's separation from her boyfriend. Taking her away from the only realm of safety she knew.

Stripped of everything important and left to the basic elements of survival. A new beginning. He was doing her a favor, giving her a new life. Kelly would just have to see it that way...eventually. Given the choice of dying at her father's hands, or living...surviving...with a new identity, Logan had no doubt which option Kelly would choose. She was going to be a mother soon, and she would choose life. Her own and her baby's.

Logan was willing to give her anything.

Envisioning a new life with Kelly and her baby made Logan smile. He felt a warmness inside his chest, a sensation too good not to hold onto. A smile emerged on his lips.

A smile which faded rapidly when he heard Kelly sniffle. She was shifting position, trying to abide by his wishes to stay low and out of sight. She was doing *everything* out of fear.

"Keep down," Logan barked, his fantasy evaporating into thin air. Kelly was driving him crazy, making Logan regret the very moment he stepped fatefully into her life.

Don't let your heart guide your mind, son.

Logan ground his teeth. His old man's words were echoing in his ears way too loudly. He wanted to make them go away, the same way he wished he could obliviate his father from his life. Permanently. It was no use. His father's words of wisdom kept drumming inside his head whether he wanted to hear them or not.

When it becomes personal, it becomes dangerous. Keep your distance.

That's all I've been doing...and I hate the way I live, Logan wanted to say.

The last time he stood eye to eye with his father, Logan wished he had the guts to kill him. To end the constant criticism, the frequent lectures on life's lessons he had no right to give. To give David Caldwell exactly what he deserved for abandoning his true family, and running back to that whore in Texas. Francesca Tulane...the bitch who had prevented his father from taking his rightful position as the head of the family he had left in the trenches.

It was all over the news she had died in the explosion at the storage facility in Texas. *Good riddance.* One last obstacle in the way if he had any chance of reconciling.

Not that Logan intended to make much of an effort. If David Caldwell wanted to make something of their relationship, if it could even be called that, then he would have to be the one making great strides. Logan didn't have the heart for it.

Despite his mother's dying wish. *Give your father a chance. Accept him. He had good reasons to keep his distance.*

Logan suddenly had a bad taste in his mouth. He wondered if his mother ever knew what he had found out about his father's secret lover Francesca Tulane. Maybe if his mother knew the truth, she wouldn't have sung his praises all these years.

Logan swerved the wheel just for spite. He had momentarily forgotten his captive in the backseat. Glancing up at the rearview mirror, he cursed seeing Kelly struggling to stay below the back window and not fall on the floor.

"You ok?"

Kelly nodded, making him feel just as worthless as he perceived his father to be.

*I am the better man...*Logan tried to convince himself.

His conscience played devil's advocate once again. *Really?*

Logan had no substantive arguments left. He was weary from waging an internal war, one he had no chance of winning...at least not while he was still holding Kelly against her will.

The clock on the dash indicated they hadn't stopped for two hours. Logan pulled the SUV to the side of the road. He circled around to the trunk and pulled out an extra blanket. Taking off his coat, he opened the driver's side rear door. Immediately he noticed Kelly was shivering. "You're cold, aren't you?" Before she could answer, he handed her his coat and the extra blanket. "Next time we stop, I'll get you some more clothes."

"Why?" Kelly asked, getting his attention before he got behind the wheel. "Why do you care?"

"You're no good to me dead."

Kelly looked away as her lips quivered. *That was it. He's taking me to my father. This is all about money.* "I should have known," was all she could think to say.

"Known what?" Logan finally put two and two together. "Oh, you think I'm doing this for some big payoff, right? Well, guess again, Kelly McBride. I'm taking you to Canada to save your life. I wish you could believe me."

They drove in silence for another hour, stopping at Ronnie's, Logan's favorite country store. Every time he made the trip to visit his friends in Ogdensburg, he made sure to stop and give the elderly couple his business. The owners were in their mid-eighties, an overly friendly couple Logan had befriended several years earlier on his first trek to Canada. Although he had to lie, telling them he was a salesman of plumbing supplies, he did it to protect them and the kindness they bestowed upon him each time he returned.

This visit would be different. The store was closed, and he would have to betray their trust. Another tie would be severed. He would never be able to come back.

Logan pulled into the back parking lot, shut off the engine and sat motionless for several minutes. He had so few friends in life he wished he didn't have to lose two more. This situation required deception, and this was his best opportunity to get what he needed without fanfare.

"Get out," he said as quietly as possible, opening the back door of the charcoal gray Range Rover. Logan offered his hand to Kelly, but she brushed past him as she climbed out. "Wait here."

Logan pulled on disposable latex gloves he had taken from his glove compartment. Clicking on the small flashlight which hung from his key ring, he shone it directly at the padlock securing the back door.

Not much of a security system, and for once, Logan was glad the couple hadn't taken his advice to change it. On his previous visit, he had pleaded with them to get a state-of-the-art wireless system, but gave up after realizing neither had any interest in learning yet another computerized function.

Logan picked the lock easily then pushed the door open, noting the familiar squeaks. The shop was getting more dilapidated every time he set foot in it. He wondered if the building was structurally safe, if the owners were just getting too old to see or care what repairs needed to be done, or if they were just determined to keep the business going until one of them passed away. Heartfelt concern for the elderly couple dominated his conscience to the point of distraction. It was then he remembered leaving Kelly outside in the dark.

"Come in." Logan held the door open, shining the flashlight on the steps. Leading her through the storage room, he nudged her towards the Ladies Room across from the cash register. "Five minutes, and then we're out of here. I'll grab some food and clothes. Here." Logan handed her a larger flashlight he had taken off the hook by the back door. "Don't turn on the light inside the bathroom. Got it?"

"Yes," Kelly replied timidly. Tugging the flashlight out of his hand, she shut the door and locked it behind her. Kelly heard him riffling through boxes, and cursing each time he obviously didn't find anything to be of use. This would only go on for so long, and then he'd come knocking on the bathroom door ordering her to get back inside the car. She had to act fast, to find something she could use to leave a message.

Before stooping to look inside the vanity cabinet, she took a moment to look at her reflection in the mirror above the sink. A mistake she shouldn't have taken time to make. Her eyes were bloodshot and puffy, her cheeks were bright pink, and her blond hair was nothing more than a nest of tangles. She looked basically the way she felt.

Get over it.

Leaving a message was more of a priority than personal hygiene. She had to get word to the police or the FBI...someway.

Opening the double doors of the small wooden cabinet, her eyes quickly scanned its contents. Cottonelle toilet paper, Tampax, Febreze, Colgate toothbrushes...a box of Tom's toothpaste. Kelly grabbed the box of toothpaste. She could barely rip it open; her fingers were shaking so badly. Glancing in the mirror one final time, she sucked in a deep breath...giving herself just the right amount of encouragement she needed.

And prayed the risk she was taking...would be worth everything.

*****

Jenna couldn't scream and she couldn't move.

Loss of mobility had stymied her ability to think clearly. Especially when the reality of what was happening seemed to encase her in vacillating waves of pain and astonishment.

She was lying naked in bed with a man she didn't know.

She recognized his voice and the general contours of his body, but that was all. Every other facet of his being was too distant, too blinding...too frightening.

She had faced danger before...experiencing the excruciating pain of a torturous knife, and a bullet burning a hole in her shoulder, but both of those horrid experiences paled in comparison.

This time...she had been hurt physically and emotionally...in alternating dimensions. Taking advantage of her commitment, her love.

Shock resonated through her body starting slowly with tiny jabs to get her attention, then with a heightened degree of numbness, paralyzing her. Shadows of unbelief moved over her like a heavy fog, and she could do nothing to cut through it. She was helpless, and he knew it.

He knew she wouldn't resist, not at first anyway. He knew she would give him everything and anything he demanded...before she realized exactly what was happening. What he was taking away...and not giving back.

She didn't want to fight him. She wanted to love him. He was counting on that.

Counting on her trust.

Then betraying it with his body. He had no intention of making love to her. This wasn't an act of passion.

"Chase...look at me," Jenna pleaded. Her voice was coarse now, strained from the tears collecting in the back of her throat. "Please..!"

Chase refused to look at her face. Whatever words Jenna was speaking were foreign to him. Almost in a different language he couldn't comprehend.

A cloudy film covered his eyes. He could barely see the outline of her body or feel the softness of her skin. She was pushing back, but he couldn't let go.

He couldn't stop what was happening.

Despite Jenna's attempts to get him back on track, to make him hear her words begging him to slow down and not hurt her...

He didn't respond...not in the right way.

To her comforting touch, to her compassionate words...to the heart-felt pleas she was crying in his ears.

And to the tears running down her face mixing with his own.

Nothing mattered...except the explicit act itself.

Why is this happening? Jenna screamed the question, hoping her mind would answer. Her body shook with confusion, twisting and turning, forcing him to stop. Any word she spoke was immediately silenced by the roughness of his lips, his hands. He didn't want to hear her, and he had nothing to say in return.

She couldn't breathe. The weight of Chase's body and the forcefulness he was exerting made her lungs work harder, striving to keep her alive. Only when she jerked her head sideways, was she able to inhale small air pockets, barely enough to sustain her. Without sufficient oxygen, Jenna knew it would only be a matter of time before she blacked out and feared what he would do in retaliation.

I have to stay awake. I have to find out why...he's doing this.

Chase seemed focused on stripping her of her dignity, forcing her to experience yet another traumatic moment in the life he had pledged to share. There had to be a reason Chase was bound and determined to destroy everything they had worked so hard to create.

Her fingers clenched the sweaty sheets as her mind spiraled. She refused to cry out anymore. She wasn't going to give him the satisfaction of knowing how much she was dying inside.

Her tender lover who had mesmerized her from the first moment they had met was drastically and horribly changing. What she saw in his eyes as he tore at her clothes, pushed her down on the bed, and restrained her hands above her head, was not the same man with whom she had fallen in love. The man with the sandy tussled hair, sexy eyes, and loving hands would never do this to her.

The drugs!

Jenna's brain kicked into overdrive. That could be the only explanation. Whatever organic compound of drugs Chase had ingested in Texas could possibly be responsible for his behavior now. Someone had slipped him another dose, more powerful this time. Making him unpredictable, uncontrollable. Turning him into a monster who wanted nothing more than to hurt the woman he loved.

She and Chase were being used for the sole purpose of someone's sadistic pleasure. Jenna's eyes flew around the room searching furtively for any type of small camera. For all she knew, this violent act against her was being recorded or streamed live. Someone...somewhere was sitting back and laughing. Enjoying what he had created.

Nausea gripped her stomach. She was being sexually attacked while some sick bastard looked on, dehumanizing her and Chase.

Maria once told her there were more crazy people in the world than sane people. Jenna fully understood the disturbing context of that revelation now. As she twisted underneath Chase's heaving body, opposing reflections were battling within her. She was angry at Chase for forcing himself on her, taking the very essence of her being...and she was equally frightened, knowing someone had the power to force Chase into submission...he was being attacked in a different way.

One man came to mind, although she knew he had plenty of people willing to do whatever he wanted for the right price.

Mason Hamilton.

If Mason Hamilton was behind this latest show of domination, then he had succeeded. He had used the man she loved as a weapon of destruction, cutting her to the core.

Hamilton had won this round.

But not the battle.

Chapter 18

"I'm in big trouble."

Ann dropped her windbreaker on the coffee table. Flopping onto the tan canvas sofa, she shook her head in disbelief. She had a bad habit of being lured to the wrong kind of man. Her record was still intact.

Jonathan Knox had revved her libido up several notches while she made the mistake of flirting with him.

Ann's lips were still tingling.

I had to kiss him...didn't I?

"Oh, yeah," Ann answered, grinning from ear to ear.

Then common sense did a double-flip and she wanted to smack herself. Her mission to keep an eye on Jenna did not include making advances towards Maria's son.

"Oh, hell," Ann groaned. Laying her arm across her forehead, she started to regret the foolish, impulsive kiss.

It felt good...so good.

"Dumb move."

I'm attracted to him. It's not purely sexual...or is it?

"No, no, no!" Ann pounded the square pillow beside her then sent it sailing across the room. She had no business getting mixed up with Jonathan Knox. There wasn't much of a chance he would reciprocate. He was too engrossed with Jenna, according to Maria. God knows she didn't need to get in the middle of that love triangle. It was too complicated as it was.

I can't get him out of my mind.

Ann grabbed the other sofa pillow and hugged it tightly to her chest. Her eyes drifted close, allowing her fantasy to come front and center. Jonathan Knox was staring at her with his electric blue eyes, holding his hand out, beckoning her...to join him. As soon as their hands clasped together, his lips were on her, inciting her to lose all control, to draw him nearer until they began to fall...slowly but purposely...

Damn, he's good...

Ann woke with a jolt as her cell buzzed. Flustered, she struggled to get her iPhone out of her front jeans' pocket. The price she paid for getting the skinny jeans with very little wiggle room.

"Hello?" Pushing the bangs out of her eyes, she sat straight up, knocking the pillow to the floor. She was still trying to catch her breath.

"Just checking in. I've been next door at the Maylors' house. Needed to make some phone calls without an audience. I was afraid Jenna or Chase might be within earshot."

"Maria!" Ann exclaimed with a tad of embarrassment.

"Anything wrong?"

"Not a bit. Everything…is just fine." Ann caught herself; she was ready to burst out laughing.

He is…so fine…

Ann rolled her eyes, so glad Maria couldn't see her face becoming flushed. "Just got back from Carney's. Met Jonathan there. He's on board with helping me keep an eye on Jenna, like you said he would be. I'm…ah…going to take a shower and get some sleep. Anything you need me to do before…?"

"No. I don't think so. I've got things covered. I'm sure Jenna and Chase are back by now. I'll go next door in a minute. Have a good night, Ann."

"You, too."

Ann tossed her cell on the sofa. "Drama, drama, drama," she muttered before heading up the stairs.

In less than a minute, she had tossed her clothes in the wicker hamper next to the walk-in closet. Her robe was still lying at the foot of the bed where she left it this morning but she didn't bother putting it on. It was a short walk from the bedroom to the bathroom at the end of the hallway. All the blinds were lowered in the upstairs windows, and Ann felt perfectly comfortable striding down the short hallway completely naked.

"Well it's not like anyone cares," she retorted sadly.

She needed a distraction. A hot, steamy shower would do the trick. Clearing her mind under a warm waterfall always worked when she was confused about a mission…or other personal dilemma. She'd feel refreshed, and relaxed right before bed.

"Just what I need."

As the steam rose steadily, a thin film of condensation covered the vanity mirror. Ann gingerly stepped inside the shower, splaying her hands against the tile. The pulsating rhythm of hot sprays was starting to hypnotize her. Drumming across her neck and shoulders, she imagined strong, supple hands encircling her waist, and seductive lips exploring her shoulders.

I want him...

Ann inhaled sharply. Her imaginary lover took form, reducing the space between them. Suddenly, she was spun around and her arms were drawn upward, positioned just right so she could arch against a chiseled, well-maintained chest. His head was bending lower, and she felt him breathing more rapidly now. The faint taste of Molson still on his tongue, he cupped her face and joined their lips.

He wants me, too...

She was floating, experiencing too many wonderful feelings she couldn't explain. He was the manifestation of all of them. Taking her body and transforming it stroke by stroke. Ann cried out, releasing guttural sighs of pleasure. Letting herself go. Savoring each and every moment, every touch of his fingertips...and praying he wouldn't stop.

Can't hold on much longer...

His hands were tightening now and she sensed the urgency building inside him. She was doing that to him, enticing him with her swaying hips, and her probing tongue. She was holding power over him.

A power he was gladly relinquishing.

Jonathan Knox cried out as Ann's hands explored his body without any inhibition. She knew exactly what she wanted, and he had no problem giving it to her.

Kissing him lightly after they had shared a few beers was an invitation so subtle yet highly erotic...neither of them could resist. The initial fusion of their lips had set the precedent for a night of lovemaking so intense and mind-blowing; Ann was scarcely able to catch her breath.

I'm losing myself...

The shower curtain ripped from its hangers. Jonathan pressed Ann's arms to the wall on either side of the shower massage. He leaned against her and lost all sense of being. Demanding lips found him, brought him back into focus, made him snap to attention. This incredible, sexy, not to mention agile woman was doing things to him he had only dreamt about. Soon he wouldn't be able to hold back, and he hoped Ann wouldn't either.

She's not slowing down...

No one had ever taken him this way before...with no regard for moderation or modesty. Ann was just as determined as he was to stretch every boundary, quickly learning every erogenous place to tease and tempt him.

Ann Bailey was without a doubt, the most artistic lover he ever had, and she was captivating him not just with her creative sexuality but with her heart and soul. She was proving she wanted him on more than one level.

Daring him to do the same.

Forcing him to forget anyone else he had lusted after...including Jenna Reed.

Jonathan sucked in air as his eyes drifted close. With each searing touch, Ann was wiping away Jenna's image until he could no longer envision her. Even the outline of Jenna's face was fading, and he could do nothing about it.

She's changing me...

Ann was too skillful, charming him in ways he never knew were possible. Her lips roamed freely. She knew what she wanted, and didn't hesitate to take it.

Water sloshed up the side of the bathtub and drenched the floor. Ann turned off the faucets. When her eyes found Jonathan's face again, all she had to do was smile.

He was awestruck, roving his eyes over her body and panting. They needed to move to her bed now, or they'd never make it.

Jonathan made the mistake of putting one foot on the water-logged bathmat and the other on the slick floor. When he lifted Ann out of the shower, he realized too late how quickly he was losing his balance. Falling together, they pushed the door open into the carpeted hallway and braced themselves for the sudden impact.

Half-laughing and half-moaning in pain, Jonathan made sure Ann landed on top. He was so afraid he would crush her and everything they had just experienced would be overshadowed by idiotic injury.

"You ok?" Jonathan asked between bated breaths.

"Never better. You?"

"God, you're amazing!"

"I'm just getting started," Ann replied with a wink.

She wasn't afraid to break the rules. In fact, she welcomed the challenge. Jonathan Knox was more than a conquest; he was toying with her heartstrings. Making her lose her good sense.

For one remarkable, unforgettable night...Jonathan Knox would be the man she would give herself to without limitation...and she would be the woman to make him lose all sense of reality.

Too much hunger was at stake.

*****

It was a big risk leaving the note.

Kelly almost regretted her actions when Logan shoved her in the car and told her to keep down while he went inside to use the men's room.

Kelly held her breath as she gripped the blanket tighter, pulling it up to her chin. Her teeth were chattering, but not from the cold air blowing in from the driver's side door. The wind was howling, making eerie noises while the trees surrounding the small parking lot were battling each other, swaying back and forth. A storm was coming, Kelly worried. A storm of aggravated proportions.

What was taking so long? God, if he found the note...!

Please help me...please don't let me die...

The wind blew the car door shut making Kelly jump. The blanket slid out of her fingers when she wrapped her arms around her belly in a protective gesture.

I'll die trying to save my baby...

The baby comes first...

Austin, I'm so sorry...

Kelly muffled her cries as her head fell downward. Even through the fierce wind, there was no mistake. Footsteps were crunching on the gravel, and they were getting closer.

I'm so sorry, baby...

Tears ran down her face while memories of Austin swirled indiscriminately in her mind. Holding hands at Sunset Beach, watching little children toss up scraps of bread for the playful seagulls. Taking an early morning walk along the beach and collecting seashells Austin insisted they keep in a glass bowl on the kitchen counter. Lying together after they had just made love, and knowing she had never felt love before until that very moment.

Good memories, so good...and so precious to her. All she had left to keep her spirit alive until...

The back tailgate creaked loudly, jarring Kelly back to her frightening reality. She sat rigid, listening to Logan shove boxes into the back section of the Range Rover then slam the door shut.

Sliding into the driver's seat, Logan turned the key in the ignition without saying a word. He had already noticed Kelly's tears when he glanced in the rearview mirror. *Damn it,* Logan cursed silently. All he wanted was to wrap his arms around her and tell her everything would be ok.

"I'm sorry," he said without thinking.

"For what?"

"You're cold. Here." Logan tossed back a sweatshirt and another blanket. "They didn't have any coats. This is the best we can do for now. Are you hungry?"

"I'm ok."

"Well, you sure don't look like you're ok. Look, we've been over this before, but I want you to hear it again. I'm doing this to keep you safe."

Nodding, Kelly wiped her face on the edge of the blanket. She focused on her breathing as the ER doctor had coached her when she was taken to Cape Regional with an anxiety attack. She had to regulate her breaths, each one nice and even. She could do this.

"I won't tie you up again. Just do as I say, and we'll make it to Canada."

"He'll find me...no matter where you take me," Kelly said with conviction. "My father won't stop. He's...relentless."

"So am I." Logan wheeled the truck back onto the paved roadway. "You're probably safer with me than with your boyfriend. I know how to take care of things."

"Meaning what?"

"I've killed men for far less."

They were driving against the wind, forcing Logan to reduce his speed or lose some control when the car struggled to stay on its side of the narrow two-lane highway. A few scattered raindrops soon erupted into a deluge. Logan turned the windshield wipers on full blast hoping they would drive out of the storm within minutes. He didn't want to pull over unless it was absolutely necessary. They had no choice but to keep moving, despite the weather.

Instead of passing through the storm, they were headed right towards it. It wasn't long before rain turned to hail pellets. Beating down on the Range Rover from all sides, the incessant noise was driving Logan crazy. Rain, sleet and snow were relatively quiet weather elements, but hail made you sit up and pay constant attention. It always reminded Logan of rapid-fire machine guns, bringing back bad memories of his limited time in the service with the Army's Special Forces. Sniper training, long hours spent in every conceivable weather condition with the goal of eliminating the weak and roughing up only the best. Government-paid and sanctioned executioners...taking out the bad guys for the greater good.

Not much different than what he was doing now, except he was on the wrong side of the fence.

Logan didn't miss his time in the Army except for the men he left behind wondering why and where he had gone when he disappeared one late night without a trace. Blending into another culture. One after another until he was so far removed from his unit and his former life, he barely knew who he was.

Like now.

Preparing to cross another border...for a new life.

Logan's eyes slowly closed. He was running on just a few hours' sleep. He needed rest. He needed time to recharge.

Kelly screamed as the Range Rover edged off the paved road towards an embankment.

Logan jerked the wheel to the left, returning the car to the road. He couldn't let that happen again, not with the weather being so unpredictable. He had to stay in control, not allowing himself to be influenced by Kelly's emotional state. "We're all right. Calm down," he said brusquely. "Just calm down...please."

Kelly pushed the hair out of her eyes, tucking her long, blond strands behind her ears. He was right. She needed to calm down, if that was even possible. Another scare like that, and she didn't know if she could fight off the anxiety building inside her.

Taking small sips from the water bottle she had been given earlier, Kelly held onto it with both hands. "If I just knew that Austin was ok...I could...deal with this." Her words faded into whispers.

"Well, I'm not exactly in a position to find out for you. Whether my house is still standing, and your boyfriend is still alive are two questions I don't have answers to. Guess we'll have to wait and see. Get some rest while it's still dark."

"How can you possibly expect me to sleep after what you've just told me? Are you crazy?"

Logan didn't mean to laugh. It was just a nervous reaction.

"Now you're laughing at me. You are heartless." Kelly refused to look at the rear view mirror any longer. He didn't deserve one more second of her attention.

"Oh, I'm definitely crazy," Logan admitted. "No doubt about that. But here's the kicker. I never was...until I met you."

Chapter 19

"You're sure? Absolutely sure?" Damian shouted gruffly into his cell. The blades from the Pennsylvania State Police search and rescue chopper were kicking up dust and making such a loud racket, Damian could hardly hear. He nodded to the pilot then held up his hand indicating he'd have an update soon.

Arriving in Stroudsburg just an hour ago by car, Damian and Jacoby had checked in with two local FBI field agents tasked with setting up a command center. Just ten minutes into their briefing, the state police called with a tip demanding their immediate attention.

"Let's go," Damian yelled to Jacoby who had grabbed two coffees inside the municipal building and was trying to juggle them and hustle at the same time. "I'll fill you in as soon as I give the pilot the coordinates."

Jacoby settled into the driver's seat, grateful he hadn't managed to spill any coffee on his new charcoal-gray pinstripe suit. He lowered the driver's side window to get some fresh air even though the wind was still whipping from the chopper. Sipping his strong black coffee with one hand, he paused to look at the map of the Pocono Mountain region supplied by the local FBI field office. If he was right and McHenry was heading to the Canadian border, his ETA was within the next five to seven hours. Not much time to work with. They needed a break, a good one.

Damian slammed the passenger door shut. "I think we just got lucky. Owners from a small general store just called the state police. Apparently when they opened up this morning, their back lock had been tampered with, supplies were stolen, and there was a cryptic message written on their bathroom mirror."

"You think Kelly wrote the message?"

"Damn sure she did. First responder sent me this." Damian showed Jacoby his phone.

5am TUE – help me!
Call FBI – D Pierce
Kelly

"At least we know she's still alive. Thank God she had an opportunity to leave a note. This has got to be very traumatizing. It's a wonder she's thinking clearly at all."

"I'm grateful she is. That gives us an advantage. Because if Kelly's still able to find a way to alert us, she'll try again." Damian smiled with a renewed sense of hope.

"When do we leave?" Jacoby asked, pointing to the chopper.

"Only when I say we do." Elias Briggs leaned against Jacoby's door and glared. "Get out of the car, Pierce."

Damian shook his head, indicating for Jacoby to keep quiet.

"Now," Briggs repeated as an armed guard yanked Damian's car door wide open. Briggs walked around the front of the car, accentuating his authoritative swagger. "This doesn't concern you, Agent Jacoby. Well, actually it does. You're now in charge. Pierce, you're relieved of duty. Turn around."

Before Damian could respond, he was roughly pulled from his seat, spun around and thrust against the hood of the SUV. Handcuffs were quickly slapped on his wrists. He fought against them, twisting his body until he turned around to face Briggs. "Enough with the theatrics, Briggs. Tell your boys to let go of me."

Briggs casually reached inside the SUV and took Damian's coffee cup. He took a swig, making a face. "Can't believe you drink this straight up, but then again, it fits your personality. You've been a bad boy, Pierce. Time to pay up for your past sins. We have rules for reasons. Taking matters into your own hands in Port Lavaca was a mistake. Breaking and entering a federally-funded facility, the attempted murder of two armed guards at said facility, unauthorized lab analysis on evidence supposedly found at said facility. Need I go on? The Director wants and expects an explanation. Accountability, Pierce. Ever hear of the concept?"

Damian's eyes flared. He twisted against the cuffs even though Briggs' two assistants were doing their best to hold him steady. "You have no idea what I had to deal with in Texas. Maria's life was at stake. I would have gone to hell and back to get her."

Briggs smiled perversely. "Then you admit you mishandled her rescue, incriminating yourself on all the aforementioned charges?"

Before Damian could answer, Jacoby stepped between him and Briggs. "Pierce doesn't have to answer to any of your charges without a lawyer present. Rules, Briggs. Gotta love 'em. Or are you purposely denying Pierce his rights, which I might add, could get your own ass in trouble?"

Briggs stepped backwards, stumbling. Jacoby's sudden show of bravado caught him off guard. At the moment, he was at a loss for words.

"I certainly hope someone is holding *you* accountable, Briggs." Jacoby stood his ground, resisting the urge to raise his voice. "If not, I'd be happy to bring that to the Director's attention."

Briggs huffed, refusing to exacerbate the heated conversation. He had no desire to tangle with Jacoby. In fact, he had gone out of his way to prevent such an altercation. "Stay out of this, Jacoby. This isn't your fight."

"Maybe not." Jacoby took a step closer, getting in Briggs' face. "Better have your *rules* all figured out this time. I'm watching."

Briggs turned on his heels, hustling straight for the van. Before he reached for the door handle, he turned back. "Just so we're clear, Jacoby. If they cross the border into Canada, you stand down. The Canadian Border Patrol can handle it. There's no reason to waste agency resources any longer."

The van's door slammed shut before Jacoby could respond. As he watched the van pull out of sight, the tension mounted on his shoulders. Speed-dialing the first number on his cell, he took a deep breath.

"Turette, I've got bad news. You better sit down."

*****

Mason paced the floor of his study with a glass of whiskey in one hand and his cell in the other. After trying several times to reach The Closer without any luck, he was beyond irritation.

"I'm telling you, Hans, the moment I no longer have need of The Closer's unique talents, I'm severing our ties. The man has the audacity to..."

"Come in unannounced?" The Closer asked as he sauntered into Mason's study. Casually leaning against the wall, he folded his arms and smugly glanced at Mason and his ever-present, incompetent assistant Hans Kliric. By the shocked look on Mason's face, it was evident he had no idea how The Closer had bypassed his expensive and supposedly, impenetrable security system. The Closer prided himself on a job well done. He had easy access to Mason's home and office, thanks in part to Suzanne Carter, Mason's former administrative assistant and lover. A woman who had been extremely cooperative when The Closer's favorite hunting knife had coerced her to reveal Mason's security codes, secret entrances, and an abundance of other worthy tidbits.

Mason nearly dropped his glass; fearful The Closer had overheard his entire conversation. "What...are you doing here?" he asked as his voice changed octaves.

"You said you wanted to see me. You left several urgent voicemails."

Mason set his glass down on the mantle. "I need you to take care of another matter...Renault. He didn't come here just for Ellen's memorial service. He has an ulterior motive, although for the life of me, I can't quite ascertain what that might be."

The Closer laughed. "He came back for you, Mason."

Mason considered The Closer's statement. "All the more reason to have him eliminated."

The Closer tilted his head in Hans' direction before answering. "Well, seeing as though you have no other *competent* allies available at the moment, I suppose the task falls to me. Where is Renault?"

"Cape May."

"How interesting." The Closer stroked his chin. "Now why would Laurence Renault go to Cape May, New Jersey? Any ideas, Mason?"

"None whatsoever."

"Then you're either stupid or totally oblivious. Which is it?" The Closer waited exactly two seconds then continued. "Never mind. I'll lay it out for you. Renault went there to see his daughter."

"I have no idea what you're talking about...*as usual*." Mason stormed towards his decanter to refill his glass.

"Stop insulting my intelligence, Mason. We both know Renault is Kelly's biological father." He glanced over to gauge Mason's reaction. "He got your wife pregnant and you raised the child to be your own. Didn't take me long to put the pieces together. I'm sure you had your reasons, none of which I care to discuss. But if you want Renault out of the picture, I can handle that."

Mason breathed a sigh of relief. "Very good. Oh, and another thing. While you're down in Cape May..."

The Closer rolled his eyes. "You want me to check in with Jenna Reed, right? Make her give me the rest of the treasure pieces? I can do that, too. Finally wrap up this mess you've created. Jenna Reed is..."

Mason waved his hand nonchalantly. "Jenna Reed is the least of my concerns at the moment. I merely thought you could take advantage of being in the same vicinity...and pay her a call. You have persuasive ways...use them in any way you see fit."

"So glad I have your permission."

*****

Hitting the Bluetooth speaker button on his steering wheel, David Caldwell smiled. His display screen positioned in the middle of the dashboard had previously alerted him with a familiar number along with a picture not suitable for public viewing.

"Miss me already, Mallory?"

"David...," Mallory began in her usual deep, seductive voice. "Come home. I'll make it worth your while."

"I'm on my way, baby. Just had to pay Hamilton a little visit."

Mallory groaned, putting an emphasis on her displeasure. "Stop dropping to one knee whenever Hamilton beckons you. It's degrading, to say the least. Besides, your time could be better spent."

"By keeping you satisfied?" David asked while expecting another raspy response. "I'm not hearing any complaints in that department unless there's something you're not telling me."

Mallory breathed heavily into the phone. "I'm lonely. How fast can you get here?" She was referring to the apartment David Caldwell kept in the heart of New York City. The top floor of a four story former linen factory he had bought several years earlier. The exterior of the building wouldn't cause anyone to look twice. The original brick was cracked in several places although his private renovator assured him the building was structurally solid.

With several elaborate and expensive enhancements, David had turned the building into a mini-fortress. Showcasing his talent with installing state-of-the-art surveillance equipment, a super-charged computer network, and multi-level security traps, he was well positioned to be alerted of any trespassers. No one came close to or entered his building without submitting to a full body scan, facial recognition program, and fingerprint analysis...without their knowledge, of course.

Privacy was paramount to his survival. Not to mention it was extremely convenient for frequent rendezvous opportunities with Mallory who was currently on assignment at the Livingston Museum of Art, just a short cab ride away.

"The bed's getting cold," Mallory teased. "By the minute...and if you're not here soon, I'm afraid I'll have to leave it to sit by the fireplace to get warm."

"I'll find you wherever you are...you know that." David inhaled sharply, imagining Mallory's sculpted body lying naked across the bed they were now sharing. Agreeing to a temporary living arrangement to test the relationship waters was working out so far. The fringe benefits were certainly outweighing the need to periodically reassure Mallory she was the only woman in his life...and she was his main priority.

"I don't know why you had to see Mason in person. It's not like he doesn't pick up his phone. I'm sure he would have been perfectly happy not seeing you at his doorstep."

"The element of surprise always gives me the advantage. The sooner I can wrap up my business arrangements with Mason, the better. I'm tired of dealing with him. The only reason I'm still holding him at arms' length is..."

"Your son."

"Yes...and I'm worried about him. Making any type of alliance with Mason Hamilton is dangerous. He's not ready for it."

Mallory chose her words carefully. "You can't keep sheltering Ben forever, David. He's a grown man. He makes his own decisions without consulting you. He makes no effort to..."

"I know, Mallory. You're right; I have been watching Ben's back for a long time. Watching from the shadows...ever since he was a young boy. I've protected him without his knowledge. That was the arrangement I made with his mother. I had to keep both of them safe."

"And you never told Francesca, did you?"

David went silent.

"You don't have to be ashamed of that, David. You've told me. That's all that matters. Come home. We'll figure it out together."

Together.

Mallory had no idea how that word tore at David's heart. She would be the one needing protection now.

Because of love.

Chapter 20

She was broken, but not defeated.

Jenna pushed herself upward to lean against her headboard, searching once again for the hidden camera. If she couldn't find it herself, she would ask Maria or Ann to search more thoroughly.

Right now all she could think about was getting out of her room without giving that son-of-a-bitch anything else to gloat about. He would see her bruises, the markings of her suffering and find sadistic humor in them. He would see her as nothing more than a vulnerable woman who had the misfortune of being attacked by the one man she loved and trusted.

The purest and deepest kind of betrayal imaginable.

Mason Hamilton would have a field day knowing he had pushed her over the edge.

I won't give him that satisfaction...

Jenna drew the torn sheet around her body. With shaking hands she quickly searched her drawers for another pair of jeans, oversized V-neck t-shirt and underwear.

Hobbling on sore legs, she made it to the bathroom just in time before throwing up. Jumping from the bed had been a mistake, and she was paying for it.

I won't let this kill me...

Jenna cried, dropping to her knees. The sheet fell to the floor when she bent over the toilet. Physically weak and emotionally scarred. A total wreck.

Forcing herself to stand, she leaned against the sink for support. She turned the faucets on full blast, splashing cold water on her face and neck.

The mirror didn't lie. It screamed silently, forcing her to look away. The scars on her chest inflicted by Kliric's knife were hardly visible. New marks were taking their place. Red splotches intermingled with black-and-blue bruises, beginning just below her neckline. She ran her fingers over them and recoiled from the tenderness.

From her head to her toes, pain radiated outward while a deeper, harsher agony swelled inside her. It would be so easy to curl into a ball, internalize her pain and withdraw completely. Pushing everyone and everything away to focus only on the part of her heart that was slowing breaking. To fall into a deep depression, foregoing substance and listening to the pleas of those left who cared about her. She could die inside so very, very easily.

Don't give up...

Jenna's eyes connected with a beam of sunshine shining through the break in the bathroom curtains. It bounced off the edge of the mirror and seemed to reach out and touch her.

Hope was still with her. It had never left. She had just been blind-sided, unable to see it.

This isn't over...

A rebirth, a rejuvenation.

All the right reasons to fight back.

Walking, bending, breathing. Jenna was hurting but she couldn't let the pain overtake her. Her mind was made up. She was going to keep moving.

Don't back down...

Jenna washed her face, brushed her teeth, then dressed quickly. Running a brush haphazardly through her unruly hair, she tossed it aside. She had no desire or energy to fool with makeup. Getting out of the house was her main priority.

Without thinking, she flung the bathroom door open and barreled out.

Almost knocking Jonathan off-balance at the top of the stairs.

"Coming or going?" Jenna asked, noticing the stubble on Jonathan's face and his unkempt, ruffled hair. Unless it was her imagination, he was still wearing the same clothes from yesterday. He had spent the night elsewhere...and she didn't know quite how to react. Jealousy never entered her mind, but strong curiosity did.

"Not sure actually. How about you?"

"Definitely going. Out. By myself." Jenna looked the other way.

"No, you're not. You're going to tell me...what happened to you." Jonathan tugged on the bottom of Jenna's shirt, revealing the abrasions just above her chest.

Jenna pushed his hands away. "Nothing you would understand."

"Try me." Jonathan blocked her way with his arm. "My God, he hurt you...again. Didn't he?"

"Take your hands off of me!"

"You're saying that to the wrong man. I would *never* hurt you. Why you let Garrett do these things to you, and not hold him accountable is beyond me. That son-of-a-bitch has gone too far this time. He forced himself on you, didn't he?"

"You have no idea what you're talking about. Now get out of my way!"

"Really, Jenna? Look at me." Jonathan held Jenna's face steady. "Stop protecting him. You deserve someone better."

"Like you?"

Jonathan hesitated. He wanted to positively give her the reassurance she needed, yet after spending the night with Ann, he wasn't in the best position to be totally truthful.

Jenna was surprised he was taking so long to answer. "Let me go, Jonathan. Please." Brushing past him, Jenna headed down the stairs and bolted out the kitchen door.

Casting glances over her shoulder, she didn't immediately notice if anyone was following her, but she didn't take any chances. Jenna darted down alleyways, hid beside and inside a few unlocked sheds, circled backwards a couple of times, and finally caught her breath inside the ominous church which anchored the top of the mall.

The polished wooden doors of Our Lady Star of the Sea seemed to beckon her to enter. A place of refuge, safety and divine mercy. Peace.

A place to hide.

Jenna stared into the empty sanctuary, amazed that candles placed on the altar were already illuminating the stained glass windows lining both sides of the church. The glow was completely and unequivocally uplifting, surreal.

A welcome respite from her otherwise harrowing life.

Jenna stood at the back of the church praying silently for Austin and Kelly's safe return, for Chase's conflicting battles threatening irreparable damage, and for her own ability to forgive...and to have enough determination to push on.

Hearing a door close on the side of the altar, Jenna's eyes flew open. She darted outside, running quickly across the street to the Acme's parking lot. A public rest room dubbed the "comfort station" was open, and she dashed inside.

Am I being followed...or just generally paranoid?

Jenna dug her cell out of her back pocket. "How far away are you?" she whispered, not wanting to draw attention in case someone stepped inside.

"Baby Girl, I've been in town all night. Left Philly shortly after you called yesterday. You're not the only one who has a beach house at the Jersey shore. My folks still rent their condo in Ocean City. I'm just up the coast. Give me about thirty-forty minutes."

"Thank God," Jenna responded with a loud sigh. "Lenny, please get here as soon as you can. I've...got a lot on my mind. I need to talk to someone...and you're the only one I can trust."

"I'll pick you up soon. Are you someplace safe?"

Jenna shrugged. "I guess so. I'm at the comfort station just off the Acme parking lot. You know where I mean?"

Lenny Lex laughed. "Yeah, I know right where you are. Keep your phone on vibrate. I'll buzz you when I'm pulling up outside. Ok?"

"Got it."

If she planned this right, Lenny could drive her around to retrieve the treasure pieces, avoiding all the drama with Jonathan, Maria, or her new bodyguard, Ann. She needed to do this without any intervention, biased opinions, or advice telling her what a dumbass move she was making. It was her choice to make, not anyone else's. Jenna alone knew where the treasure pieces were buried, and she was the only one who could make a bargain with Mason Hamilton.

Trading the last three treasure pieces for the safe return of Austin, Kelly...and Chase.

Mason Hamilton had turned her into a vindictive, calculating vigilante seeking revenge for the pain he had caused. The people he had manipulated and the ones whose memories she was honoring.

The game had to end. No one else needed to die, or be hurt. She could prevent anything else from happening.

There was no turning back.

Her cell buzzed inside her jacket pocket, jarring her out of her trance. She had completely lost track of time.

"I'm here, Baby Girl. All you need to do is…"

"Fast enough for you?"

Jenna had barely fastened her seatbelt when Lenny sped off, running the red light at the corner and hanging a right onto Lafayette. "Don't kill me, Lenny Lex," Jenna cautioned as she righted herself in her seat.

Lenny took off his scruffy Phillies baseball cap and tapped Jenna lightly on the head with it. "Wouldn't dream of it, Baby Girl." He gave her the once over. "Looking good…sort of." His smile quickly turned into a frown. "I'm worried about you…but I have your back."

"I'm ok…I think."

Lenny took a sharp right on Union then pulled to the curb. "Talk to me, Baby Girl. Why do you need a gun?"

"Did you bring it?" Jenna asked without answering.

Lenny nodded. Reaching over to open the glove compartment, he pulled the .38 from a small leather pouch. "Listen to me, Jenna. This is serious shit you've got yourself into if you need a weapon. You don't have a license to carry. You see where I'm going with this?"

Jenna swallowed hard taking the pistol in her hands. "Is it loaded?"

"No." Lenny grabbed the gun out of her hands. "I'm not that stupid, contrary to popular belief. I don't plan on giving you any bullets until you tell me what's going on."

"I have to get to New York."

"Not good enough. Try again."

Jenna crossed her arms. "I…need to make a trade. You know about the treasure pieces, right? Austin has probably told you."

"Yeah, yeah, yeah. I know…enough. But I still don't understand why you need a gun when you have no idea how to shoot one, unless you've taken up a new hobby."

"Not exactly. I want to be able to protect myself."

"Nothing wrong with that, Baby Girl."

Jenna relaxed her shoulders. "Then we're cool with this?"

"I didn't say that. I just agreed with you about protection. That's where I come in. I told you; I've got your back."

Jenna shook her head. "I can't get you involved in this, Lenny."

"I'm already involved. Now, where are we headed?"

"To get the treasure pieces."

Suddenly, Jenna could hear her mother's words echoing in her ears. She was a young child again, playing her favorite guessing game as she and her mother walked along the beach. The same guessing game leading her to several prime hiding spots for the treasure pieces.

"I'm thinking of a place where the big red trucks sleep," Lois would say with a gleam in her eyes.

"I know it, I know it!" Jenna hopped up and down, tugging on her mother's hand.

"Are you sure?" her mother asked, trying to hide her smile.

"Yes, Momma, the fire station. The big red trucks are asleep until the siren blows. It's loud. It hurts my ears."

Lois picked up her daughter and swung her around. "You are so smart, my little girl."

Jenna grinned. "Take a right on Washington, Lenny Lex."

This was the right thing to do…with or without the gun.

She had to keep moving. Every minute mattered.

*****

Austin woke with a jolt, disoriented. He was cold, hungry and irritated by the pounding noise vibrating through the car.

Raising his head from the backseat where he had crawled at three in the morning to get some sleep, he couldn't believe his eyes.

A state police cruiser had pulled up beside him, and the trooper was banging on the rear windshield trying to get his attention.

"Are you alright, sir?" the trooper asked repeatedly. "Please step outside the car."

Austin scrambled to find his shoes and untangle himself from the coarse wool blanket he had found in the trunk. When the Tahoe started to sputter, he knew it was time to give up the fight. The gas gauge was on empty.

Stumbling out of the backseat, Austin realized too late what he looked like. A crazy man in bloody, disheveled clothes.

Before he knew what was happening, the trooper had unhitched the strap on his gun holster.

"Stay where you are, sir," the trooper commanded. "Back against the car." He took a step backwards, waiting until Austin had complied. "Now tell me what's going on. Why did you pull your vehicle to the shoulder? Don't you have a cell phone?"

Austin's body began to shake. "No time. We have to find my fiancée. He's taken her. God, help me, please! Call Agent Damian Pierce. He's with the FBI, D.C. office. Please! There's no time to lose! My name is Austin Reed."

The trooper took a step closer to get a better look. "What's the blood from, sir? Are you hurt?"

Austin nodded then shook his head. "Yes...no. I'm ok. I'm worried about my fiancée, Kelly. She's pregnant. For God's sake, please call the FBI. Now!"

Not smelling alcohol or noting any dilation of Austin's eyes, the trooper keyed up his walkie. "Marge, you there? Run these plates." He stepped backwards to read the license plate. "PA Tag 42012. And Marge, call the FBI. See if there's a Damian Pierce in the D.C. office. Thank you."

Austin sagged against the trunk of the car. "Thanks."

"Don't thank me yet. Just tell me what's going on. Why did you pull over? Engine trouble?"

"Empty tank. Guess your next question will be where's the key to the car? Hot-wired. Drove right through a barbed wire fence. Maybe you should cuff me now and get it over with," Austin said as he leaned forward against the trunk and put his hands behind his back. He glanced over his shoulder to see the trooper returning to his car, realizing he was talking to himself.

In a few minutes, the trooper returned, offering a cup from his thermos. "Welcome back to civilization, Mr. Reed. I'm Trooper Danny Barnes."

Austin was at a loss for words, but gladly accepted the coffee.

"Looks like you have quite a fan club, Mr. Reed. Couldn't get ahold of Agent Pierce, but I was patched through to an Agent Jacoby. You know him?"

Austin wiped his mouth on the back of his hand then handed the empty cup back to the trooper. "Yeah, I know him."

"Well, he's very happy to hear you're ok. He's heading up an investigation to find your fiancée. Apparently, Agent Pierce had to return unexpectedly to Washington. Jacoby's got some strong leads. He wanted me to tell you."

Austin's eyes glistened. "They haven't found her yet."

"Just a matter of time, sir. The FBI is good at what they do."

"I'm sure they are." Austin slumped against the car. He hadn't noticed the blood seeping out of the tear in his pant leg. He was too preoccupied with worrying about Kelly to pay attention to the deep cut in his leg which had begun to bleed again.

"You need to get to a hospital, sir," Trooper Barnes advised. "We have a paramedic en route. Just hang in there. Maybe you should sit down." Trooper Barnes opened the door to the back seat and helped Austin inside. "They're not far. Should be here in a couple of minutes."

"He took her," Austin moaned. "She's pregnant. Almost four months. God, we can't lose the baby!"

Trooper Barnes was quick to sympathize. "Got one on the way myself. Don't worry, Mr. Reed. I'm sure you'll be reunited with your fiancée very soon. Keep the faith."

That's all I can do, Austin muttered to himself, never hearing the ambulance arrive or the paramedics coming to his rescue. His last conscious thoughts were focused on Kelly and their baby...right before he passed out.

Chapter 21

"You can't hold me, Briggs, unless you charge me...and I have a feeling you dragged me back here just to annoy me and jeopardize the success of my mission. Do you have any idea the chance you're taking?" Damian yelled at the glass separating the interrogation cell from the viewing room. He was certain Briggs and his cronies were on the other side of the glass making smartass remarks at his expense...and he couldn't do one thing about it.

Damian was tired and thirsty. His repeated requests for water and access to a phone were flatly denied. He knew what they were doing. He had done it himself...many times. An interrogation technique used frequently and with little repercussion. Wear down the suspect until he started to talk, thereby increasing the odds he would incriminate himself.

Try all you want, Briggs. I'm not giving in...

Chained by his wrists to a steel bar on top of a small table, Damian was unable to stand straight or lean backwards in his chair. No matter how many minutes or hours passed, Damian found the courage he needed to put up with his unauthorized containment. Briggs would be brought to his knees eventually. Made to answer for his inappropriate actions.

One way or another.

Payback time. Not only for himself, but for Maria's sake also. Damian had cringed each time Briggs had gone on and on about Maria's incompetence during the five hour car ride back to D.C. Damian kept quiet; shouldering the accusations without additional commentary knowing full well Briggs was goading him.

As he purposely pushed Briggs' outlandish comments to the back of his mind, Damian concentrated on another angle. Besides jockeying for his next elevated position, Briggs seemed determined to bring down both Damian and Maria.

Why?

Was there even a remote possibility Briggs was dirty? Had he aligned himself with Mason Hamilton or The Closer? Or was he motivated by something else altogether?

Damian couldn't be sure. Briggs was always so bound and determined to abide by every rule in the book. Maybe he was breaking a few on the side.

Briggs had connections, influence and opportunities. He was frequently called to the Deputy Director's Office to provide reports, recommendations, and to assist with prosecutions if warranted. He had access to confidential documents, and high level clearance. He could demand access to any FBI office, storage facility, or computer files on a whim. All in the name of justice.

Damian's own revelation struck him hard and silent.

Briggs could be the mole or the one calling the shots.

Damian cursed as the writing on the wall became perfectly clear. He and Maria were about to be screwed, and unless a miracle happened, their chances of surviving in the Agency were minimal.

If Briggs wanted a fight, then that was exactly what he would get. Damian clenched his teeth and yanked on the cuffs. He wasn't going down without a fight. There was too much at stake.

"I want my lawyer!" Damian yelled as he stood hunched over, kicking his chair out from under him. "Now, Briggs. Now!"

*****

"We've been over this, Mallory. You can't come with me. Not this time."

Mallory pouted. She punched the pillow next to her as she sat against their teakwood headboard. "You're being stubborn, David. You know full well you need me. I don't know why you have to be so bull-headed and…"

David cut her off as he hastily zipped his black canvas duffel bag. "I do need you…to stay here and keep an eye on Mason. I want to know what he's up to every minute of every day. I can't take a chance he's going to switch gears and send Hans or one of his other goons to go after Ben."

"Ben will see someone coming before they get too close. You taught him that."

"If he was by himself, I wouldn't have a reason to worry, but he's got a distraction. Kelly McBride. No man in his right mind would…"

"She's *that* beautiful?" Mallory asked as flecks of jealousy flickered in her eyes.

"She's not you, Mallory, so don't worry about it. But, yes, Kelly McBride is beautiful and Ben would be a fool not to notice." David turned to walk out of the bedroom, then stopped when Mallory slipped her arms around his waist. "You're safer here." He kissed the top of her nose.

"But I'm also *alone* here. I can't make love to you over the phone. We've tried that, remember? It's not satisfying enough…for either of us. Besides," she said playfully as she stroked his cheek. "You just might miss me."

David chuckled as he tickled her in the ribs. "I already miss you." He changed the subject hurriedly knowing he was within seconds of pulling her underneath him and forgetting everything else. "I'll be home soon. I don't expect this job to take too long. Renault should be an easy target. He's right around Mason's age, maybe a few years older. No potential threat, except it wouldn't surprise me if he's got a couple of bodyguards. Either way, it's nothing I can't handle. Malcolm and his team will be there to back me up. Oh, and you'll love this. Chase Garrett might also be an unlikely accomplice."

Mallory jerked back with a wary look on her face. "Chase Garrett? Jenna Reed's boyfriend? What have you done, David?"

"Speeding up the process, that's all. Mason wants the treasure pieces, and the sooner I can put them in his hands, the faster I can sever our business ties. The only way to make Jenna Reed sit up and pay attention is to attack her where it hurts her the most. The core of her vulnerability. The man she loves."

Mallory was dumbstruck.

"Garrett got a few doses of my special blend. We experimented down in Texas just for kicks. Last night he came full circle."

"What happened?"

"Garrett attacked her…and we got it all on camera. Haven't had a chance to watch it yet. Should have uploaded by now. I'll check it out when I get back."

"How…?" Mallory was speechless.

"My guy in Cape May set it all up. Installed the camera in Jenna's bedroom when no one was home. Quite ingenious on his part, I have to say. Might have to give him a raise." David laughed.

Mallory still couldn't believe her ears. David was unscrupulous, she knew that. But installing cameras to purposely record someone's private sex life was beyond anything he had ever done before. David was venturing down a path too immoral even by her standards.

"How could you do that?" she asked, her voice quaking. "Do you record…us?"

"Of course not, Mallory. Why would you ask such a thing?" David sat back on the bed, letting his arms drop. "You trust me, don't you?"

"I thought I did." Mallory suddenly felt very cold…alone in a room with a man she had given everything to…her body, her heart…and her trust. For the first time since she had met David, she was hesitant to respond. "You went too far, David."

"Don't judge me, Mallory." David turned away, retrieving his duffel. Blankly, he stared into Mallory's misty eyes. "I did what had to be done. I always do. *Whatever* that entails. You've known that from the start. I haven't changed."

"But your methods have. You're turning into a man…who frightens me. I love you, David, but I can't…"

David stopped at the doorway. "That's your first mistake, Mallory. Loving me."

And before she could respond, he left slamming the door behind him…and wondering if Mallory would still be there when he finally returned.

*****

"Yes, I have her. No need for back-up right now. I'll keep you posted."

"Stats every hour if you can. Be careful."

"You got it, boss." Lenny popped his cell back into his jeans, then wiped the sweat off his forehead. Close call. He couldn't afford to let his guard down in front of Jenna. Not yet, anyway.

Jenna was running back to his Lexus. Within twenty minutes, he had driven her to three separate places around town so she could retrieve the last three treasure pieces. Lenny had stayed in the car each time at her request. Jenna had been quite adamant that no one needed to know the secret hiding places she had chosen, and Lenny couldn't help but respect her for not wanting anyone else to be involved at that level.

But she was also assuming the full responsibility and the full risk. An extremely dangerous move.

Jenna threw herself in the passenger seat and gave Lenny the thumbs up. It was done. She had successfully found all three treasure pieces without drawing attention to herself. Now they could head to New York.

"You know I wouldn't be a good person unless I tried to talk you out of this one more time."

Jenna tried to smile. "You are a good person, Lenny. Or you wouldn't be here right now. I do appreciate your concern, but I know what I'm doing. I just need to keep moving before I lose the momentum."

Lenny checked his rearview mirror. No one was following them; he had made sure of that by circling the block a few times, cutting down an alleyway, and hiding in a hotel parking lot. "You're going to need more than momentum, Baby Girl. Facing Mason Hamilton is like signing a death warrant. He'll snap you in two before you can figure out what's happening. This is a suicide mission…but I think you already know that, don't you?"

Jenna stared out the side window, listening to Lenny's words of wisdom and letting them fade into a cautionary silence. "I'm the only one who can end this…Hamilton knows that." She withdrew one of the little gold animals, the monkey, and held it up for Lenny to see. "He wants this, and I'm going to give it to him, but first he's going to agree to release my brother, my best friend…and somehow bring Chase back to me."

"Is Chase missing?"

"He might as well be. He's lost to me. I have to get him back…there has to be a way." Jenna leaned against the headrest.

"What happened, Jenna? You seem…very distracted, and I know it's not just because of the treasure pieces."

Jenna looked away, refusing to answer.

"You need to trust me, and listen to me. Can you do that?"

"I told you before…you're the only one I have left to trust." Jenna's eyes fell to her hands, cradled in her lap.

Lenny pulled the car to the side of the road. "You know I think of Austin as my brother…and you as my sister. I would do *anything*…for both of you. I want you to know that."

"I can't ask you to risk your life. That's my call to make. But I will let you drive me to New York. Then you can take off."

Lenny tossed his baseball cap in the back seat. Pushing his dark bangs backwards, he knew he had to come clean. "I can't do that, Jenna. I can't leave you alone. It's not just your fight. It's also Maria Turette's…and I work for her."

Jenna stared in surprise as the words sunk in. "Just what I need…another bodyguard."

"You got it, Baby Girl. I'm here to stay."

*****

He had made it…a phenomenon all its own.

One final exertion of energy had been enough to propel him to leave the Reeds' beach house a few hours earlier while it was still dark, get his bearings, and find the safe house set up by his partner.

Chase had initially balked at the idea when she had suggested they needed a safe house in Cape May, but now he truly appreciated her rational thinking. His partner had come through once again, making him realize just how much he relied on her.

Chase's sweaty palms slid off the edge of the kitchen island. He fell to the floor as his knees buckled. Writhing in pain, he reached towards the nearest chair but was unable to move any closer. Each time a seizure incapacitated him, Chase felt like he was having a heart attack. Darkness cloaked him and before his body shut down, Chase wondered if he would ever wake up again.

That would be the easy way to go.

A coward's way out.

After what he had just done to the woman he loved, he deserved nothing less except for maybe a bullet in his brain. If he couldn't pull the trigger himself, Chase was sure Knox would do the honors. Hands down.

He had taken Jenna's dignity away. Stripping her, bruising her...using passion as a lure, only to trick her into submission. Hideous images replayed in his mind, and Chase cried out wishing they would stop punishing him. Reliving the tragedy from Jenna's standpoint was killing him more so than the poisonous drugs flowing through his veins.

In one fateful act, he had severed what was left of their relationship held together only by a thread of commitment. Jenna had forgiven him for lashing out at her in Texas, but there was no way she could do the same now.

Initially shocked by his roughness and his brutal passion, Jenna had willingly allowed him to restrain her hands above her head. With one hand, he had held her down, and with the other...

Chase banged his head against the floor, punishing himself for taking advantage of her trust. There would be no going back. Not now.

His stubbornness to forget the past had come back to haunt him in the most horrible way possible. Too driven to let go, he had pushed Jenna in harm's way...making her take the brunt of his frustration.

All because of revenge.

Damian had tried to talk him out of such a doomed mission, but he hadn't listened. He was getting too close to stop now. The drugs he had somehow ingested were an organic blend with scopolamine as a major component. The Closer had been known in the past for experimenting with drug compounds...incapacitating his victims right before he went in for the kill. Too crazed by the drugs, they never felt The Closer's knife upwardly thrust and twisted. Death was almost a welcome relief.

Chase forced himself not to dwell on that possibility. He was committed to play along, to allow The Closer to use him for whatever sinister purpose he had in mind. To catch him once and for all.

His partner had even begged him to reconsider.

Why didn't I listen? She's right most of the time...

Sacrificing himself for the greater good seemed like a noble idea at the time. As Chase thrashed on the kitchen floor, unable to control his muscle reflexes, he wondered how much longer he could withstand the drugs before his body was paralyzed. Never figuring out how they were being absorbed into his system was making him half-crazy anyway.

Chase rolled over onto his back. He stared into the muted darkness wishing it would overshadow him, forcing him into a deep sleep. Opaque shades in the small retro kitchen were pulled down to the edge of the windowsills, preventing even the most curious neighbor from seeing inside. Blinds were closed on all the windows; giving the house the appearance its owners had left their summer vacation home for the season. Just another vacant beach house, protected only by an alarm system as evidenced by the Allied Home Alarm sticker on the front door.

The house was exactly one block down and one street over from the Reeds'. Another quiet street where pedestrians were more frequent than cars. A good place to hide out.

His partner had chosen well.

"You look like crap."

Chase opened his eyes slowly. He knew from her tone she was angry. Might be better to lay low, so to speak, and keep quiet.

"Don't think I'm going to give you an ounce of pity. You did this to yourself. I'm just saying…"

"I get it," Chase moaned. He deserved everything she wanted to dish out.

"Just in case you're interested, Jenna is missing. I lost her trail about an hour ago. She's not picking up her cell. We have no idea where she is…you know any reason why she'd leave?"

Chase felt like a hammer had just hit his chest. "She left because of me."

"Please tell me you finally came to your senses and told her the truth…who you really are. She just left because she needs to clear her head, right?"

Chase shook his head. "That's not what happened. It's a lot worse. I hurt her…very badly."

His partner wasn't flinching. In fact, she barely responded. She knew.

"Jonathan told me."

"Knox doesn't know half of it. I doubt Jenna would confide in him…at least about those details. He's making assumptions that he has no right…"

"Jonathan said she had bruises all over…"

"I didn't hit Jenna. At least I don't think I did. Everything was happening so fast."

"Think, Chase! She certainly didn't get black-and-blue marks from rolling around in bed with you."

Chase winced as he tried to stand. "We...I...got too rough. *Very* rough. Jenna...didn't fight me at first but I...couldn't stop."

"Oh, God, please tell me you didn't..."

Stabbing pain jerked Chase's body. He swayed unsteadily until his partner helped him to a chair.

"I attacked her. Is that what you want me to say? Ok, it's out in the open now. I regret what I did. I regret it all. From the first moment I tricked her into believing I was an author on a book tour, to falling in love with her and putting her in danger. Hurting her in ways I can't even begin to explain. I wish to God I could turn back the clock. If I could, I'd never put Jenna through any of this."

"She loves you, you know."

"Not any more. It's over." Chase laid his head on the round aluminum table, too ashamed to look into his partner's eyes. "I've lost her. I was too obsessed with finding The Closer...and now I have nothing left."

"You're wrong about that. You have me. I haven't figured it out yet, but we'll get through this somehow. Hopefully, you'll get an opportunity to apologize to Jenna. Even if she doesn't want you anymore, she deserves to hear the truth. I'm not giving up on you. That's what partners are for."

Ann Bailey laid her hand on Chase's back, keeping it there until she felt him nod his head in gratitude.

Chapter 22

Tumi's cell buzzed inside his jacket pocket. He smiled the moment he recognized the caller ID. "Markus, it is good to hear your voice. Please tell me you have called to provide much needed and perfectly timed good news."

Markus paused. "Sadly no, my friend. I wanted to update you. Miss Jenna is missing. She left earlier today and has not returned. Maria is quite upset. She is unable to reach Jenna by cell phone and she is planning to leave shortly for Washington, D.C."

"Yes, Markus, I am quite aware of Maria's travel plans. Phillip and I are staying in Maria and Damian's house awaiting her arrival. We have plans to meet Thomas later this afternoon."

"Thomas Movell?"

"Yes, Markus. Thomas Movell, my old friend. You remember him, I'm certain. He will be quite instrumental in facilitating Damian's release. I trust him completely. Now please tell me more about Jenna's disappearance. This concerns me. She has blatantly disregarded Maria's advice to not venture far from the beach house. I sincerely hope she is not taking matters into her own hands. Your thoughts on that matter?"

Markus chose his words with great thought. "She has been quite traumatized by the absence of her brother and friend. Additionally it appears she and Chase have parted ways. Perhaps Miss Jenna no longer wishes to be at the beach house and has gone back to her apartment."

"I hope that is not the case. However, should Jenna return, please call me immediately or ask her to call Maria. You are our eyes and ears now, Markus. I am relying on you, my friend."

"As you wish."

Tumi rubbed his forehead, laying his cell on the coffee table. He barely looked up when Phillip joined him and offered him a cup of tea. "Thank you," he said with hesitation.

"You are troubled. What did Markus say?"

"Jenna is missing. He does not know where she went or if she is in trouble. Apparently, she and Chase quarreled which could have precipitated her hasty departure. Their relationship is very fragile...like a cracked piece of fine china. I am fearful it will break in two with the slightest touch. Unable to be fused together again despite their tired efforts."

Phillip nodded slowly. "Then what is to be done, Tumi?"

"I do not know. Perhaps it is fate. Jenna and Chase may not be destined to be together. This could be the beginning of separate pathways they must take."

"Love may win."

"Love may not have a chance, Phillip." Tumi drained his cup and set it aside. "On another matter, I expect Thomas at any moment. I am anxious to hear this plan concerning Damian. Elias Briggs has no authority to hold my brother without substantiated charges. I fully intend to seek his badge when all is said and done. Do you not agree?"

"For certain. Briggs has overstepped his boundaries. I am positive Thomas will provide us with clarity regarding Damian's false imprisonment, and a plan to facilitate his release."

Tumi forced a smile. "Be careful, Phillip. You may not wish to venture down the road Movell has travelled. Suffice it to say, his methods of extraction may seem unconventional. He will surprise you, as he has done consistently in the past. Movell is more elusive than I am."

Phillip was intrigued. "Then I await his return with open arms. You have other reservations I assume regarding Briggs."

"Many in fact. Briggs did not act alone. If I had to guess, I would make the assumption Raymond Konecki is involved to some degree. Movell does not trust him. He interacts with Konecki only when necessary." Tumi walked to the kitchen to place his cup and saucer in the sink. As he returned to the living room, he caught Phillip's worried glance. "Do not fret, my friend. All will be well. I am fully convinced Movell will take the appropriate actions to free Damian very soon."

"Your trust in Movell in unwavering."

"Indeed. I trust him with my life...and my brother's. Now please inform the team leaders to be on alert. Movell may need back-up."

*****

"In and out, Malcolm. Nice and clean. You take care of Renault's body, and then I'm on to my next assignment. Finding Jenna Reed and talking some sense into her."

Malcolm stifled his laugh. "You? Talking sense into someone? This I have to see for myself."

"I was using a figure of speech." The Closer peered out the front window of Malcolm's small house in West Cape May. "You know I don't mince words. Talking is not my forte."

"As I well know. You only call me when you need something."

The Closer folded his arms, locking his stance. "You're not complaining, are you? I thought you rather liked hanging out at the beach, pretending you were the manager of a hardware store while in reality, you're just as cold-blooded as I am. You just have a better alibi."

"And you left yours at home, I take it? Mallory must not be too happy about that."

The Closer took a seat on Malcolm's worn checkered sofa and put his feet up on the scratched coffee table. Malcolm's taste in furniture left a lot to be desired. "She's not. But I'll make it up to her…like I always do."

"Must be hell on your love life," Malcolm added sarcastically. Mallory Kincaid was tantalizing to the eyes, body and soul. Her only flaw was that she was indelibly dedicated to the wrong man.

The Closer disregarded Malcolm's smartass remark. He snatched the TV remote lying next to his foot and starting hitting buttons. "I'm not discussing our sex life with you, so go fuel your warped fantasies someplace else."

Malcolm laughed. "I just might do that."

The Closer didn't flinch although secretly he wished he could smack the silly grin off of Malcolm's face.

The air in the small room suddenly got heavy.

Malcolm changed the subject. "Let's switch gears and talk strategy. My guys have been tracking Renault since you called. He's got two bruisers following him around with bulging jackets. Safe bet they're packing at least one gun or maybe more.

Anyway…he's keeping a low profile, not drawing any attention to himself. How do you want to play this?"

The Closer thought for a moment. "One by one. We'll take out the guards first, and then go after Renault. I…have someone coming in for an assist."

Malcolm raised his eyebrows. "A partner? Thought you said Mallory was staying at home."

"This is a special *circumstance.*"

"Details?"

"None you need to know about. Just make sure your crew is ready to go when I call." The Closer continued to look straight ahead.

"I just want to make sure my guys don't walk into anything they can't handle."

"Then maybe you need to think twice about who you hire. I don't foresee any problems out of the ordinary. Standard clean-up job. If your men find the need to improvise, I'll make sure they're adequately compensated. End of discussion." The Closer focused on the baseball game, turning the volume higher. Out of the corner of his eye, he noticed Malcolm retreating to the kitchen.

Just as well…

Malcolm had the annoying habit of trying to get tidbits of information out of conversations meant for another purpose. Either he was overly curious, or he had ulterior motives, neither of which were important enough to spend time worrying about. Malcolm was reliable and that's all that mattered.

Except when he made personal references about Mallory…

Maybe it was nothing and he had misread Malcolm's body language and facial expressions. Malcolm never mentioned having a woman of his own, but that was a topic The Closer had no interest in discussing. What Malcolm or any member of his team did on their off-hours was entirely up to them.

Unless it became his business for an entirely different reason.

*****

"I'm dining in Cape May as we speak."

Laurence Renault laid a linen napkin across his lap with one hand and cradled his cell phone in the other. A long-time aficionado of fine dining and exquisite wines, he had firmly disregarded Raul's advice to be sequestered in a hotel room.

There were too many unique Victorian dining establishments he simply had to try. The concierge at the Southern Mansion where Renault and his two bodyguards were staying had recommended the 19th century Washington Inn for an early dinner. Tables were elegantly decorated in the five-room restaurant set on the lower level.

"Have you completely lost your mind?" Jonathan Knox shouted so loudly, Renault had to pull his phone several inches from his ear.

"Jonathan, I'm touched by your concern."

"Don't misinterpret my annoyance. I just can't wrap my head around the fact you're stupid enough to set foot in Cape May. Kelly isn't here. She's been kidnapped. The FBI is..."

"What!" Renault jumped to his feet.

"Surprised you didn't know that by now. I would think it would be the talk of the town," Jonathan continued. "The FBI just found Austin in the Pocono Mountains, central Pennsylvania. Kelly is still missing. The FBI thinks whoever has her might be taking her to Canada."

"They're certain she's still alive?" Renault waved his hand at Raul and Jason to sit back down at the same time he took his chair.

"A note was found in a general store, and the FBI has reason to believe Kelly wrote it. There's no need for you to stick around Cape May. I'm...not sure how long it's going to take to get Kelly back. When she does get home, neither she nor Austin will need any more drama in their lives. Go home, Renault. Nobody wants you here."

"Harsh words, Jonathan. I'm offended; however, I understand you're under a great deal of stress worrying about my daughter. For that, I will forgive you."

"I don't care about your forgiveness. I want you out of Kelly's life...and mine. Believe me; I'm sure the FBI would be happy to learn..."

"You're forgetting the bond we have, Jonathan. Certainly you wouldn't take the chance of dragging your good name through the mud along with my own. Think carefully before you make a move that will adversely impact you."

"Spare me the fatherly advice which is entirely self-serving on your part. I'm fully capable of making my own decisions."

Renault gestured to the waiter to pour from the bottle of wine he had selected earlier. He was elated to find a 2003 Valdicava Brunello di Montalcino on their wine list, one of his personal favorites to compliment a filet mignon stuffed with crab imperial. Raul and Jason were perfectly content with their imported beers, but Renault had always preferred the finesse of wine to accompany every evening meal. He wasn't about to let Jonathan's callous remarks spoil his dinner.

"Then I shall not linger on the subject. Do as you will. In the matter of my daughter, I will expect updates as they become available."

Jonathan choked. "What? You definitely have a few screws loose. If you think for one minute I'm at your disposal, you're more of a fool than I originally thought. If you want updates, watch the news. I'm not your go-to man for inside information at the FBI."

Renault chuckled. "No, I suppose you're not although you seem to be very well-connected." Renault took a sip of wine allowing the heady aroma to fill his nostrils and the velvety smoothness to envelope his mouth. He was temporarily distracted.

Jonathan had since hung up.

Renault replaced his phone. He held up his glass. "Now, shall we enjoy our dinner, gentlemen? To good fortune and happy reunions."

Raul and Jason looked at each other guardedly before clanking their beer bottles against Renault's wine glass.

"You seem rather calm, sir." Raul kept his voice low.

Renault dabbed the corners of his mouth with his napkin. "There is nothing I can do at the moment. My daughter's fate is in the hands of the FBI who, according to Jonathan, are in fast pursuit heading towards Canada. When we're back to the room, I shall contact a few allies in Montreal to see if they can lend their services should the matter be perpetuated across the border. Otherwise, I must simply wait for news."

Once again, Raul and Jason exchanged wary glances.

"It is out of my hands," Renault added with a touch of sadness. "I can only pray my daughter is found very soon."

"And...if she's not, sir?" Raul ventured to ask.

"Then I shall personally seek out and find the men responsible...and deal with them accordingly. I've stayed in the shadows long enough, gentlemen, and I have no intention of remaining there any longer."

Chapter 23

"You're mad at me. I can see that."

"You have no idea." Arms folded, Jenna sat rigidly against the car door, staring Lenny down. "Might as well get this over with. Drive me back to Cape May. Isn't that what your boss wants you to do?"

Lenny had been her last hope. When it finally sunk in that he was an undercover agent on Maria's team, Jenna was ready to throw in the towel. She had no one else to rely on who wasn't already mixed up in her crazy drama.

She was on her own.

"Turette's a good person, Jenna. You of all people should know that." Lenny paused to make his point. "If you want to go back to your beach house, I'll take you there. Might be a little lonely, though. Turette's on her way to D.C."

"I...don't understand."

"Pierce got into a bit of trouble. He was yanked off the search and rescue mission by SAC Briggs, a major pain-in-the-ass. Sneakiest bastard in IA, if you ask me. Always trying to make a name for himself. Doesn't care who he steps on in the process." Lenny gritted his teeth in frustration.

"IA?"

"Sorry. Internal Affairs. Might as well be called *IP*...Internal *Police*. That's basically what they are. Paper pushers who can't function in the field. Get their jollies finding fault with the people who put their lives on the line every day. Makes me sick to think what Briggs is putting Pierce through. Some trumped-up charges, no doubt. Just another way for Briggs to draw attention to himself. For all I know, he's probably itching to take Turette down, too. Like to see that happen." Lenny snickered. "Turette doesn't back down. She'll give Briggs a run for the money. Would love to see that."

Jenna sat dumbfounded, unable to respond.

"So," Lenny continued. "Turette's racing back to D.C. to see what she can do. Hopefully, this will get resolved quickly so

Pierce can get back in action. At least he's got Jacoby picking up the slack. Anyway…when you called me…"

Jenna regained her stamina. "You immediately called Maria, didn't you? I should have known. All these years…I should have known. There was always something I couldn't explain about you, Lenny. I tried to tell Austin…but he just thought…oh, never mind. Why does it matter anymore?" Jenna closed her eyes as her head drooped.

"Hey." Lenny reached over and shook Jenna's arm. "It matters a lot. You and Austin are like family. I don't give up on family. So here's what we're going to do. If you still want to go to New York and drop off your *cargo*, then we'll do it together. I got a buddy who flies tourist choppers around Philly. He's based out of the Philly airport. Owes me a couple of favors. He'll take us to New York; save us some driving time."

"Maria's ok with this? I find that hard to believe."

Lenny tried to hide a smile. "She told me to stick close to you. I'm just following orders, Baby Girl." Lenny waved his hands, trying to imitate a rapper.

Jenna couldn't help but laugh. "You've been in Philly too long, Lenny."

"Gotta fit in, Baby Girl. Listen, about all this trust stuff. I got your back…and Austin's. That's all you need to worry about. Don't get hung up on thinking you can't trust people. Most people have good intentions. So, what do you say we head up to Philly, grab a beer at O'Clarian's, for old times' sake? Then when my buddy calls, we'll hitch a ride to the big city."

"Ok." Jenna took in a deep breath. "Now that everything's out in the open, are you going to tell me your real name?"

"And spoil the fun, Baby Girl? Never."

Lenny winked and revved the engine. It was time to go.

*****

Mallory pushed open the heavy, double-paneled doors to David's study, taking a moment to view her surroundings…and reconsider what she was about to do. She had never been invited to his inner sanctum before. His *command center*, David liked to call it. It was forbidden territory, at least she thought it was.

David had never come out and said she couldn't go inside; Mallory just didn't want to. But tonight was different.

He had shocked her beyond anything she had ever experienced, and that was saying a lot. Mallory had tried many times to understand David's rationale for having his man in Cape May install a camera in Jenna Reed's bedroom, but each time she came up empty. What David had done, or authorized to be done, was nothing short of indecency...bordering on pornography.

She knew David wasn't a saint by any stretch of the imagination, but this act of control and manipulation was well beyond what was necessary to get the job done. He had purposely invaded Jenna's privacy while at the same time drugging her boyfriend to do the unthinkable.

Mallory couldn't get over it. She was deeply traumatized, imagining herself in Jenna's position. Never before had she ever related to one of David's victims in such a personal way, but this time Mallory wrestled with the moral implications.

Mallory held her breath. Taking a few steps inside the great room, her eyes adjusted to the muted lighting. Rich mahogany paneled walls darkened the windowless room with only recessed lighting illuminating three-quarters of the space. A flat-screen was mounted on the wall directly in front of her. It was the largest TV she had ever seen, and Mallory guessed it had to be at least seventy inches. She wondered if it was a TV at all, or just a huge monitor for displaying multiple computer screens at one time. Below it was a long counter that ran along the length of the wall. Filled with CPUs, monitors, printers, iPads, recording equipment, and sparsely placed table lamps, there was barely any room for a few note tablets and pens.

Whatever David did in here he never shared with her, and for a few moments, Mallory was offended. He had promised to make her a priority, yet he was still finding ways to exclude her from his life.

Maybe it was better that way.

Not knowing what David Caldwell did in the early hours when he left their bed and retreated to his private chamber was another mysterious wall between them. If she really did know the truth, it was quite possible, she'd be hurt by it.

Like now.

Mallory moved closer, stopping just short of the tall leather swivel chair pushed against the counter. She ran her fingers across the top, and she immediately inhaled the faint scent of his woodsy cologne. She missed him; missed the comfort he gave her when his strong arms held her tightly and she felt completely safe.

Mallory's eyes flew open. She realized she was hugging the back of the chair, and she let go so forcefully it spun away from her. Pushing her hair out of her face, she fell into his chair and booted up the CPU. For some insane reason, the initial start-up screen wasn't password protected, and she paused. David was too clever not to put several levels of security in place, especially when it came to his private electronic files.

"Is this a trick, David? To test my loyalty? Guess what? I don't care if I pass your little tests."

Mallory clicked on the icon for David's email account. She scanned the most recent entries. Sure enough, there was one which caught her eye marked *JRVideo*. Without hesitating, Mallory double-clicked and the video began.

At first she couldn't make out what was happening because the room was dark and the audio appeared to be distorted. Two figures appeared on the side of the screen but their faces and movements were only caught by side views. They were twisting back and forth, and Mallory was having a hard time hearing or seeing much of anything. After a few minutes, they came into full view directly in front of the camera which was centered on the bed.

What happened in the next several minutes made Mallory gasp, cry and almost fall out of the comfort of David's chair. She was appalled, frightened and angry all at the same time. Emotions swirled so rapidly inside her, she was finding it hard to breathe and watch the monitor. She knew there was a way to convert the video to the big screen overhead, but there was certainly no need for that. She couldn't imagine broadcasting this horrendous video to begin with, let alone enlarging it for a better view.

It was too graphic for words.

Mallory's stomach couldn't take anymore; she had to turn it off.

Without a moment's hesitation she hit the delete button. Making sure a copy wouldn't be saved in the pc's trash bin, she searched for the back-up file, and promptly destroyed that as well.

Whoever sent the file to David most likely had saved a copy, but at least Mallory had taken the first steps to make sure David knew how upset she was.

Until she could tell him in person, and then based on his response, she'd decide if she could forgive him at all.

*****

"B, C or D section? Guess it's my choice."

Lenny pulled into the general parking lot for departures at the Philadelphia International Airport. His friend hadn't been too clear as to where they were supposed to meet; only telling Lenny to park anywhere he wanted then give him a shout on his cell. "If you want to use the ladies room, now would be a good time." Lenny scrolled through his caller list as Jenna got out of his Lexus.

"Ok, I'll be right back."

Lenny watched Jenna cross the four-lane bypass road from his side view mirror. He turned his attention back to his cell. Once again his friend's phone went right to voicemail. Time to leave another message.

"Hey, Jon. We're here. Parked outside of Southwest." Lenny leaned under his visor to find the section sign. "We're in section C. Call me back and let me know if you're coming to us, or we need to find you. Later, man."

Jon was most likely in the middle of his pre-flight checklist, ignoring any incoming calls. Lenny chuckled, remembering Jon's favorite phrase, *I don't stop for nothing or nobody when I'm checkin' the chop.*

"Goofball," Lenny snickered. He and Jon Hafton went way back to their high school days. Jon had been his friend longer than anyone, and he was still the same. Laid back, easy-going, same as Lenny. Except Jon didn't practice night maneuvers, hang out at the firing range in the wee hours of the morning, or learn three different languages on Rosetta Stone for his job.

Life was much simpler before he had signed on with the FBI, Lenny recalled. Bound and determined to go into law enforcement after college, he had attended one seminar by a visiting FBI agent and that was that. Before he could cancel his Eagles season tickets, he was shipped off to Quantico for training, never imagining he would end up right where he had begun...in the City of Brotherly Love, Philadelphia.

What goes around, comes around...his mother used to say, and she was right on a dime that time. Besides, it made sense. Turette knew his background. She had done her homework. He was a Philly boy, born and raised. If any of her team could blend into the scenery, Lenny was her best shot.

Lenny leaned back against the headrest, and closed his eyes. He had driven down from Philly yesterday evening, and now he was back again in less than twenty-four hours. Turette had been right once again. Jenna was on the verge of breaking down, and would undoubtedly start to make irrational decisions. He needed to stick to her like glue, especially after she had given Ann Bailey the slip.

Lenny couldn't imagine how pissed Ann must be feeling. It was embarrassing, to say the least. Losing your target was an insult, a sign you needed to brush up on your tracking skills. Not something you wanted on your record. Although from what he understood, Ann Bailey wasn't exactly on anyone's record...at least not by the FBI's standards. She was on loan from the CIA *unofficially*, someone Turette had enlisted to help...under the radar.

Just like the rest of us, Lenny mused. *Under the radar, or hovering just above it.*

Hitting the redial button and getting the same result, Lenny tossed his cell in the console's cup holder. It was going to be a long day. Even if Jon finally got his act together and called him back, the trip to New York would take a couple of hours. They'd have to find a place to stay, and then he hoped he'd be able to stall Jenna long enough until he could get some back-up from the Manhattan Field Office. All he needed was Jenna to make a sudden move without thinking, and all hell would break lose.

History would repeat itself. Jenna had almost been killed the last time she dared to face Hamilton on his own turf. Lenny wasn't about to let that happen again.

Not on his watch.

Lenny snatched the newspaper from the backseat to check the sports scores of yesterday's games. Making a mental note to call his brother and check on the date they were supposed to go watch the Phillies play Atlanta, Lenny stretched his arm out the window to get some fresh air. He was suddenly absorbed in an article about the Phillies' manager who wanted to rethink his latest lineup.

"Leave it alone," Lenny retorted. "Stupid shit. Why anyone would want to mess with…"

The first tranquilizer dart hit the side of his neck without warning. Lenny's hand flew upward just as the second dart was fired. His arm went slack at the same time his vision began to blur. "What the…?"

Words he didn't recognize were spewing from his mouth. When his eyes closed and his body sagged, Lenny's last thought was of Jenna.

And how he had failed to keep her safe.

*****

Snapping the tight latex gloves over his bulky hands was more trouble than it was worth. The car was going to be torched anyway.

Do as I say, Hans.

Mason's words droned in his ears like an incessant mosquito.

Hans Kliric growled. He stormed towards the Lexus parked just a couple of spots to his right. Far enough away not to be noticed but close enough for a direct shot. Two shots hitting the target both times.

Mason would be pleased.

The parking lot was practically abandoned. Passengers from a recent flight had found their cars and departed at least twenty minutes ago. Only a few cars parked randomly were taking up space in Lot C. Hans had waited patiently as Mason had told him to do, and his shots had been accurate.

The small darts were barely visible, and Mason had ensured him there was no way they could be detected by the security cameras which spanned the entire parking lot at regular intervals. Hans had no time to worry about the cameras; right now, his task was to get into the Lexus, push his victim out of the way, and get on the highway as quickly as possible.

The only thing that was bothering him was wondering if Jenna Reed had spied him inside the airport just minutes ago.

It was a stupid move. If Mason found out what he had done, Hans knew he would pay the price for it. But he couldn't help himself. Seeing Jenna Reed again was well worth the price of a tongue lashing, or privileges being taken away.

He had to follow her.

Hans had kept back at a safe distance. Watching Jenna move down the corridor was more than he could take. He wanted to reach out and grab her, force her inside an empty room and make her scream. His mouth went dry thinking about Mason's promise. Once Hans had the treasure pieces in his hands, Mason didn't care what happened to Jenna Reed, paving the way for Hans to fulfill his twisted fantasies.

As Jenna disappeared inside the ladies room, Hans came to his senses. It wouldn't be too long before she returned to the Lexus. He had to make his move. Opening the driver's side door, he laughed as loud as possible just in case anyone passed him. "You drunk again? I drive. I get you home."

Hans crumbled the newspaper, flinging it into the back seat. He hoisted his victim's body up and over the console with very little effort. Hans poked the man's chest with his finger as if they were sharing some sort of private joke.

Hans looked around the parking lot once more. No one was looking in his direction. Good. Mason would be happy.

Within seconds, the Lexus was heading towards the toll gate, leaving a worn Phillies baseball cap in its place on floor marker 54.

Hans fought the urge to grin profusely when he handed the cashier the ticket stub and a ten-dollar bill. He blended into traffic, gradually increasing his speed until he hit the I-95 interstate. Then and only then did he allow himself the luxury of speaking Russian, priding himself on a job well-done.

Mason would be pleased. He had followed directions, and there had been no problems. The only thing left to do was to find the drop-off point and set the car on fire.

*****

Jenna regretted her decision the moment she got in line at the Starbucks kiosk. Each of the six people in front of her was ordering a latte of a different variety. Double-shot espresso, flavored syrup, soy milk, non-fat milk, no milk at all, whipped cream, chocolate shavings...not one person simply ordered a plain coffee to go. Customers didn't seem too impatient to wait, while they contented themselves with checking messages or Facebook entries on their cells.

According to her watch, she had taken exactly five minutes inside the ladies room, and at least twice that amount of time standing in line. If it wasn't for the fact she had rushed out of the house without any breakfast or her usual two cups of coffee, she would happily turn around and zip back to the car. Her growling stomach was dictating her decision to stay in line. Shifting position for the third time, Jenna sighed. It was amazing to think how many people passed her by, not giving her a second glance. Having no friggin' idea what she had gone through in the past forty-eight hours.

Caffeine withdrawal was clawing at her nerves. Making her think crazy thoughts. Imagining Hans Kliric was walking through the airport. Jenna stopped herself from laughing.

Get a grip, Reed. You're tired, sore and your mind is play- ing tricks on you. You have an undercover FBI agent across the street waiting for you, and airport security has passed the Starbucks twice already.

Kliric's not here. Get over yourself.

Five more minutes evaporated from her life, and she was still three spots back. She couldn't take it anymore. The person at the counter was asking every conceivable question about the ingredients in the new Skinny Double Espresso Caramel Laced Latte. *Milk, coffee and sugar, dude. Get a brain.*

Jenna dashed out of line. Coffee could wait. Crossing at the pedestrian lane, Jenna stood rigid in her tracks. The Lexus was gone and in its place was Lenny's overturned baseball cap.

Every breath left her body.

Kliric was here...and he had found Lenny.

Chapter 24

Logan pulled into the Exxon off of Interstate 81 and breathed a sigh of relief. They had just passed Watertown, New York. A couple of more hours to Ogdensburg. It was almost over. Kelly would soon be safe.

He would have plenty of time to plan their next move.

There was just one problem. His friends weren't answering their home phone or their cells. Something was up. Zach and Trevor never disregarded his calls before. They were the most reliable friends he had, if he could call them friends at all. They were indebted to each other, trading favors when the need arose. He crashed at their place whenever he wanted, or had a reason to hide in Canada until the dust settled on a recent hit. They used Logan's connections in Europe to purchase and sell handguns on the black market. Nothing big or bulky, just small weapons they could easily smuggle in and out of countries in humanitarian health kits.

A friendship of convenience, Zach would say. Logan agreed without question. Logan had their house key on his key ring, and he wouldn't hesitate to help himself to their hospitality whether they were home or not. They knew him well enough to stock the fridge with beer and food before they took off for parts unknown. Clean towels and sheets would be piled in the spare bedroom, and their extra car would have a full tank of gas.

Simple requests were always honored. Logan had no reason to doubt they would come through for him again. That wasn't what was bothering him.

Not being able to reach either Zach or Trevor made the hairs on his neck stand to attention. *An early warning sign, maybe?*

No way, Logan muttered silently. Zach and Trevor both knew the drill. If they were compromised in any way, they were to call or text him immediately with the code phrase *gone fishing.*

No calls or texts. He was jumping to conclusions, making assumptions he had no business making. Everything was fine.

Zach and Trevor were busy; they'd call him back as soon as they could.

You're going to drive yourself crazy.

"I'm already there."

Logan didn't realize he was talking to himself until an older man using the pump right next door looked in his direction and shook his head. Logan shrugged as he hustled into the Exxon's convenience store.

Act normal. Blend in.

Being on the run and swapping identities the way most people change their clothes was getting old. He was tired of what his life had become. Always looking over his shoulder, shielding his eyes, changing the way he walked and talked.

It had been this way for five years now. He was getting good at it, regardless. Not one government agent or international police officer had been smart enough to catch him. He was *le cameleon* in France, *el impostor* in Spain, and *der Schurke* in Germany. The chameleon, the impostor or the rogue…all suitable nicknames. Logan laughed when he had first heard them or read about himself in the national press pages in each country. He had international notoriety, or at least his reputation did. Not one country had ever posted his picture. He was too clever for that. He had mastered the art of disguise at an early stage, always well-equipped to change his appearance at a moment's notice.

Crossing over to Canada and changing their identities would be easy. He just needed to stay a few more miles ahead of the FBI, and everything would work out. As long as Kelly continued to cooperate.

Up to this point, she had done everything he told her to do. She was protecting her child the only way she could. Logan admired her for that. As he sauntered into the mini mart, he glanced backwards. Kelly was still asleep in the backseat, the blankets tucked up to her chin. She looked peaceful. Her long, blond hair flowed over the top of the blankets, covering part of her face. Her hands were lying in her lap, loosely draped over a half-drained water bottle. Sheer exhaustion and never-ending tension had finally claimed her.

Logan stared longer than he had intended. Kelly's serene pose reminded him of a marble statute outside a small church in an

Irish village he had stumbled through last summer. *The sleeping angel*, Logan mused. *My sleeping angel.*

If only she could be...

A horn blasted behind him from the drive-through car wash. Obscenities followed, then doors slamming. The coin-operated keypad wasn't working apparently, or someone had punched in the wrong four-digit code.

People and their petty frustrations. Logan shook his head. He pulled out two twenties and a ten from his wallet. Getting in line to pay for his gas inside the mini-mart, he whistled, hoping the line would move faster. The sooner they were back on the road and out of the public eye, the better he would feel.

His attention was drawn to the small flat screen mounted in the far corner above the cash register. The volume was turned down but CNN was providing the current news feed on the bottom ticker.

Logan's mouth dropped open. Kelly's picture took up practically the entire screen with an inset picture of his old army mug shot. National news. Multi-state manhunt. Canadian border patrols notified on alert.

Logan turned his head aside, thankful he was the last person in line. Pressure in his chest was telling him to get out of there right now.

"Fill up, sir?"

"What?"

Logan stuttered, avoiding eye contact.

The cashier, a middle-aged woman with tufted brown hair showing more gray than brown, shot him a disparaging look. "Are...you...filling...up?" Emphasized staccato words demonstrated her apparent irritation of having to repeat herself.

"What...pump?"

"Five." The temptation to follow his short answer with something a bit more flagrant was on the tip of his tongue. He laid the bills next to the register, and left without another word.

Stay calm. Walk slowly.

Logan wanted to run back to his car. His heart was pumping in double-time. Jamming the nozzle into the gas tank and putting the clip down on the handle, he yanked the back door open.

"Wake up!" Sliding next to Kelly, he draped his arm around her and bent his head. "Stay still. I'm not going to hurt you." He held her tighter as she flinched. "I…just saw a news report on the TV inside." Logan tilted his head towards the convenience store. "We have to get out of here…fast."

Kelly shook, praying he was too distracted to figure out what she had done. She squeezed her eyes shut, putting up with the way his body was pressed close to her. He was breathing on her neck. Nervous breaths…keeping in time with his rapid heartbeat pounding against her chest. He was too close…every second repulsing her.

Hearing the pump click off, Logan scrambled out of the car. He was due $1.87 in change. "Screw it." He couldn't take a chance the cashier would remember his face; the odds of probability increasing if he went inside for his change.

Logan maneuvered the Range Rover back onto the highway. He wasn't stopping again. Hitting redial on his cell, Logan tried again to reach Zach and Trevor. He would keep trying until one of them answered.

He wasn't giving up.

Too preoccupied with driving and hitting keys on his cell, Logan never saw the small smile emerging on Kelly's face. She had turned away from him the second he exited the back seat, unable to contain her excitement.

She had left a second clue.

Pretending to be asleep, Kelly made her move the exact moment Logan went into the store to pay for gas. She had found a ballpoint pen stuck inside the fabric pouch on the back of the driver's seat. Noticing a few gas receipts lying on the ground next to the pump, she quickly retrieved one and wrote a message. Keeping her eye on the store, she snuck between the pumps and placed the note underneath the black, plastic nozzle flap on the pump directly behind the one Logan would be using.

Hoping the next customer would take a moment to read it and notify the owner of the gas station, Kelly returned to the backseat, covered up, and pretended once again to be asleep.

Never giving Logan the slightest indication she wasn't doing exactly as he had told her.

*****

"Austin, try and think."

203

Agent Brett Jacoby was trying to be calm but he didn't have Turette's finesse. She was much better at getting people to talk, to provide even the most intricate details under stress; a skill he definitely lacked and was the first to admit.

"It's very important for us to locate McHenry's hideaway. We don't have much time. If McHenry is headed for the Canadian border, he's got a head start."

"Then why are you wasting your time trying to find his house? Shouldn't you guys be more concerned about heading up to the border?" Austin rubbed his eyes again and tried to focus. "I'm sorry, Agent Jacoby. I don't mean to tell you how to do your job."

Jacoby took the criticism in check. He knew it wasn't personal and he wasn't offended. Austin Reed had been through hell and back, and his nightmare was far from being over. "We've already alerted the border patrols, and we've got agents en route. I'm just trying to cover all the bases. Finding McHenry's hide-out might provide additional evidence as to his long-range intentions."

Austin took a couple of deep breaths, wincing from the pain every time he moved and the stitches on his chest pulled in resistance. Twenty-nine stitches, to be exact, on his neck, chest, arms and legs. Between the bandages and the bruises, he looked like he had been on the wrong side of a drunken bar fight. "Ok," he said, trying to shift to a better sitting position in the hospital bed.

Taken to the Pocono Medical Center in East Stroudsburg, he had received excellent care. The nurses and doctors were extremely attentive and compassionate. As soon as they learned he was the fiancé of the kidnapped pregnant woman broadcast on local and national television stations, Austin also received their sympathetic well-wishes for Kelly's safe return.

"The roads all looked the same except there was a turn-off to a gravel road. At first it was just a dirt road off the highway, then when we got a few yards in, the ground started to get bumpy. I remembered seeing a sign for Bushkill Falls. It wasn't much farther down the road that we turned off."

"Which side of the road had the sign for Bushkill Falls? You're doing great, Austin."

"Right. Yeah, it was the right side."

Jacoby keyed up his iPad to reveal the Department of Transportation's detailed map of the Poconos. He zeroed in on the tourist attraction Bushkill Falls. "Was there a blinking light on the road?"

Austin nodded.

"How far after the blinking light did the car turn?"

"Less than a mile."

Jacoby gently clapped Austin on the shoulder. "Good job, Austin. You've just helped us narrow the search. I'm going to step outside your room for a few minutes to talk to my partner, Thompson. Then I'll stop back in to say good-bye before I leave. I know it's hard right now for you to just stay here and wait for news, but we're moving as quickly and strategically as possible. We don't want to scare McHenry into doing something stupid and jeopardizing Kelly's safety. So, bear with us, please."

"Just bring her back to me," Austin added before Jacoby turned to leave.

"That's what I plan to do."

Jacoby hurried out the door, leaving Austin to sink back against his pillow and stare out the window. His private room was cheery enough, with its bright yellow wallpaper border and artificial Boston fern in the far corner. But his mood was recognizably somber, leaving him depressed and on edge. Overhearing Jacoby's conversation did little to lift his spirits, although he was the main reason the FBI now knew where to search.

"Thompson?"

"I'm here. Where are we going?"

"Route 109. There's a blinking light at the Bushkill Falls Road intersection. Get a couple of units to head out that way; widen the search to where the vehicle was found, and track backwards. I want every inch of highway accounted for, any dirt pathways investigated. If you find a gravel road, tell the guys to proceed with caution. Pick me up at the front door. I'm on my way there now."

"Copy that," Thompson responded, keying off.

Jacoby pushed the door open to Austin's room. He stuck his head inside and waved. "I'm heading out. Thompson's picking me up in a few minutes. I have the phone number to your room. The moment we have an update, I'll call you."

"Thanks," Austin replied before the door swung back. All he could do now was wait...and worry.

*****

Jacoby stared at his cell while he rode the elevator down to the hospital lobby. He was hesitating to call Briggs for good reason. This whole business with crucifying Pierce and Turette was eating at him. It didn't matter if Pierce hadn't been entirely forthcoming about what took place in Texas; Jacoby completely understood the *need-to-know* mantra. He didn't ask too many probing questions. There was no reason for it. He trusted Pierce too much to doubt him.

This whole mess with Briggs at the center made the Texas mission take on new meaning. If there was even the slightest chance Briggs had ground to stand on with his accusations, Pierce would be put through the ringer. Coming out with a few black marks on his record would be the least of it.

Briggs had made it clear he was out for blood.

Why? Briggs had to be acting on orders from above. Someone in the higher ranks at the FBI had a vendetta against Damian Pierce, or he was acting on orders from an outside source; that had to be it. Turette's theory about David Caldwell being The Closer was making more sense every time Jacoby thought about it. Caldwell had money and influence, two prime factors for blackmail or making someone re-think their loyalties.

Jacoby's phone buzzed with a text reminder from Briggs stating his latest report was an hour overdue. So tempted to send a reply telling Briggs where he could stuff his reports, Jacoby disregarded the order and pocketed his cell. "Let's move." Without even a cursory acknowledgment towards his partner, Jacoby slammed the door to the SUV.

Thompson knew better than to push. Tension was running high, and manners were taking a backseat. "Field techs just called. State Police found the gravel road. Scanning the perimeter now. Told them to wait until we get there to search the house. Reed wasn't kidding. He tore the fence apart at the seams. No wonder he was banged up pretty good."

"How far away?"

"Ten minutes tops. Just popped the address into the GPS. How's Reed doing?"

Jacoby took his iPad out of its protective sleeve. "Shaken up. Hurting. Got a ton of stitches, and he's weak because of the blood loss. He'll be ok if he doesn't go crazy. Must be frustrating to just sit back and wait."

"I hate sitting still."

Jacoby laughed. "It's a good thing Turette hasn't needed us for any stakeouts lately. You were going crazy the last time we had to sit around for hours in South Carolina. Remember?"

"She still owes me for that."

"Good luck trying to collect. Turette's up to her neck with other problems. Briggs is doing his best to build a case against Pierce. He's pushing for a panel of inquiry. You and I both know that's not good."

Thompson shot his partner a worried glance. "Turette got a plan in mind?"

"She's meeting with Carile, and someone else he's brought in. Thomas Movell. Ever heard of him?" Jacoby scrolled through his updated probability calculations.

"Name's familiar for some reason. Can't place him. You?"

Jacoby shook his head. "Same thing. I remember the name Movell from a few years back, but I can't pinpoint the details."

"Maybe you never got the details. Could be a cover up."

Jacoby looked up from his iPad. "Oh, don't start with the conspiracy theories, Mick. You have a basic distrust of every-one."

Thompson's laugh bellowed. "I trust you, don't I?"

"For the most part." Jacoby's attention was drawn to a cloud of black smoke emerging from the tree tops directly ahead of them. "What do you think that is?"

Thompson craned his neck, keeping his hands firmly gripped on the steering wheel. "Not sure, but we're driving right towards it." He handed Jacoby his phone. "Tap the first number on the call history list. Belongs to one of the field techs who rode out with the state police. He called me a few minutes ago."

Before Jacoby could find the number, Thompson's phone buzzed. It was the same number calling. Jacoby hit the speaker button.

"What's happening?" Thompson asked before the caller had time to speak. "We're seeing black smoke. Something on fire?"

"Affirmative. The house was rigged. We had two guys inside. Not sure..." the team leader paused. "Just called for the fire department. We're afraid the flames are going to hit the trees. Might be quite a mess by the time you get here. How far out are you?"

Jacoby checked the GPS. "Three miles. This is Agent Jacoby. Make sure no one else goes inside. Bomb squad already alerted?"

"Yes, sir."

Jacoby tossed his cell on top of the dashboard. "McHenry knew we'd find the house. He expected trouble, just like he's been three steps ahead of us ever since. After I see what's going on, we're heading back to base. I want a chopper to take us to Ogdensburg. We're going to block every road, and trap him."

Jacoby turned back to his iPad. Somewhere between here and Canada McHenry was making his final approach, and the FBI's window of opportunity would shortly be closing. Jacoby vowed he wouldn't give up trying to catch him...even if he had to cross the border himself and go rogue.

Some men were worth killing at any cost...and McHenry had just joined the party.

Chapter 25

Chase's head rolled to one side while his eyes fluttered open. It didn't take him long to figure out he wasn't in the safe house any longer.

His arms weren't budging and neither were his feet.

He was someone's prisoner.

Attempts to twist his arms and legs free were useless. Whoever had tied his arms behind the back of the chair and shackled his ankles to the chair legs knew what he was doing. What was bothering Chase more was the gap in time he was missing. The last thing he remembered was his partner Ann Bailey encouraging him to move from the kitchen table to the sofa in the living room. Then she had left, telling Chase she would check in on him later. Surely she had remembered to lock the door behind her.

Someone was watching...and waiting.

Whoever had captured him did so while he was unconscious. To minimize retaliation, not that he was in any shape to defend himself. He could barely move.

Still, his captor had been smart enough to track him, restrain him, and transport him to another location without raising suspicion. Someone knew the tricks of the trade.

Chase wracked his brain for any slight recollection of details. He had none. He had passed out at the safe house and woke up lashed to a chair in a room he didn't know.

Scan the site for details. Commit them to memory. Analyze every angle.

Chase went through the standard operational checklist in his mind. The room was small, maybe twelve by eight feet at best. An old metal table was to his left, just inches from the doorway. It was empty except for a couple of paint cans and a roller tray. In the far corner, rolls of tarp were stacked haphazardly against each other next to a box of paint brushes. Along the opposite wall, at least two sets of painters' overalls were draped over the only other chair in the room. Down the wall to his right, turpentine cans were neatly stored in a plastic storage tub.

One or more professional painters used this room for storage.

Chase's mind flew to a conversation he and Jenna had with Kelly right before they were headed to Texas with Damian. Kelly had mentioned she had noticed a painting van parked between the Reeds' beach house and the Maylors' next door right before Austin had been taken to New York.

Was it too coincidental he was now confined to a room full of painting supplies?

Chase wondered if the two incidents were possibly connected. Different crimes committed by the same man or his accomplices. The same criminal he had been trying to track down for several years.

The Closer.

If he could just free his hands from the rope bindings, Chase had a chance of getting out of there. Chase's eyes flew around the room again. He had missed it the first time.

Stuck inside the box of paint brushes was a box cutter. All he had to do was push his chair towards the box, topple the chair, grab the box cutter and free himself. He had been in stickier situations before. He could do this.

The chair creaked when he rocked it. Chase jerked his body to the left and then the right trying to gauge the best way to move himself in the direction of the box on the floor. Finally, he was able to slide the chair sideways an inch at a time. A slow, steady process but one Chase hoped would yield the desired result. Freedom.

Several minutes passed. He was making progress, sweating and grunting all the while. It was hard work, moving his own weight and the chair's little by little. Scraping across the concrete floor, Chase focused on his goal, never taking into account the noise he was making. With every push, the metal stabilizers attached to the bottom of the chair legs made a high-pitched sound echoing off the walls.

A sound heard beyond the storage room.

A concept he realized two seconds too late.

The door flung open and fists immediately connected with his face, sending him and the chair back several feet. It would have fallen to the floor if someone with large brown hands hadn't stopped it.

"I don't think we've been properly introduced."

Chase fought hard to focus. His head was spinning.

"Do you think that is wise?" The man behind him spoke, and Chase reeled, recognizing the voice immediately.

"Come now, Markus, don't you think our guest should know exactly who he's dealing with?"

"I know who you are." Chase spit out a clump of congealed blood. "So you can dispense with the formalities."

"Straight to the point. I can appreciate that." The Closer stared at Chase, wondering if the comment was based on reputation alone or something else altogether. Finally, he took a step closer to get a better look. A strange familiarity struck him hard; he just couldn't place it. "We've met before, haven't we?"

Chase remained silent, refusing to answer. Memories of his family's vacation in Talkeetna, Alaska flooded his brain. He was seven and his sister was five in 1988 when their parents had taken them on what would become their last family vacation. He remembered it vividly now as if he had been transported back in time. All the snow, so much of it in fact, his mother had complained she would never want to leave southern California again ever in her entire life. His father had laughed, telling her and their children they were going to have the experience of a lifetime. How frightfully true that statement had become.

Instead of enjoying family-bonding time with his parents and sister, the vacation had turned into Chase's worst nightmare. The lodge they had chosen happened to be the hiding place of an international hit man the federal authorities had finally tracked down. Within hours of their arrival, Chase and his family had become unwilling pawns in a battle of survival as they and the other lodge patrons were held hostage at gunpoint. To aid in his escape, the hit man had set the lodge on fire, making his victims move from room to room in a hurried manner until mass pandemonium ensued. Units from local fire and police departments in addition to a barrage of FBI and CIA agents joined forces for the rescue efforts, but it seemed like all they were doing were getting in each other's way.

If it hadn't been for the heroic efforts of the one female FBI agent and her team, Chase was certain no one would have come out of the lodge alive.

Special Agent Maria Turette had arrived, issuing commands with such authority, every fire, police, and paramedic stood at attention. She quickly organized the rescue teams, gave them strategic orders, and stood at the helm of the command center telling each unit when and where they would take control. Within less than two hours after her arrival, the lodge had been infiltrated, the hotel guests rescued unharmed, and a manhunt initiated.

The hit man was never found.

Apparently, after security cameras had been further analyzed, he had escaped donning a paramedic's uniform and steering the ambulance off into the sunset. An embarrassment for the FBI.

Instead of receiving accolades for her brave efforts, Turette had been reprimanded in public by a supervising agent. Accused of mismanaging her priorities, Turette had been tongue-lashed for allowing the number three fugitive on the FBI's Most Wanted List slip out of her fingers. She had chosen the preservation of civilian lives over capturing a hit man. Even though it was a benevolent move, the fact remained she had allowed an extremely dangerous criminal to escape.

Chase had tried to intervene, running between the agent and her boss, screaming that she had saved a lot of people and they should be happy. But as he had been pushed back into the arms of his mother, he was forced to watch as the female agent hung her head in shame while cameras snapped and microphones were jammed in her face. She composed herself within seconds, smiled briefly, and provided praise for the brave men and women of Talkeetna who had risked their lives and performed a good deed.

Chase had been amazed by her humility, and the gracefulness by which she conducted herself. He promised himself one day he would find Special Agent Maria Turette and thank her once again for saving his family.

Instead, he had taken a pot shot at her while he was in Texas under the influence of the same drugs flowing through his veins.

Now he was staring back at the man who had caused his family's turmoil in Alaska, Maria's kidnapping in Texas, and most likely the attack on the museum in New York at the beginning of summer.

The Closer. The man he wanted to bring to justice more than anything.

Chase jerked from the unexpected smack to his head.

"Garrett, do you have any idea why you're here?"

Chase refused to answer. He wasn't going to give The Closer the satisfaction of finding out his true identity.

The Closer dragged the other chair to the middle of the room and straddled it. "Well, then. I think it's time we talk about that."

*****

Thomas Movell waited patiently, glancing down at his watch only a time or two. He was seated in his rented BMW 528i in a public parking garage three blocks from the FBI building in downtown Washington, D.C. The dampness from last evening's downpour was still lingering in the air, making him miss the warm, comforting climate of Jamaica. Fall in Washington brought with it fluctuating temperatures, frequent rain storms, and the ever present annoyance of leaves sticking to the bottoms of shoes.

Movell made a promise to himself; one he fully intended to honor. He would stay as long as necessary in the States at the request of his best friend Tumi Carile; however, the moment his presence was no longer required, he would take the very next flight back to his homeland. Of course, he knew that wouldn't be anytime soon.

Rectifying the wrongful imprisonment of Damian Pierce, finding the traitors within the FBI, and restoring order to the livelihood of the people Tumi cared most about, would take time and patience, definitive strategies, and reliance upon his loyal network of allies. He had his work cut out for him.

As his hands rested calmly on the steering wheel, Movell watched the familiar female figure emerge from the stairwell. He smiled, beckoning her forward with a slight nod of his head.

Maria Turette still carried herself the same, Movell marveled. No matter how many years passed, she still had the same slim, petite figure many women lost when they hit their late forties. According to Tumi, Maria had a passion for kick-boxing which Movell found to be quite amusing. Nonetheless, he admired Maria for pursuing a hobby she enjoyed which also yielded her the benefit of a well-defined physique. Movell had no doubt Maria Turette was the envy of other female agents half her age.

Maria's physical attractiveness wasn't her only endearing quality, Movell considered. He had always admired her tenacity, her devotion to her husband and her job, and her never-ending outward displays of kindness. She was quite remarkable, and Movell made a point of telling Damian Pierce those very words whenever he had the chance.

"Thomas, thank you for coming." Maria reached over and kissed him gently on the cheek. "Damian and I...will appreciate whatever you can do."

Movell clasped her hands and tilted his head slightly. "I consider you and Damian to be family. I will do whatever is in my power to take care of my family. Do not worry. Tumi, Phillip and I are formulating a plan. You must trust our judgment, Maria. Can you do that...unconditionally?"

"Of course." Maria turned in her seat to give him her full attention. "What do you need me to do?"

Movell shook his finger. "You must not...work with us directly. Elias Briggs already is reviewing your track record, and will find any cause necessary to relieve you of command permanently. As it stands, you are currently on administrative and medical leave. As long as we can divert his attention, your status will remain the same. Do not underestimate him, Maria. Briggs has ways of turning the tables to his favor. I do not trust him. These charges against Damian were not brought by him directly. He received orders from a higher level to initiate the inquiry. I have my suspicions, and will share them when I have finished conducting my own research. In the meantime, I would ask you to stay at home, make as few public appearances as possible, and make sure you stay away from the FBI."

"I want to see my husband, Thomas. The FBI has no right to hold him if he's not being formally charged. They've already kept him over the allowable time frame. We have to get him out of there."

"To which I am fully devoted, my dear Maria. Allow me to..."

"Damn it, Thomas! It's driving me crazy just waiting around!" Maria fisted her hands in her lap. Lifting her eyes, she softened her tone. "I'm sorry. I...shouldn't lash out at you. You came here to help. Today hasn't been one of my better days. I'm not sure how much Tumi has filled you in. Kelly is still missing, Jenna won't answer her cell, and two of my agents never made it to Cape May."

Movell patted Maria's hand. "You are troubled. Rest assured I will resolve the matter concerning Damian's confinement as quickly as possible. Then I shall proceed with my private investigation with or without Raymond Konecki's cooperation. I beg for your patience. Please understand I must tread lightly, and discreetly."

"Konecki? The man you saved in Florida? Are you sure, Thomas? I haven't heard anything that would indicate…"

Movell raised his hand stopping Maria. "Raymond Konecki is not the man he appears. I assure you, Maria. Do not trust him under any circumstances."

"That won't be a problem. I've learned not to trust too many people. Hazard of the job, I guess."

Movell laughed. "I suppose that it is. Rest assured, I will find out if Konecki is involved. Ironically, he's given me the green light to investigate the men in your unit. I explained to him I'm under the impression a traitor lurks within. He was willing to give me access to your team."

"And what have you found?" Maria asked nervously.

"Nothing at the moment. I am more concerned about facilitating Damian's release. Your home may be compromised. Go to this address." Movell took out a small notebook from his jacket pocket. He wrote down the address of the hotel where Tumi and Phillip had relocated after leaving Damian and Maria's home. "Wait for me to call. I promise you, Maria, I will find the answers you seek. Now, let me get to work."

*****

Damian sat on the hard wooden bench inside the holding cell, cracking his knuckles. Hours of constant, repetitive questions without food and water had drained him. A technique he had used himself on many occasions. The sad part was, he couldn't just get up and pour himself another cup of coffee to ease the tedious routine. He was at the mercy of Briggs or one of his deputies who obviously didn't care if he had food or water.

215

So much for the Agency taking care of its own.

It was one thing to publicly parade him around in shackles, but to keep him in Holding over the regulated timeframe was inexcusable. Briggs was playing a game, and unfortunately, at the moment he held all the cards.

For what? Damian wondered, drumming up various theories. Briggs was either taking orders from a level or two above him, or he had a vendetta which included blackballing Damian and Maria. Or he was just being a pain-in-the-ass, throwing his authority around in case anyone was paying attention.

None of the notions seemed to make any sense.

Damian pressed his back against the cold, concrete wall, trying to rationalize Briggs' allegations. The breaking and entering part, he got. But a federally-funded research facility? Attempted murder? Wrongful use of lab resources?

Right. Give me a friggin' break! Damian swore, pounding the bench. Someone had gotten to Briggs, fed him a bunch of bull, and then convinced him to rack up the charges. *But who?*

Damian wracked his brain to remember the chain of command in Briggs' division. Gene Stafford? No, he had retired a few months ago. Joe Rifton? No, he had transferred late last summer to California. Raymond Konecki. Had to be. Damian pondered that idea for several minutes. How Briggs could act upon Konecki's orders and not question the validity of them was senseless. Unless…Briggs was the one being threatened or even blackmailed.

It was plausible, Damian concluded. Maybe Maria would know the inside track about Konecki.

Maria.

Shutting his eyes, Damian pictured the last time he had looked into his wife's soulful eyes. They had argued, he had forgotten to kiss her good-bye and he had felt incomplete ever since.

"Visitor, Pierce." The security guard announced as he unlocked the door.

Damian's heart began to beat in double time. *Maria's here!*

"My apologies for not arriving sooner."

Damian's shoulders sagged with disappointment. Although he was very grateful Tumi had sent his most-trusted envoy,

Thomas Movell. If anyone could figure out a way to get him out of Holding, Movell was his best chance.

"Maria sends her regards. I did my best to relieve her fears. The problem...will be *facilitated*."

Damian met Movell's eyes and nodded. He knew the meaning of Tumi's catch phrase, used by all his ambassadors. *Say no more.*

Movell bowed slightly and pressed the buzzer to alert the guard. He closed his fist and held it tightly against his chest, sending Damian yet another nonverbal signal.

We will act...soon. Be ready.

Chapter 26

Jenna couldn't remember the past twenty minutes. They seemed to vanish inexplicably. One moment she was standing in the parking lot across from the departures terminal of Southwest Airlines, and the next she was seated in the office of Airport Security.

"Let me get this straight, Ms. Reed. You *think* you saw a man strolling in the lobby who *might have* looked like someone who took a knife to you a few months ago. Now he's gone, the man you came to the airport with is gone, and you do not have a flight reservation. You can see why I'm a little...confused." The security manager laced his fingers behind his head and leaned back in his swivel chair. Nothing about this young woman's story was adding up, and he was thirty minutes shy of his smoke break. He didn't have time for this. "Let's wrap this up so we can both get on our way."

Jenna wrung her hands. She had no idea who to call for help. Maria had gone back to D.C., she couldn't remember Ann's last name, and Jonathan's cell phone number wasn't picking up.

Chase? Absolutely not.

No matter what was happening right now, she couldn't even begin to think about another interaction with Chase.

Another name came to light, and she took a bold chance speaking his name. "Agent Brett Jacoby with the FBI. Can you call him please?"

The security guard stopped drumming his fingers on top of his desk. "The FBI? You want me to call the friggin' FBI? Lady, are you on something?"

"Please. Just call the FBI's main number and ask for Agent Brett Jacoby. I'm sure he'll take my call. He's searching for my brother right now."

"You brother is wanted by the FBI?" The security manager smiled sarcastically. "This keeps getting better and better."

"No, damn it. Agent Jacoby is searching for my brother and my best friend. They were kidnapped from Cape May."

Either the woman sitting across from him was using the latest news flash to stimulate her heightened sense of delirium, or she was telling the truth. He religiously watched CNN in between patrols, and the story of the kidnapped pregnant woman had caught his attention more than once. Grabbing the phone, he hoped he wasn't making a mistake. "This is Officer Frank Tyson with Airport Security at Philly International. I need to be patched through to the FBI. Agent Brett Jacoby."

"Yes, Sir. Hold, please."

Officer Tyson covered his mouthpiece. Spinning around, he shot Jenna a stern look. "I'm warning you. If this is nothing but a prank, the cops are going to haul your..."

The operator interrupted. "Sir, Agent Jacoby will be on the line when I hang up."

Tyson's feet hit the rubberized mat underneath his chair with a thud. His posture straightened, and he cleared his throat. He was dumbfounded, and hoped he didn't manage to make a total fool out of himself by stuttering.

"Agent Jacoby here. To whom am I speaking?"

"Uh...Officer Frank Tyson, sir. Airport security, Philadelphia International Airport."

"What can I do for you, Officer Tyson? I'm in a bit of a rush."

"Yes, sir! I can completely understand that. I...uh...sir, a woman here wants to talk with you. She mentioned you by name."

Jacoby's patience was dwindling. "What woman, Officer Tyson?"

Jenna had about all she could handle. She circled Tyson's desk, yanked the phone out of his hand and held up her hand. "Jacoby, it's Jenna. I need your help!"

Tyson stumbled out of his chair, sending it sliding across the floor. It banged against his metal filing cabinet, making a loud noise. Tyson stood with his hands on his hips looking like he could spit fire.

"I'm stuck at the Philly Airport. A friend of Austin's was driving me here. I just know him as Lenny Lex. He said he works for Maria. He's gone. His car's gone. God, Jacoby, I think I saw Hans Kliric! Maybe I'm just going crazy." Jenna ran her fingers through her hair in desperation.

"Calm down, Jenna. I'll take care of this. By the way, I don't think you're going crazy. With everything going on, it doesn't surprise me that Kliric is making an appearance. How he found you, I don't know. My initial guess is that you have a tracking device somewhere on you or Kliric somehow found out about Lenny Jankovich. By the way, Lenny is part of Turette's team. I'm sorry you had to find out the hard way. We'll put out a BOLO on him and his car. Right now, Jenna, I need you to hold tight. We found Austin; he's getting medical attention for some cuts and bruises at the Pocono Medical Center. Otherwise, he's fine. Put Officer Tyson back on the phone. I'll arrange a transport for you so you can get to your brother."

"What...about Kelly?"

Jacoby hesitated. "We're still searching, but the gap is closing. We're making good strides. Let me talk to Tyson and I'll get things rolling."

"Thanks, Jacoby. I owe you one." Jenna handed the phone back to Officer Tyson with an apologetic look on her face. "Sorry," she mouthed before taking her seat.

Officer Tyson reached for a pencil and scribbled some notes on his desk blotter. "Yes, sir. Right away, sir." Hanging up, he stuck the pencil behind his ear. He had a new respect level for the woman standing across from him. "FBI connections? Must be nice." Officer Tyson hung up, giving Jenna the once-over. "How did you manage that?"

"Long story. Believe me, you don't want to know."

The phone rang before Tyson had taken his hand away. "Yes, sir. We'll be right there." Getting up, he motioned for Jenna to do the same. "Follow me, Ms. Reed. We're going to get you on your way."

"Might need to stop and get a coffee first. Not sure if I can drive without some caffeine."

Tyson chortled. "No, Ms. Reed. You're not driving any-where. You're going by police helicopter. You'll get to the Poconos in less than an hour."

"Jacoby came through." Jenna eased into a smile, swearing she'd never take her friends at the FBI for granted ever again.

*****

Jonathan didn't believe in harboring regrets. At least not when it came to satisfying personal needs. He chose his sex partners well, never giving in to lustful one-night stands, or being callous to underappreciate the woman he was waking up to the next morning. He had always prided himself on being a gentleman even if he realized the relationship wouldn't last more than a few days, weeks or even months.

Standards of decency never entered Jonathan's mind last night. Not once. From the moment Ann Bailey placed her hands on him, he had almost welcomed the euphoria of totally losing control.

Obsessed cravings were gnawing at him once again, pushing coherent thoughts aside. He saw one face and one body...and he wanted Ann Bailey more than anything. More than the air he breathed.

How and why he had left her bed at such an early hour was weighing heavily on his mind. No sound reason was evident. Only confusion.

Ann Bailey scared the living daylights out of him. No other woman had ever physically and emotionally drained him completely. When they finally landed in her bed at two a.m., Jonathan fell asleep as soon as his head hit the pillow. For four solid hours, he slept with his arms draped across Ann's hip, exactly where it was when he woke to the sound of her annoying bedside alarm.

Ann didn't budge, nestled against his chest, making it quite an effort to leave her side. When Jonathan reached over to turn off the alarm, she breathed deeply, almost sighing. Kissing her gently on the cheek, Jonathan rose slowly and headed for the bathroom.

Sidestepping the torn shower curtain, the drenched bathmat, and a couple of bunched-up towels tossed in a corner, Jonathan couldn't help but laugh. It looked like a war zone, and they certainly had done battle.

He was still sore from where Ann fell on top of him, and then proceeded to work him over in the hallway. Jonathan made a quick survey of his body, thankful there were no obvious bruises. Just a bruised ego telling him he needed to get in better shape if he intended to pursue Ann Bailey for more than one date.

Actually, their chance encounter hadn't quite qualified as a date. Although Ann had denied it twice, Jonathan was sure there was more than one reason why she happened to be at Carney's last evening, not to mention on the next barstool.

Ann Bailey hadn't been entirely truthful with him. Jonathan wondered if telling the truth was in her repertoire altogether. She was CIA, and if nothing else, he understood her reluctance to lay all her cards on the table at once. In any regard, she intrigued him. Excited him. Made him want more.

Wants and needs. The perpetual see-saw of life. Jonathan debated what to do. He was in need of a good shave, and a few more hours of sleep. Which was never going to happen if he returned to Ann's bed.

No way whatsoever.

The only thing he could think of was dragging his tired body across the street to the Reeds' and getting under an extremely hot shower. Memories of being in the shower with Ann brought a wide grin to his face. Never again would he turn on the faucet and not think of the water streaming down Ann's body and the way she pulled his hips closer with firm, decisive hands.

Grabbing his clothes where he had dropped them in the hallway, Jonathan dressed as quickly as possible just outside her doorway. He poked his head around the doorframe, taking one last look at her naked body. Ann had rolled over on her side facing the far side windows. The soft rise and fall of her silhouette beckoned him, and it took every ounce of willpower not to rush back to her bed.

Hurrying down the stairs, Jonathan's mind played devil's advocate. He was acting like a coward and a fool.

We just met. We're sexually compatible...extremely compatible, but that's probably as far as this will go.

She works for my mother. Too weird of a connection.

I still have feelings for Jenna, don't I? Jenna needs me.

Needs and wants...

But there was no denying the passion...and the aftermath. His body was still tingling. Ann Bailey had done her best to persuade him he needed to look no further. And at this early hour with the subtle essence of her lavender bath oil still clinging to his nostrils, Jonathan had a hard time believing any reason was good enough to keep them apart for long.

Until he met Jenna at the top of the stairs, and his heart stopped. A rush of shame fell over him. He avoided her eyes. He knew she could tell he was just getting in, and probably wondering with whom he had spent the night. Jenna knew...but she didn't say a word.

She was too focused on getting away from him or just running away in general.

Jonathan punched the tile in the shower as the water began to roll down his back. Jenna had the tell-tale signs of sex gone bad, and he blamed Garrett entirely for abusing her. Slapping her in Texas was just the beginning. Chase Garrett was a time bomb rigged to explode. From the look in Jenna's eyes, Jonathan had pretty much guessed correctly. Garrett had taken his frustration out on her...*again.*

What can I do? She won't listen to me...

Jenna had many endearing qualities but stubbornness wasn't one of them. Jonathan berated himself for not stopping her, trying one more time to get through to her. Jenna had pushed him aside, refusing to hear another word.

I should have tried harder...she needs me...

Exhausted, Jonathan fell into bed. He didn't realize until several hours later, his cell was missing. It had to be at Ann's. Probably fell from his pocket. God knows he wasn't keeping track of anything last night. Surprising enough, he had remembered all of his clothes.

Jonathan knew he had another stupid grin on his face well before he stared at himself in the mirror. Maybe he had unconsciously left the cell at Ann's. A prime excuse for seeing her again.

To apologize for leaving her bed without saying a word or leaving a note. So much for being a gentleman. Jonathan doubted he was capable of it, at least when he was in Ann's presence. The way she had acted last night, it was clear she preferred a rogue to a gentleman any day.

Visions of Ann's vibrant body were making Jonathan delirious. He combed his wavy hair, letting his bangs fall almost over his eyes. Dressing quickly in a light blue polo shirt, his favorite Levi jeans, and seasoned Dockers boat shoes, he was almost ready to go. He dabbed a few drops of Clive Christian 1872 cologne on the sides of his neck hoping Ann would notice. Checking his image in the dresser mirror, he whistled. He felt like a new man.

Ann is definitely the reason for that.

S.A. Van

It was crazy, but he could still taste her, feel her...like they had never been apart. He was craving her, wanting to kiss her and put his lips all over her again.

Jonathan knocked rapidly on Ann's door. All she had to do was look at him and he'd be gone.

If she wasn't too mad at him.

As the door opened, Jonathan didn't wait to find out. He barged in, wrapped his arms around Ann's waist and kissed her until she pushed gently against his chest. "I...ah...left my cell."

"Not exactly the greeting I was hoping for. I don't know, something a little more romantic, maybe?" Ann inhaled Jonathan's cologne, closing her eyes. He was sexier than she had remembered from last night. "You missed breakfast," she teased.

Jonathan responded with a second kiss. "I missed *you*." His lips grazed her ear.

Ann pushed him back. Her eyes were dark, unreadable.

Jonathan didn't understand.

"Seems like you missed someone else...a little more. Is that why you left? Guilty feelings? So that's why you're here now. To apologize...for using me when you can't have who you really want?"

Jonathan stopped Ann before she could finish. He drew her hands up to his neck and kissed her deeply. Then he pulled back abruptly. "I didn't run back to Jenna, and I sure in hell didn't use you. The way you were attacking me last night, I was beginning to think it was the other way around." He laughed, then stopped when he noticed Ann turned away. "I'm sorry...for what it's worth. I won't apologize for making love to you but I will say I'm sorry if you thought I left because I was having regrets. You worried for nothing, Ann Bailey."

Jonathan tugged on Ann's chin to make her face him. "Something else is bothering you?"

Ann nodded. "Jenna is missing. I screwed up...again. I...was too tired to pay attention. I saw her leave this morning, and I tried to keep up with her, but...I lost her. Maria is not going to be happy at all. I told her I could handle everything. What if something happened, Jonathan? What if...somehow Hamilton's men got to Jenna...and I wasn't there to protect her? I really suck at this bodyguard stuff."

224

Jonathan pulled Ann back against his chest. "Jenna knows this town better than all of us. If she ditched you, she did it on purpose. She didn't want you to follow her. I don't know why she would take such a risk, but she's not the easiest person to figure out. Believe me, I've tried...unsuccessfully. Don't beat yourself up about it. When Jenna's ready to come back, I'm sure she'll have a good explanation."

Ann leaned against Jonathan's chin. "She's not coming back...not just yet anyway. Jacoby called; they found Austin and he's at the Pocono Medical Center. Jenna apparently hitched a ride with an undercover agent and somehow got to the Philly airport. She's en route now to the Poconos by helicopter. I've got to get up there."

"Want some company?" Jonathan asked, stroking her cheek.

"Not this time. I'll be working." Leading Jonathan to the front door, she picked up his cell from the small pedestal table flanking the entranceway and placed it in his hand. Kissing him lightly on the cheek, she playfully shoved him backwards. "You have to go. I need to get ready."

Jonathan nodded, then surprised Ann by pulling her closer. He kissed her, not wanting to stop for anything. He wasn't sure if his actions were based on fear for her safety, or something altogether different. "Come back to me, Ann Bailey. We have unfinished business." Jonathan winked then headed down the steps.

"Yes, we do." Ann flew up the stairs. She had less than twenty minutes to get ready before agents from the AC Field Office were picking her up. "We most certainly do."

Chapter 27

The walls were moving. Clockwise first, then a few seconds later...counter-clockwise.

Sweat dripped down his cheeks, wetting his lips. His tongue lashed out, welcoming the moisture. The dryness of his mouth had been so irritating while practically every other area of his body was drenched in perspiration or blood.

Chase fought the incessant urge to heave. Vomiting all over himself would make matters worse. Grinding his teeth, he prayed the pain would subside, if only for a minute or two. Enough time for him to catch his breath.

Wishful thinking left him discouraged.

He had no choice; it was time to beg.

"Make it stop." Words echoed, striking him from all sides. His breathing had slowed, and his mind was shutting down. Soon he would either be dead or unconscious...on his way to being dead.

Stabbing him with a needle this time, the drugs flowed faster into his bloodstream. The side effects were almost instantaneous, making Chase experience the rush of adrenaline and the heightened fears stemming from the hallucinations which followed.

Millions of tiny beetles crawled out of paint cans, skimming across the floor, moving closer and closer. All at once they attacked his shoes, running up his legs, burrowing themselves in his pant legs. They were biting him, eating at his flesh. Inching higher. He could feel them rippling across his stomach, hanging on despite his frantic efforts to force them off his body. Finally, they stopped...just a few centimeters from his heart.

What were they waiting for? Positioning themselves for the kill? In three quick seconds, they would be tearing at his heart.

Cold water splashed his face. Chase shook it off, panting. His eyes were drawn downward at his shaking body.

The beetles were gone...just as suddenly as they had appeared. They were never there to begin with. He had imagined it all.

Gasping for air and to see past his dripping hair, Chase blinked several times. A cool cloth was placed on his neck. Too soothing for words, Chase leaned back to soak in the much-needed relief.

It lasted all of a minute.

Another needle jabbed the vein in his neck where the cloth had been ripped away. His skin began to itch uncontrollably followed by an intense burning sensation. His fingers stretched and tingled, wanting to scratch, tear, and destroy. Chase cried out, begging his captors to peel away his fiery skin, or take a knife to his throat to end it all.

He wanted to die.

Another bucket of icy water hit him squarely in the face, waking him once again from his delirium. A soft towel was draped over his shoulders just as his head fell forward.

"Just so we have an understanding." The Closer cut the ropes binding Chase's wrists. "I control you. I determine if you live...or die. You do exactly as I tell you. Are we clear?"

Chase nodded, wanting so badly to have enough energy to rise from his chair, grab The Closer around his neck, and strangle him with his bare hands.

"Good." The Closer started to leave, then changed his mind. "Markus will fill you in. You're going to help us on a job. Oh, and Garrett, if you need yet another reminder of what the drugs can do to you, Markus would be more than willing to play the video of you attacking your girlfriend. You lost control, Garrett. Sexual assault carries several years in prison, and I doubt you'd survive. We wouldn't want this little video to find its way to the Feds, would we?"

Chase stiffened as The Closer's threat finally sunk in. Somehow Markus had placed a camera in Jenna's room and caught him forcing himself on her. Chase looked away, acknowledging his guilt with silence.

"I didn't think so." The Closer gestured to Markus to untie the ropes binding Chase's ankles. "Get him ready, Markus."

Chase focused his eyes on a crack in the wall in front of him. He had no intention of looking at Markus directly. He was a traitor, choosing the wrong side of justice. And most likely he would suffer the same fate as The Closer. Death...at Chase's hands.

*****

"Bad news, Turette."

Jacoby counted to ten in his head. He had enough to deal with at the moment, but keeping his boss in the loop was always a priority…even when he technically didn't have to tell her a thing. He had bonded with Maria Turette the first time he met her. She was new at supervising her all-male team, and Jacoby knew if he didn't step in and show her a major level of respect, none of the younger, less-experienced agents would do the same. He was the first agent to gain her trust and he was damn sure he'd be the last one to lose it.

"What is it?" Turette snapped, immediately regretting her tone of voice. "Sorry, Genius, didn't mean to take my…"

Jacoby paused once again, waiting for her initial reaction to abate. "No problem. I know your nerves are frayed. We're all on edge. I just wanted to bring you up to date. We found Janko-vich's car…or what's left of it."

"Doesn't sound good."

"It's not. Delaware State Police reported the car was set on fire at the first rest stop down from the Philadelphia Airport. Recovered one body. ME's on site now."

Maria held her breath.

"Male. Early indicators point to the possibility it could be Jankovich. Will know more when the ME has a positive ID. Thought you'd want to know as soon as possible."

"Thank you." Maria struggled for the right words. "Have someone call me when the ME knows for sure. I…should be the one making the call to his family. I hate this, Jacoby! I should be there with you. Damian should be there. We're both sidelined and you've got your hands full. I'm so sorry."

"Nothing I can't handle. I'm just filling in. Soon as you and Pierce are back on board, I'm fine with handing back the reins."

"We owe you. I mean that. When we get back…"

"I can have your corner office?"

"Right now, you can have whatever you want."

Jacoby laughed. "I'm making a mental note of that, Turette. Maybe a new paint job will be in order."

"Don't push your luck."

"Don't worry. I'm not. We need all the luck we can get."

Maria went silent again.

"Still there?"

"Yeah, I'm still here. Just thinking...about how grateful I am you're sticking by me...and Damian. I know I don't tell you that often..."

If Turette really knew Jacoby was assigned to her unit because he actually reported to her husband, she might change her tune. But it wasn't the time to tell her, and Jacoby swore he was leaving that little bit of news to Pierce. Then he was getting as far away as possible when the fireworks started.

"Don't need to tell me; I've got your back. That's what partners are for. By the way, Thompson's up here."

"Your right arm." Maria chuckled.

"Left would be more accurate. He's like a raging bull, scaring the shit out of everybody. Running around making sure weapons are checked, radios working. Pumping up the junior agents. You know how he is. Thompson's watched too many Rambo movies."

"You wouldn't want him any other way. Tell him to watch your back since I can't. That's an order."

"Got it, boss."

*****

"He's not going to be happy. You shouldn't be here."

Malcolm stood in his doorway feasting his eyes on Mallory Kincaid. At first when she called, Malcolm thought it was a joke, a way for Caldwell to test his loyalty. That theory was now shot to hell.

Mallory stomped her foot in annoyance. "Are you going to invite me in or not, Malcolm?" Tired and irritable, Mallory's patience was diminishing with every sullen stare she had to endure from David's long-time business partner. She huffed, brushing past him with the assumption he would bring in her luggage.

Malcolm wasn't the least bit fazed. Mallory more than made up for her lack of pleasantries by tempting him with her looks and seductive curves. He could care less if she insulted him all day. It was well worth the time he could spend ogling her and fueling his fantasies.

Malcolm dragged her heavy suitcase, dress bag, and travel tote into his modest living room while keeping his eyes planted on Mallory's every move. She was pacing, obviously annoyed and he just hoped her latest fight with Caldwell was enough for her to come to her senses. She could do better. Much better, in fact.

Turning around, Mallory stood with her hands on her hips. "You actually *live* here?" Gaping at the nondescript living room, Mallory was shell-shocked. The purely functional room held nothing to be desired. A checkered canvas sofa and matching armchair ripped at the seams, a scuffed-up mahogany coffee table, a couple of cheap silver floor lamps, and a small wicker trash can filled to the brim with empty beer bottles and cans. The only item in the room which didn't appear to come from the clearance rack of a bargain store was the fifty-inch flat screen mounted in the far corner. A bachelor's house, totally devoid of a feminine touch, thereby lacking frivolous and welcoming amenities.

Malcolm merely laughed. *How spoiled you are,* he wanted to say. Instead, he mocked her, waving his arm. "Make yourself at home."

Mallory had no desire of ruining her favorite silk skirt by sitting on Malcolm's dilapidated furniture. The sofa was stained in several spots; Mallory assumed it was beer, or something else equally disgusting. The armchair was littered with remnants of a newspaper, and she was afraid to discover what lurked underneath. Deciding it was probably in her best interests to check out the kitchen, Mallory barged forward.

Malcolm followed close behind. "Thirsty?" He opened the fridge, withdrawing two beer bottles. "Sorry...I'm all out of *champagne*. Beer will have to do."

Mallory shook her head. "Not now. I need to speak with David. Where is he?"

"Do I look like his babysitter?" Malcolm uncapped the Heineken, and took a seat. "He comes and goes; doesn't bother to check in with me until he needs my services. I guess he thought it was safer to bunk here. But I am curious, Mal. Why are *you* here?"

"For answers."

Malcolm laughed, dribbling beer down his shirt. "This should be good. You and I both know Caldwell only tells us what we need to know. If he's keeping something from you, then he has his reasons. As far as I know, he's out doing recon. Got a job coming up that requires *special handling*."

Mallory caught the reference but didn't comment.

"Probably better if we don't know the details. I just do what he tells me. You should learn the same. Beginning with...staying out of his way when he's working. You can't come on every job, Mal."

"I didn't ask for your opinion, Malcolm."

"I'm not the enemy. You should know that by now." Malcolm opened his second beer. His attention was drawn to Mallory's stylish outfit which hugged her near-perfect body, her perfectly-coiffed hair, and the shine on her immaculate, manicured fingernails. Mallory was accustomed to being pampered, being treated like a lady, and living a high-end lifestyle. No wonder she was suffering from culture-shock stepping inside his house.

"Are you listening to me, Malcolm? Apparently not." Mallory brushed a dark strand out of her eyes, then tossed her hair off her shoulders. "I asked you...if you saw the video?"

"Have no idea what you're talking about."

"Really? I find that hard to believe." Mallory studied Malcolm's eyes. Either he was a better liar than she was giving him credit for, or he hadn't been brought into the loop about the distressing video.

"Caldwell doesn't trust me enough to tell me everything. I'm sure you can relate."

Mallory disregarded the insinuation. She was too busy giving the small kitchen the once-over with obvious disgust. Cluttered counters, empty pizza boxes stacked on a spare chair, and two trash cans on the verge of overflowing. She couldn't wait to move on to better accommodations. As soon as David returned, that would be the first order of business. "I would think with all the money David pays you, Malcolm, you could...elevate your standard of living."

"Is that your way of telling me my place is a dump? I can't exactly stand out, Mal. All part of the job. I have to *blend*. You know what I'm saying?"

"Blending is one thing; this is...oh, God, where do I begin?"

"With me." David Caldwell stood in the back doorway with his arms folded. He shot Malcolm a glance indicating he needed to leave as quickly as possible.

"David." Mallory jumped to her feet. Gripping the back of her chair for support, her legs went weak when she saw the look on his face. Malcolm was right; David wasn't the least bit happy she had defied him, turning up at the most inopportune time.

"Why are you here, Mallory, when I specifically asked you to stay in New York?" He circled the table, taking his time. Tension sizzled between them.

Mallory stepped backwards, catching her heel against the chair leg. When her body began to sway, David reached out to firmly grasp her arms. His frustration was evident as he continued to hold her at a distance. Still, it felt good to be touched by him even under the circumstances. Mallory felt herself leaning towards him. "If you want to kiss me, just do it and get it over with."

Roughly, David pulled her into his arms. When their lips touched, all semblance of Mallory's intentional disobedience flew out of his mind. For the first time since his departure, he openly admitted to himself how much he missed her. Allowing them both some much needed air, David broke their kiss. "Can't stand to be away...even for a few days?"

Mallory lifted her eyes. "Is that a question, or are you finally willing to admit you need me?"

David answered her with another searing kiss. "You know I need you; that's not the issue here."

Mallory pulled back, breaking away from David's arms. "I...needed to talk to you about something. I couldn't do this...over the phone."

"Are you leaving me, Mal?" The taboo subject was on the table now, where it should have been from the start. "If you want out; I'll understand. You shouldn't have to put up with me."

Mallory fell against David's chest. The torment on his face was tearing her apart. "I love you, David. It's never been easy between us, and I doubt it ever will be. You owe me some answers, though, starting with the reason for making that horrible video."

David let her arms drop. "That's what this is all about? The video? Let it go, Mallory. It's nothing more than leverage. Something to hold over Garrett. A *motivational* tool. Stop making this into something it's not. But I am curious...how did you manage to view it?"

"If you don't want me to see things like that, don't ask me to check your email while you're away. Unless you wanted me to find it. Is that what this is, David? A test of my loyalty? Well, you've got your answer. If this makes you think less of me, deal with it." She turned away, refusing to lock eyes with him.

Folding his arms around her waist, David laid his head on her shoulder. "Don't push me away, baby. I don't want this to come between us. I haven't even seen the video. Markus just gave me...an *overview*, so to speak. I'm sorry you were upset about it. Sometimes...what I have to do isn't...who I am. You know me, Mal. I would never...do anything like that to you...or us. I care about you too much."

Mallory's eyes filled with tears. "It was...awful, David. It was bad enough watching what was happening, but knowing you had personally created the drugs making Garrett act that way...made me sick."

"I've sheltered you, Mallory, for so many reasons. Selfish ones. I wanted you to see me only one way. Now you know all there is, and I can see how much it hurts you."

"You can't protect me from everything. I want to get past this. I don't want to lose you." Mallory's voice was breaking; she was losing ground. Standing up to David was harder than she imagined. Mallory never felt David's arms tightening around her. She was too distracted with disturbing thoughts. Conflicting ones making her heart the cornerstone of defeat or hope.

"Let me go."

David immediately released her. He walked to the other side of the table, putting a careful distance between them. "You're putting up a wall, Mal. If it doesn't come down soon, it's going to destroy us."

Mallory's eyes burned. "You're the one who put up the wall, David. Not me. This is all about you." She stalked past him. "I need some fresh air."

From his vantage point across the street in one of his painting vans, Malcolm watched Mallory storm out the front door and run down the street. Caldwell wasn't following her; another sign they had argued and the almighty son-of-a-bitch had won another round.

Your loss, my gain, Malcolm mused, pulling the van away from the curb. It was time to show Mallory what she had been missing all these years wasting her time with David Caldwell.

Chapter 28

"I will take responsibility for the prisoner."

Thomas Movell's rigid posture and level tone commanded authority although he had no legal means to stand on. This was all about appearance and showmanship. Traits he had mastered over the years and used proficiently to maneuver himself and others out of unpleasant situations. "Your services, Lieutenant, are commendable. I shall put a letter of recommendation in your file immediately upon my return."

The first-level security officer beamed with embarrassment. "I...appreciate that, Mr. Movell. But I...don't have that high of a rank. I'm just a Security Officer."

"However, you exude qualities of leadership. I am certain the next time I visit; you will have achieved a higher ranking." Movell hid his smile, knowing his compliments were winning over the gullible young man.

The guard wiped the silly grin off his face as he followed Movell to the elevator and pulled Damian along with him. "You...ah...finding your way around town ok, Mr. Movell? If not, I could take you on a personal tour. I get off at seven. You let me know, ok?"

"An offer I would greatly consider had I not already made plans." Pushing the button for the second level of the parking garage, Movell exchanged a slight smile with the guard. He purposely avoided making eye contact with Damian.

"You...ah...want me to come with you, Mr. Movell? I mean...transporting a prisoner by yourself...doesn't sound too safe, if you know what I mean."

"I never said I would be alone. Thank you for your offer." Movell was quite aware a camera was monitoring his every move, mounted inconspicuously in one of the ceiling panels. He needed to remain calm, show no emotion, and most importantly not make any gestures which would later be construed as some type of signal.

As the bell rang indicating they had reached their destination, the doors opened on cue and they stepped outside. Blustery, cool air drew their attention to scattered leaves swirling upward, imitating a mini tornado. There was no escaping the ever present abundance and annoyance of leaves and other debris collecting in parking garages, and in many other crevices within the city.

Movell disregarded the crunching noise his feet made walking in his usual, determined stride over several clusters of dried leaves. His demeanor rarely changed; projecting confidence and quiet resolve. Qualities he had mastered to mask his true intentions. He certainly didn't want the security guard returning to his post, and notifying Briggs of any improprieties.

"Sir, where is your car?" The guard asked, still holding onto Damian's left arm.

"Over here." Unit Chief Raymond Konecki stepped out from behind a black Chrysler 300 sedan. "Thank you, Officer Davis. We'll take it from here."

The guard let go of Damian's arm abruptly. He took a step backwards, unsure if he needed to salute. Unit Chief Konecki was very high up in the ranks, many pay grades above his own. He had no reason at all to question his authority. "Yes, sir. I'll return…to my…post now unless…you'll be needing…anything else?" He didn't mean to stutter, but being in Konecki's company made him entirely too nervous.

"No, Officer, that won't be necessary. Mr. Movell and I will take it from here. We appreciate your offer." With a wave of his hand, Konecki dismissed the guard. Withdrawing a small key from his jacket pocket, he unlocked the cuffs restraining Damian's wrists. "Get in the backseat," he said in a low voice. Nodding to Movell to join him in the front seat, Konecki got behind the steering wheel, trying to hide his grin.

When Movell had first called him and explained his plan to rescue Damian Pierce from FBI custody, Konecki had almost doubled over in laughter, telling Movell he had several screws loose. He had tried to talk Movell out of such a foolish notion, telling him he was an idiot to mess with Elias Briggs, but Movell wouldn't take no for an answer. As Konecki reversed the car, and drove it slowly past the elevator, he noticed the guard had his cell phone up to his ear.

That could mean only one thing.

*****

"Stop here." Movell pointed to a parking space in the far right corner of Garage Level Three. All three men scrambled to the commercial freight elevator used primarily by the custodial staff and repair technicians. It was the only elevator not monitored on a continuous basis by the security department. Keys were needed to access the elevator, registering the user's identity in a separate database than the mainframe. According to security personnel Movell had interviewed as part of his liaison research project, the logs were reviewed nightly by the crew who had the misfortune of drawing the short straws for the graveyard shift. Log review was more of an insult than anything, and the least favorite job task of any of the guards. Needless to say, it had the lowest priority, and Movell was betting on that theory, giving him more than sufficient lead time.

Three large, metal containers on wheels had been pushed to the back of the elevator. Movell nodded to Damian and Konecki to get inside while he did the same. Banging on the side of the elevator, he didn't flinch when three men dressed in Harris Heating, Ventilation and Air-Conditioning overalls stepped inside the elevator without saying any words. Movell hadn't quite closed the door panel before one of Tumi's team pushed the button for the boiler room.

In quiet succession, the metal storage units were pushed one by one into the small confines of the boiler room located on the first level just behind the lobby. No one looked their way, obviously distracted by the chaos ensuing at the front of the building where Elias Briggs was barking orders. The men in the HVAC uniforms moved swiftly, closing and locking the door behind them.

Movell was the first to emerge, and he took the time to shake hands with all three men who had aided in their escape. Peeling off their overalls, they handed them to Movell, Damian and Konecki, who put them on as quickly as possible over their own clothes. Hats bearing the Harris HVAC logo, and sunglasses were produced from a storage bin on an overhead ledge. Within minutes, they exited the back door, climbed into the back of a truck bearing the same name of the heating and air servicing company.

Two of Tumi's team were already wearing buttoned-up shirts with the same emblem on the pocket. They moved to the front cab, and turned on the engine, pulling slowly into traffic. The third man stayed behind to wipe down the metal storage units, eradicating fingerprints or DNA. Once he was done, he would simply walk out the back door with the multitude of other federal employees at the standard lunch hour at noon.

Hearing two sets of three knocks coming from the front panel, Movell relaxed his shoulders. "We're clear. We can drop you a few streets over, if you like, Raymond. There's no need for you...to implicate yourself any further."

Konecki held onto an overhead strap to keep himself from falling off the small bench not meant for a man his size. He wondered how Damian and Movell were able to keep from sliding sideways. "I don't mind driving with you, Thomas. I haven't had this much fun in a long time. Makes me see how easy it is to break out of FBI custody. I might want to recommend that further measures be taken to augment our security detail. You're putting us to shame. I'm sure you're aware of that." He laughed slightly.

"It was not my intention, I assure you. I merely observed, took notice of opportunities, and used them to our advantage. Damian was being held without formal charges; he should have been released several hours ago. I...facilitated the matter; that's all."

"My apologies, Pierce." Konecki reached over to shake Damian's hand. "No hard feelings. I had no idea Briggs was...depriving you of your freedom without abiding by the necessary protocols. He's always such a stickler for that. Perhaps he was allowing his personal feelings to get in the way. I'd offer to reprimand him for that, but as you can see, that would bring up my involvement in Movell's little scheme. Don't think I'm ready to jump into the lion's den just yet. You understand?"

Damian nodded without saying a word. He had been coached by Movell to play along with whatever Konecki was saying, letting it roll off his back. Movell had his own suspicions of Konecki, and when he agreed to help Damian escape, he knew they were justified. Konecki couldn't be trusted and needed to be kept on a short string.

Movell tapped Konecki's foot with the side of his shoe to divert his attention. "When we stop to change trucks, it would be advisable for you to depart, Raymond."

"No argument from me, Thomas. You're calling the shots here. Besides, I may be called upon to clean up the mess Briggs has most likely gotten himself into. He allowed a prisoner to just disappear on his watch. Have to admit, it might bring him down a notch or two on the ego-meter. Something that should have been done years ago. Anyway, I would imagine I'll have my work cut out for me. The sooner I get back, the better."

"Very well." Movell hit a couple of keys on his cell and brought it up to his ear. "How much longer until we exchange vehicles? I see. Thank you." He turned to Konecki. "We'll be stopping in ten minutes."

Konecki took another look at Damian who was purposely avoiding eye-contact. He wondered why but didn't let on to Movell how much it bothered him. Pierce was holding back, refusing to talk. Probably on Movell's direct orders. He made a mental note for future reference.

As the truck slowed to a stop, Movell, Pierce and Konecki got to their feet. The back panel door opened and they hopped out finding themselves inside a huge warehouse containing rows and rows of identical Harris HVAC trucks, the largest supplier of heating and air units in the metro-area as well as the neighboring states of Maryland and Virginia.

Konecki stood with his hands on his hips as a black Chrysler 300 pulled alongside of him. It wasn't his own private vehicle. He noticed immediately it didn't have the keypad locking system on the passenger door. This was merely an imposter, another way Movell had camouflaged the escape.

"This is where we part ways." Movell extended his hand. "I may not see you again for quite some time, Raymond. As always, you remain in my thoughts. Stay well."

Konecki clapped Movell on the back. "And you, Thomas. Stay...safe." He would have uttered a few parting words for Pierce but Konecki assumed he was already being loaded into a waiting truck for the next leg of their journey.

As he watched Movell walk down the first row of trucks, Konecki got inside the waiting car. Assuming his driver was one of Tumi Carile's men, he didn't make the mistake of dialing his cell. There was no need.

He had already made the necessary plans.

Movell wasn't the only one with secret agendas.

*****

"Are you still getting the tracking signal, Kliric?" The Closer asked for the third time. "Please tell me you know how to follow the little red dot on the screen."

"Yes. Red dot. I see it. It's moving. I follow red dot."

The Closer huffed loudly. Mason Hamilton's inept side-kick was driving him crazy as usual. No matter how many times he tried to convince Hamilton that Kliric was better off dead, the argument was stifled mid-stream.

"Good, Kliric. You keep following the red dot until you find the girl. Then you find the treasure pieces. Just think how happy Mason will be if you are successful in returning the last three treasure pieces to him." The Closer was on the verge of losing his temper.

"Yes. Good to keep Mason happy."

"That's right, Kliric. That's what you're aiming for...keeping Mason happy. Oh, and Kliric, Mason could care less what happens to Jenna Reed after you take the treasure pieces from her. She's all yours."

The Closer held his cell away from his ear. Hearing Kliric make disgusting slurs in Russian was more than he could take. He had to get off the phone. He had other more pressing matters demanding his attention. Babysitting Mason's watchdog and reviewing his assignments were a complete waste of his time and efforts. "I want you to call me, Kliric, the moment you have the treasure pieces in your hand. You understand?"

"Yes." Kliric resented the implication. The Closer treated him like a child at times. Repeating sentences, raising his voice, deepening his tone. He could take directions. He could obey. The Closer should not be treating him this way.

"Glad to hear we've come to an understanding." The Closer ended the call, tossing his cell phone on the bed in Malcolm's guest room. Glancing down at his watch, he swore loudly.

Practically the whole day had been screwed.

First the unavoidable drama with Mallory, then her hasty departure. Malcolm's unexplained disappearance. Now all this stupid banter with Kliric.

He didn't need all these complications. Mallory should have stayed in New York, keeping an eye on Hamilton. Malcolm should have answered his cell phone on the second ring. And Hamilton shouldn't have put Kliric on a job he couldn't handle.

The Closer checked Malcolm's cabinets for something stronger than beer. Either Malcolm was holding out on him, or he actually drank as cheaply as he lived.

"All you have to do is ask." Malcolm dropped his car keys on the kitchen table and stripped out of his jacket.

"Where have you been for the past two hours? I've been trying to call you. Mallory took off, and I have no idea how to find her."

"First of all, my phone died. Thought my back-up battery was in the van's console, but it wasn't. Secondly, I went for a drive to check out some escape routes. Don't like taking the same roads all the time. Never know when the painting vans might be caught on camera or the locals start getting curious. As to Mallory...why is that my business? If you can't keep your woman in line, that's your problem. Have you tried calling her, or are you waiting until she calms down and calls you? You two are quite a pair. Neither of you want to budge."

"Just what is that supposed to mean?"

Malcolm shrugged. "Never mind." He changed the subject. "What about a tracking device? Don't you have Mallory's phone tapped?"

"No."

Malcolm leaned against the kitchen counter, totally amazed. "You're kidding me, right? You keep preaching to me all the time about putting trackers on the phones of my guys, and you have the nerve to stand there and tell me you're not tracking your girlfriend. I think I've heard it all now."

"I don't have any reasons not to trust her. Mallory has been very loyal to me. This is...just a misunderstanding. Once she comes back, I'll smooth things over. It's just annoying; that's all. I don't like to fight with her. Somehow I always feel like I'm on the losing side." David took the beer Malcolm offered him.

"Did she take her luggage?" Malcolm asked.

"No."

"She'll be back for sure. No woman leaves her luggage behind."

"How are you so well-versed with the female perspective when you never seem to have a girlfriend?" David took a long drink, waiting for Malcolm's answer.

"Grew up with five sisters. I paid attention. As to female companionship, well, I..."

"I really don't want to know." David tossed his beer bottle in the trash.

"Maybe you need to pay attention. Mallory is..."

"I don't pay you to lecture me, Malcolm. Just do your job and we'll get along just fine." The Closer kicked the chair in front of him out of anger, toppling it over.

"If you break my furniture, I'm adding it to my bill."

"If I break your neck, you won't need furniture." The Closer stormed out of the kitchen, taking the hallway to the left. It led to the storage room where Markus was sitting outside reading a magazine.

Anticipating The Closer's question, Markus looked up. "He sleeps now."

"Good. Get some rest yourself; he's not going anywhere. We move out tonight. You take out the bodyguards; I'll get Renault. Garrett might be useful. Take him with you."

Markus bowed.

"I'm relying on you, Markus, once again."

"My pleasure. You will be happy to hear it was very easy to install the camera in Jenna Reed's bedroom. Everyone was out of the house; it took me only minutes. I'm assuming it provided the...results you were hoping for?"

The Closer drummed his fingers against the doorjamb. Remembering Mallory's heated accusations, he downplayed the whole ordeal. "I haven't seen it yet. You did keep a copy?"

Markus shook his massive head. "No. I did as you told me to do. I uploaded the file to your email address, then I promptly deleted it from the camera's memory card and the file history on my laptop. No evidence remains here. Isn't that what you wanted?"

"Yes, Markus. What about the tracer?"

"I placed it inside Jenna's watch. She will never know it's there. She leaves her watch on the dining room table every night along with her keys. Another easy task."

"Glad to hear it, Markus." The Closer clapped him on the back. "This is just the beginning of a long, mutually-beneficial partnership. I don't take good people for granted."

"Really?" Malcolm walked behind The Closer and gave him a slight nudge.

"Don't start, Malcolm."

Chapter 29

"Sis, I'm glad you're here." Austin hugged Jenna until both of their faces were wet with tears. "I can't lose her, Jenna. I just can't."

"I know, Austin. It's hard sitting here and doing nothing. We have to…" Jenna lost her train of thought as Austin closed his eyes in defeat.

At the hospital, the loneliness had sent Austin into a deep depression. Even the presence of his sister couldn't lift his spirits. He had no interest whatsoever in looking at TV, reading magazines, or eating. He wanted Kelly, and nothing else would do.

Jenna rubbed Austin's shoulder until he opened his eyes again. "They'll find her, Austin. Jacoby is good at what he does; we have the best of the best searching for her. You can't give up hope."

"I finally…" Austin's voice choked. "I finally found someone who loves me back, Jenna. Kelly's perfect…in my eyes. She's so good to me. I just can't bear the thought of…oh, God, I can't even say it."

Austin's eyes fell to his lap, and Jenna felt like she was on the verge of crying again. She had never seen her brother so despondent. She had no idea how to cheer him up.

She could barely form words of her own. Maybe a change of scenery would do them both good. "Why don't we go for a walk? Come on. It will give us something to do instead of just sitting in here and moaning."

Austin begrudgingly swung his legs over the side of the bed. He leaned against Jenna as she wrapped her arm around his waist. "Sis, not so tight." Austin winced as Jenna relaxed her hold. "I'm sorry. It's just that the stitches keep pulling, and the nurses are stingy with the pain meds."

"Did it ever occur to you they might be trying to wean you off of them? Codeine can be additive, Austin. They're doing their best to help you transition to something a little less strong. Cut them some slack. I hope you haven't been rude to them. The staff here seems extremely nice and attentive."

"I'm sure I haven't been the best patient," Austin grumbled as he allowed Jenna to lead him out of his room.

One of the nurses immediately looked up from her desktop and shot Austin a wary look. "Good to see he's up and about," the nurse chimed as they shuffled past.

"I'll take good care of him," Jenna called over her shoulder. "He won't get too far without me."

"Truth is...I've *never* gotten far without you." Austin stopped in his tracks to look Jenna in the eyes. "You've always been here for me. Thanks for that."

"You're welcome." Jenna got silent. She was withdrawing, unable to find the right words.

"You're not telling me something," Austin announced as he slowed to another stop. "I don't think it has anything to do with Kelly. Something else is bothering you. I can tell. Why won't you tell me what's going on? Sis, you're here for me. I want to be here for you."

Jenna's arm slipped from Austin's waist and she reached for his hand. Leading him to the small lounge right before the elevator bank, she waited until he had taken a chair. "I don't even know where to begin, Austin, and you have so much on your mind right now. I don't need to burden you...with something else."

"You made a promise to me...at Mom and Dad's funeral that you would always stand by me in good times...and not-so-good times. I promised to do the same. Remember?"

Jenna blinked back tears as she looked out the window at the darkening skies. "Yes, of course I remember. But, Austin, I just don't know how to..."

"It's about Chase, isn't it?" Austin made an attempt at guessing. "He's not here with you. Something's happened...or he'd be by your side. Chase loves you, Jenna. Don't ask me how I know that, but I do. He's crazy about you. I saw it the first time you were together."

Small droplets of rain started to dampen the windows, making Jenna wonder if a storm cloud had been following her for the past several months. It never ceased to amaze her how the weather matched her current mood. Soon there would be a downpour, and the floodgates of her resolve would break. Austin would have to be the one comforting her, not the other way around.

"Chase...isn't himself. He's...changed."

Austin could see his sister shaking where she stood. "What do you mean? How has Chase changed? You're not talking about the drugs again, are you?"

Jenna's silence and avoidance of his eyes gave Austin his answer.

"He...hurt you, didn't he? Worse...this time?" Austin asked as his words stuck in his throat. "You don't have to tell me if it's too painful for you. Just come over here."

Austin held out his hand and Jenna readily took it. She fell to her knees and laid her head against his knee. Sobbing, she could hardly feel his hand stroking her back. She was too lost to feel anything. The same numbness that had overshadowed her when Chase had left her was returning to haunt her again. She couldn't move.

"I'm sorry I brought back sad memories. I shouldn't have pushed you. You're going to be ok, Jenna."

I don't know that I'll ever be ok. Something inside me has changed.

Jenna stared into space, continuing to tune out Austin's words of reassurance. As the rain pounded the windows, Jenna found herself wanting to punch something as well. To take her anger and frustration to a physical manifestation. Destroying something just for the hell of it. Lashing out...with no reservations.

Just once, Jenna thought. *It would feel good.*

"Jenna?" Austin's voice penetrated her trance, getting her attention. "Don't zone out on me. I need you."

"I'm right here, Austin." Wiping her tears on Austin's pant leg, Jenna lifted her head and tried to smile. "I'm not going anywhere. I just needed a few minutes." Getting to her feet, she dusted off her jeans. "I'm...not ready to talk about it yet. It hurts too much. Come on," she said, changing the subject. "Let's walk some more. Maybe it will take my mind off some things I don't need to dwell on right now."

As soon as she started to pull Austin to his feet, her cell buzzed in her jacket pocket. She didn't recognize the number. Debating whether to answer or not, she finally gave in. "Hello?"

"My God, Jenna! Are you alright? It's Ann."

Relief washed over Jenna's face. "I'm ok, Ann. Is Maria on your case because you're not here with me? I'm fine, really."

"Well, you're not going to be if you don't listen to me very carefully. Is Austin with you? Are you in his room?"

Jenna's face tensed. "Yes. No. I mean, we're taking a walk down the hall. What's going on?"

"Get Austin and find a place to hide. Now, Jenna! Kliric is walking in the front door!"

*****

Markus had no idea where Malcolm was going. He had been driving for the past twenty minutes heading towards the Villas, not far from the Cape May-Lewes Ferry. He had circled back; sat in the McDonald's parking lot for another ten minutes talking on his phone, then took his time driving past the strip mall. Either Malcolm had figured out he was being tailed or he was just driving around killing time.

Based on Malcolm's shady reputation, Markus felt certain Malcolm was purposely driving in circles.

"He's on Bayshore Road now," Markus reported to The Closer through his speakerphone. "He must know I'm following him. What do you want me to do?"

The Closer huffed loudly, causing static to transmit over Markus' car speaker. "Keep on him. I don't care what he thinks. He needs to explain himself. He's got plenty to do, and shouldn't be wasting his time and mine taking a joyride. Besides, I'm very interested in hearing more about his apparent interest in my woman."

Markus remained silent. He had no intention of touching that subject. Mallory Kincaid was beautiful; there was no doubt about that. The Closer was right; Malcolm had crossed the line if he was coveting the boss' woman. Any intelligent man could see that.

"Call me back if he doesn't head back to town in the next half hour."

"As you wish." Markus hit the end call button on his phone. Malcolm was playing with fire if he dared to make his desires known. The Closer, of all people, wasn't someone to have on your bad side. As Malcolm ran the next traffic light, Markus hesitated to follow. He certainly didn't need to get a ticket, and he was quite sure out-of-state cars were monitored more so than the locals. He waited his turn, then when the light turned green, he crossed the intersection, keeping his eyes peeled. Sure enough, Malcolm's car hadn't gotten too far. The next light hadn't cycled fast enough and he was caught behind a slower driver.

Markus grinned, keeping a steady eye on Malcolm's car even though he was two positions back. It might be better to have one car as a buffer, keeping a wider distance so Malcolm would be distracted. It was a good plan.

Malcolm was staying within the speed limit as Markus watched from a distance. When Malcolm turned onto Route 9, he made a hasty left turn into a residential development. Two blocks ahead, Malcolm made another sharp turn without a turn-signal. By the time Markus approached the same intersection, Malcolm's car was nowhere to be seen.

Markus idled the engine at the end of the street, deciding whether to go left or right at the dead-end. He chose left only because he had read an article about crowds having the tendency to go right at amusement parks when they first opened. It bore no relevance at all to his current situation, but logically, it justified his move.

Abruptly, he realized why the majority of people turned right. The left turn took him to a dead-end at the back of the development. Hurriedly, Markus reversed to retrace his steps. Once he had turned the car around, he sped along at a good clip. He was flying by houses on either side of the road, trying to check their driveways for Malcolm's van. He would have missed it altogether, had it not been for The Closer buzzing his phone. Slowing the car to a stop along the curb, Markus caught a glimpse of the back of the van parked in a garage with the door half-way shut.

Markus backed up slowly until he was several houses away, fearful that Malcolm would recognize his silver Ford Expedition. When he had reversed all the way to the intersection, Markus pulled around the corner. His phone was buzzing again. "Sorry I did not answer the first time. I was moving the car."

"Did you find him?"

"Yes." Markus switched the phone to speaker then grabbed binoculars from the back seat. "He pulled into a garage at a house I do not know. Perhaps one of his crew lives here? I'm just off of Route 9. Not far from the Marina. I will text you the address."

"Unless he's hired someone else, none of his men live up that way. They're all locals living in town. Not far from Malcolm's house. I have no idea what he's doing up there."

"Maybe he's visiting a woman."

"The way he was looking at Mallory, he probably needs a woman right now. Sit tight. I'm on my way."

Markus focused the binoculars on the front door of the brick rancher with the detached garage. He wondered why the garage door hadn't been closed all the way. Maybe it was stuck, or maybe Malcolm had wanted him to find the van. Maybe this was a set-up, and Markus knew better than to venture off on his own. If The Closer wanted to barge right in on Malcolm, then that was his choice...or mistake to make.

Markus scanned the front of the house for any movement along the front windows. Drapes had been hung on either side and thin sheers muted his ability to look directly into the house. No lights had been turned on unless they were in the back of the house.

It was apparent the owner took no pride in the upkeep. The lawn was definitely in need of a good cut, the honeysuckle bushes on either side of the steps were overgrown, and a garden hose was sprawled across the walkway. If anyone lived there, they were either lazy or hadn't been around for a while.

Markus ran through possible scenarios in his head. *Was this Malcolm's secret hideaway that even The Closer wasn't privy to? Or was Malcolm meeting with someone who had a different agenda? Maybe Malcolm had a side business just in case The Closer got tired of their arrangement?*

All of the reasons were plausible. Malcolm was always a little secretive, purposely leaving out details Markus thought he needed to know. Malcolm obviously didn't trust The Closer's newest associate, but Markus was fine with that.

He didn't trust Malcolm either.

*****

"I'm on my way to you, Jenna! Hide some-where...anywhere, just get out of sight! Back-up is on the way and I've called hospital security. Don't take any chances. Go, now, Jenna!"

Ann's words were still echoing in her ear as Jenna pulled Austin into the nearest family bathroom and locked the door behind them. She put her finger to her lips to silence his protests.

"What is going on? Who was on the phone? Why do you look so scared?" Austin was whispering questions faster than Jenna could answer them.

She tugged on Austin's hand, keeping him as far away from the door as possible. "We're being followed. Kliric is here. How he found me, I have no idea. But he's here, and we have to find a way to outsmart him until help arrives."

"Jacoby?"

"No. Ann Bailey. She's with the CIA, and...believe it or not, she's my bodyguard. Maria thought it was a good idea," Jenna added. Maybe if she had heeded Maria's warnings and not taken off without Ann, she wouldn't be in danger now. "Anyway, Ann has tracked Kliric here. She may have just saved our lives by giving us the heads-up."

Austin rested against the wall, never taking his eyes off of Jenna's face. "This all goes back to that letter, doesn't it? I told you to leave it alone, but you never listened to me. Now, we're all still paying the price for it. I know you think you're doing the right thing keeping these treasure pieces hidden, but Jenna, enough is enough. Think about what you're doing...please. Is it worth our lives?"

"Austin, please don't ask me that now. I can't possibly give you the answer you want to hear. Too much has happened in the past couple of days. You don't know the half of it. Yes, you're right. This all started with the letter I found at the beach house, and yes, we're all still dealing with the aftermath. I'm incredibly sorry for that."

Tense silence drifted between them.

"Sis, what else happened?"

Jenna cleared her throat before continuing. "I called Lenny Lex...and asked him to get me a gun." She paused when Austin's eyes popped. "Then I asked him to take me to New York. I had this crazy notion to take the rest of the treasure pieces to Hamilton.

To bargain with him somehow to leave us alone. Lenny drove me to Philly, took me to O'Clarian's and tried to talk me out of it. When I kept pushing him, he finally agreed to take me to the airport where one of his buddies stored his helicopter. Lenny promised to stick by me when I faced Hamilton. I think something happened to him...and I blame Kliric for that. While I was inside the airport using the restroom and trying to get some coffee, Lenny waited for me in the parking area. I swore I saw Kliric walking through the airport lobby, but at the time I thought it was just my imagination running wild. So just to make sure I wasn't totally insane, I ran out to check on Lenny. His car was gone. I called Jacoby, and he told me you were here. He arranged for a chopper shuttle. I think...Kliric got to Lenny."

"What are you saying, Jenna? Are you telling me Lenny Lex is dead?" Austin's words caught in his throat.

Jenna looked away. If Lenny hadn't survived Kliric's attack, then he was another casualty for which she was indirectly responsible.

All because of the letter and the treasure pieces...

Her vision blurred. "We don't...know that for sure, Austin. But there's something else you need to know about Lenny, and I hope this doesn't change your opinion of him." Jenna took a deep breath. "He was working for Maria. All this time, and for as long as you've known him, Lenny was an undercover agent assigned to keep an eye on you when you moved to Philly. Maria had promised Mom she would always keep a watchful eye on us. I'm not sure who else was watching us from the day we were born, and at this point, I don't care. It can't help but make me paranoid about everyone I've ever known."

Austin was awe-struck, trying to comprehend everything Jenna was saying at one time. "Lenny? My best friend from Philly was an undercover agent? Well, he was very good at his job. I never knew, Jenna. Looking back, I probably could remember some times when Lenny seemed to have all the answers, and I just took them for granted. This is unbelievable."

Jenna closed the space between them. "My life has been unbelievable, Austin, ever since the beginning of summer. In more ways than one." Her phone vibrated with a text. "Ann's here. She just got to the lobby." Jenna sent a reply giving Ann their location. "She'll scan the first floor, but we need to keep moving. Let's go." Jenna grabbed Austin's hand and gave it a reassuring squeeze.

Opening the door just a crack, Jenna stuck her head out slowly. Kliric was nowhere in sight but she didn't take that fact for granted. Before she made the decision to head for the stairwell, Ann buzzed her again.

Stay where you are. I'll come to you.

Jenna turned the lock, and took a step backwards, bumping into Austin. "Ann wants us to stay put. She's on her way."

"Can you trust her, Jenna?"

"As much as I can trust anyone at this point, Austin. I see no reason not to trust Ann. I've become very cynical when it comes to the trust factor. I've been burned too many times."

Austin saw the torment in Jenna's eyes. "It amazes me that you haven't gone off the deep end by now."

"Believe me, I'm getting close."

A light knock and the toggle of the doorknob made both of them jump.

"It's me, Jenna," Ann called from outside the door. "Open the door."

Jenna met Austin's eyes then grabbed his hand, opening the door with her other one. Ann greeted them with a nod as Jenna focused on the gun Ann was carrying. Her heart skipped a beat. "What do you want us to do?"

Ann motioned Jenna and Austin to follow her to the stairwell, trying to keep her gun as close to her right leg as possible. Even though it wasn't concealed, she hoped the hospital staff had received their silent text alerts telling them not to react when she passed by. All she needed was Kliric getting wind that he was being tracked, and he could figure out her location. "I just came up the stairs from the lobby," she said in a low tone. "So unless Kliric doubled back, we should be ok."

As soon as they had entered the stairwell, Austin stopped them at the landing. "I'm just slowing the two of you down. Get out of here while you can."

"Austin, stop being…," Jenna started to say.

"Austin, we're not leaving you," Ann interrupted. "I'm Ann Bailey, by the way. I'm sure Jenna has told you about me. Hopefully, not all of it is bad." Ann shot a half-smile in Jenna's direction. "Let's go down one level. Minor surgery wing. There should be more opportunities for hiding places besides these open-air environments on the patient floors."

"That might be a problem," Jenna added, catching Ann's attention. Her eyes were drawn to Austin's pant leg. He was bleeding badly. The overexertion must have torn his stitches.

"No problems, only solutions," Ann said with as much confidence as she could muster. She couldn't let Jenna and Austin see the true picture, or they'd be too frightened to move at all.

Kliric had the upper hand...and he was coming for all of them.

Chapter 30

Logan suddenly veered right onto an umarked intersecting road. He was nearing the outskirts of Ogdensburg, and it was time to get off the main highway. If there were roadblocks set up, Logan was sure the FBI would be monitoring the three major interchanges leading into the city. He just needed to bypass them, and take an alternate route. He had many choices, and he doubted the FBI or the local police had enough manpower to monitor each and every road, paved or otherwise leading into Ogdensburg.

As long as he planned carefully, Logan was confident he would be able to sneak in unnoticed, as he had done many times before. Under the radar and only at night when visibility was impaired by darkness and even the best trained officers were tired from the monotony of stake out detail. He had come to rely on that theory more than once.

Logan had given up trying to reach his friends by cell. It had to be an omen that something wasn't quite right. Logan could feel it in his bones. The premonition that almost always preceded a mission full of risks and liabilities. He was getting the same vibe now.

A tell-tale sign demanding his full attention. Despite taking every conceivable precaution to minimize the risks of being caught, Logan didn't need a high-tech program to see the writing on the wall. As long as Kelly was in tow, his chances of escaping were severely limited. At first, he had believed they could travel undetected if disguises were clever enough, but the voice of reason kept jabbing him in the side of the head. Any pregnant woman remotely matching Kelly's description would catch someone's eye. Then all eyes would be drawn to her companion.

A scenario too risky to be considered.

Logan looked over his shoulder. Kelly had fallen asleep, or was pretending to be. She knew every mile was taking them closer to a showdown with the federal and local authorities, making her extremely nervous. She could do nothing more than to let it play out, helpless to do anything which might alter her fate.

Without words, Kelly had conveyed her fear, trembling in the back seat until she collapsed from exhaustion.

He was the one holding the key to her survival, and she knew it. She was going to live or die based on a decision he had to make alone.

Logan wished he could turn back time. He would never have stalked Kelly and Austin, intruded into their most private moments, and kidnapped them. He would have refused to do Mason Hamilton's dirty work, and retreated to Europe where he could change identities and hibernate until it was safe to surface again.

Instead, he was being forced to make a critical decision, one based purely on personal stakes with secondary regard for the woman he coveted. Kelly was everything he wanted, and nothing he could have freely. She had made it very clear she was fully committed to Austin, reaffirming Logan's assumption Kelly would never give herself to him. He would have to take her by force, something he promised himself he would never do.

Logan faced forward again. He couldn't look at Kelly and think clearly anymore. She would continue to be a distraction on or off of U.S. soil.

A distraction he couldn't afford.

*****

"Get the chopper ready."

Jacoby dropped the binoculars from his eyes. "Mick, he's figured it out. McHenry's known for anticipating the obvious. He puts himself into the mindset of whoever's tracking him. I don't think he's going to come to us; we'll have to go to him. Take the chopper and span out about three miles. Anything that looks out of the ordinary, I want to know about it."

"You got it." Thompson gave a quick nod, then whirled his hand in the air indicating to the pilot to crank up the engine. His two team leaders fell into cadence alongside of him. All three men ran against the wind holding onto their baseball caps, ducking the overhead current. The noise was deafening at such close range.

They never heard Jacoby's warning before it was too late.

The helicopter jumped several feet off the ground and exploded into a ball of fire, scattering metal particles into the air.

Everyone on the ground, police, fire and rescue teams were brought to their knees in one orchestrated motion. Unit leaders yelled commands, attempting to manage the chaos as best they could. Fire crews hustled to move their engines closer, hoping they had brought enough of a water reserve to at least bring the flames under control before they engulfed the entire dry cornfield. Police sirens wailed to alert bystanders to get back as far as possible as foot patrols formed a human perimeter.

The damage had been done and no one had seen it coming.

"What the hell!" Jacoby yelled from behind the door of the police cruiser he had used for cover. He could hardly see past the smoke and uniformed bodies running back and forth. "Thompson!" Jacoby shouted. His throat and eyes were stinging from the smoke. "Somebody, find Thompson!"

Fighting through the barrage of rescue personnel, Jacoby headed in the direction he had last seen his partner go. Almost colliding with a paramedic, Jacoby stopped in his tracks when he finally saw the clearing.

Mick Thompson and his two team leaders bound for the chopper had taken the brunt of the blast. All three men were now lying on the ground covered in blood and soot. None of them were moving.

Jacoby fell to his knees then grabbed Thompson's hand. "You stay with me, Thompson! That's an order!" He squeezed Thompson's hand as hard as he could, trying to get some type of response. "Don't you dare give up, Mick. I won't let you give up."

"Sir, I'm going to ask you to step aside," the paramedic said authoritatively, dropping his medical bag at Jacoby's feet. "I want to do my best to help your friend, but you need to give me some room."

Jacoby reluctantly got to his feet, nodding in acknowledgment. "What are his chances?"

"I can't answer that, sir. He's breathing and he has a pulse, both of which are good signs. Looks like a fighter to me, so that's also going to work in his favor. Doctors will know better when we get him to ER. The truck's pulling up now. If you'll step aside, we'll get him on the stretcher, and get him help as soon as possible."

"Yes, of course." Jacoby sidestepped the other paramedic hustling over with the stretcher. "He's my partner. Take good care of him."

"You got it," the paramedic replied, never looking up from his patient. Fixing an oxygen mask over Thompson's face, he laid the small canister on top of his chest. "One, two, three...lift."

Both paramedics ran alongside of the stretcher towards their ambulance. Within minutes, they had loaded Thompson on board, shut the doors, and were navigating their way across the cornfield in the direction of the paved roadway. Two other ambulances followed closely behind.

Jacoby stood rigid watching the ambulance convoy fade into the distance. As much as he wanted to ride along with Thompson, Jacoby knew his place was here. "Get me another chopper," he said to the Ogdensburg Chief of Police who had been designated as his local point person. "I don't care who you have to call. I want another chopper here in the next twenty minutes. You got that?"

"Yes, sir!"

As the Chief hurried away in the direction of his cruiser, Jacoby surveyed the damage to the chopper, or what was left of it. Shaking his head, he swore McHenry would pay one day for what he had done. Especially if Thompson didn't survive.

The explosion was nothing more than a diversion, and a good one at that. Jacoby and his multi-jurisdictional team never saw it coming. In all probability, McHenry was probably well over the Canadian border by now with Kelly McBride in tow.

If she was still alive.

Another casualty Jacoby would hold over McHenry's head until he had the chance to blow it off.

*****

"Good work. Ben should have the extra time he needs now to change course. Keep in touch, Langston."

David Caldwell glanced over in Markus' direction after he tossed his cell on the dashboard. Just minutes earlier, he had pulled up behind Markus' Expedition and joined him in the front seat. "I'm sorry, Markus. I didn't mean to ignore you. Had to check in with one of my pilots. He took care of a little diversion for me close to the Canadian border. Seems my son was driving straight towards an ambush...and I had to pull some strings to get the matter...eradicated." Caldwell's lips edged into a smile.

"Then your son should be very grateful."

Caldwell laughed. "Ben doesn't believe in gratitude. At least when it involves me. We're on opposite ends of the spectrum, so to speak. Doesn't want to take my advice. Wants to figure things out on his own which isn't a bad thing as long as he makes the right decisions and isn't compromised. But when he's distracted by a beautiful woman, he doesn't think straight."

Markus nodded. "Perhaps it is the way you give advice that causes him to...keep his distance. Do you not agree?"

"I'm sure you're right about that, Markus. My son and I have never communicated well. Guess that's a flaw in both of our personalities, or in his case, an inherited one." Noticing a light had just been turned on in the front room of the house, Caldwell took the binoculars from Markus and focused. It was still too hard to determine if Malcolm was the shape appearing behind the curtains. "What do you make of that, Markus? Do you think Malcolm knows we're watching him?"

"I am not sure. I have not seen anyone peer out the windows and look in our direction. This is the first time a light has appeared through the windows. Are you ready to confront him?" Markus reached for his gun stuffed under his seat.

Caldwell rubbed his chin, considering what to do. Except for his own distorted theory of Malcolm's mysterious behavior, he had no just cause to burst into someone's house, accuse Malcolm of wrongdoing, and end up making an ass out of himself. Then again, if Malcolm was doing something behind his back, he was perfectly justified in finding out what was going on. Checking his watch, he cursed silently. Waiting for Malcolm to make a move could take all night. He didn't have the luxury to waste time and neither did Markus. Within a couple of hours, Markus and the clean-up crew were heading to Renault's hotel.

"Go back to the house, Markus, and get some rest. Make sure Garrett is pumped up and ready to go. You know what to do. I'll stay here for a little while longer. I might call Malcolm to check in and see what he says. Based on his answer, I'll decide what to do."

Caldwell slowly exited the SUV, taking the binoculars with him. Returning to his Volvo, he immediately regretted not switching cars with Markus. The sedan's leather seats were extremely comfortable but sitting lower didn't give him the same vantage point. Forced to lean over the console and turn his head sideways, Caldwell grumbled. This whole situation could have been avoided if Malcolm was a little more forthcoming about his mysterious absences.

Such a waste of time.

Spying on Malcolm was taking too much effort. He had better things to do than sit in a car and debate the loyalty of his employees. Caldwell checked his watch then picked up the binoculars again. One more sweep of the property and then he'd have to decide to pack it in, or make a move.

Zooming to the maximum level, Caldwell scanned the front of the house, steps, lawn and driveway leading to the detached garage. At first he had been surprised to see the garage door partially shut, but dismissed the notion Malcolm had done it on purpose to hide the painting van. He had mentioned on several occasions, he kept the vans out of sight whenever possible; not wanting the locals to think it was an actual *painting* business.

Turning his focus towards the driveway, Caldwell almost lost his grip on the binoculars. Lying in the driveway not far from the van's tires was a small object shining reflectively into the lens.

Mallory's diamond bracelet. A gift he had given her when she had returned home from Venice just weeks ago. She had never taken it off...until now.

Malcolm had brought Mallory here against her will...or she had come of her own accord. He had to find out...*now.*

Caldwell got out of his car to survey his best point of entry. Circling around the back of the house seemed like a better solution, unless of course any of the neighbors had dogs in their back yards. It was worth a shot regardless. Even dogs could be quieted with a tranquilizer dart.

Caldwell pulled up on the backseat cushion to reveal an access panel to the trunk. Primarily designed to allow space for longer pieces of cargo, the small hidden compartment also provided a prime hiding spot for his weapons.

Withdrawing his favorite hunting knife encased in its sheath, Caldwell strapped it quickly to his right leg. Dressed all in black, as was his customary attire, he grabbed a black baseball cap from the floor of the backseat. Setting his phone to vibrate, he zipped it inside the left pocket of his North Face nylon jacket. In the right pocket, he stuffed a small tranq gun. Finally, he pulled out his second most prized possession, a SIG P226 SCT with a rear night-sight. He was ready for anything or anyone keeping him from finding Mallory.

Circling around towards the common ground between the front and back properties, he made his way towards the back of Malcolm's house, fourth from the corner. No dogs or children in sight. Caldwell breathed a sigh of relief. He could make his presence known at his own choosing using the element of surprise as an added advantage.

Stopping at the corner of Malcolm's garage, Caldwell searched the back of the house for obvious surveillance equipment positioned just under the rain gutters or slightly above the window frames. He saw none. The only light above the back door was a single bulb inside a cheap lantern-style compartment. No motion-sensors and no hidden cameras, at least at first glance. Malcolm had purposely disregarded his advice regarding basic security procedures, or he was too lazy to be bothered.

Idiot. Caldwell chimed silently, as he drew his binoculars up again to peer through a side window into the kitchen. Trying to second guess Malcolm's logic, Caldwell gave up. If his presence was detected another way, then so be it.

Malcolm needed to explain himself.

As he inched closer down the side of the garage, Caldwell stopped suddenly. He bent down to pick up Mallory's bracelet then stuffed it inside his jeans. It took every ounce of willpower to hold back and think strategically.

What is he doing to her?

Did she run to Malcolm to get away from me?

Jealousy pounded Caldwell from all sides. Making his way to the back door, he listened for a few seconds before turning the doorknob. Surprised it wasn't locked, he slipped inside the kitchen. Clicking on the SIG's night scope, he moved slowly to gauge any possible traps or room sensors. Satisfied his presence hadn't immediately been detected, Caldwell pushed forward into the sparsely-furnished living room. Next, he ventured down the hallway which led to two small bedrooms. Checking closets and under beds, Caldwell quickly determined whoever was in the house had gone below.

Muffled sounds drew his attention. Retreating to the kitchen, he stopped briefly at the top of the staircase which led to the lower level. The noises were louder now.

Stuffing the SIG into his back waistband, Caldwell withdrew his knife. Cautiously, he descended the steps one by one, stopping half-way down. Straining his ears, he tried to decipher what was being said behind the closed door at the bottom of the stairs.

"I think you'll look better in the candlelight totally naked," Malcolm quipped as he stroked Mallory's hair. Slowly unzipping the back of her sleeveless dress, his eyes feasted upon the black-and-red striped bra and panties she was wearing. Finally, as the zipper stopped at the lower part of her back, Malcolm sucked in a deep breath. The object of his most heated, unrequited desire was trembling in front of him.

Her arms had been drawn upward and latched together with a leather belt attached to a rope pulley. While still unconscious from the anesthesia Malcolm had given her after she was tricked into getting inside his van, Mallory had been hoisted to a standing position.

Waking to find herself in such a vulnerable position, Mallory had elicited only one terrified scream before Malcolm stuffed a rag in her mouth. A tug on the rope was an additional punishment, pulling her arms higher. Her toes were barely touching the cement floor now.

She was a puppet dangling on a string...and Malcolm was her master. She could do nothing to change her fate. It had been sealed the moment she foolishly accepted a ride from Malcolm two blocks from his house. Too upset with fighting with David, Mallory had never suspected Malcolm would harm her.

She was finding out the hard way.

Malcolm took a step backwards to admire his handiwork. She was his now, and he could do whatever he wanted. He snickered, grateful for once he had pulled one over on David Caldwell. For years he had endured Caldwell's self-righteous, overbearing comments and slurs, making him inferior. Now, he had the upper-hand, taking what he wanted from the woman Caldwell had callously tossed aside.

Still, the momentary bravado Malcolm was enjoying did little to take the edge off of the anxiety building inside him. Glancing nervously at his watch, he expected Caldwell to call any moment and tell him to get the crew ready for the Renault job.

Returning his attention to Mallory, Malcolm slit the thin straps of her dress, and then watched it fall to the floor. He licked his lips, kicking the dress out of his way.

Mallory dangled in front of him, clad only in her underwear. Tantalizing him with her body and the tears streaming down her face.

It took seconds to slice away at her bra straps and toss the remnants aside. Malcolm ran his hands down the sides of her breasts, amazed by the perfect shape of her body. He never wanted to stop touching her. His hands slid lower, stopping at the curve of her waist.

She was exciting him, with every inch of skin he explored. Mallory was the epitome of every woman he had lusted after but dared not approach. She was his from this moment forward even if it meant keeping her a prisoner.

He had needs, and Mallory would satisfy all of them. So mesmerized by her vulnerability, Malcolm continued to caress her body. He was drawing her back against his chest, breathing in her fear. With every whimper, he pressed her closer.

Distracted, Malcolm never heard the noises coming from the stairwell. His heart was beating so fast, he couldn't focus on anything else. Slipping his fingers under the waistband of Mallory's panties, Malcolm closed his eyes.

In the next few minutes, he would make Mallory forget the hurt her former lover had caused. He would erase the name of David Caldwell from her lips and her mind. There would be no reason for Mallory to want anyone else. Malcolm pressed her body backwards more forcefully this time. He couldn't take it anymore.

He had lost the ability to breathe.

Blood dripped down the back of his legs, staining the floor beneath him. Malcolm fell forward on one knee, trying to reach behind him. He knew who had thrust the blade into his back.

David Caldwell stepped in front of Malcolm, nodding first at Mallory. "You disappointed me, Malcolm. You went after the wrong woman. You wanted her from the beginning, didn't you? You were just waiting to make your move. Waiting until I pushed her away. Come to think of it, a back stab is the easy way out."

The moment Malcolm struggled to look Caldwell in the eyes, he knew what was coming next.

Two bullets in quick succession blasted Malcolm in the face and the heart. His body dropped seconds later and went still.

Refusing to waste another moment looking at his latest victim, Caldwell caught Mallory around the waist with one arm. Lifting her as gently as possible, he unlashed the belt freeing her arms. She slipped down his body, too exhausted to hold on.

"Thank you," she whispered when the gag was pulled from her mouth.

Cradling her face in his hands, David exhaled against her forehead. "You're ok, Mallory. I have you and I'm never letting go."

Chapter 31

Laurence Renault sat straight up in bed, suddenly awakened by an overbearing sense of dread. He listened, waited. Grappling on the bedside table, he breathed easier when his fingers clenched around the TAG Heuer Carrera watch with the luminous hands.

A little past two in the morning.

Rarely did he have trouble sleeping, but tonight he had not gone to bed with a restful mind or body. Too many troubling factors were causing internal debates on his conscience. Truth. Lies. Betrayal. Love. Hate. Fear.

Fear. I know so much about fear…and yet so little.

Oh, he had put on a good show for his compatriots, Raul and Jason at dinner, giving them no reason to worry. The FBI could handle Kelly's rescue and all would be well.

A charade masking his own internal fears of hopelessness.

He could do nothing for her; that was certain. Calling a few contacts in Canada would ease his mind, but certainly not increase her odds of survival. Raul and Jason couldn't possibly understand. *How could they?* Neither had children. Neither had to worry excessively about the welfare of another individual they would die to protect.

Raul and Jason were good men nonetheless, Renault assured himself. They were well paid to watch his back, and anticipate any type of dangerous situation. Bodyguards, not family.

Family. Ellen. Kelly. My future grandchild.

Renault dwelt on the meaning of *family* for several minutes. It was all he could do to steady his nerves. To think of something pleasant…*anything* to take his mind off the fear.

Of death…and dying.

An eerie sense of foreboding loomed within the shadows. The heavy tapestry drapes had been drawn tightly against the windows, allowing only small pinnacles of moonlight to sneak through. It wasn't the darkness that scared him. No, he had never been afraid of the dark. It had always been the perfect backdrop for his sinister deeds.

Yet now, the darkness seemed to taunt him in ways he could not explain.

Renault reached for the light next to his bed. Calmness returned slowly to his startled frame. His body was starting to relax again, finding no substantiated reason to react otherwise. He was worrying for nothing. There was no threat. He was perfectly safe.

Raul and Jason had said goodnight to him hours ago. Most likely they were sound asleep in the room on the opposite side of the suite. A common area consisting of a small sitting area, wet bar, and a small refrigerator separated the two bedrooms. Surely if he had the need to call Raul and Jason, they would draw their weapons and come running.

There was simply no conceivable rationale for the goose bumps rising on his arms, or the elevation of his heart rate. None based on logical assumptions anyway.

Just a gut feeling Renault had always trusted. The one true measure he relied upon time and time again. It had never failed him.

Mason had once called it his gift of the *sixth sense*, the uncanny way Renault always could tell well in advance if something wasn't quite right. He could immediately change course to avert disaster. Part of his livelihood. The part which had kept him alive, even when the rest of the world assumed he was dead.

Another charade. Another mask.

The digital clock on the bedside table advanced another hour. Time was drifting by. Minutes of his life escaping to another dimension where so many times he wished he was, holding Ellen once again. She had been taken from this world too soon and he continued to ache for her.

Why had Mason seen the need to snuff out her life after all this time?

Struggling with possible answers and the inability to fall back to sleep, Renault opened his wallet. He had only brought one picture of Ellen with him, and another one of Kelly, taken when she was ten years old. Riding her bike around the circular driveway in front of her home, Kelly seemed relatively happy. She was radiant as a little girl. Her long, blond tresses tied with a pink ribbon to match her short set and the shoelaces on her sneakers. His beautiful daughter, deprived of the love she rightly deserved.

Renault sadly gazed at the worn photograph. He had lost so many years imprisoned by his own identity, and Mason Hamilton's selfishness; he hardly knew how to function as a freed man. How could he possibly introduce himself to his daughter now? Maybe Jonathan Knox was right. Maybe the best gift he could give his daughter was not to complicate her life any more than it already was.

Kelly had suffered enough. If her captor had successfully taken her across the Canadian border, then he was just as relentless as Mason. Renault made a mental note to have Raul find out what was going on in the morning. Too much time had already been wasted. His daughter and his future grandchild's lives were at stake. The FBI had been given too much leeway, and they still hadn't gotten their man.

Renault shifted further down on the pillows. He was going to try to fall asleep again. Perhaps then he could finally drift off with no worries.

After several minutes, he gave up trying.

Fastening the robe around his waist, Renault walked into the common area with only the lamp from his bedroom lighting his way. He took a small carton of milk from the micro-fridge, and a glass from the tray on the nearby table. Sitting on the sofa, he poured the milk slowly into the glass and took a sip. His eyes adjusted to the dimly-lit room then wandered in the direction of the adjacent bedroom.

Renault found it quite odd the door to Raul and Jason's room was half-way closed. Unless they were afraid they wouldn't be able to hear him, he wondered why the door was intentionally left open. Rising to satisfy his own curiosity, Renault made his way to their doorway, then stopped abruptly.

Neither bed was occupied. Raul and Jason had left the suite...leaving him without protection.

Renault tensed, hurrying back to his room. Panic gripped him, making him spin in opposite directions. Fumbling inside his suitcase, his fingers closed around the barrel of his gun. All he had to do was release the safety, point and shoot. Easy enough.

Unless your hands were shaking and you were afraid to die.

*****

Jonathan watched the shadows dance along the windowsill of the upper floor bedroom. He couldn't sleep. Being alone in the Reeds' beach house was quirky enough. One by one, everyone had left, and he didn't know what to do with all his free time. He didn't know anyone else in Cape May, and it seemed foolish to hang around not knowing when everyone would return.

The logical thing to do was go back to New York. Deal with Mason's incessant ramblings about his ineptitude as the heir-apparent at H-K, and become distracted with mounds of paper-work. Anything was better than moping around waiting for news.

Jonathan sat in the dark, attempting to find a reason to stay, but none came to mind. He wasn't needed here.

Pulling his suitcase from under the bed, Jonathan began to pack his clothes. His laptop was still downstairs on the dining room table where he had left it last evening. He'd check the airport schedule over coffee. It was too unnerving sitting around doing nothing. At least in New York, he could put his mind to work or go to the gym.

Packing took exactly five minutes. Stopping at the landing at the top of the stairs, he couldn't help but notice the door to Jenna's room was slightly open. He had to know what happened. Why she had purposely disregarded his comments about the bruises on her body.

As her bed came into view, Jonathan dropped his suitcase at the same time his mouth fell open.

Jenna's room was a mess. The bed covers were twisted. The sheets were torn, and ripped clothes were hanging over her wicker trash can.

Rage pulsated through every limb. He wanted to tear Garrett apart, and for once, revel in giving him the same amount of pain he had already inflicted on Jenna.

"Damn you, Chase Garrett," Jonathan swore as he tore his eyes away from the rumpled bed covers. "Damn you for coming into her life."

Jonathan's heart ached and he felt physically drained. It was too early to be up and moving, yet he couldn't sit still any longer. Especially after what he had just seen.

Forcing himself to leave Jenna's room, he grabbed his suit-case and hurried down the stairs. He would grab some coffee, make a plane reservation then get on the road. Even if he had to sit in the Atlantic City airport for the next several hours, it would be better than being in the same house where Jenna had been attacked.

As he opened his laptop and waited for the Wi-Fi signal to light up, his cell buzzed inside his pocket. Wondering who could be calling him at such a strange hour, he answered, not bothering to check the caller ID. "Hello?"

"Knox, listen to me. I don't have much time."

Jonathan clawed at the phone, fighting the urge to destroy it.

"Are you there, Knox? This is important. I need you to pay attention," Chase Garrett demanded.

"I'm here. What do you want?"

"You, Knox. I want you to meet me at the lighthouse…in one hour. Do you know how to get there?"

This was the opportunity he had been waiting for…a final showdown with Chase Garrett. To make him pay once and for all for the pain and suffering he had caused Jenna.

"One hour, Garrett. I'm looking forward to it."

*****

Leaving Jenna and Austin in the stairwell with her spare gun hadn't been Ann's first choice.

Austin's leg wound severely hampered their mobility. Blood was running down his leg and onto the floor. He was leaving a trail that Ann felt certain Kliric would figure out soon enough. Instead of hiding, Jenna and Austin were now the bait as Ann sought frantically to draw Kliric out, confront him, and take him down.

Holding her gun with both hands in a lowered position, she scanned the floor, sweeping left to right. She had instructed the main desk to alert all nursing units Kliric was armed and extremely dangerous. They were to take no chances, and do their best to protect themselves and their patients. Doors to all rooms were to be closed, and the centralized desk stations were to be vacated.

Three pods down the corridor, Ann stopped in her tracks. Apparently, this wing hadn't received the urgent message. One of the nurses was standing in the middle of the circular desk area holding a clipboard and writing notes. It was as if this section of the building was conducting business as usual, or they were completely defying the order for lock-down.

Ann approached cautiously, and as she got closer, the nurse lifted her head. Her eyes were bloodshot, and the look of panic on her face told Ann everything she needed to know.

Except where Kliric was hiding.

Kliric rammed into Ann with such force, she was almost catapulted in the air. Slamming against the wall of the first patient's room, her gun fell out of her hand. Kliric pressed her head to the wall with one hand, and motioned to the nurse with his other.

"Now," he commanded as the nurse came forward bearing a needle. "Do it now."

The needle punctured her arm despite Ann's attempts to wriggle free of Kliric's hold. She fought hard, twisting her body back and forth as she tried to free her elbow. Angling her shoulder downward, she had almost reached the point of countering Kliric's strong-armed defense.

Even her most practiced Krav Maga moves couldn't help her now. As the drugs seeped into her bloodstream, dizziness took hold. Ann felt her body losing all resistance. Within seconds, she was incapacitated. Nothing more than a rag doll laying on the ground...at Kliric's feet.

She had lost her weapon, and the ability to fight.

Before her eyes closed, her last thoughts were of Jenna, Austin, Maria...and Jonathan.

Kliric spat on the ground next to Ann's body. He wasted no time shoving the nurse aside. When she cowered in a nearby corner, Kliric fought the urge to snap her neck. Mason had told him to get the job done with as little damage as possible. He was to kill no one unless it was unavoidable. Kliric growled, kicking Ann's limp body out of spite.

Removing the tracker out of his pocket, Kliric refocused on his task at hand. Finding Jenna Reed. The signal indicated she was still in the building. Not far.

"Good," Kliric uttered. He was getting closer; he could feel it. Very soon he would have Jenna Reed right where he wanted her, begging for mercy.

Kliric hurried towards the stairwell at the end of the corridor. The signal was getting stronger. His heart was racing as the anticipation grew inside him. Very soon he would be touching her skin again, tracing the lines where his knife had scarred her. Kliric breathed heavily. She was right behind the stairwell's door.

The lion had been led straight to the prey.

With gusto, Kliric tore open the stairwell door.

The stairwell was empty.

Except for a small watch lying on the floor in the corner.

Kliric erupted with Russian obscenities. Jenna Reed had tricked him. She would pay dearly for this deception. With her life. Once he satisfied his perverse sexual desires, he would kill her, making her suffer as much as possible. No one made a fool out of Hans Kliric.

Especially a woman.

Kliric stomped on the watch, then noticed the tracking signal on his remote had vanished. He had no idea where Jenna Reed was hiding, if she was even still in the hospital. He had wasted his time searching for her. It was time to go.

Mason had specifically told him to avoid any contact with the police. If he was caught and interrogated, he was to say nothing. Kliric knew firsthand what happened to people who dared to defy Mason Hamilton. He had no intention of putting himself in that predicament. All he could do now was find a way out of the hospital without drawing any more attention.

Kliric hustled down the stairs, then stopped at the main level. As he scratched his head and debated what to do, Kliric's eyes dropped to the floor. He saw red droplets leading down the staircase and towards the corridor on the left, the Physical Therapy Wing.

Curious, Kliric quickened his pace. He drew his gun, sidestepping the bloody trail. It stopped briefly at the glass door labeled *Aqua Therapy Pod*. Kliric peered inside. The room consisted of three small pools, several benches, and carts piled high with towels. The tiled floor was slick with water. Kliric took his time, maneuvering alongside of the larger pool. The chlorine irritated his nostrils, a smell he had always hated, reminding him of swimming lessons forced upon him as a child.

Making his way to the back of the pool area, he came to the locker rooms. Once again, a reddish trail stained the floor in front of him. Whoever was bleeding had taken refuge here.

Kliric felt his adrenaline building. It wouldn't be long now. He would find her. She was still here. Thinking she was outsmarting him by hiding. Kliric snorted.

He was the one outsmarting her.

Bloody smears led him towards the men's locker room. Approaching with his gun aimed straight ahead, Kliric kept his eyes glued to the floor. This was too easy.

The spots stopped in front of a storage cabinet labeled *SCRUBS AND LINENS.*

Without another thought, Kliric powerfully pulled on the cabinet's handle.

"Get out," he said with a wave of his gun. "Now." His finger anxiously hovered against the trigger.

Austin climbed out slowly as pain radiated from his leg. He wasn't moving fast enough.

Kliric grabbed the front of Austin's robe. Slamming him against the side of the wall, he shoved his gun against Austin's head. "Where is she?" he demanded.

Austin shook his head, too afraid to speak.

"Ten seconds to give answer."

"I...don't know."

"Wrong answer." Kliric smacked Austin against the head with the handle of his gun, drawing blood. "Tell me where she is. Next time I pull trigger."

Austin winced from the pain. "I...really don't know where she is. She left me here, and took off."

Kliric swung Austin around, then rammed his gun against Austin's back. "Then we find her together."

Austin nodded without saying another word. His leg hurt so badly with every motion, but he wasn't about to let Kliric go after Jenna by himself. He pushed on, dragging his throbbing leg. If it was the last thing he did, he had a chance to stall Kliric, giving Jenna enough time to escape.

Austin didn't hesitate. He was quite possibly making the ultimate sacrifice, and for his sister he was willing to do it.

Just as Jenna had done earlier when she had found a place for him to hide...before heading out to face Kliric on her own.

Chapter 32

The gun felt so heavy in her hand.

Jenna had already dropped it twice, and silently cursed her clumsiness. An inherent flaw she just couldn't overcome...especially when her nerves were on fire.

Preoccupied with worrying about Austin's leg; she hadn't paid close attention to Ann's brief instructions. Something about holding the gun steady, expecting a kickback, whatever that was. At best, she remembered to point, shoot, and run.

Wounding Kliric would be the goal, giving her enough time to get away, retrieve Austin, and hopefully make it to the front door when the police arrived. Fatally shooting Kliric was only a last resort. As much as the son-of-the-bitch deserved what he got, Jenna didn't want his death on her conscience. However, if the decision came down to Kliric's life or Austin's...or even her own, Jenna knew she'd have no choice.

She had to find Ann. Either she wasn't picking up her cell because she was too busy tracking Kliric, or he had taken it from her.

Jenna forced herself not to think in those terms. To believe Ann had been overpowered by Kliric would mean she was on her own. A concept she didn't want to entertain, considering her odds of survival.

Taking the elevator, Jenna stepped off with the gun pointing straight ahead. The corridor was empty and a bone-chilling silence greeted her. Kliric had passed by this way; she was sure of it. She felt his presence hanging heavily in the air, making her palms slippery.

Moving cautiously towards the first nursing station, Jenna's attention was drawn immediately to the heel of a shoe protruding from behind the section divider. Rounding the corner, she couldn't believe her eyes.

Ann was on the floor, lying in a contorted position.

Jenna rushed forward. She gasped, falling to her knees next to Ann's body. "Ann! Oh, God...are you ok?" Jenna shook

Ann's shoulder, her eyes searching desperately for any signs of blood.

"She wasn't shot," a meek voice called from behind a partially closed door. The nurse finally emerged, joining Jenna on the floor.

"Are you sure?" Jenna asked.

The nurse nodded, wringing her hands. "He...made me...give her a sedative. That's all. I...gave her the lowest dosage, just to knock her out. Won't last long, I promise. I...was afraid what he would do to her...and me, if she didn't pass out. I...I had no choice."

"I'm not blaming you." Jenna sat back on her heels, as relief washed over her. "Help me get her to a chair. How long before she wakes up?"

"Any time now. But she'll be groggy. Don't know if she'll be able to stand or walk for a while. I...found her gun after he left." The nurse pulled the gun from the pocket of her scrubs, handing it to Jenna. "Are you with the police?"

Jenna nervously laughed. "Hell no. But now I have two guns and I just deputized myself. The man who did this is still out there. I'm sure he's still searching for me. I'll just have to find him first. Please continue to keep an eye on her. When she wakes up, tell her to call Jenna." Jenna pulled Ann's cell out of her pant's pocket and gave it to the nurse. "Don't let me down. You watch her. Got it?"

The nurse nodded, trying to break into a smile.

Taking off in the direction of the elevator, Jenna's thoughts centered on Austin. In the haste of searching for Ann, she had completely forgotten how much his leg was bleeding, and the blood dripping all over the floor.

Her heart pounded inside her chest. Punching the button for the main level, Jenna paced. She had to get Austin, wrap his leg, and somehow move him to another hiding spot.

When the elevator doors split open, Jenna stood frozen with fear.

Kliric stood just a few feet away with his gun pressed against Austin's head. "Leave guns there," Kliric barked, pointing to the floor of the elevator. "Go this way." He motioned for Jenna to head towards the Aqua Therapy room. "Walk fast. Now."

Jenna exchanged a worried look with Austin without saying a word. She was too afraid Kliric would retaliate, shooting Austin just to get back at her.

Once inside the pool area, Kliric shoved her forward. "Locker room," he said. "Go there...now."

Jenna took the doorway to the right into the women's locker area. Kliric hadn't been specific, and at this point, she doubted he cared where he killed both of them.

"Stop." Kliric's voice echoed off the walls. He pushed Austin to the floor inside the first section of lockers, and grabbed Jenna around the throat. "We talk...privately."

Kliric dragged her towards the back area of the lockers, just in front of the shower rooms. Stopping across from the sinks, he let her go. "Give me treasure pieces. Mason wants them."

"All this time, Kliric, I thought what you really wanted was *me.*"

Snarling, Kliric stepped closer. "Treasure pieces first. Then I take what I want. You." His eyes bore down, threatening her.

"Not on your life." Jenna backed herself against a wall. "I'll tell Hamilton where they are; not you."

"You tell *me*...or you die."

Kliric's slap sent Jenna sliding sideways. She shook it off, hoping her head would stop ringing long enough for her to form coherent words. "Hamilton won't be happy; you know that, Kliric. If you kill me, he'll never find the treasure pieces. Take me to him."

"Get up." Kliric started to reach for her arm.

Jenna saw the chance she was waiting for. She sprung up from her sitting position and barreled into his legs. Kliric lost his balance, sending his gun sprawling into the first shower. Jenna got to her feet faster than Kliric could manage, and as he was regaining his stance, she firmly kicked him between the legs.

Screaming obscenities in his native Russian, Kliric fell backwards, hitting his head on the edge of the sink. Dazed, Kliric lay motionless.

Jenna scrambled to find his gun. As she stepped over his body, she couldn't help herself. She drove her foot hard against his ribs, just for good measure.

Fleeing the shower room, Jenna leaned against a locker for a few seconds to catch her breath. "Austin!" Jenna cried, moving as quickly as she could with the fear in the back of her mind Kliric wouldn't stay down for long. Finally reaching her brother, Jenna grabbed him around the waist and forced him to his feet. Just as they were nearing the pool area, she heard voices in the outside corridor. The police had finally arrived.

Thank God!

Two officers with their guns drawn ran towards them just as Jenna and Austin cleared the doorway. Dropping to her knees, Jenna pointed behind her. "He's…in there. Hans Kliric. Here." Jenna handed Kliric's gun to one of the officers. "I…disarmed him."

Both officers exchanged surprised looks. "Are you the CIA agent?" One of them asked.

"Hell no." Jenna laid her head against Austin's as her eyelids drooped. "Not in a million years."

*****

"Time to get out."

Logan yanked open the back door of the Range Rover harder than he planned. It practically bounced back at him and he caught it with his arm. Motioning for Kelly to step outside, he resisted the temptation to touch her. He had made his choice.

The choice of a survivor.

A journey he had to travel alone.

Opening his Swiss Army knife, Logan paused to look deeply into Kelly's eyes. "I'm sorry."

Kelly slumped against the car, her legs shaking so badly she could barely stand. This was it; her last moments on earth…and she didn't know what to say.

Meaningful words escaped her as thoughts of the life she was leaving behind flashed in front of her. Austin…their baby…living at the beach…Jenna…being with her best friend…and her brother Jonathan. Memories of better times, of laughter, love and loyalty were fading as each second of her life clicked away. She would never hold her baby, kiss it good-night, or rock it to sleep. She would never look into Austin's eyes again and see their future, or make love to him again. Every good part of her life would end swiftly as soon as Logan drew his arm and stabbed her. She would die here, on a deserted road not far from the Canadian border, her blood seeping into the ground.

No one would be able to save her. Only miss her.

Kelly started to fall as Logan reached out to grab her arm. She didn't understand. *Why was he hesitating, prolonging her agony? Did he have to be so stone cold in her last moments alive? Did he have to treat her as horribly as her father? A fitting ending,* Kelly thought. Logan would no doubt recant the way she died in vivid detail, and Mason would take great pleasure hearing the news.

"Do it," she said as her mind finally accepted her fate. "Right now. Don't wait any longer."

Logan took both of her arms and held them steady. Only then did he look into her eyes, offering her a smile. "I'm not going to kill you, Kelly McBride. No matter what you think of me, and what you'll tell other people about me, I want you to know, I never wanted to hurt you. I wanted to keep you safe. I was trying to get you to Canada to keep you away from Hamilton." Logan stopped, suddenly at a loss for words. "But I can't take you any further. You don't belong with me. You belong with the man you love…and your baby."

Kelly trembled. If Logan hadn't been supporting her, she would have fainted, falling fast on the ground. "I thought…all this time…I thought all you wanted was…Oh, God, I can't believe this!" Her eyes released a deluge of tears and her head dropped to her chest. So overcome with relief, Kelly didn't realize Logan was placing a cell phone in her hands.

"I…have to say good-bye now. I'm going to dial 911 and when the operator comes on, you need to give her this address." Logan pulled a small slip of paper from his pocket. "Right down this road about a half mile is a farmhouse," Logan said as he pointed east. "That's the address I gave you. The FBI or the police…shouldn't have any trouble finding you."

The realization of what Logan was saying finally made sense. He was abandoning her on the side of the road. In the middle of nowhere. She had no idea where she was, and if the phone would even work. Kelly tensed, not letting go of Logan's hand. "Don't leave me out here alone. I…"

"You'll be fine; I promise. Here." Logan took the phone and dialed 911. Within seconds, an operator's voice answered. "Now's your chance, Kelly. Your chance to be rescued."

Logan took one step away, then turned back. He kissed her quickly on the cheek, ran to his car and sped away.

Kelly turned away from the dust kicking up in her face. She couldn't believe her good fortune. Just minutes earlier, she had anticipated her own death. Now as the operator's reassuring words echoed in her ear, she struggled to speak.

"Yes," Kelly stammered, watching Logan's car disappear in the opposite direction. "I'm...ok. My name is Kelly McBride. Please send someone to get me!"

The operator responded immediately. "I have your GPS signal. Help is on the way, Kelly McBride. You're going to be fine."

*****

The truck slowed to a stop much sooner than Movell anticipated. Something was wrong. Reaching down to roll up his pant leg, he withdrew a small handgun from the ankle holster strapped to his leg.

Damian sat rigid on the opposite bench. "What's going on, Thomas?"

Movell checked his watch. They had been travelling less than an hour. The rendezvous point was two hours away. Something had occurred making the driver stop and turn off the engine. Motioning for Damian to join him on the right side of the truck, he attempted to pull apart the partition separating the cab from the cargo area. It was locked. A bad sign.

Both men raced to the back of the truck. Reaching for the dual handles on the inside of the paneled door, they pulled upward. No luck. Apparently, the door was locked from the outside. It only budged six inches or so.

Damian flattened himself on the floor while Movell jiggled the door handle. "My guess...it's padlocked." He jumped to his feet. "Someone wants us to stay put."

"Indeed," Movell said as he considered several options, all of which pointed in Raymond Konecki's direction. Dropping to his knees, he waved Damian away. "Hold the door steady." Movell lay on his back, reaching his hand underneath the door.

He had procured an app on his cell phone several weeks ago enabling the device to act as a mirror. Never realizing he would use it so soon, Movell was grateful he had listened to Tumi's advice to download the app.

Movell reached his long arm under the door, moving the cell in various directions until he viewed the lock on the door. Damian was right; it was a simple padlock. Drawing his arm back, Movell tossed his cell beside him then reached for his gun. Taking precise aim, he shattered the lock on his first shot.

Damian yanked hard on the door handle, breaking it free.

"Nice shot, Thomas. Ever think about joining the FBI?" Damian chuckled as both men leaped off the back of the truck.

"I do not think Tumi would be happy if I left the brother-hood."

"Probably not." Damian clasped Movell on his back. "Let's get out of here."

Movell stopped Damian in his tracks. "We must proceed with caution. Something is amiss." He gestured Damian to follow him, retreating to a wooded area several yards behind the abandoned truck.

They were at a weigh station, somewhere along interstate I-95 Movell guessed. They were alone. Movell's two team leaders who were supposed to be driving the truck were nowhere sight.

Movell's instincts reacted on cue. As soon as he smelled the familiar odor of gasoline, he and Damian took off running as fast as they could.

The blast knocked them both to the ground. Smoke billowed around them, irritating their eyes and throats. Trying desperately to stand, Damian helped Movell to his feet.

"Called that one, didn't you?" he asked, brushing debris and soot from his clothes. "I owe you, Thomas."

Movell bowed his head. "You owe me nothing. I am certain you would have done the same. You are my friend's brother; say no more."

"All the same, thanks."

Movell watched the flames begin to dissipate. "Raymond is to blame. I am certain of it."

"Konecki? How can you say that? He helped me escape. He wouldn't have risked his career if…"

Movell interrupted. "Raymond knew exactly what he was doing. He holds many cards, Damian. None of which he plans to play without a reason."

Damian was dumbfounded. "What about Briggs?"

"Elias Briggs is a scapegoat, much like you and Maria. I know, he acts pretentious and his swagger is...egotistical at the very least. However, we both know Briggs doesn't have the level of authority necessary to bring charges against you. Your rank is too high. My suspicions lie with Konecki. He has means and opportunities. It would be very easy for him to twist the truth, and bend the ear of the Director."

"You may be right, Thomas. Although, thinking of Briggs as a scapegoat isn't setting well with me. He's an ass. Don't expect me to rally for his cause."

Movell shook his head. "I would do no such thing. Just keep in mind, Briggs may be well-positioned to help us...should we be able to convince him his boss is acting inappropriately."

"You have your work cut out for you, Thomas."

"Of that you can be sure." Movell pulled his cell from his pocket. "Tumi, my friend. Yes, Damian and I are safe. Please ask Phillip to track my phone and arrange for a transport. We have not...reached our destination as originally planned. We are at a weigh station on the interstate. Approximately forty-five minutes south of D.C. *Car trouble*, you could say. Thank you."

Damian looked surprised when Movell handed him the cell.

"Isn't there someone you wish to call?"

Movell smiled as Damian looked down at the caller ID Movell had selected from his call list.

Maria.

*****

"You amaze me, sis." Austin tugged on his sister's hand. Back in his hospital bed after having several stitches replaced, Austin was grateful for Jenna's heroic efforts, and the other good news he had received.

Kelly had been found and was on her way to him, due to arrive at any minute.

Austin's compliment wasn't enough to get Jenna's attention. She continued to stare blankly out the window, lost in many thoughts. Despite her efforts, Kliric had gotten away. By the time the police searched the Aqua Therapy wing, he had vanished. A back door to an outdoor track was hanging open. Somehow Kliric had circled back to the front parking lot, and drove away while the police were barging into the lobby.

"You're a million miles away." Austin tried again.

"I'm sorry." Jenna turned her head towards her brother. "Guess I'm a little worn out." She sat back in the guest chair, rubbing her eyes. She had failed to stop Kliric, allowing him the freedom to do Mason Hamilton's bidding, and no doubt traumatize her at some future time. She had outsmarted him to keep Austin safe, but it hadn't been enough to ensure Kliric's capture.

The treasure pieces weighed heavily on her mind. Sticking her hand into her jacket pocket, she withdrew one of them, the monkey. Holding it in her palm, she showed it to Austin. "Not worth risking our lives for, is it?"

Austin took the small gold figurine and gazed intently at it. "Apparently Mom thought so. She risked her life for these treasure pieces...or at least keeping them out of Hamilton's hands."

Austin's comment blared like a trumpet. With all the drama and craziness taking up so much of their time, Jenna had completely forgotten to share the news about Lois Reed. Although Maria and Ann had warned Jenna not to say a word about Lois being alive, Jenna felt Austin had a right to know just like she did. For too long they both had been kept in the dark while secret agendas and secret agents ruled their lives for them.

The truth was exactly what they both needed.

"Austin, I have something...to tell you," Jenna began as she stood up. She took the gold monkey and placed it back in her pocket. Covering Austin's hand with her own, Jenna took a deep breath.

"That's going to have to wait." Ann Bailey barged in, purposely interrupting. "Austin has a visitor." Ann leaned against the door to prop it open, grinning from ear to ear.

Kelly took two slow steps then rushed to Jenna and Austin's open arms. Hugs and kisses followed as Ann closed the door.

Austin was the first to speak although his voice was shaky. "How...did you get here so fast? I didn't think I would see you so soon."

"Jacoby…arranged for a helicopter ride. I…"

Austin's worried look stopped Kelly immediately. "Was…that safe…for the baby? Oh, God, Kelly…please tell me you and the baby are ok!"

Kelly laid Austin's hand against her stomach. Then she leaned closer to kiss him. "We're fine," she whispered. "We're both fine."

Jenna draped her arms around Kelly's shoulder to hug her. "Well, I'm glad to hear that, too. We'll catch up later. I have a lot to tell you." Jenna winked at Austin, then left the room to give them some privacy.

Austin relaxed against the pillow, pulling Kelly down with him. After a few moments, she lifted her head to look at him. Neither said any words for what seemed like the longest time. They didn't have to; holding each other was all that mattered.

Finally, Kelly broke into tears. She had done her best not to fall to pieces when the FBI picked her up on the side of the road until this very moment. Now that she was able to look into Austin's eyes with the knowledge they were all going to be ok, her body wanted nothing more than to collapse. Tears drenched her face even though Austin did his best to kiss them away.

"I'm sorry," she said, wiping her cheeks dry. "Guess I couldn't hold it together any longer."

"Oh, Kel." Austin moved across the bed to give her just enough room to lie next to him. "It's over. We're together, and the baby's fine. That's all I care about."

"Me, too. I love you so much," she said as his arm tightened around her. She was back where she belonged.

In Austin's arms.

Chapter 33

"Damn it, Damian. Don't scare me like that...*ever again.*" Maria fought back tears. "We're getting too old for this."

"Sweetheart, I called you the first chance I got. Thomas and I were...a little distracted." Damian chose his words carefully. He was riding in the backseat alongside of Tumi's team leader Gerard. Phillip was driving, and Movell was seated up front. It was awkward holding a private conversation.

"I'm sorry," Maria apologized as she leveled her voice. "I...just miss you and I was so worried. When I was told I couldn't see you...and they held me back at the main security gate, I can't tell you how livid I was. If it wasn't for Tumi and Phillip, I probably would have lost my mind by now."

Damian covered his cell with his hand. "How much further, Phillip?"

"If traffic cooperates, less than an hour."

"Did you hear that, sweetheart? Less than hour."

"Good." Maria's voice was softer, calmer. "Then we can get on the road before dark."

Damian paused in responding. "Where are we headed now?"

"Back to Cape May. For Kelly and Austin's wedding. You're giving away the bride, or did you forget, Mr. Pierce?"

Damian smiled. Despite all the chaos the last several days, something good was coming out of it. "I didn't forget. I'm looking forward to it. I'd better go. I'll see you soon. I love you."

"I love you, too, Damian." Maria laid her cell on the side table between the two sofas in Tumi's suite. "Thank you," she said in Tumi's direction. "I don't know how I could ever repay you or Thomas, but I am grateful, Tumi. Thank you for bringing my husband back to me."

Tumi nodded. "Thomas deserves all the credit, I assure you. His quick thinking probably saved both of their lives. I am honored to have him as my friend."

"I like the company you keep, Tumi." Maria got up to walk into the extra bedroom. "I'd better get my suitcase ready to go, so we can get on the road." Before she turned to leave, her cell buzzed.

Tumi quickly handed it to her. "It's Jacoby," he noticed by glancing at the caller ID.

"Please tell me you have good news." Maria stood frozen in her tracks. "Is Thompson out of surgery?"

"Just got out a few minutes ago. The doctor said he was very lucky. If he hadn't been wearing his Kevlar vest, I'd be calling you from the morgue. Thought you'd like to know. How are you holding up?"

Maria felt the air returning to her lungs. "Better now. Tell Thompson to rest up. If he tries to jump out of bed, shoot him. That's an order. Damian's on his way back; should be here any minute. The wedding is back on, and we're headed to Cape May within the hour. I don't want to jinx it, but this is the best day I've had in a long time."

"Glad to hear it. As soon as Thompson is out of ICU, I'm heading back to base. Getting settled into my new digs. Say goodbye to your coveted corner office, Turette. It's a thing of the past."

"You wouldn't dare..."

"Try me." Jacoby was ready to burst at the seams. "I have a little bit of clout now...rescuing Kelly McBride. I might even requisition a new high-back leather chair. Have to say, the one in your office is looking pretty worn. Not the right image we want to promote in the unit. Probably not even worth re-cycling at this point."

"Touch my chair and I'll haul you in the ring. Need to practice my kickboxing anyway. Get ready to take a beating."

Jacoby howled. "I'll take it under advisement. Have a good time at the wedding, and then get your ass back to D.C. I have a feeling Briggs' case against you is about to fall by the wayside."

Maria rolled her head from side to side, a relaxation routine she had learned years go. "Let's hope so. I miss being there."

"Well, don't let this rumor get started...but I have a feeling the guys miss you, too. Stay in touch."

*****

"Logan, so good of you to call."

Mason sneered as he hit the speaker button on his cell phone. "No lengthy apologies are necessary. Your inability to follow orders is nothing more than youthful rebellion. I can see past your indiscretions."

"I didn't call to apologize. I wouldn't give you the satisfaction. Don't ever try to manipulate me again. I don't have the patience for it."

"I have to say, Logan, I am quite disappointed. I expected much more from you. I am perplexed as to why you failed. Perhaps you were influenced on a personal level. Kelly won you over with her charms, didn't she?"

Mason Hamilton was leading into forbidden territory, and Logan wasn't falling for it. Not this time.

"The risks outweighed the benefits. I saw no reason to put myself in the FBI's limelight. I got out of a sticky situation before it turned ugly."

"If you had followed my orders the first time, all those unpleasantries could have been avoided. Should you wish to redeem yourself, I have another assignment you may want to consider."

Seconds ticked away. Finally, Mason broke the stalemate. "I'm assuming you wish to regain some sense of dignity. Elevate yourself to a new standing. I can help you achieve that."

Logan still did not answer. The amount of trust he had for Mason Hamilton was miniscule at best. Still, it didn't hurt to hear him out. He needed to recoup some recent expenses. "What did you have in mind?"

"Splendid!" Mason clapped his hands together. This time Logan McHenry would have no choice but to obey his every command. Or take his chances with the FBI. Once Mason found out where Logan was hiding, all he'd have to do was call his contact at the FBI.

And Raymond Konecki would take it from there.

*****

"Are you sure?"

David paced the entire length of the living room in the condo his pilot owned just outside of Avalon. After coming to Mallory's rescue, the last place he wanted to go was Malcolm's house. Any reminder of that son-of-a-bitch and what he had almost done to Mallory was too much to take.

David's mind drifted away from his conversation. Every time he looked at Mallory, his heart skipped several beats. As much as he tried to deny it, Mallory held his heart. He had killed for her and he was willing to die for her. If that wasn't love, he didn't know how else to describe it. But once he said *I love you* to Mallory, there would be no turning back. She would want to be with him despite any risk, even if a situation turned deadly.

"If I have to repeat myself again, I'm hanging up," Raymond Konecki emphasized, louder this time. "You're obviously distracted. Far be it for me to take up your precious time since your time is all that matters. I merely called to give you an update. Now, either listen to me, or find out on your own."

"Just tell me Pierce is dead; that's all I want to hear. If Movell was another casualty, so be it. Tell me you saw Pierce die with your own eyes."

"Why would you think for one minute I would jeopardize my life or my career by being in the same vicinity of a car explosion? No, if that's what you're asking. I was not present when the truck exploded. I did not see Pierce die. However, my contacts tell me..."

"Not good enough. I want proof Pierce and Movell are dead. When you can get that for me, you'll get your money." David continued to walk across the floor, stopping only when he locked eyes with Mallory. He tossed his phone on the sofa, then sat down beside her. In all the years he had known her, David had never seen Mallory so vulnerable and scared. Pushing one of her dark strands behind her ear, he kissed her cheek. "You want something to eat...drink?"

Mallory laced her fingers with David's, laying her head against his shoulder. "I just want you."

"You have me, Mallory. I'm right here."

Mallory turned her head to gaze into his eyes. They held an intensity she had never seen before, or maybe she had just been too afraid to see it. Fear. For her.

And love...whether he could say it or not.

David Caldwell was in love with her.

*****

All Chase Garrett had managed to do was get in the way.

At first Markus had been skeptical of The Closer's order to bring Garrett along to take out Renault's bodyguards, but now he was downright irritated. Garrett should have just kept out of sight in the van. Instead, he had followed Markus into the hotel's bar, made some lame excuse he had to use the restroom, and then didn't bother to show up again until the van was ready to pull out.

Garrett was a liability. Markus couldn't understand why The Closer insisted on keeping Garrett around...or alive for that matter. Part of the big picture Markus wasn't privy to which made him fume even more. He had enough to worry about without Garrett's little Houdini act.

Taking out Renault's bodyguards.

Markus had watched them from a distance as they drank their beers at the bar. Then, as The Closer coached him, another man in the cleaning crew simply walked by and asked the bartender to slip them a note. They both exited the bar abruptly, heading straight for Renault's suite on the second level. At the top of the stairwell they were greeted by Markus and two other members of the cleaning crew.

The men were silenced within seconds as needles were jabbed into their necks. Just enough of a sedative to make them appear drunk, they were hustled back down the steps, through the kitchen, and out the back door. Markus hopped into the driver's seat of the van, surprised to see Chase already in the passenger's seat.

"Where have you been?"

"Men's room. Felt sick. Probably all the drugs you're dosing me with. Better drop me off at the house before I throw up in the van."

Markus checked his watch and hissed. He really didn't have time to make a side trip, but there was no way he wanted to ride around with vomit in the van in addition to the two bodyguards' bodies. "The Closer will not be happy we are wasting time. I will not pull into the driveway. You will jump out as soon as I pull along the curb. Do you understand?"

Chase nodded, grabbing his stomach for effect.

It wasn't long before he was standing on the sidewalk watching Markus fly away in the van. Chase knew he had no control over what happened to Renault's bodyguards. In order to maintain his cover, it was necessary to look the other way, even if it meant not interfering with murder.

Choices have to be made sometimes...even when you're stuck with no good options...

Another piece of advice courtesy of his partner. Who wasn't picking up her cell.

There was no time to lose.

He needed Knox.

*****

"You feel good, sweetheart." Damian nuzzled Maria's neck. "So good. I missed you."

Maria grinned as Damian lifted her gently off the ground. "Now that we've established how strong you are, you can put me down."

Laughter filled the room. Tumi stepped forward to embrace his brother and sister-in-law. "I am grateful you are safe, brother; however, it is not necessary to knock me off my feet."

"Nice to know family and friends are watching out for us."

"Our pleasure," Phillip quipped. "You're leaving now, I presume?" He gestured toward the suitcases stacked by the door.

"Yes, we are." Maria squeezed Damian's hand. "Unless you want a shower first? We don't have to leave this very minute."

"Only if you take one with me."

Maria suspected her face was turning red by the mischievous smiles surrounding her. "Behave yourself, Mr. Pierce. I can see that incarceration did nothing to curb your devious behavior. Perhaps a longer stay in confinement would..."

Damian stopped Maria's playful teasing with a lip-smacking kiss. "That's one way to distract you. I can think of others." He tugged on her hand, winking.

"We'll...be back in a little bit," Maria announced, pulling Damian toward the back bedroom.

"Don't bet on it," he called over his shoulder.

Tumi gestured for Phillip and Thomas to join him in the seating area. "You second-guessed Konecki, Thomas. I must commend you for your quick thinking and expertise in devising a rescue mission."

"Konecki is not to be trusted. I knew this the first moment I met him. He thinks he is in control, manipulating our relationship. I shall let him continue to think that way, and use it against him. Konecki will continue to make mistakes. I will be watching and waiting. When the timing is right, he will step into his own web."

"I appreciate your confidence, Thomas. However, I caution you to act with prudence. Konecki has reached a level of authority which is well-respected. Bringing him to his knees will not be an easy task."

Movell bent his head in acknowledgment. "I will approach the challenge with due diligence, my friend."

"Then all you need to do is ask, and I shall provide any assistance you may need."

Movell took a wine glass offered by Phillip. "Thank you. Suffice it to say, I will counter every step Konecki makes until he is tired of dancing with me. Failure is not an option I am contemplating. You have my word on it."

"You are as tenacious as ever, Thomas."

"And you, my friend, are protective as ever. It is no wonder our friendship has stood the test of time. We are family; are we not?"

*****

Jonathan's entire game plan had been shot to hell.

Chase Garrett had turned the tables. A move Jonathan had never expected.

Meeting Garrett at the lighthouse was going to be a slam dunk. Convincing himself the only right thing to do was beat Garrett to a pulp, Jonathan had pumped himself up on enough caffeine and adrenaline to get the job done. Garrett didn't stand a chance. For all the pain he had caused Jenna, and all the annoyances Jonathan was forced to endure, Garrett had it coming.

Hard and fast. No holds barred.

Garrett was going to fall flat, moan and groan, and Jonathan was going to enjoy every minute.

His plan was flawed from the very beginning. All Garrett had to do was say those four little words.

"I need your help."

Jonathan had stopped himself from taking another step. Garrett's admission had thrown him off-guard, and Jonathan wondered immediately if it was done on purpose.

"Did you hear me, Knox? I'm asking for your help," Chase repeated, taking a step closer.

Jonathan shot Chase a puzzled look, almost afraid to hear any more details. Curiosity got the best of him. He couldn't hold back. "My help? For what?"

"To save Jenna."

Jonathan was struck dumb, unable to move.

"Knox, can I count on you, or what?"

"I..."

"I don't have a lot of time. You have to give me your answer. Now." Chase checked his watch. If he didn't return before Markus, he'd have a tough time explaining why he had taken off in one of the painting vans.

Jonathan stood rigid, trying to focus. "Save Jenna from what, Garrett? You? You seem to be the only one causing her pain and heartache. Believe me," Jonathan said as he rolled up his jacket sleeves. "I'm ready and willing to do the honors."

"There's more I have to tell you, Knox, so I need you to shut up and listen. Jenna needs to be protected, and I...won't be there to do it. I'm counting on you to take care of her...when...please do this. Please listen to what I have to say."

Jonathan relaxed his stance. Garrett was speaking in riddles, but when it came to Jenna's safety, they were both on the same wavelength. "I'll do it, Garrett. For Jenna. Not for you."

Chase took two steps closer and stuck out his hand. Getting Knox on board was half the battle. "Then listen very carefully...because what I have to tell you is going to blow your mind."

Jonathan braced himself for a logical explanation. One based upon truth, clarity, and above all, common sense. Why Chase Garrett had been acting strangely for months, taking his frustrations out on the woman he loved, and disappearing into the night.

What Jonathan heard in the next several minutes stunned him beyond words and defied the laws of nature.

Chase Garrett was going to sacrifice himself.

Although he was willing to bet Garrett had left out quite a few intricate details, Jonathan had no problem zeroing in on the main facts. Chase Garrett was an undercover agent. He had been chasing an elusive assassin known as The Closer for several years internationally and also in the States. Whenever Chase tried to get close enough, The Closer seemed to be three steps ahead of him. Just recently when Intel surfaced again indicating Mason Hamilton had ties with The Closer, Chase was once again summoned to follow the trail.

The trail which led straight to Jenna Reed and Blackbeard's treasure pieces. Chase befriended Jenna to find out what she knew...then succumbed to falling in love with her. The Closer used their union to his advantage. Drugging Chase in Texas and again a few days ago, The Closer had every intention of forcing Chase to convince Jenna to give up the last three treasure pieces.

Chase agreed to play along, to get one chance to bring The Closer to justice. But in doing so, he would have to betray Jenna's trust. To ensure he went along with The Closer's plan, Chase received a modified dosage of the drugs, making him uncontrollable. Without elaborating, Chase admitted he had hurt Jenna physically and mentally.

The only way to right the wrongs he had committed was to capture The Closer. He needed help, and Jonathan was his only hope since he hadn't been able to reach his partner.

Ann Bailey.

Jonathan's brain snapped into overdrive. Ann hadn't shared that little piece of information with him, and for good reason. Ann wasn't just a bodyguard; she was a spy, too.

Jonathan's head was spinning.

"I know what I'm asking you to do will risk your life. I don't have another option. You're it, Knox. You're all I have. Please do this for Jenna if not for me."

"Garrett...what if you don't come back?"

"Then love her, Knox. Don't stop loving her. Do that for me." Chase disappeared behind the lighthouse before Jonathan could comprehend what he had just heard.

Chase Garrett was ready to die to protect the woman he loved.

Chapter 34

"I'll get our rental."

Ann and Jenna made their way down the ramp from the plane. After landing in Atlantic City, they bypassed the baggage carousel. Both had travelled to and from the Poconos with just the clothes on their backs.

"Thanks," Jenna called as Ann headed straight for the Enterprise counter. "I'll find you after I hit the ladies room."

Ann sighed when she saw the line wrapping around the rental desk. She had the authority to pull rank and requisition a security detail, but drawing unnecessary attention to herself and Jenna wasn't in their best interests. Instead, she got in line, took out her cell and speed-dialed Maria.

"Just wanted you to know, we're back in Jersey. Where are you?"

"Not as far as I hoped to be." Maria glared at her husband then broke into a smile. "We only left D.C. a couple of hours ago. Hopefully, we'll arrive in Cape May in a few hours. Everybody ok?"

"As far as I know. Jenna and I flew down together. Austin and Kelly will hopefully be leaving tonight or first thing tomorrow morning. Are you sure we still have enough time to pull off this wedding? Going to be cutting it pretty close."

"I think we can manage. Weddings are happy times. With all the craziness going on, I think we all need to throw ourselves into the festivities, and push the drama to the backburner for a few days."

"Couldn't agree with you more." Ann hesitated to say another word. She knew Jonathan was the best man, and being in the same room with him without flirting was going to be extremely hard. Kelly and Austin's wedding wasn't the time to reveal their new *relationship*. Especially when Jenna was probably going solo.

Ann's mind drifted to her partner. She had promised Chase she wouldn't call him; he would have to reach out to her if he needed help. Her phone log indicated he had called several hours ago, but didn't leave a message.

Ann was afraid to even begin speculating what that could mean. There were too many possibilities. For all she knew, Chase could be dead, stabbed in the back by The Closer, or so damaged by the drugs, he wouldn't be able to recite his name.

The stubborn fool, Ann mused. She had tried, and so had Damian. Tried to reason with Chase, to make him see he didn't have to handle things on his own. But he wouldn't listen. He didn't want anyone else to take the risk he was willing to accept.

An admirable quality, but also a stupid one. *Chase should have known better*, Ann continued to tell herself. Should have taken his own advice. He was forever reminding her not to forge ahead without adequate back-up, or taking too many risks. *You're not invincible, despite what you think of yourself.*

Ann bit her lip, wondering if Chase still had his blinders on. He was certainly acting that way. Bull-headed, he could dish out the advice, but not take it.

"He's going to wind up dead," Ann said out loud, then shifted her stance, wondering if anyone standing next to her had overheard her comment. She was startled when Jenna touched her elbow.

"Surprising enough, the line in the ladies room was shorter than this one."

Ann frowned. "Looks like it's going to take a few more minutes. I checked in with Maria. She's hell-bent on moving forward with the wedding; if you're up to it, I mean."

"Oh, yeah. I'm up to it. I need something positive to focus on for a change. How about you? I'm sure you could use a distraction."

Ann wasn't sure how to respond. Her mind was instantly drawn to the physical distraction she was craving wrapped in Jonathan's arms . "Whatever you need me to do," she replied, putting on her best poker face.

"I'll start a list when we're in the car. I think the three of us can do this. We might not get any sleep the next couple of days, but we'll have fun putting the wedding together. Kelly and Austin are going to be so surprised. I can't wait to see the looks on their faces when we tell them the wedding is still on!"

Ann smiled. "You're a good person, Jenna Reed. Glad I got to know you...in a round-about sort of way."

*****

The moment had arrived. The one she had waited so patiently for...was finally here. The promise she made to herself many years ago was coming to fulfillment. And she would take great pleasure in it.

Killing Laurence Renault. Feeling the life drain from his body would give her such deep satisfaction. A feeling she had stored inside her for over thirty years. Planning his murder had never left her conscience for even one day.

He had made such an impact on her, and her family. This was restitution time. Renault would pay for his past sins, and she would feel no remorse whatsoever. It was time.

Close to forty now, she had survived the ridicule as a child, bearing the scars on her neck that never healed properly. She had learned to accept her deformity with honor, casting aside the wary glances and the ludicrous comments. She chose to wear silk scarves which soothed her tender skin, and covered the remnants of the worst day of her life. Even the deaths of her parents, spaced ironically six months to the day, paled in comparison to the horrific suffering she had been forced to endure as Laurence Renault wielded his shiny knife.

While Mason Hamilton stood by and did nothing. He was next on her list. When he stared soullessly into space and took his last breath, only then would she allow herself to feel complete gratification. Her revenge would be fulfilled.

Her life...could finally go on.

As she stood in the shadows of the stairwell, she casually glanced out the small side window facing the ocean. She vaguely remembered a time when laughter hung in the air, and she had no cares in the world. Happier times full of love and trust.

All shattered in an instant. Her innocence was forever severed the day Laurence Renault and Mason Hamilton came into her life. Her father had a very important position as the Head Curator of the Brussels Museum of Antiquities and Fine Arts. He would take her for private tours, showing her the most amazing artwork spanning centuries. Paintings, sculptures, abstract pieces she couldn't understand at such a young age. He was in charge of keeping watch over them. A job he enjoyed immensely until one night his family paid the ultimate price.

Awakened slightly after midnight, the curator, his wife, and young daughter were forced from the tranquility of their home, threatened at gunpoint, and taken to an old textile warehouse where the torture began...and never quite ended. Even though her family was extremely fortunate to escape with their lives, their happiness and livelihood was forfeited. Her father had agreed to give up the museum's most coveted pieces, several original paintings by the artist, Gauguin, to Hamilton and Renault in exchange for his daughter's life. Replicas were swapped with the original pieces, and even the most discerning tourists and art aficionados didn't take notice.

It was only after an insurance audit several years later, that the forgeries were discovered. By then the originals had exchanged hands so many times on the black market, they were assumed to be lost forever. Someone had to be blamed, and even though the evidence pointed away from her father, his own guilty conscience made him break down and admit his part in the theft. Just hours before he was formally charged, he hung himself in the very storage room the paintings had passed through before being placed in Renault's truck.

Her mother had been overcome with grief and shame, and suffered multiple health problems until she, too, passed away suddenly from a heart attack in her late thirties.

At sixteen, she was an orphan, forced to deal with the demons that haunted her memories. She was taken in by her kind aunt, on her mother's side, who was like a second mother to her. Had it not been for the comforting arms of Aunt Marie, she knew she would have ended up either in an asylum, or worse yet, on the streets of Brussels begging or offering her body in exchange for food.

It seemed like another lifetime, but it hadn't been.

Memories so raw and tingling she could almost feel the rush of the air and the ice cold steel against her throat. She raised her hand instinctively as if the blade was taunting her again. A responsive action she had repeated so many times it had become second nature. The constant reminder she had fought so hard to erase from the very essence of her soul.

The scars, inside and out, would continue to plague every facet of her life. She had never married, never bore children. She had been too afraid that someone she loved would face a similar tragedy. Although the likelihood was relatively remote, she could not help herself. Every time she began to develop feelings for a man, she caught herself and hastily ended the relationship. It was too painful to perpetuate something that would never come to fruition. Yet, again and again she had tried.

Tried to overcome her fears with the hope of discovering her taste for revenge would diminish over time. It had not. It was still as strong today as it had been the night Laurence Renault and Mason Hamilton had taken away the purity of her childhood.

Now as she crept slowly down the corridor, she was empowered to do what had to be done. To atone for the atrocities these men had committed, she alone had to take their lives. They had enjoyed living for too many years already, undeserving and worthless that they were.

In the end, they would die just like any other man or woman. No amount of power or wealth could give them one extra breath. She reveled in that thought, meticulously inching towards Renault's doorway.

He wasn't expecting her; she was sure of it. But when his two bodyguards did not return in a timely manner, he had to be suspicious. So he would be prepared, armed most likely, and consciously expecting an attack. She had planned for that. To second guess his actions, no matter how contrived they were, she would be ready. She had to be.

She knocked gently.

"Who's there?" Renault called, his voice noticeably shaking.

"Hotel management," she replied in a perfected American accent. "May I come in, sir? I want to make sure everything is according to your expectations. We are required to make periodic checks of all suites. It will only take a moment of your time."

Her tone was calm, polished and soft.

Renault straightened his tie then exhaled loudly. He had worried for nothing. Certainly if the hotel manager was coming to pay him a visit; there was no cause for alarm. He would give her a glowing review of the hotel's accommodations and the restaurant, and then bid her good-day. He was getting tired after being awake off and on for most of the night and early morning hours. Soon he would have no choice but to take a nap and forget such foolish notions. Jason and Raul were grown men. If they felt the need to search out female companionship and leave him alone for one night, they were entitled.

"Yes, of course." Renault opened the door, gesturing for her to enter. "I must say, I am quite impressed by the suite, your staff, and…"

As Renault turned his head toward the windows, she struck.

The red silk scarf unraveled quickly due to the thin, flexible wire encased inside. Before Renault knew what was happening, the scarf had been looped around his neck, the strands twisted in opposite directions and pulled tight. In seconds, he had dropped to his knees.

With every choking sound he made, she pulled harder perfecting the technique she had practiced so many times on unsuspecting animals. Killing a man well past his prime wasn't much more of a challenge. As Renault fell forward, she placed one boot firmly against his back and pressed down as hard as she could.

Renault's fingers clawed at his neck, trying to disengage the ligature. It was no use. The filament of the material was too silky, and he was unable to get a firm grip underneath the wire. His hands were bloody and slippery. Slightly arthritic, Renault found it quite difficult to navigate past the garrote slicing into his neck.

Death was approaching, and he could do little to ward it off. Airflow to his lungs was being eliminated with each agonizing second that passed. He knew it was only a matter of time. The female assassin had caught him off-guard. She was confident, cunning and highly trained.

Had she been sent by Mason Hamilton?

Letting Renault slip from her grasp, he rolled sideways. Grasping his neck with both hands, he stared blankly into her face. He had seconds to make a connection, to figure out who she was and why she had been sent to kill him.

"Do you not recognize me?" She asked as her eyes pierced his own. "Perhaps this will remind you." She unbuttoned the top of her blouse to reveal her scarred neckline, waiting for a response.

Renault's eyes fluttered as he struggled for every remaining breath.

"You should remember me quite well. I have never forgotten you. I have waited many years for this moment. To see you one last time...to be the one who takes your final breath away. Let me refresh your memory. Brussels, a cold December night, 1978. You and Mason Hamilton took me and my parents to an old textile warehouse. You...cut me here," her hands splayed across her neck, as she forced them not to shake. "You tortured me until my father agreed to your terms. You...changed me. I had never known hatred before that night. You gave that to me...and the desire to kill. I've thought of nothing else...since then. Do you want to hear how I plan to murder Mason Hamilton?"

Her words fell silent. Laurence Renault was dead.

*****

"Why am I not surprised?"

Mason stared intently at Hans, hoping he had misunderstood. When Hans was flustered, he frequently resorted to speaking half-English, half-Russian, a language so convoluted Mason didn't have the time or patience to decipher.

"Let me get this straight, and please correct me if I'm wrong. The Closer told you how to track Jenna Reed, you obviously found her, yet here you are without the treasure pieces. I'm finding it rather difficult to understand how a man of your stature could possibly be outsmarted by a young woman. You have the advantage of size, strength, and I'm assuming you were carrying at least one gun and a knife. However, here we are...discussing your failed attempt to bring me what I want."

"Mason, I...tried..."

"Hans, did you see the treasure pieces? Was she carrying them?"

Hans vigorously shook his head. "I did not see the treasure pieces. You must believe me. I had to act quickly. The police were coming. I had to leave...before they got to me."

Mason waved Hans away. He was disgusted with Hans' failure but at the same time, he blamed The Closer for such a risky move. Hans should never have been tasked with approaching Jenna Reed in the hospital setting. He was the proverbial bull in the china closet.

Hans shouldn't be held accountable. He was...

Mason stopped himself. He was doing it again. Defending the incompetency of his loyal dog. A trait he could never quite give up, much to The Closer's dismay. Yet where was The Closer in all this? Still hanging out at the beach, taking his dear sweet time to kill Renault when he should have finished the job and taken off in Jenna Reed's direction.

Mason wasn't having the best of days. The men on his team were disappointing him left and right, but he didn't have the energy to bring anyone else on board. He knew deep down Logan McHenry had potential; he just had to hone his skills and reaffirm his loyalties. The Closer on the other hand, had the skills but was lacking in any type of loyalty except his own. Hans was and would continue to be the wild card, loyal to the end but dumb as dirt.

Mason felt the tension rising in his neck. His team was disjointed at times, but each man had redeeming qualities. Perfection was a misconception, and he had spent countless hours trying to convince himself how hard it was to find a true ally.

At one point in his life, Mason thought he had met such a man. Charismatic, influential and deadly. Laurence Renault embodied those qualities and many more. Mason Sr. had thought so, and had implored Renault to teach them to his son.

It didn't take long for Mason to see Renault's true colors, and the concept of perfection was cast aside. Renault was nothing more than a con artist who had convinced Mason's father he could perform a miracle for the right price. Oh, Mason had figured out early on Renault hadn't agreed to tutor him free of charge. Transactions in his father's ledgers were all the proof he needed. Renault had been swindling Mason Sr. out of a sizable chunk of cash and securities. The sad part was the old man had turned his cheek, refusing to acknowledge he had been duped. Only when Mason shoved the ledgers in his face, did his father sit up and take notice. By then it was too late. The damage had been done.

Renault had gotten away with it. Exploiting the Hamiltons by taking their money and by taking Mason's wife. Renault had to pay for his indiscretions.

Mason regretted the failed attempt on Renault's life, once again employing incompetent men to do his bidding. A cycle that was repeating itself.

He'd have to take charge now. Make his intentions clear. Specify there would be no further failures or all three men would be held personally accountable.

The time for allowing Jenna Reed to call the shots was over. She needed to be put in her place.

Preferably in the ground alongside of Agent Turette.

Chapter 35

"He suffered…immensely, in case you're wondering."

The woman with the red silk scarf never flinched when The Closer entered Renault's suite. She was seated just a few feet from Renault's body, sipping his expensive champagne. Her posture was relaxed and poised.

Not quite what The Closer had expected.

She had been somewhat aloof when they had originally communicated by phone. A conversation set up through one of his European connections who knew better than to waste his time unless the fee and the job warranted his involvement. She had deposited the required stipend in his Australian bank account with the understanding it was non-refundable should he decide not to take her case.

Intrigue had won him over in the end, especially when she had insisted she perform the task herself. All The Closer was being asked to do for the sum of ten million dollars was to find a way to get rid of Renault's bodyguards, dispose of Renault's body once she was done with it, then wipe down the suite. He couldn't pass up the opportunity. So little work for a lot of money.

Not to mention the chance to meet this woman in person.

As he stooped down to view Renault's body, she shifted in her position to draw his attention. "It's obvious you knew what you were doing."

"I practiced."

The Closer stood up, taken aback by her forthright admission. "I didn't realize you and I were in the same business. My apologies for underestimating…"

The woman looked away. "I wasn't clear. I've never killed a *man* before. I was trained in this…*art*, shall we say. Perfected my craft…on animals. A man is just a larger animal, in *many* regards. However, I only foresee the need to use this talent one more time."

The Closer nodded, understanding completely. "Mason Hamilton."

"Yes," she replied, setting her flute glass on the crystal tray behind her. "I will be leaving shortly for New York. I may…need your assistance, as we previously discussed." She rose and extended her hand. "Expect my call."

"I don't even know your name," The Closer commented.

"Nor do I care to learn yours. This is purely a business arrangement. There is no need to exchange anything other than contact numbers and of course, your preferred method of payment. Anything else would…" Pausing, she ran her fingers up his jacket. "Complicate matters. Don't you agree?"

Staring into her eyes longer than he anticipated, The Closer took a step backwards. She was flirting with him, or at least she appeared to be. Her overt familiarity was making him uncomfortable; a feeling he rarely experienced.

She excited him, but not from a sexual standpoint.

Her mannerisms and confidence level were similar to his own. For a brief moment, he envisioned taking her on as a partner in the truest sense of the word. This woman, with her obvious skills in stealth and murder, had a potential to elevate herself as his peer.

A feat no one had ever done before.

She was captivating him minute by minute, and The Closer almost regretted the fact she was moving closer to the door. He wanted to talk with her more, to propose a more well-defined arrangement combining their talents, making greater use of…

As his eyes swayed in her direction, he realized he was alone.

She had disappeared as silently as a ghost.

A trait he also shared.

It was imperative he got to know her better. It would drive him crazy until he did. She was refined, cool and calculating. The perfect personality to become his partner.

He would make it happen…somehow.

But not today. He had other more pressing matters on his mind. Markus was waiting outside with the clean-up crew ready to transfer Renault's body and work their magic inside the suite. Mallory was waiting for him to return to Avalon, and he needed to finalize plans with Chase Garrett.

So much to do in a short window of time. Yes, he definitely needed a partner. As soon as possible.

S.A. Van

*****

"Where are you?"

Ann was beyond angry. She was livid.

She and Jenna had just arrived in Cape May. Dropping Jenna at the curb, Ann had pulled the car across the street in the one-car driveway next to her rental property. As soon as she had opened the front door, and tossed her purse on the dining room table, her cell had buzzed.

"Do you have any idea how worried I've been? Damian and I both have been trying to reach you for the past several hours. My God, Chase, when we didn't hear from you we thought..."

"I'm fine, Ann. Stop hyperventilating. You're going to give yourself a migraine. Listen, I can't talk long. The Closer and Markus are due back any second. I don't want them hearing anything."

Ann counted to three before responding. "Then don't play games with me. Tell me where you are and I'll come get you. The deeper you get in, I won't be able to pull you out. You know that, damn it! Stop trying to take him out without back-up. Believe it or not, some protocols are worth observing."

"I know what I'm doing. You should have more confidence in me, partner." Chase lowered his voice.

"That's not the issue here, and you know it. You're keeping us out of the loop on purpose. You don't want to drag us down with you; I get that. It's commendable, but otherwise, it's stupid and irresponsible. Besides, it's time you tell Jenna the truth."

"We...didn't part on good terms. I'm not sure how much she told you, but I...hurt her, Ann. There's nothing I can possibly say...to make Jenna see how sorry I am. She's...better off without me. Probably should be with Knox. He thinks he loves her, and she's obviously attracted to him."

Ann cringed. Jealousy flared inside her like a freshly lit match. One night certainly didn't entitle her to feel this way. Actually, it hadn't even been a night; only a few, extremely passionate hours she wished to God she could replay in slow motion. She didn't want to share Jonathan Knox with anyone, especially not the woman she had promised to protect.

"Jenna loves you, Chase. I don't think she's ever stopped. You just need to remind her how you feel...despite what

302

happened. And no, I didn't get all the details, just a basic overview. I couldn't very well take up your defense without telling Jenna you're my partner. That's probably better coming from you or Damian."

Chase took Ann's words to heart. Jenna did deserve the truth, and now she was ready to hear it. If she would consider seeing him...one last time. "Alright. Let me think about it."

"You need to do more than just think about it. Jenna needs to hear the explanation only from you, Chase. It won't mean anything unless you tell her what's going on."

"I have to go. I'll call you as soon as I can. Ann...thanks."

Chase ended the call only seconds before Markus barged through the back door of Malcolm's house looking like he was ready to crush something or someone with his bare hands. Chase stepped backwards just in case.

Markus pulled two beers out of the fridge, slamming one down in front of Chase. "It's done," he grumbled, staring off into space. He didn't stop drinking the beer until it was gone. "If I had known what was involved, I probably wouldn't have agreed to..." Markus stopped mid-sentence, finally realizing Chase hadn't touched the beer. He grabbed it from the table. "The Closer should be here any minute. He wants to talk about the treasure pieces...and how you're going to get them from Jenna Reed." Markus fell into a nearby chair. "You won't like it."

Chase held his ground. "What do you mean by that?"

"You'll see." Markus laughed, shaking the table. "I won't spoil the surprise."

Chase pretended to ignore Markus' comment. He helped himself to a beer, setting another one down in front of Markus. "I don't like surprises." Chase folded his arms and locked his eyes. "Tell me what you know, Markus."

"As you wish." Markus drained the third bottle. By now, he was starting to feel relaxed, and he really didn't care if Chase found out what The Closer was planning. "The marina...two days. You need to make sure Jenna Reed is there with the treasure pieces. Shouldn't be a problem for a man of your...romantic charms." He snickered.

"She doesn't need to be there. I can get them from her. Why are we waiting two days?"

"So many questions, Garrett? I can see how eager you are to please me. I'm impressed." The Closer leaned against the archway in the kitchen crossing his arms.

Markus sat straight in his chair. He wondered how long The Closer had been eavesdropping. "I shouldn't have...," he stuttered.

The Closer waved his hand. "Not a problem, Markus. Garrett has been initiated into the fold. You can share whatever information you have with him. He's going to be very instrumental in bringing this little matter to a close."

Taking a seat at the head of the table, The Closer looked back and forth between Markus and Chase. He had their attention, and before he returned to spend time with Mallory, he saw no reason to keep them in suspense any longer. "Jenna Reed just returned to Cape May, and from what our audio relays are providing, she will be helping to plan her brother's wedding. If you reappear now, Garrett, she'll be too flustered to do what you ask. No, waiting two days will be just the timing we need. It will give us a chance to get organized, finalize our plans, and take whatever actions are needed to get the job done. Markus was right; it's going down at the marina. That gives us an opportunity to set a distraction before making an escape. The locals flock to the lobster restaurant on the pier. They won't have a clue what's going on until it's too late. By the time the cops or Coast Guard gets there, we'll be long gone. I'll go over the details tomorrow. Right now, my woman is waiting."

The Closer got up to leave, but stopped before he reached the back door. "Get some rest, both of you. Once this gets rolling, we'll be non-stop for over twenty-four hours. I need you to be sharp and ready."

As soon as he heard The Closer pull out of the driveway, Chase rose to his feet. "I need to go in to town."

Markus' head was starting to spin. All he wanted was to fall into bed, not caring where Chase was headed. The Closer didn't leave any instructions about leaving the house. "Get more beer," he mumbled as he sauntered down the hallway.

Chase didn't wait for Markus to reconsider. He grabbed the keys to one of the painting vans and barreled out the driveway. As soon as he had cleared the entrance to the development, he pulled over and speed-dialed Ann. "Change of plans. I have a little time.

Ask Jenna to come to Sunset Beach now. Please, Ann. This may be the only chance I get."

*****

Chase drove as fast as he could down Broadway, making a right onto Sunset Boulevard. It hadn't taken him long at all from Malcolm's house, probably less than five miles. Now it was the waiting game.

A game he had little chance of winning.

The prize was so far out of his reach, he wondered why he was even trying. Jenna's love for him had been destroyed, and the best Chase could hope to do was explain who and what he was…on a professional level.

Perspiration dampened the back collar of his shirt, and with each minute that passed, he grew more agitated. Markus had promised to stop drugging him if he didn't cause any problems. And so far, he was almost a full day away from the seizures.

Chase withdrew his wallet, taking out a strip of pictures he and Jenna had taken at the arcade's photo booth. Remembering that night brought a smile to his face. Playing games at the arcade and cashing in their tickets for a goofy prize they ended up giving away to a little girl too young to play skee-ball. Their moonlit walk on the beach where Jenna had bent down to untie his sneakers, and when she looked into his eyes, he wanted to marry her right then and there. Afterwards, when they lay in bed listening to the sounds of clopping hooves as the horse-drawn carriages passed the beach house on their way back to the stables, Chase knew he wouldn't love anyone else.

She's the perfect woman…for me.

Chase replaced the pictures then shut his eyes. Imagining Jenna running alongside of him on the beach, shooting him her infectious smile filled him with warmth and happiness. She had fascinated him from the first moment they met, and he had never been the same.

How can I possibly admit to her we didn't meet by chance? That I orchestrated the whole book signing frenzy with a few phone calls to Towson University's Drama Department. That I tracked her because of her mother's involvement with Mason

S.A. Van

Hamilton, and Hamilton's connection to The Closer. How can I
tell Jenna I used her for the sole purpose of getting revenge?
Chase didn't have time to formulate any answers.

A car was pulling into the parking lot, and before he looked
back to see who was driving, Chase raced up the steps to the
nearby concession stand. Holding his breath, he prayed he would
somehow find the right words.

"I'm here," Jenna called after shutting the car door. "Where
are you, Chase?"

Chase peered from around the corner of the wooden deck.
"Here." Sticking his hands in his pockets, his head dropped. He
couldn't bear to look at her. He had no right to look at her.

Jenna climbed the three steps, taking her time on each one.
When she stepped on the landing, Chase moved quickly to the far
corner. He was acting like he was afraid of her, instead of the
other way around. She didn't understand at all, and kept her
distance. "You...wanted to talk?"

Without lifting his head, Chase nodded. "I...wanted you to
know...some things. I...have to be...honest with you, Jenna.
You deserve that."

Jenna took a step forward. "Damian arrived a half hour ago.
The first thing he did was...sit me down for a long talk. I...know
who you are, Chase. Damian explained a lot to me; some things I
still can't believe. This is a lot to take in. He...told me you work
for him on some kind of task force. You...are and have been
working undercover to catch The Closer. Damian also told
me...what The Closer did to your family when you were just a
boy." Jenna's voice softened.

Was it pity? Chase wondered.

"Damian also said...you're a good man. You...want to get
The Closer so badly you allowed him to drug you. Is that right?"

Chase nodded again, keeping his head lowered.

"Damian is afraid for you...that you're getting in too deep.
He thought...maybe I could talk you out of...whatever you're
getting ready to do. He thinks you're taking too much of a risk,
and you..." Jenna choked on her words. "Might die. Please don't
do this, Chase."

"You shouldn't care that much about me, Jenna. What I did
to you was...something no one should forgive. You...would be
better off with...someone else." Words felt like leaden balls in his

306

mouth. Chase was having trouble continuing. With his eyes lowered, he didn't notice Jenna walking towards him.

She reached out gingerly and cupped his face in her hand. "Look at me," she whispered. "Please."

Chase slowly raised his face to look into her eyes. Once they held such promise, sparkling every time they talked about spending their lives together. Now, Jenna's dark brown eyes were filled with an endless pool of sadness which he mistook for grief. "I'm...sorry," he mouthed, unable to say the words out loud.

Jenna leaned her forehead against Chase's, a gesture she had done so many times before. The feel of his skin rejuvenated her, scared her, and made her tremble. She knew he could feel her shaking against him, and how much he was probably fighting the urge to touch her. She was tormenting him.

Jenna pulled away. She had repeatedly told herself as she drove the short distance to Sunset beach, she wasn't going to dredge up angry feelings or start their conversation with resentment. Chase had hurt her physically and emotionally; there was no doubt about that. But she knew deep down he would have never touched her that way if drugs were not flowing through his body and mind, making him half-crazy. She blamed The Closer or whoever he had hired to slip Chase the drugs and most likely install the hidden camera Damian had found in her bedroom. Ultimately, Mason Hamilton was the one she held accountable.

The man with whom she had fallen in love was as much a pawn in Hamilton's twisted game as she was. By Chase's hands, she had suffered...and at Hamilton's command, she had been betrayed.

I can't push him away...I'm still in love with him.

"We...need to get past this," Jenna asserted. "You're pushing me away...and I won't let you." Without another word, Jenna pulled Chase into her arms, holding on tightly. "I haven't stopped loving you."

Chase sagged against Jenna's body, making them both sway. They landed against the railing, finding each other's lips. Jenna was taking the lead, kissing him without holding back. The floodgate of confusing emotions had broken, and she felt liberated. Free to love Chase again without any reservations. Free to trust him with her heart, knowing he was a good man, a man worthy of everything she could give.

"Come back with me," she said, gasping for air. "I want you. We need to be together. Right now, Chase."

Chase ran his hands through Jenna's hair. "Not yet, Jenna. Please trust me on this. I have to do something else. I can't get into the details with you."

"It's dangerous, isn't it? Damian said…"

Chase held her gaze. "Yes. I'm not going to lie to you. There's been too much of that happening to last a lifetime. I'm…still working undercover. I need to be for just a little while longer."

Jenna began to protest, and Chase silenced her with a long, deep kiss. "I love you, Jenna Reed, and I promise you, once this is over, we'll be together. Nothing…will keep me away from you. So, rest up. Because when I take you…"

"Promises, promises." Jenna nuzzled Chase's chin. "How much longer? I'm barely able to control myself now. Maybe you should be the one to rest up!" She managed to smile.

"A couple of days, that's all. Think you can keep your libido in check until then, Ms. Reed?" Chase teased as his fingers tugged on the edge of her lacey green thong.

"I'll do my best, but don't push your luck. I may be forced to take my sexual frustration out on the next handsome man who walks down my street."

"I'll keep that in mind." Chase nervously checked his watch. "I…have to go, Jenna." He tugged both of her hands until they slipped around his waist. Laying his head against her neck, Chase breathed deeply, wanting to remember Jenna exactly this way for the rest of his life. "You feel so good."

"Then don't leave me," she pleaded, squeezing him. "Stay with me and let Damian handle…whatever needs to be handled."

Chase sighed, weighing his options. He didn't have any. If he didn't go back, Markus would inform The Closer. Jenna's life would be at stake and The Closer would stop listening to reason. Staying with Jenna would mean Chase signing her death warrant.

Pulling her hands away from his body, Chase pushed back the tears he wanted so desperately to cry. He couldn't let Jenna watch him fall apart or she would refuse to leave him. "Two days, Jenna Reed." Chase kissed her fully, and when they had parted, he memorized every detail of her face.

"Two days, and then I want you to say yes when I ask you to marry me."

Chapter 36

"Welcome home!"

Kelly and Austin were hugged and kissed by Maria as soon as they stepped inside the beach house.

"So glad to be home! What smells so good?" Kelly asked.

"My husband is cooking...so beware! How he gets spaghetti sauce all over the kitchen and on himself instead of keeping it in the pot, I'll never know. Don't worry...I'll make sure he cleans up. We're having meatball sandwiches and salad for lunch. Hope you're hungry!"

"Starving," Austin added. "I'm glad you're here, Maria. You too, Damian."

Damian waved with one hand and stirred the simmering pot with the other. "Austin, next time you pull a daredevil stunt, you might want to avoid fences. But, hey, if it gets you some TLC, then go for it."

Maria promptly swatted Damian's butt. "Don't listen to a word he says. He's just trying to cause trouble. Believe me; I know how to put him in his place. You two go relax in the living room, and we'll call you when the sandwiches are ready. Jenna had to run out for a little bit. Should be back any time now."

When Austin and Kelly left the kitchen, Maria peered through the curtains.

"Stop worrying, sweetheart. Jenna's fine. It's broad daylight. She and Chase need to talk things out."

"About what? He hurt her, Damian. First in Texas, now here. Of course, I'm worried."

"You don't have to be." Damian dried his hands on a dishtowel, then slung it over his shoulder. He grabbed Maria squarely by her shoulders. "Chase works for me. He's on the Joint Task Force. He's been working undercover for months, ever since we got word Mason Hamilton was up to his tricks again. When you told me Lois was being threatened last December, I knew it would only be a matter of time before Hamilton set his sights on Jenna and Austin."

Maria did a double-take.

"I knew you had Lenny watching Austin in Philly so I needed to make sure Jenna was being watched as well. We placed a few long-term substitutes at her school to keep an eye on her during the day, and then at night, the same agents took turns following her. When she announced she was spending the summer in Cape May, I had to act quickly. We found out she was friends with the editor of the local paper down here. Can't remember the girl's name...Lacey, maybe? Anyway, she agreed to get in touch with Jenna and ask her to interview Dr. Chase Garrett, the *travelling author*."

"I can't believe you did this."

"I had to, Maria. Intel indicated Hamilton had enlisted The Closer. Chase needed to get close to Jenna to protect her. He didn't plan on falling in love with her." Damian paused to stir the pot again. "There's more. Chase has history with The Closer; he wants to catch him one way or another."

"Let me get this straight." Maria's tone stiffened. "You sent one of your operatives to protect Jenna? Well, he hasn't done a very good job. She's been tortured and shot. She can't take much more, Damian. I'm telling you right now. This has got to end. Jenna deserves to hear the truth."

"Chase is telling her right now. We're close, Maria. Very close. Within the next twenty-four to forty-eight hours, we could have The Closer in custody."

"He's here? Oh, God! Why do you keep me in the dark so much?"

Damian closed the gap between them and drew Maria into his arms. "Because, sweetheart, whether you want to admit it or not, I do my best work in the dark."

Maria pretended to fight off Damian's affection. "Well, Mr. Pierce, if you don't start leveling with me, you're going to start spending time *alone* in the dark. Starting with tonight. Don't push any more of my buttons." Maria finally let Damian kiss her in the one place which always drove her crazy.

"Threats will get you nowhere, dear wife."

"Damian," Maria whispered in a husky voice, "go stir the pot before it boils over."

"That's incredibly sexy, you know that?"

*****

"I wonder where Jenna went." Austin exchanged a worried look with Kelly.

"She's with Garrett." Jonathan bounded down the stairs and into the living room. "Am I too late for a hug?" As Kelly stood up, Jonathan pulled her into his arms. "I'm so glad you're ok. You too, Austin. It's good to have you back."

"Glad to be back. How are you doing, Jonathan? Managing to stay out of trouble for a few days?"

Jonathan debated how to answer Austin's innocent question, as explicit thoughts about Ann Bailey riveted his mind. "I did the best I could, under the circumstances."

Under the sheets, actually...

"So, we're really going to pull off this wedding, aren't we?" Jonathan changed the subject. "Should be fun. Lots to do, though. As soon as we're done lunch, Damian and I have a long list of errands to run. Starting with picking up the tuxes. Think you can let him out of your sight for a little while, sis?"

Kelly smiled, nudging Austin's knee with her own. "I think I can handle that...as long as you keep an eye on him."

Austin and Jonathan didn't get a chance to respond.

"Lunch is served!" Maria laid a huge platter of meatball sandwiches in the middle of the dining room table, then retreated back to the kitchen. "I'm bringing iced tea," she called over her shoulder.

The wonderful aroma sent everyone rushing to the table. Damian carried in a large salad bowl and two bottles of dressing. Plates, silverware and napkins were already in place.

"Hey, Damian, how soon can you get ready?" Jonathan produced a list from his pocket. "We need to pick up the tuxes, drop off checks to the florist, the photographer and the Inn. This is going to take a while."

"As soon as we're done eating." Damian caught Maria's glare as she distributed the beverages. "Cooking is an art, sweetheart." He playfully wrapped one arm around her waist and squeezed gently.

"And you're not Van Gogh, so don't even think about delegating the cleaning duties to the females in the house. As soon as you're done *eating*...you'll be *cleaning*. I'm sure Jonathan and

Austin can handle the other errands. They can swing back and pick you up to get the tuxes. See? Problem solved."

"Austin, now's the time to think twice about the move you're about to make," Damian teased. "No offense, Kelly."

Kelly smiled as she wiped her mouth. "I'll let that slide. If Austin and I have as many good years together as the two of you, we'll be perfectly happy. Now, if I can just find my brother a good woman..."

Ann barged in the front door as if on cue. She was carrying two boxes from the Cape May Bakery. When everyone's eyes fell on her, she looked back in amazement. "What?"

Jonathan's jaw fell open and a meatball rolled back onto his plate. He caught it quickly then stuffed it back in his mouth, diverting his eyes to his fork.

"Hi, Ann." Kelly stood and held out her hands. "Here, let me help you." She took the boxes and set them on an empty chair stuck in a corner. "Three men in the house, and all they can do is stuff their faces. So much for manners. Come and join us. There's room here next to my brother."

Jonathan coughed, grabbing his water glass.

Kelly shot him a quizzical look, as if to ask *what is your problem?*

Jonathan waved her off, moving his chair slightly so Ann could maneuver hers without bumping into him.

"What's in the box?" Damian asked, soaking up some leftover sauce on his plate with the last piece of his roll. "Dessert, I hope. Please tell me you got cannolis."

"Yes. Cannolis, cupcakes, chocolate cheesecake and some Italian butter cookies. I wanted tiramisu cups but they were all out. That's the box on top. The one on the bottom is filled with breakfast treats for tomorrow morning. Cinnamon buns, fruit pastries, apple turnovers...I can't remember the rest. The cashier was filling the box so fast, I lost track."

Maria groaned. "My dress only stretches so far. This is going to be quite a challenge."

"I know what you mean," Kelly chimed. "I just hope my dress *still fits*. The last time I tried it on..."

"The seamstress said she was going to allow for a few more inches, Kel. Don't worry." Austin covered Kelly's hand with his own.

"Your fitting isn't until tomorrow morning," Maria added. "Treat yourself."

Kelly was the first to open the box. "Hmmm. Too many choices. How about you, Ann? Care to indulge?"

You have no idea, Ann was tempted to say. Brushing against Jonathan's arm propelled her backwards in time. Memories of falling in slow motion entwined with Jonathan's wet body was making her heart race. "Cookie, cupcake, or cannoli?" Kelly repeated, sensing something was definitely going on; she just couldn't place it.

"Ah…cannoli, please." Ann took the small Italian delicacy and placed it on her plate. She offered the box to Jonathan and when he took it from her, their eyes met.

Maria noticed the silent interchange. She was at a loss for words; assuming Jonathan's only love interest was Jenna. But as she stared at her son for a longer time, she could see how he could be attracted to Ann. She was pretty, athletic, personable. A perfect match for him…except for the fact she was a CIA operative.

Jonathan had no idea the type of life Ann lived, but Maria could definitely relate. Calls in the middle of the night. Last minute assignments. Putting your career ahead of your personal life. Ann Bailey could never give Jonathan what he needed as long as she was married to the Agency. Stability. Family. Love. Not in the job description she had chosen. Her job was too demanding. Until she was ready to let her heart make the right commitment, Jonathan didn't stand a chance.

"Maria?" Kelly tapped Maria's hand to get her attention. "I was just wondering if we could hit a few shops on the Mall while the guys are out?"

"Of course!" Maria answered, embarrassed she had been lost in her thoughts. "Do you want to wait for Jenna?"

"I'm here!" Jenna called as she dropped her packages on the kitchen table and hurried into the dining room. She bent down to kiss Austin then Kelly. "Glad to be home?"

"Sis, you have no idea." Austin moved over one seat so Jenna could sit between him and Kelly.

"Missed you." Jenna hugged Kelly around the neck.

"Well?" Kelly asked, putting Jenna on the spot.

"I saw Chase," Jenna began as all eyes magnetized on her. "And he's going to ask me to marry him!"

"Going to...?" Kelly asked. "When?"

"In two days...and I'm going to say yes!"

Maria exchanged a wary glance with Damian at the same time Jonathan and Ann stared at each other. Austin and Kelly were the only two people at the table not clued in.

"Why is everyone looking that way?" Austin asked. "Aren't you guys happy for my sister?"

Damian broke the uncomfortable silence. "We're very happy. I guess...this just took us all by surprise. Chase is a good man."

"So where is your *good man*, Jenna?"

Jenna hesitated in answering. "He's busy, Kelly. Very, very...busy."

*****

"Any last minute advice for the groom?"

"Keep your woman happy...and you'll be happy." Damian paused as he pulled in front of Richardson's Formal Wear. "Oh, and one more thing..."

"If this is the sex talk, I think we have that covered."

"Whoa...too much information." Jonathan exited the back seat, heading straight for the front door of the tuxedo shop.

When he caught up to him, Damian smacked Jonathan on the side of the head. "I was going to say...before I was so rudely interrupted...make sure you tell Kelly you love her *every day*, Austin. Don't miss an opportunity. Or your day will get progressively worse."

"Speaking from personal experience?" Jonathan joked.

"Let's just say some lessons are learned the hard way."

"Gentlemen!" The sales associate clapped her hands to get their attention. "If you'll follow me into the changing rooms, I'll pull your tuxedos. Right this way."

Jonathan held back, stepping in Damian's way. "I need to talk to you about Renault."

"What do you know, Jonathan?"

"I know...he's Kelly's father. Mason used Kelly and her mother as eye candy for the media. Renault pulled me aside at

Ellen's memorial service. He told me more than I probably needed to hear. I'm afraid he's going to show up at the wedding, and ruin everything."

"You don't have to worry about Renault."

"Hey, you guys coming?" Austin called.

"In a minute," Jonathan replied. "Why shouldn't I worry?"

Damian gripped Jonathan's arm, leaning closer to keep his voice down. "Renault is dead. Found by a couple of hunters on a private reserve not too far from here. My resources..."

"Chase Garrett? Relax, Damian. Garrett told me who he is and what's going on. He also told me Markus is a traitor. But Garrett didn't mention anything about Renault. Are you sure?"

"Chase may not have known at the time you spoke to him. But he did confirm The Closer was intending to kill Renault. I have that straight from Chase's partner."

"Ann Bailey."

Damian folded his arms. "Is there anything you don't know?"

Jonathan looked away. It was time to lie. "That just about sums it up, Damian. We better get back to Austin. He..."

Damian stepped in Jonathan's path. "You know I'll find out...eventually. Better tell me now before someone else gets hurt...including yourself."

Jonathan shook his head. "That's all I've got."

"You can be a stubborn bastard when you want to be."

"Funny. I've always thought the same about you." Jonathan tore away from Damian and headed to the changing rooms. He had made a promise to protect Jenna. Telling Damian what Chase was planning could complicate matters. Jonathan couldn't take a chance on that.

A promise was a promise.

*****

"Maria, I...need to apologize."

Jenna struggled for the right words. They were waiting inside Rose's Victorian Bridal Shop while Kelly had her final fitting.

"No, you don't. I had no right to keep the truth from you about your mother. I thought at the time it was the right decision, but in retrospect, it wasn't. Lois was...*is* my best friend. She was there for me from the start and I promised her I would repay her somehow. Instead, I just made things worse by lying to her children. Does Austin know, by the way?" Maria held her breath.

"No, not yet. I don't want to spoil the wedding. I am sorry, Maria...for not trusting you. I was wrong to lash out at you and Ann. You've both been trying to protect me. I do appreciate that. It's taken me up till now to realize just how much."

"Then let's move forward."

"I don't know what I'd do without you, Maria."

"And I don't know what I'd do without *either* of you." Kelly approached their chairs, standing with her hands on her hips. "What do you think of my wedding gown?"

Maria and Jenna stood up in a synchronized motion. They were mesmerized by how beautiful Kelly looked with her blond hair cascading down the back of the strapless gown. She was radiant, her wide smile extremely contagious.

"Well?" Kelly twirled slowly. "What do you think?"

Jenna reached for Kelly's hand. "You look...amazing! Austin is going to..."

"He's already seen it, Jenna. You were still in Texas. He came with me to pick it out. It's not going to be a surprise." Kelly frowned.

"Oh, he's going to be surprised when we get done with you," Maria quipped. "Trust me; he won't remember the details of your dress. Just how to get it off of you."

Kelly blushed. "Your turn, Jenna. Try on your Maid of Honor dress." Kelly instantly regretted not including Maria in the wedding party, especially since she had asked Damian to walk her down the aisle. "Maria, I..."

Maria picked up on Kelly's embarrassment. "Don't you think someone needs to keep the men straight? I'm your girl. Besides, I brought my favorite dress to wear to the wedding. One that I know for a fact makes my husband drool."

Hearing her phone buzz, Maria stepped next door into the bridal accessory room. "How are you doing? We'll be done here in another twenty minutes or so."

Ann caught her breath. "Fine...I think."

"You don't sound fine. Everything ok?"

"This wedding stuff is hard work."

Maria looked at her watch. "Well, you've got at least another hour to set up for the shower. Once Jenna gets the seamstress to check her dress, we're heading over to the Inn. I crossed that off Jonathan's list. Thought we'd be better suited to answer questions regarding candles and table linens. I don't trust the guys to handle that. We'd be sitting with paper napkins and citronella candles as centerpieces."

"You should have been a wedding planner."

"Hardly." Maria laughed. "When Damian and I got married we had even less time. We were racing down the aisle right before a policy change was signed barring agents from marrying. I'm not kidding! We said our vows in less than ten minutes, and then the policy took effect at noon. I'm not complaining. I love him, even if he drives me crazy."

"You've stayed together all these years. That says a lot. I hope to have that one day with someone."

"You will. Find yourself a good man...and hang on tight."

"I plan to. Bye!" Grateful they hadn't activated the video chat feature on their smartphones, Ann wiped a bead of sweat running down her cheek. Her face was getting hot, but she had no time to fantasize about Jonathan right at the moment.

Not only was Ann in charge of decorating the beach house for Kelly's bridal shower, but she had to take time for one more phone call. To Lois Reed.

Helping Lois witness her son's wedding was going to take every trick in the book, and probably a few covert maneuvers.

None of which the CIA had prepared her for.

*****

"Here's your beer." Chase dropped a twelve-pack of Guinness on the kitchen table.

"*Irish* beer?" Markus' disapproval was evident.

"My beer run, my choice. Want one?"

Markus waved his hands. "No. Next time get Red Stripe, Jamaican beer. Sit down. The Closer just called."

Chase purposely lowered his eyes.

"Tomorrow night. Seven o'clock. Slip #5 at the marina. The boat is called *Trace*. He will be waiting for you...and Jenna Reed."

"That wasn't the plan. I was to get the treasure pieces from Jenna. He knows that."

"His plan, his rules."

Chase gripped his knee under the table. This was something he hadn't counted on.

It was too late. He was out of options and out of time.

Jenna was going to be the bait.

Chapter 37

"I can't believe you had the time to pull off a bridal shower, Jenna! You, Maria and Ann are incredible! Austin and I were so surprised. It means a lot to us how all of you are helping us with the wedding. I can't..." Kelly pushed back a few tears. "I can't find the right words to thank you."

"You just did." Jenna wrapped her arm around her best friend and smiled. They were both sitting on Kelly and Austin's bed. The house was very quiet, giving them a rare moment of privacy. The men had gone next door to the Maylors' to dress, leaving the Reeds' beach house to the ladies. "We're having a lot of fun with the preparations. It's just what we need. A breather from all the drama." Jenna reached into the pocket of her robe and pulled out two small boxes, one tied in peach ribbon, the other in dark green. "I have something for you."

Kelly could hardly get out the words. "More...presents?"

"Something *old...and new*. Maria has something *borrowed* for you, and Ann's taking care of something *blue*. I think we've got all the bases covered." She laughed.

"Oh, Jenna!" Kelly held her breath as she withdrew a dainty silver bracelet with tiny pearls separated by filigree. With shaking hands, Kelly laid the bracelet in her palm then looked up to catch Jenna's smile.

"This is *something old*," Jenna said as she unclasped the hook and refastened it around Kelly's wrist. "It was my mom's. My grandmother gave it to her on her wedding day and I...want you to have it. Besides, when I get married...you can let me borrow it. We'll just keep it in the family, ok?"

Kelly nodded as tears soaked her face. "Thank you, Jenna. I know this will mean a lot to Austin, too. He was really choked up last night when he was telling me how much he wished your parents could have seen us get married. I know it's supposedly bad luck to see the bride the night before the wedding, but I just couldn't let go of him. He needed me last night."

"I don't believe in any of that superstitious stuff anyway," Jenna said with sincerity. "We've all had enough bad luck the past few months. I think we're due for some good times. Now, open the other box...and no more crying...not just yet!" Jenna grabbed the wicker tissue box from the nightstand. "Oh, well...go ahead. We haven't done your make-up yet!"

Kelly turned her attention to the second box.

"And this is *something new*," Jenna added.

Kelly opened the lid slowly. She pushed aside the small piece of tissue paper to reveal a pair of silver and pearl earrings which perfectly complemented the bracelet. She couldn't believe how delicate and beautiful they were.

"When you first told me you and Austin were getting married, I took the bracelet to one of the jewelers in town. He specializes in creating one-of-a kind pieces, and he was able to create the earrings to match the design as close as possible. I was very pleased...and I know my mom would be, too. I hope you like them."

"Jenna, I love them...and you! Thank you so much!" Kelly grabbed Jenna around the neck. She couldn't believe this day had finally come. Jenna would be her sister-in-law in just a few hours. Everything she had hoped for was coming together. She was so excited.

"You're going to be a beautiful bride, Kelly. And the wedding...oh, I can't wait!" Jenna jumped from the bed and pulled Kelly up with her.

"Let's see if Maria and Ann are up. Might as well enjoy a peaceful breakfast before we all start going a little crazy!"

*****

"What did you say?"

Mason Hamilton loosened his tie, as his heart rate jumped to a dangerous level. He was starting to hyperventilate, and his throat was getting dry.

"She left you a calling card, Mason." The Closer flipped the small plain card between his fingers. "She said you would remember who she was. I suppose you want me to read it?"

"Get on with it."

The Closer could just envision Mason pacing back and forth with his cell phone on speaker, and his hand hovering above his whiskey decanter on the mantle. Mason was so predictable. "The card says *You are next* on one side and *Remember Brussels* on the other. Mean anything to you?"

Mason swallowed hard. "Yes." His fears had come full circle. The young, helpless girl who haunted his dreams was coming to kill him.

She had succeeded in murdering Renault, a miracle in its own right. Renault had let down his guard, or he had been tricked into it. Either way, this woman had accomplished the impossible. Revenge at the highest level.

Mason stood frozen, staring into space. His own fatality looming before him, Mason wondered how much time he had left.

"I want you up here...now!" Mason shouted. "Forget the whole Jenna Reed business and get on the road as soon as we hang up. I need protection, and you're the only one...I trust with my life."

"I suppose I should be flattered," The Closer replied unconvincingly. "But here we are again, Mason. Your timetable is not *my timetable*. I'm trying to get you the treasure pieces once and for all. Enough with the game-playing. You know I don't have the tolerance for it. It's going to end tonight. Once I'm done with that, I'll head up your way. In the meantime, I'll send a few guys to watch your house and your office. Team leader's name is Langston. They should be there within the hour. You stay inside with Kliric and don't open the door until Langston gets there. You understand?"

Mason turned to Hans Kliric after he tossed his cell on the mantle. "Tell the staff to leave the premises immediately. Then bring up the guns from the storage closet."

"You are...worried, Mason."

"Yes, Hans, I am worried. But The Closer assures me his team is on the way. We just need to...take necessary precautions until they get here." Mason nervously ran his fingers through his thick, silver hair.

"I will protect you, Mason," Hans added, confidence exuding from his massive chest. "No one will hurt you."

"I have no doubt about that, Hans. However, we must be prepared. Someone is coming to kill me...and I intend to stage a counterattack at any cost."

*****

"Are you completely out of your mind?"

Ann stared at Chase, seething. "It won't work, and you're going to scare Jenna half to death."

They had been arguing for the past several minutes in the kitchen of her rental. Chase had snuck inside the back door, telling Ann he could only stay a few minutes. He was already well past his deadline. If he didn't get back soon, he knew Markus would be out hunting for him.

"It *will work* as long as you do your part." Chase sidestepped Ann to double-check both of the Glock nine-millimeter pistols she had placed on the dining room table. Part of her cache stored in the basement by the elusive *"S"* prior to her arrival. "You need to have more confidence in me. I know what I'm doing."

Ann shrugged, knowing she was wasting her breath. "I trust you, partner, but this is suicide. You're not listening to me and I'm pretty sure Jenna's pleas fell on deaf ears as well. Think for one minute what you're doing...and how she'll feel if...you don't come back."

Chase held Ann by her shoulders. "I love Jenna, you know that. If I let my feelings for her get in the way...I'll be too distracted. He'll escape...again."

"Not if we plan this right. If we have enough undercover agents on site, there will be no place for him to go."

"He's not stupid, Ann. He's thought this through very carefully. I can't take a chance he'll start shooting and innocent people will get in the way...including Jenna. We have to do this my way."

"Chase, let me call Damian. For God's sake, he's right across the street. He can be here in two minutes."

"No. If you call him now, he'll insist on taking charge, and that will screw up the wedding. You know how he is, Ann."

Ann shook her head in frustration. "Yes, I know how the both of you are. Bull-headed and stubborn. Risk takers to the max. Now you're taking a risk with Jenna's life. That's totally unfair to her. She has no say in it whatsoever. You know she'll come running the moment you call...or I give her the note you've written. She won't hesitate to run right into the line of fire."

"Jenna will be safe. You'll be there to protect her." Chase stuck both guns into a small duffel, then looked around to make sure he had the extra supplies Ann was also providing. "I've got Knox on board. He won't let anything happen to Jenna; believe me."

Ann turned away so Chase wouldn't see the pain in her eyes. She was worried for Jenna and Jonathan's safety, but at the same time, twinges of jealousy were threatening to surface. Too many emotions were hitting her all at once.

Chase was out the door before she had a chance to wish him good luck.

*****

When the three-piece strings ensemble starting playing the wedding march, Jenna's eyes flew immediately up to the picture-perfect sky. Pillowy clouds were scattered randomly like puffs of cotton on a light-blue felt background. Even the sun was cooperating, beaming down just the right amount of brightness and warmth to add a golden radiance to the day.

Jenna turned back and winked at Kelly before she started her walk down the white runner. She smiled, hoping Chase was somewhere in the crowd watching her from a safe vantage point. Trying hard to keep a smile on her face as she walked, Jenna's heart trembled.

Chase had been confident, but she had seen the fear in his eyes. *He's going to be fine. He's going to be safe. He loves you. After today, we'll be together.*

Jenna forced happy thoughts to the front of her mind. After today, it would be over. Chase would capture The Closer, Damian and Maria would charge Mason Hamilton with several crimes, and her family would be safe again.

This time tomorrow, I'll be in Chase's arms...

Jenna was at the bottom of the wooden steps now. She closed her eyes briefly, saying a prayer for Chase and one for the bride and groom. She lifted the hem of her long gown and slowly ascended the steps. When she reached the top of the gazebo, Jenna's eyes widened when she saw her brother.

Austin stood straight with his hands clasped and the widest grin on his face Jenna had ever seen. Jenna couldn't believe how handsome he looked. He was clean-shaven, probably at Maria's insistence, and his hair was tousled with gel. Not quite *GQ* material, but she was absolutely sure Kelly would be notably impressed.

As Kelly reached the top of the gazebo, she handed Jenna her bouquet of peach roses, white daisies and baby's breath. Then she kissed Jenna on the cheek. "You're next," she whispered, watching Jenna blush.

Exchanging vows at the gazebo behind the Washington Street Mall was the setting for Kelly's dream wedding. She had told Jenna the first time she and Austin had climbed the steps to the gazebo, she had known she wanted to marry him. Then when he kissed her and a small group of tourists applauded, she felt like her dream could actually come true.

Kelly was already in a trance and barely heard Damian wish her well, lift her veil, and kiss her cheek. When he placed her hand inside Austin's, she felt like she was floating, never wanting to come back down to earth.

"You take my breath away." Austin lifted her hand to his lips, then laced their fingers together.

"I love you," Kelly responded, allowing Austin to lead her a few steps forward in front of the pastor.

After he greeted the wedding party, the pastor began the ceremony with a prayer. As the wedding guests filled in around the bottom of the gazebo, Maria looked around and wondered what was keeping Ann. In a few minutes, she felt someone touching her elbow. "You're late," Maria noted.

"Couldn't be avoided." Ann tugged on the hem of her gray chiffon dress. It seemed so much shorter than she remembered when she tried it on a couple of weeks ago. At the time she wasn't wearing four-inch heels. She wished she wasn't wearing them now.

All for the look...

And to make Jonathan pay attention. If he ever got the chance. Jenna looked stunning in her peach, floor-length silk gown. It flowed seductively, accentuating her curves and revealing most of her back. Jonathan would be a fool not to notice.

He has no business noticing...

Jenna had made it quite clear she intended to marry Chase. Jonathan needed to get his priorities in check. She wasn't just going to stand by and let him...

Damn, he looks good...

Ann couldn't take her eyes off of him. Although Jonathan looked enticing in his tailored tuxedo, Ann much preferred to remember what it was like to lie next to him without clothes getting in the way. She sighed, a bit too loudly, catching Maria's attention.

"They look lovely, don't they?"

"Who?" Ann asked, shifting uncomfortably.

"The bride and groom...and the best man...and the Maid of Honor."

"Absolutely." Ann smiled, staring straight ahead.

"Nice dress." Maria glanced sideways at Ann, sensing her uneasiness. "Must be a bitch walking in those heels, though. I can't do that anymore. The price you pay for fashion catches up to you real quick. Guess you can kick them off at the reception if you want. I think it will be pretty laid back."

"I just might do that." Ann scanned the crowd for anyone who looked out of place. She wondered if Lois Reed was in the crowd and how she was holding up. Ann's heart ached for Lois, wishing the circumstances were different, and she could be on the gazebo, standing just a few feet away.

Ann focused again on the wedding ceremony. The pastor was reading from the Bible now, and telling the couple how love would see them through to the end of their days. At the end of the minister's message, he asked Kelly and Austin to face each other and hold hands. Rings and vows were exchanged quietly as both Austin and Kelly were so overwhelmed, their voices were cracking.

The pastor smiled and placed his hands on both of their shoulders, giving his blessing. "It is my pleasure, Austin and Kelly, to unite you as husband and wife." He leaned a little closer and winked. "Now...it's time for the kiss."

Austin didn't immediately kiss Kelly as everyone expected. He traced the sides of her face with his fingers, drawing her face upward. He kissed her softly at first, then as he tasted the tears on Kelly's lips, he stopped. "I will always love you," he said, pausing for a few seconds. Then before Kelly could say a single word, Austin crushed her lips, only stopping when they both needed air. "I *never* want you to forget our wedding kiss. Never...*ever*."

Kelly reciprocated by pulling Austin's face closer for another powerful kiss. "No chance of that happening...*ever*."

Hearing loud applause and whistles, Austin finally released Kelly into Jenna's waiting arms. In the process, Jenna dropped her bouquet and Kelly's. "Clumsy again," she muttered as her face reddened.

"It's ok, sis. Today, you can be as clumsy as you want. I'm on cloud nine and plan to stay there as long as possible. I have the woman I love and my family right here. Today is a great day!"

"How about a hug for the best man?" Jonathan stepped forward and pulled Kelly into his arms. "Congrats, sis. I'm very happy for you." He kissed Kelly's cheek as she held on tighter. "You look very, very beautiful." Jonathan turned his attention to Austin and stuck out his hand. "Austin, take good care of her. I'm counting on you."

Austin beamed with pride. "I won't let you down, Jonathan. I promise."

Damian met Maria half-way up the steps so they could congratulate the couple together. "We're so happy for both of you!" Maria kissed Austin on the cheek as Damian did the same to Kelly.

"The trolley's coming!" Ann called. As soon as Maria had raced up to greet Kelly and Austin, Ann had taken a few minutes to once again search the crowd. Lois had blended perfectly into the group of on-lookers, just as Ann thought she would. Whatever disguise Lois had chosen, she wasn't recognized at all by anyone in attendance. Ann was duly impressed.

Lois and Maria were professional spies, even after all these years, and nothing they did would ever surprise her.

The white wedding trolley, sponsored by the Cape May Mid-Atlantic Center for the Arts, had just pulled up along the curb. Cascades of silk roses in peach and white with dark green leaves decorated both sides. Large white bows were on the front and back of the trolley. Even the driver was smartly dressed in a black tuxedo with tails and a top hat decorated with the colors of the wedding party.

"All aboard!" With a dramatic wave, he gestured for the bridal party and guests to follow. As soon as everyone was seated, the trolley took off, clanging its bell along the way.

From a safe distance several yards away, a woman dressed in worn jeans, a brown corduroy jacket and Vera Bradley sunglasses couldn't suppress her smile any longer.

Or her tears of joy.

Lois Reed had just watched her son get married. A feat she never would have undertaken without Ann Bailey's help.

A favor she promised to return one day.

Chapter 38

Sparkling white lights dazzled the entranceway.

Twilight was emerging, bringing with it a romantic ambience only a seaside Victorian hotel could capture.

The Inn of Cape May.

Grand and gracious. Stately and regal.

Known for its signature purple awnings, dozens of one-of-a-kind antiques and heirlooms decorating the lobby and corridors, and the hearty welcome of its staff, it was no wonder the Inn was one of the town's most popular venues for wedding receptions.

No wonder it had been Kelly and Austin's first choice.

With the backdrop of the rolling surf and the setting sun, it was a picture-perfect setting for a late afternoon wedding reception. As the hotel's staff hurried to fluff bows and adjust floral cascades, curious onlookers gathered on the sidewalk and across the street.

The wedding party would be arriving soon. No one wanted to miss catching a glimpse of the bride in her flowing gown. Or the smile of the groom as he held onto her hand. Happiness was contagious, and as the crowd continued to grow, their excitement intensified.

The clanging of the trolley bell could be heard from a few blocks away. Any minute now, it would round the curve onto Ocean Avenue. Tourists were getting their cameras ready. Children were jumping up and down. The staff of the Inn scrambled to take their places. It was time to welcome the bride and groom!

As the unmistakable wedding trolley pulled alongside the curb at the Inn, everyone on board gazed out the windows and gasped in surprise. To their delight, the Inn's staff had taken the liberty to stand on either side of the white runner and were clapping.

Jenna was the first to embark alongside of Jonathan and Damian. Maria was next, followed by Ann, who stepped aside to take a picture of Austin and Kelly exiting the trolley. Ann kept backing up until she could get a better focus. Her left heel sunk into the grass just inches off the sidewalk. As she started to lose her balance, she felt a familiar and reassuring hand reach around her waist.

"Falling for me already," Jonathan whispered close to her ear.

Ann sucked in a deep breath as she lowered her camera, missing the Kodak moment. She turned, pushing Jonathan further back into the crowd. "Don't sneak up on me like that."

"That wouldn't be a threat, would it Agent Bailey?" Jonathan winked, catching Ann's inability to ward off a smile.

"Of course not. When I *threaten* you, Jonathan Knox, you'll damn well know it."

"I already know it. I'm hoping you'll do it again...*very soon.*"

Ann withdrew his arm and stepped away, trying to distance herself from his intoxicating cologne. "Dancing with the Maid of Honor?" Sarcasm mixed dangerously with jealousy.

Jonathan uttered a quick laugh. "You're sexy when you're riled up. Actually, you're sexy anyway. Love the dress, by the way." He leaned closer. "I'd like it better on the floor by your bed."

Before Ann could recover, Jonathan strode off in the direction of the reception. Flustered and frustrated, Ann could do little but stuff her camera inside her clutch and follow him.

*****

Jonathan stopped at the bar for a double martini, then entered the banquet room. The reception was just getting started. Wait staff were offering trays of various hors d'oeuvres. The champagne fountain was flowing like liquid sunshine, and the bride and groom were still in the midst of getting hugs and well-wishes.

As he scanned the room, Jonathan stopped momentarily to stare at Jenna. She was holding a glass of white wine and laughing. She was happy. For the first time since they had known each other, Jonathan sincerely believed Jenna was truly happy.

Even if Garrett wasn't right beside her.

Jonathan felt the hairs on his neck stand to attention. Chase Garrett would be risking his life in a few hours, and depending on that outcome, Jonathan knew his life was about to change.

If Garrett was successful in capturing The Closer, then the wheels would be put in motion to bring down Mason. Jonathan would have to return to New York immediately to assume the leadership of H-K, while Jenna and Chase would get officially engaged.

Maybe that's the way it should be, Jonathan thought, finally acknowledging what he'd known all along. *Maybe Jenna isn't the girl for me...maybe I just need to look a little farther...*

As Ann walked straight past him to take her seat, Jonathan caught his breath.

It didn't take him too long to consider the other possibility...*if Garrett fails, and something happens to him, I promised him...I would take care of Jenna...and love her.*

Jonathan downed his drink, wishing it would dull his senses a lot faster. When Jenna looked his way and their eyes met, Jonathan felt like he had been hit by lightning. It was a different sensation this time, pain and pleasure rolled into one. He needed fresh air as quickly as possible. Racing outside to the deck, he would have fallen to his knees if Damian hadn't been quick enough to catch him.

"One drink and you're doubling over? Maybe I should get one." Damian laughed. He clapped Jonathan on the back. "You ok? Weddings used to make me nervous, too. Always thought people were wondering when I would be next, the single girls trying to latch onto me for a dance, the other guys hoping I'd leave early." Damian paused, finally noticing Jonathan wasn't paying a bit of attention. "What's going on, Jonathan?"

Jonathan stumbled into a nearby chair to catch his breath. "I...don't know, Damian."

Damian sat next to him. "I think you do. You know more about what's happening with Chase than you're letting on. Do yourself a favor and tell me what..."

Jonathan stood up, straightened his jacket and ran his fingers through his hair. "Don't lecture me, Damian. I know what I'm doing."

"Well then, *Best Man*, get yourself inside and dance with the Maid of Honor. Start looking like you're having a good time."

Jonathan knew better than to continue arguing with a man twice his size. He brushed past Damian, grabbed two glasses of wine from the bar, and walked back to his table. Setting a glass in front of Jenna, he tapped her on the shoulder. "Take one sip and then we're heading for the dance floor." Jonathan held out his hand, waiting for Jenna's response.

Surprisingly, she did exactly as he suggested. Jenna placed her hand in Jonathan's and allowed him to lead her onto the dance floor. As she laid her hand on top of his shoulder, she noticed immediately the tension, or excitement...surging through both of them. "You know...we don't have to do this. There's nothing in the wedding guide that says it's mandatory the Maid of Honor has to dance with the Best Man."

Jonathan avoided Jenna's gaze. "Forget it. I've been told by two people already the Best Man should dance with the Maid of Honor. Might as well keep the peace." Jonathan changed the subject, still looking away. "You look beautiful, by the way. Peach is definitely your color. And your hair ...*wow*."

"Funny how you can give me a compliment without looking at me. What's going on with you?"

Jonathan took a deep breath before tilting his head towards Jenna. There was so much he wanted to tell her, and so little he could. "Weddings make me nervous. Ok? I've admitted it."

Jenna couldn't contain her laughter. "Afraid some sexually-charged woman is going to sweep you off your feet? Better learn some self-control, Jonathan Knox."

Jonathan eased his grip on Jenna's waist, widening the distance between them. "I think I need another drink."

"Song's over anyway."

Without another word, Jonathan escorted Jenna back to their table. He winked at Kelly, then rose again when she beckoned him with her finger.

"Time for a dance, big brother. You can't deny the bride so don't even think about protesting." Kelly laughed as she pulled Jonathan back to the dance floor.

"You snagged me just as I was heading back to the bar. You owe me, sis."

"Sorry. Thought I'd better grab you for a dance before you started swaying by yourself. You look a little pale. Everything ok?"

"I'm great," Jonathan lied.

"Dinner is served," the hotel banquet manager announced as he strode into the middle of the dance floor just as the song ended.

After taking Kelly back to her seat, Jonathan took a glass of champagne from one of the servers. He raised his glass high in the air. "To the bride and groom. May you always love, laugh and live like a passionate fire that has no end. Appreciate life to the fullest as each other's best friend. And find comfort and joy in knowing the other will bend. To Austin and Kelly, a happy life! Congratulations!"

As everyone raised their glasses, Jonathan drained his in a single gulp. He bent down to kiss Kelly's cheek then stretched his hand toward Austin. "I'm jealous, you guys," he said with a smile, then headed back to his seat.

Maria patted Jonathan's hand. "I'm impressed, Best Man. Good job with the toast."

"Thank you." Jonathan waved to the server to bring him another glass of champagne.

"Looking to get drunk?" Jenna raised her eyebrows.

"No," Jonathan replied. "Just mildly buzzed."

Before he had taken a sip, Jonathan felt his cell vibrate inside his pocket. Unless he was mistaken, he knew who was texting him.

It was show time.

And Chase Garrett was calling all the shots.

*****

Staring was rude, but she couldn't help it.

Not one bit.

Ann was uncharacteristically irritated. Thinking for one moment she could lure Jonathan away from Jenna had been nothing but overconfidence. Now she was being forced to sit in the same room and watch him rub elbows or any other part of Jenna's body he could get away with. At the very least, he could be nonchalant about it, but apparently that wasn't his style.

Jonathan Knox exuded sexual prowess just by blinking his eyes, and Ann had fallen for it. How Jenna could appear to be so calm and collected sitting only inches away from him was beyond Ann's comprehension.

.A. Van

Jonathan was making every hair on her body stand to attention, not to mention striking her libido up several notches. He looked so handsome in his tuxedo. When he had wrapped his arms around her in the alleyway just a short while ago, she inhaled the unmistaken scent of his cologne, Clive Christian 1872. A very unique and exhilarating scent for which few men could justify spending over three hundred dollars a bottle.

Unique and exhilarating.

Suited Jonathan perfectly. *Handsome and sexy.*

God, she could go on and on.

Fantasizing and rationalizing about Jonathan was only complicating matters.

Stop it, Ann repeated over and over silently. She didn't need any more drama to deal with. Jenna still needed protection and Chase was in way over his head, so much Ann worried she'd never be able to help him.

As conflicting priorities battled within, Ann was too lost in her thoughts. Mindless table conversation went on without her while she focused on her obligations, personal and professional. It was the only way she could think of to get through the reception without giving herself a migraine, and keeping her jealousy twinges in check.

God knows she had plenty of them. Shock waves were riding up and down her body each time Jonathan leaned back to glance in her direction...with his arm draped casually around the back of Jenna's chair.

Was he doing that on purpose? Ann wondered.

Jonathan didn't seem like a hurtful person, but she had rebuffed him in the alleyway. She had every reason to. Jonathan Knox couldn't have it both ways. Despite her previous bad choices in male companions, she had too much self-respect to allow someone to use her just for sex.

Ann's lips twitched. She suddenly became overheated. Jonathan was looking her way again, and this time she couldn't pull her eyes away.

Coward, her conscience reprimanded.

Needing air desperately, Ann rose from her seat and headed outside through the lobby. Her appetite had been ruined, although she did manage to taste the chicken fricassee, finding it to be extraordinarily good along with the almond-crusted green beans and potatoes in the puff pastry.

Once fresh air hit her face, she was able to breathe again.

Which lasted roughly ten seconds.

Her cell was vibrating.

Her partner was calling.

Chapter 39

Dead fools were the worst kind.
Their lives were over, but the people who cared about them
continued to suffer...for years to come.

Ann had recited this lecture several times trying to talk some sense into him, and he hadn't listened.

Too headstrong for reason to seep through the crevices of his already tortured mind, and too bullheaded to admit his partner was right.

Chase adjusted the binoculars. His nerves were raw. He was fighting the urge to call off the whole undercover mission, grab Jenna and make a run for it. Letting The Closer go would always haunt him, and this fact alone made him reconsider. Gut-wrenching remorse would hit him the exact moment he left the marina.

He couldn't give in to temptation. He had made his decision.

The world would be a safer place because of what he was prepared to do. Chase used that encouragement to re-focus. Cursing his inability to come up with an alternate plan, Chase shifted uncomfortably in his crouched position. He should have just asked Jenna for the three treasure pieces and told her the entire truth. They were the bargaining chips The Closer had demanded. She would have gladly handed them over without a second thought.

Second thoughts were dangerous mistakes.

Another one of Ann's mantras she felt the need to share quite often. Amongst others.

"You're right, partner," Chase mumbled. Peering out from his vantage point at the marina, he scanned the dock again. He had arrived just shy of two hours before The Closer was scheduled to appear. Enough time to get his bearings from his hiding place inside the marine mechanic's storage room directly across from the first pier off the dock. The shop had closed at noon due to weekend hours, and Chase had no problem bypassing the deadbolt and standard lock combination. *Lock Disengagement 101*, as Ann liked to call it, was a quirky class taught at Langley most people tried to ignore. Chase had gone under protest, later realizing how beneficial a few little picks could be after being the only person to successfully unlock every single deadbolt in record time.

He often kidded Ann he had chosen the wrong profession, and could probably be making at least double his salary on the flip side of the law. Her usual response was she'd be the unlucky agent assigned to track him down, and no amount of lock-picking tools would help him at that point. *Checkmate*, Ann Bailey-style.

"Hope you get here in time, partner."

Chase glanced at his watch. Right about now Ann had to make her move, and it wouldn't be an easy one. She had to convince Jenna to leave Austin and Kelly's wedding, retrieve the treasure pieces, and get to the marina within the hour.

To save his life, that's what the note would say, and Jenna wouldn't hesitate to act immediately. He knew her all too well. She'd rush in without thinking, putting herself in harm's way...all because she loved him.

And she had no idea he had set her up.

*****

"It's happening."

Ann stepped next to Damian as he stood by the champagne fountain with his arms folded. Maria had left for the ladies room informing him they would be taking in the next dance, and he needed to stay put until she returned.

"Now?"

"As soon as I can get Jenna to the marina." Ann shifted her posture, swearing she was giving up four-inch heels forever.

"I'm coming with you."

"That's not a good idea."

Damian lowered his voice. "You work for me, remember?"

"Yes, boss. You never let me forget. But right now, you need to listen to reason. Chase has this all planned out. If you show up, The Closer will be spooked, make a run for it, and this whole sting will go under. I don't like it any more than you do, but he's my partner. I can't let him down. I'll text you once Jenna and I get to the marina."

"What?" Damian asked louder than he intended. He backed up, gesturing for Ann to do the same.

Ann casually glanced around to see if anyone in the near vicinity was paying attention. Satisfied the other wedding guests were otherwise engaged with dancing and laughing, she resumed her conversation. "That's part of the grand scheme. Chase needs Jenna to deliver the treasure pieces to the marina. He's going to use them to bargain for her life with The Closer. Personally, I don't like making deals with assassins but Chase sees this as his prime opportunity to take down his nemesis. I'm worried, Damian. I'm not going to sugarcoat it for you. Chase is in too deep this time. I don't know if I can pull him out alive."

"The Closer picked the marina because he knows he'll have the advantage. He could be hiding on any boat with a clean shot as soon as Jenna steps on the dock. You have to stay with her, Ann. Don't let Jenna out of your sight for one minute. Do you hear me? I'll get Maria and we'll be just a few steps behind you. I'm already packing." Damian lifted his jacket to show Ann his shoulder holster.

"Only you would wear a gun to a wedding, Damian Pierce." Maria's voice matched the furrow on her brow. "Care to explain yourself?"

Ann took her cue and backed away. There was no way she was getting in the middle of that little discussion. Taking a deep breath, she marched straight to Jenna's table and tapped her on the shoulder. "Got a minute?"

Jenna looked up with dazed eyes. Three glasses of champagne were her limit, and she was dangerously eyeing the fourth. "Please tell me I'm not slurring my words...yet."

"Not yet," Ann replied in a serious tone. "Come with me, Jenna. I really need to talk to you...privately."

Jenna started to wave to Austin and Kelly then realized they were back on the dance floor. She allowed Ann to pull her out of the banquet hall, but finally stopped when they were almost to the front door of the lobby. "What is going on? First Jonathan leaves, then you disappear. Ann, please tell me..."

"It's Chase, Jenna." Ann withdrew a small folded piece of paper and placed it in Jenna's hand. "He gave this to me with instructions to hand it to you right about now."

Jenna unfolded the note with shaking hands. She read it silently as tears filled the corners of her eyes.

I'm sorry, Jenna. Please believe me. I need you to come to the marina at seven o'clock sharp. Bring the three treasure pieces with you to Slip #5. The Closer will kill me if you don't come.
  I love you.
      Chase

Ann held Jenna's arm as she started to sway. "We don't have much time. We have to go, Jenna."

"I...should say something to Austin...and Kelly. Don't you think?" Jenna searched for an answer in Ann's eyes.

"No, Jenna. There's no time for that. Besides, we don't want to upset them on their wedding day. We'll explain later. Right now we need to leave, get changed at the beach house, grab the treasure pieces, and race over to the marina. You still have them at home somewhere, don't you?"

Jenna nodded nervously. "Yes. I never got the chance to put them back in their hiding places. I just stuck them..."

Ann interrupted. "Don't tell me. Let's just get moving."

"How...did Chase give you this note?" Jenna was certain she was feeling the effects of the champagne, but something wasn't adding up. "When...?"

Ann shut the driver's side door, reversed her Camry rental, and kicked up stones in the gravel parking lot as she pulled out onto the road. "Long story. One we don't have time for right now." She noticed Jenna was holding her head. "Headache?"

"Too much bubbly. Should know better. The price I pay for having a good time. Lesson learned, a little too late though. God, Ann, please tell me Chase is going to be ok! I can't..." Jenna's voice trailed. "I can't let anything happen to him! I love him."

Ann gripped the wheel, embedding her nail prints in the leather. "I know you do, Jenna. And Chase loves you...I...just know it."

Within minutes, Ann had managed to dodge traffic and get them back to the beach house. As soon as she stepped out of the car, she pulled off her heels, swearing silently she'd never wear them again. "Jenna, get changed and find the treasure pieces. I'm

S.A. Van

going across the street to put on my jeans and sneakers. I'll be right back. Lock the door behind you and don't open it to anyone but me. Got it?"

Ann didn't give Jenna a chance to answer. She darted across the street, raced up the front steps, then tossed her shoes in the middle of the living room. She was out of her dress and flying up the stairs in less than ten seconds.

At best they had thirty-five minutes to get to the marina.

She prayed her partner wasn't stupid enough to do anything before she got there.

Including getting himself killed.

*****

"I won't be long."

David Caldwell zipped up Mallory's suitcase and placed it by the front door of the condo along with her other two bags. Mallory never travelled light despite David's repeated requests to simplify her luggage. Telling Mallory she'd have to suffice with one carry-on was sure to ignite another argument. Something he was shying away from for as long as possible.

"When I get back, we're hitting the road. My pilot is meeting us at a landing strip about an hour from here."

Mallory shot David a worried look. "Mason has you wrapped around his little finger, David. Admit it. He calls and you jump. I wish you would just tell him to go..."

"Mason won't be a problem much longer."

"Why not?"

"Because he won't be around to annoy me. Looks like I'm not the only one who has a taste for revenge. The woman who murdered Renault...the one with the red silk scarf...she..."

"A silk scarf? Don't you think that's a bit melodramatic?"

David shrugged. "She wears it to hide her scars, Mallory."

Mallory was noticeably confused. "I'm sorry...her *what?* She's disfigured? If Renault did that to her, then he got what he deserved." Mallory's hand flew to her neck and she shivered.

David wrapped his arms around Mallory from behind. He kissed the back of her head, then spun her around to face him. "According to her...by the way, she won't tell me her name...anyway...Renault tortured her with a knife in front of her

340

parents. Mason stood by and did nothing. That's why he's next on her hit list."

"She'll save you the trouble." Mallory searched David's eyes. As usual, they were dark and cold. Never wavering. A fortress she wanted to break through more than anything. "Once Mason is out of the picture, maybe we can go back to Europe. Take up where we left off." She started to smile as David's hands moved up her back.

"Sure you want to do that? I'm serious, Mallory. Think about it. I'm too hard of a man to love."

"I'm up for the challenge, David."

David kissed her nose. "I'm sure you are. We'll continue this conversation when I get back." Before Mallory could latch onto him and detain him any longer, David rushed out the door. All the way to the marina he kept wondering about the woman in the red silk scarf and how unaffected she appeared to be after murdering Renault. Then David's thoughts shifted to Mallory, and how vulnerable she was. If the woman in the red silk scarf ever found out how much Mallory meant to him, she could use that information to her advantage.

And Mallory would never be safe again.

*****

"There's something else you should know…about me and Chase."

Ann waited for Jenna to absorb those words before she continued. As expected, Jenna's mouth dropped wide open.

"You…and Chase…?"

"It's not what you think. We're not romantically involved; never were. He's my partner…and we both report to Damian."

"Does…Maria know that?"

"Not yet. I don't know why Damian hasn't told her, but for the meantime, I'm asking you to keep his secret. Maria needs to hear this straight from her husband…so he can explain why he felt the need to keep her in the dark all these years."

"Wouldn't want to be there when that unfolds."

"Me neither." Ann made a face. "Damian was offered a very lucrative position with the FBI which led to the creation of the Joint Task Force, or *JTF*, as we like to call it."

"I'm a little confused. Don't *you* work for the CIA?"

Ann laughed. "More or less, depending on what day is it! Actually, I'm part of JTF, too. Trained with other CIA operatives, then did a couple of tours with the FBI, finally ending up in London with the Interpol boys. Chase and I met several years ago when JTF was looking for some new recruits. We've been partners ever since. As for Damian...he's got agents reporting to him in the States and internationally. That's how he's been able to keep tabs on The Closer. He's pretty high in the ranks, Jenna, and I'm pretty sure he hasn't told Maria about that. He maintains a small office in D.C., a couple floors above her unit. It's just a quasi-branch of JTF, but it's a good enough cover. Anyway...to get back to how I fit into the picture. When Maria asked Damian for a recommendation...a female agent to watch over you, well...let's just say, he picked one of his own."

"This is mind-boggling, Ann."

Ann turned her head to respond, then jerked it back again. She swerved the car, avoiding being hit by an oncoming driver too busy to take her cell phone out of her ear. "Sorry for the NASCAR move. You ok?"

Jenna nodded, catching her breath.

"Reminds me of a time when I had to hug a lot of curves during a stint in Germany a couple years back. Learned pretty damn quick how *not* to fall off a mountain going eighty miles an hour. Of course, the arms dealer I was tracking..."

Jenna checked the clock on the dash. Seventeen minutes to go. She had gone from happiness to craziness in less than an hour. *A new personal record.* "I'm sorry. What were you saying?"

"Sorry. Got off on one of my tangents. Bad habit. Did you bring the three treasure pieces?"

Jenna pulled the gold animal figurines out of her jacket. "This is it...Blackbeard's treasure...well, part of it. Hamilton has managed to get the other two."

Ann stole a glance in Jenna's direction, sensing her uneasiness. "Chase will end this tonight, Jenna. He'll get The Closer, and you'll finally be safe. The two of you can get on with your lives."

"I hope you're right. I don't know what I'll do if..."

"He knows what he's doing," Ann lied. Only sheer luck would help her partner tonight.

They arrived at the marina five minutes later.

"Ready?" Ann asked as she opened Jenna's door.

"Ready," Jenna said with heightened determination. "Let's go."

Epilogue

Holding your breath doesn't make time go any faster.
Ann's advice echoed loudly in his eardrums.

Chase exhaled loudly, choking to get in as much air as possible. He had no idea how stuffy it could get in the mechanic's storage room with the doors and windows shut. It was practically unbearable, and he had already stripped off his jacket. Not much else to do except sit and wait.

For chaos to erupt.

On The Closer's timetable, not his own.

Chase had very little patience when it came to stakeouts, and tonight was no exception. At least when Ann was on the same assignment, he had someone to talk with...and complain to until she told him to put up or shut up. Everyone needed a nudge, and Ann fit the bill. All in all, she was the best partner he could ever ask for. Even if she did feel the compulsion to sling a few dissertations his way from time to time. Most of them were justified, Chase had to admit. Especially the ones she was probably thinking or saying this very minute.

Six-fifty. Ten minutes to go.

Once again, the binoculars snapped to attention, zooming in on every possible section of the dock in Chase's viewing spectrum. Just a couple of restaurant patrons strolling down the walkway from the Lobster House hand-in-hand, leaning in closer for a quick kiss.

Chase slowly lowered the binoculars and set them aside. His last kiss with Jenna was crossing his mind and hanging on for dear life. He remembered exactly how good she felt in his arms, the light scent of her freshly washed hair, and the hope in her eyes. She had given him another second chance, and was depending on him to keep his promise to come back to her.

Yet here he was, within minutes of facing the man who had caused his worst nightmare. Chase didn't need special technology to calculate his chances of survival. He already knew the probable outcome, and it wasn't in his favor.

Chase had known from the start he was being used. The first time in Texas when the drugs were discovered in his body, and the tox screen indicated an unusual organic drug compound, he had no doubt The Closer was behind it. He had sent a message then, and he was sending one now.

I'll do whatever I want, and you won't catch me.

Chase grimaced. He had put up with the drug reactions, the excruciating seizures and the mind tricks which caused him to lash out verbally and physically. He had withstood the ridicule from Markus, and the condescending remarks from The Closer. And he had endured a forced separation from Jenna after he had attacked her, causing both of them massive heartbreak and pain.

Those reasons alone were enough to take down The Closer with a single shot, not to mention the running list of crimes in his repertoire. The man needed to be killed, plain and simple. A long, drawn out court case would only exacerbate the inevitable. Chase could save the taxpayers thousands of dollars if he would just pull the trigger, and not think twice about it.

That was the problem. He couldn't help but think about it. If he killed The Closer without a clear need to defend himself, he would be the one on trial. He'd be ostracized by the agency, thrown in jail amongst some criminals he most likely had the pleasure of putting behind bars, and he would never feel the comfort of Jenna's arms again. He couldn't do that...not to her and certainly not to himself.

No, Chase thought with conviction, *this has to be done by the books*. If The Closer provoked him, and there was no other way around it, then he would discharge his weapon with just cause. He'd never be able to look Jenna in the eyes with a clear conscience otherwise. He was one of the good guys. At the very least he wanted her to remember him that way.

Chase peered out of the small rectangular window cut into the metal door. The darkened skies loomed heavily in the distance, and he wondered if the marina always looked this way at night, or if a storm was headed to the coast. Switching to night vision on his binoculars, he panned sideways to catch any suspicious movement.

Water lapped against the dock, sending ripples towards the anchored boats. A storm was coming, Chase figured. Not just one created by Mother Nature. He couldn't help but wonder if Knox was shaking in his boots, and the thought made him laugh a little. The irony of it all. Knox was the last person Chase would have ever thought of as an ally, yet he was the only one who came to mind who would also give his life for Jenna.

Walking to the back entrance of the mechanic's shop, Chase stuck his head out through the crack in the door. "Knox, stay sharp. Stay out of sight until I call you. Jenna can't know that…"

"I've got it, Garrett. We've been over this three times now. I'm not Bond, but I think I can follow simple instructions. You call; I come running, grab Jenna and get her the hell out of here. Right?"

Chase nodded. "I'm counting on you, Knox. Don't let me down." Chase shut the door and returned to his viewing position. Unless The Closer had arrived in the past two minutes, he was satisfied he hadn't missed anything. He didn't have time to speculate. Jenna was approaching from the right, as he had instructed Ann to coach her. As she crossed in front of the seafood take-out window, Chase noticed Ann taking her position just inside the side door of the restaurant. Her gun was drawn and she was holding it down close to her leg.

Chase breathed a sigh of relief knowing his partner was close enough to back him up. What he couldn't see was Markus directly behind Ann telling her not to move or he'd ram a knife into her back and puncture her kidneys.

As Jenna moved closer to the dock, Chase glanced back at Ann and her face told him all he needed to know. She had been compromised. He was on his own to protect Jenna.

Chase couldn't take it any longer. He couldn't do this. He couldn't send Jenna to her death because of his own personal quests.

"Jenna!" Chase darted from his hiding spot and ran toward her. "Knox, now!"

Jonathan came running on cue, and did precisely what Chase had told him to do. He grabbed Jenna around her waist and dragged her backwards while she fought to get free. Stopping at the corner of the mechanic's shop, he finally let her go when she bit into his forearm. "Why did you do that?"

"To get you off me! Chase, what's going on?" Jenna clung to Chase's arm, surprised he wasn't reacting to Jonathan's daring move. "Tell me right now what's…"

"Did you bring the treasure pieces?" Chase asked hurriedly.

"Yes, but, Chase…"

"Jenna, this is important. Listen to me very carefully." Chase snatched the monkey figurine out of her hand and closed her fist around the other two. "Knox is going to get you out of here, and I'm...going to take this to The Closer."

Jenna tried to shove the other two gold animals into his hand but Chase backed away. "Take them! They're blood money and I don't want them anymore. For God's sake, Chase, this can end tonight! If you give them to..."

"He won't stop, Jenna. Hamilton won't stop even when The Closer gives him all the treasure pieces. Can't you see that? You have to keep the last two...they're your insurance policy...to keep you safe."

"But I thought...the note said...if I didn't bring them...?"

"It was a ruse, Jenna. To get you here. To draw him out. Nothing more. I...needed you...as the bait." Chase started to back away.

"Garrett! It's time."

Chase spun around. There was no mistake who was calling him, beckoning him to Slip #5. He had only seconds left. "Jenna, please go with Knox. He'll keep you safe. Just remember...I love you."

"No, Chase! Don't leave me! You promised...come back to me!" Jenna twisted from side to side trying her best to wriggle free from Jonathan's hold. "I need you! Chase!"

"Now, Knox! Get her out of here!" Chase took off in the direction of The Closer's voice, never looking back. As he neared Slip #5 where the *Trace* was anchored, his chest tightened. Her last memory of him was yet another betrayal.

"Get up here, Garrett. Let's get this done." The Closer stood on deck with one hand on the wheel.

Chase climbed up the side ladder and stepped onto the deck. Just as he turned around, he heard the familiar crack of a gunshot and felt the whiz of a bullet narrowly missing his head.

"Next time I won't miss. Now that I have your full attention, I believe you have something for me. Toss the treasure pieces on one of the seats, then step back. Needless to say, I'm a little disappointed you chose to disregard my explicit orders. I was hoping to wrap up this mess today. Not a problem, though. I can always come back and pay Ms. Reed another visit. I've grown quite fond of the Jersey shore."

As The Closer turned his attention to the dock, he smiled sadistically. "Looks like your girl might be joining us after all."

Chase took advantage of The Closer's distraction, wishing to God Jenna hadn't been crazy enough to follow him. Barreling into The Closer head first, Chase knocked him off-balance. As the two men fell to the deck, Chase did his best to keep The Closer's hands from reaching the knife sheath attached to his belt.

Chase sucked in a breath as The Closer's punches landed squarely against his jaw. He blocked as many as possible, and although they were evenly matched in terms of fight maneuvers, The Closer's slightly taller and heavier physique gave him the advantage. Chase was slammed against the rung of the metal ladder, and his head started to spin. Dazed, he dropped the gold monkey figurine to the deck.

"Chase! Tell me you're alright!" Jenna called frantically from the pier. Relying on another one of Maria's self-defense maneuvers, she had kicked Jonathan just below the kneecap then shoved him backwards, breaking free.

Chase froze. Jenna was too close to the boat. An easy target for a knife or gun.

"Your fight is with me. Leave her alone!" Chase staggered to regain his stance, ready to lunge forward.

The Closer stuffed the monkey figurine into his pocket and withdrew his knife. "Fine with me, Garrett. But I am curious, where are the other two treasure pieces? If your girl still has them, you know I'll have to take them from her. That was our little understanding, wasn't it? I thought I made myself perfectly clear."

Chase deflected the first thrust of the knife, hoping he had used enough force to knock it out of The Closer's hand.

"Not good enough, Garrett. Do you honestly think you can out-fight me?" The Closer ducked, then thrust the knife upward in the opposite direction.

Blood spurted from Chase's right arm. As The Closer drew back to steady himself for the kill, multiple sirens caught his attention. There was no time to finish what he had started. The police would be swarming the marina very soon, and his chances for escape would be next to none. Shoving Chase backwards against the railing, The Closer hit the throttle and the boat lurched in reverse. As soon as he had a clearing, he turned the boat to the right, then propelled it forward. He had just passed the first marker, giving him five minutes.

Turning backwards to look at Garrett, The Closer's mouth dropped open. The deck was clear. Garrett had fallen overboard when the boat took off.

One less problem to deal with, The Closer mused. Within a minute, he had cleared the second marker, the last row of boats. Markus would be in position, taking aim.

Stripping off his shirt and pants, he tossed them to the deck. Picking up the gold monkey, he stuffed it inside the zippered front pocket of his wetsuit. Lifting the seat closest to the wheel, he grabbed his diving mask and hoisted an oxygen tank onto his back.

It was time to go.

While the boat was still moving forward, The Closer flipped over the side of the boat, holding onto a small cable he had draped earlier. As he slowly drifted beneath the surface of the water, he wondered if he would encounter Garrett's body floating somewhere below. A fleeting thought lasting only a few seconds. He had less than two minutes to clear the swell of the boat's pathway and dive deeper.

Counting the seconds off in his head, The Closer swam towards the rendezvous point.

At precisely the appointed time, he heard a loud crack followed by an ear-piercing explosion. Climbing back onto the dock behind a barricade of crates and a large trash receptacle, The Closer stepped out of his wet suit, and changed into the clothes laid neatly in a pile. He didn't have to look back. He knew exactly what had happened.

The gas tank of the *Trace* had just erupted, shooting flames straight up into the air.

*****

Jenna couldn't hear herself screaming anymore.

Sirens were blaring; police were running up and down the dock shouting at the top of their lungs. Paramedics were trying to fight through the crowd that had rushed from the restaurant.

Mass pandemonium had taken on a life of its own.

In the middle of it all, Jenna had fallen to her knees.

Nothing she experienced over the past few months could compare to what she had just witnessed.

Chase had sacrificed himself for her.

In one fateful moment, Chase had locked eyes with her for the very last time. Seeking solace and forgiveness for what he had done to her in the past, and for leaving her now...alone.

No one had ever loved her more.

Jenna bent her head to her chest, willing her eyes to cry more tears. She needed the sweet release from the pain rocking her from the inside out.

Not even the torture of Kliric's razor-sharp knife, or the bullet piercing her shoulder in Texas could mirror the incomparable agony shooting through every nerve in her body. She was incapacitated, unable to move her smallest finger.

She was shutting down.

Only her mind seemed to be functioning. Words she desperately wanted to say were nothing more than silent whispers trapped between trembling lips...

Don't let him suffer. Let him think of me.
And the way we loved...
Through hurt and pain.
Seeing only each other...
And hanging on to promises...we'll never keep.

Familiar voices were talking to her all at once. Jenna couldn't distinguish one from the other. She couldn't feel anything.

Not the strong arms supporting her, the two gold animal figurines stuck inside her jeans, or the note someone had hastily placed between her fingers.

She was moving...or being carried.

It didn't matter what was happening. Nothing would ever matter again.

The man she had fallen in love with was gone.

And inside...she was dying, too.

*****

Keep your chin up...

The Jenna Reed saga continues in Counterpoint.

CPSIA information can be obtained at www.ICGtesting.com
Printed in the USA
LVOW11s2307080415

433779LV00031B/1142/P